SCARS AND SEAMS

ALL THE QUEEN'S KNAVES BOOK THREE

KATE SPARKES

SPARROWCAT PRESS

For Mike

Sorry about the roller skate

Aster crouched among the bushes outside the garden fence and checked her gold pocket watch. Eleven o'clock precisely, which meant the man in the bedroom upstairs should have been dead five minutes ago. He would have been, if not for the dog.

She'd been watching its master for three weeks and had known the big brindle fellow in the yard would be an issue. The people Aster had been hunting for the past three years were cautious sorts, and a single guard dog was a small obstacle compared to what she'd faced in the past. She'd asked Eamon to brew a simple sedative potion that would knock the brute off his paws for a few hours, leaving him at best well-rested when he woke after his master's death and at worst embarrassed over his professional failure.

The problem was that the dog was a fighter in more ways than one. Aster had seen him snarl at the mail carrier, had watched as local children cried over balls kicked onto the property that they'd never recover, and had almost needed to avert her eyes from the gleeful violence after a pigeon dared to land in the yard. She'd tested the dog, tossing rocks over the fence in the dead of night and watching as he woke and investigated, the short hair on his back standing in a thick line down his spine as he growled a warning at the offending stone.

And on top of all that, it seemed he was as stubborn as a rusty lock.

Getting the potion into the dog had been simple. His master kept him hungry enough to make him mean, and Aster had splurged on a nice steak that had gone down so quickly the dog likely hadn't tasted the potion. But now, twenty minutes later, he was still wobbling in circles around the flagstone-paved yard, his tongue hanging out from between his fearsome teeth.

Finally he pitched forward and rolled onto his side.

Aster gathered the familiar weight of her cloak around her, scaled the fence, and dropped silently into the scraggly garden bed on the other side. The house's sole occupant could afford a home in one of Queen's Run's middle-tier neighbourhoods, a guard dog, and a maid who would arrive at nine tomorrow. A gardener to draw anything but weeds and neglected wisps of shrubbery from the soil, however, seemed out of his reach.

Aster didn't feel the least bit sorry for him.

The dog's big barrel chest rose and fell in a steady rhythm as Aster crept closer. She risked a sharp click of her tongue to get his attention and braced herself to run, but the dog didn't so much as twitch. Once she'd checked to make sure his lolling tongue wasn't going to block his airway, she moved silently on toward the narrow brick house.

The night was unusually warm given that they were quickly approaching the longest one of the year, but Aster wore her hood up. Her cloak was made from soft fabric in a red so dark and deep it blended with the shadows and hid the old bloodstains on its hem, and though it offered no extra protection in the form of armour or enchantments, she felt safe in it.

No other disguises tonight. Even if her prey saw her face, he wouldn't be telling anyone what he'd seen.

The bedroom was on the second floor. Its occupant had taken the precaution of removing the roof that had once sheltered the back door, which, along with every window at ground level, was a masterpiece of security. The rear of the house was uglier for the loss, but it made good practical sense. Until tonight, no one had broken in.

Aster climbed the rough stone wall, choosing hand and toeholds carefully. She wore trousers and a tunic beneath her cloak, which allowed her to move more freely than the dresses she usually wore. Still, it wasn't as easy as it should have been.

Her muscles cramped and ached. Jagged pain tugged at every scar on her body, from the pale starburst that stood out against the brown skin of her left thigh to the thin line that traced over her right eye from her scalp to her jaw. It wasn't enough to distract her yet, but she'd need healing soon. She'd been putting it off, not wanting to interrupt weeks of surveillance with the inconvenient side effects of Eamon's magic, but the long days and nights were taking their toll.

Too much strain. Too much pressure. Not enough rest.

Only two more to go after tonight, she reminded herself, and kept climbing.

Only three remained of the family responsible for her current physical and mental state. Two of them had died more than a decade ago at her grandmother's cabin, when Eamon had saved her from them. Six more had fallen by her hand in the past three years. They'd been scattered across Andonia, but one by one she and Eamon had hunted them down and Aster had taken the lives they owed her. And now, finally, it was time to deal with those she'd located closer to home.

The blood on her hands didn't trouble her. These people were like rats, able to escape through the tiniest holes in whatever net the police set for them, vanishing into new identities in new cities whenever their crimes threatened to catch up with them. It took a special sort of person to deliver justice to their kind, and doing so had been her mission since Eamon had taken her in.

She wished she could remember any of it. But like the memories of every other painful experience she'd had since that day, the details of each kill had vanished when Eamon's healing took away the rest of her pain. It was the one flaw in the enchantment that had saved her life—one that wouldn't have been necessary if not for these people.

These so-called wolves.

If not for them I'd be whole, body and mind. The thought was enough to push her onward.

Aster's heart pounded, strong and steady, as she held tight to the window frame with one hand and pulled Eamon's enchanted dagger from its sheath on her belt. The blade glinted silver in the moonlight, and the line of gold down its centre glowed with dull fire as it always did when it was about to taste blood.

Soon.

Though she didn't remember the other kills, everything about this felt familiar—the tension, the way every part of her seemed to lean toward the task at hand, the perfect focus, the lack of fear even as her mind whirred, considering angles and anticipating obstacles.

The memories were gone, but the experiences were still a part of her somewhere far below conscious thought. It had always been enough before. It would be enough now.

She used the tip of the blade to carve a thin circle into the glass, then pressed harder on the second pass. She'd practiced at home dozens of times, from different angles and on different types of glass, and when she felt the magically sharp blade had cut deep enough she pushed against the window, sending the circle of glass onto the window seat, where it landed with a soft thud. She reached in and unlocked the window, slid it open, and climbed inside.

Though her legs still ached, Aster crouched beside the

window until her eyes had adjusted to the deeper darkness inside the room. She watched for movement, but there was nothing. Just a bed with an ornately carved headboard, a sturdy writing desk covered in papers, a massive armoire in the far corner, a washbasin, and a settee upholstered in dark fabric at the end of the bed. No more dogs. No guards. As expected, a dark-haired man slept alone. Aster crossed the room, her flat leather boots making no noise, and checked that the bedroom door was locked. There shouldn't have been anyone else in the house, but she wasn't in the habit of taking chances.

She adjusted her grip on the dagger's handle and approached the bed.

He—Pietro Ilcone, formerly Quin Daggersmith, Ren Amudsen, and a handful of other names—was a surprisingly attractive middle-aged fellow, with dark lashes and an aristocratic nose that balanced the strength of his jaw. His well-formed lips parted in sleep, appearing innocent and peaceful as a child's.

It seemed unfair that anyone with so ugly a soul should be allowed to show so pretty a face to the world.

Do it, Aster told herself. She had strict instructions from Eamon to kill quickly and not to converse with the doomed party. He said it was always this way and that she'd always followed the rule. These people spoke with forked tongues and lied off both ends, and their skill in manipulation was a good part of the reason Aster took their lives instead of turning them in to the police.

But she hesitated.

It seemed wrong for a person to die without knowing why. Eamon's dagger would make the procedure relatively painless given its sharp edge and Aster's knowledge of anatomy. She could have him drowning in his own blood or bleeding out before he knew she was there, or she could slice directly into his brain and end him with even less fuss.

But something deep in her gut said it was cheap and cowardly to not let an enemy see the end coming, no matter what Eamon had ordered.

Justice will be done, she told herself. *Time is passing, and I need to get back—*

He opened his eyes.

Aster had the dagger at his throat before he had time to understand that she was there. "Show me your hands." The rasp of her voice filled the room, though she spoke quietly.

Ilcone's eyes widened, then quickly narrowed.

"Hands." Aster pressed the tip of the blade to his skin, and a bead of blood welled up around it.

He raised them above the blankets and rested them palms-up on his pillow. "Who are you?"

She frowned down at him, though he wouldn't see it in the shadows of her hood. "Are there so many possibilities that you can't guess?"

"You never know what people will get upset about nowadays." He'd recovered any sliver of composure he might have lost when he woke with a blade to his throat and now peered up at her with interest. "If it's about those women, you've got it wrong. Every marriage was legal, and every bride willing. I can't help it if I've had bad luck with marrying poorly constituted ladies."

Aster gritted her teeth. Eamon was right about these people. They'd moved on to new kinds of business since the day they'd left her for dead, but not one of them had left their criminal ways behind. They still preyed on the weak and helpless and valued coin over human life.

"Not those women," she said. "One grandmother and one little girl. About eleven years ago. You and your family took advantage of the old woman. You stole her property and kept her to serve you, then you killed her before you moved on to your next victim." Aster lowered her hood with her free hand. "Then her granddaughter came to the door, and you had another loose end to tidy up."

Ilcone flinched, then sat up, hands still raised beside his head, eyes narrowed. "No. There was a girl there, but she—" Even in the moonlight Aster saw the blood drain from his face. "You should be dead."

"I should." Aster didn't offer him more than that. He already knew Eamon had heard screams from the cabin as he'd been out cutting wood and had fought the criminals until they fled. He didn't need to know about the magic that had saved her.

Or about how parts of her *had* died. She'd lost every memory of herself before the moment she woke up in Eamon's home, every bit of it wiped away in the desperate enchantments that had healed her body. She didn't know what her grandmother had looked like, or who her parents were, or who she might have been if not for this man and his family.

It might please him to know it, and that wouldn't do.

"What a day that was." Ilcone reached slowly toward the little table beside his bed. "Mind if I have one last smoke?"

"I do."

Ilcone sighed and shifted his weight on the mattress, but returned his hand to its proper position beside his head, though he didn't lie back down. A shrewd look came into his eyes. "You're the one that's been picking us off?"

"I am." There was no point lying. If there was life after death, he'd find out the truth from his family soon enough.

"But there are at least two more of us left." He flashed her a conspiratorial smile that might have been charming under other circumstances. "I'm not the one you really want. I wasn't in charge that day."

"I know."

Ilcone sighed. "Gods, kid. *I should, I am, I know…* you're quite a conversationalist, aren't you?"

"You're wasting time." Aster kept her voice calm and even, and she didn't correct the insult. At eighteen she was an adult, but she supposed it must still hurt an old swindler like this one to stare death in the eye and see someone so young looking back. "I'll give you one minute to make your peace with whichever of those gods you think might still be willing to listen to you."

"No." Ilcone glanced down at the dagger. "Listen. I know where she is. The one who put us after old grandma in the first place. Her daughter, too."

Aster allowed herself a small, smug smile. "I know where the daughter is. I'll be seeing her tomorrow."

She'd been keeping an eye on that one, too, between shifts observing Ilcone's comings and goings.

"But not the one you really want," Ilcone said. "Let me go. I'll tell you everything you want to know, and then I'll disappear. It'll be up to you what you do with the information."

Aster gritted her teeth. This was why Eamon said not to talk to them. Just a few minutes after meeting her, Ilcone knew her vulnerable points.

But Eamon has leads. We'll find her without losing him.

"I didn't come here for information. I came for justice. Can you give me back my grandmother's life?"

The charm drained from Ilcone's expression, leaving a sneer of open, bitter rage. "How many people need to die to pay for one old hag?"

He moved quickly, dropping his hands and reaching under his pillow, drawing out a hunting knife. It had barely cleared the blankets before Aster moved, letting her years of training take over without giving conscious thought a chance to interfere. She drove the dagger deep and opened his throat, releasing a flood of blood that appeared black in the moonlight from the window.

Ilcone dropped his knife and pressed his hands to the wound as though he might hold back the life that spilled from him, then collapsed sideways onto the mattress.

At least it was almost an honest fight.

It could have been cleaner if she'd struck while he slept, but her conscience felt clearer for giving him a chance to try. She waited for a moment, curious to see whether some unexpected emotion welled up in her. Something shameful, perhaps, like regret or guilt, that she'd kept secret after past kills and Eamon didn't know to warn her about when she forgot.

There was nothing but the relief of the job being done and another name crossed off her list.

With her deep hood pulled up to shadow her face, Aster went to the window and checked to be sure the dog was still sleeping, then sheathed her dagger and riffled through the papers on the desk. There wasn't much of interest. Ledgers relating to business that wasn't her concern, a stack of cash he presumably kept for emergencies like the one he'd have faced if she'd let him walk away tonight, and a few pieces of jewellery he'd likely taken from the wives he'd conned into marrying him just weeks before each of their untimely deaths.

There was a letter, though, in an unsealed envelope bearing an address in Embercliffe.

M—

I found her. I'm willing to negotiate.

—R

And in the desk drawer, a business card with the name of a curiosity shop in another part of town that Aster had become quite familiar with over the past few weeks.

Aster pocketed both items, pleased with her discoveries. The card didn't tell her anything she didn't already know, but the letter was the freshest sign they had of where the last wolf might be hiding. If she moved quickly, this might all be over soon.

She checked on the body, then scouted the house quickly as she made her way down to the back door. There was nothing else of interest. If Ilcone had been a rat, his bedroom was his nest. The rest of the house was just for show.

She unlocked the back door and stepped out into the night, then paused next to the dog on her way through the yard. His paws were twitching like he was trying to run in a dream. Aster checked her watch again. The maid would be by in the morning. The dog seemed to like her well enough, at least from what Aster had seen. She'd take care of him.

In a few moments Aster had scaled the fence again and vanished into the shadows.

A black horse and carriage waited a few blocks away on a narrow street with tall brick buildings looming over both sides. A thin man in a threadbare suit leaned against one of the doors. He tipped his equally ratty top hat to Aster as she approached. "Ready?"

Aster took a roll of bills from the pouch on her belt and handed it over. "It's safe to go in the back way as long as you don't disturb the dog. Body's in the bedroom at the top of the stairs. You'll want to remove the mattress and bedding, but I think the mess is contained otherwise."

She watched and tried not to feel disgust over the transaction as he licked his fingers and counted through the bills.

I killed a man, she reminded herself. *He's just taking care of the body.*

He tried to peer under her hood, and Aster looked away.

"Going to cost a little extra," he said. "If there's clean-up involved."

"I'd have thought you'd be satisfied with being paid twice." Aster took a step closer. "I know how you make bodies disappear, Mister Andrews. You're going to sell it to the medical school. I don't care."

In truth, she did care. Resurrection men were a blight on the city, digging up fresh graves so the student doctors would have cadavers to take apart and put back together. Eamon said it was necessary, as most folks wouldn't donate the bodies willingly and medicine for the living was more important than the dignity of the dead.

Still, standing on a dark street with a grave robber made Aster's skin crawl.

She pulled out a second, smaller roll of bills and handed it over. "Here. Final offer. The body disappears, the mess goes with it, and if there are any questions, you never met me."

He didn't bother to count this one. "Fair enough. I suppose you're saving me a bit of trouble and some dirt on my suit." He grinned, revealing gleaming white teeth that seemed too big for his mouth, and tipped his hat again. "Pleasure doing business with you, dear lady."

Aster walked away as quickly as she could without drawing attention. She kept the letter but tore the business card into tiny pieces that she divided between several trash bins.

If the police did come, the last thing she wanted was them showing up with questions before she had a chance to kill Jesamyn Windram.

CHAPTER TWO
ASTER

The building on the corner before her was far larger and grander than the house Aster had just left behind. She paused before she stepped into view of its many windows, looked over a group of coach drivers who stood in a tight circle near the line of carriages that filled the circular drive, and scanned for anyone else who might see her in her cloak and trousers. The stately brick structure beyond the drive, two storeys tall with a high mansard roof, had been one of the finest homes in the city until its recent conversion to Queen's Run's newest museum. Now it housed artefacts instead of people and had become a popular location for parties, weddings, and charity fundraisers like the one that occupied so many people inside that night.

Lamplight glowed warm behind a dozen windows at the front of the museum, illuminating the glittering glass baubles and pine boughs that decorated their sills and the equally dazzling guests in the rooms beyond. From a distance, it was hard to pick out faces, but the wealthy folks inside the house were a symphony of styles and bright colours. Dancing couples passed by the windows in shimmering ballgowns, ornate robes with wide sashes, and suits in an array of jewel tones, each of them trying to outdo the others.

Like peacocks, Aster thought, and smiled. She clung to the shadows and hurried to Eamon's carriage, which was parked near the front of the line. None of the coachmen noticed her, and in a moment, she'd unlocked the door and slipped inside. She closed the curtains and shed her cloak and clothing, then lifted one of the seats to reveal the party clothes she'd stowed there earlier.

There wasn't much room to move, but she'd designed everything from her underclothes to the gown to make it possible for her to dress without assistance. It wasn't so different from the rest of her wardrobe in that regard. She and Eamon lived alone, with no maids to help her on any day, whether it was for a party or a walk to the shops. She tightened the corset to shape her athletic frame and pulled on the simple underskirts, then fit her tired feet into dancing slippers of pale silk.

The dress, sewn from pale gold cloth, had long, fitted sleeves and a simple neckline that came up to just beneath her collarbone and covered most of her scars. From the waist up it fit her like her favourite gloves. Below that, the underskirts gave it a wider shape, though nothing as voluminous as what was strictly fashionable at these extravagant functions. It was lovely, but wouldn't draw undue attention, and that was just as Aster liked it.

Clothing was useful no matter where a person went. Some outfits were better for sneaking and slaying, some for fitting in with the wealthiest folks in Queen's Run, and Aster liked wearing either in the right time and place. She'd spent most of her life becoming comfortable in both roles and played her parts well.

It crossed her mind that the role she felt more comfortable in would soon become redundant, but she set that aside. For the rest of the night, Aster the Hunter didn't exist. There was only Aster Islington, the orphan girl who had taken her guardian's last name because she didn't have one of her own, who had grown into such a credit to him in the years since.

A shy girl who didn't make many friends or let anyone get close to her.

A clever girl who impressed local tutors but so often travelled with Eamon and took her lessons elsewhere.

A scarred girl, what a shame, just imagine how beautiful she might have been.

She knew everything they said about her. So many questions, so many mild criticisms framed as concern, when they could be bothered to think of her at all.

Aster dug a small mirror out from beneath the seat, then stowed her hunting clothes away. She couldn't see her whole reflection, but the mirror was large enough for her to get a good look as she freed her dark curls from the braid that had contained them on her mission and twisted them around her fingers until the riot of volume looked more *forest goddess* and less *windswept adventurer.*

Then the last piece of her costume. She'd tucked a little pot of gold powder into her reticule earlier and now drew it out, twisted it open, and carefully drew a line down the left side of the scar on her face, then blended it over both eyelids. It glowed against her skin and sharpened her dark eyes in a way that pleased her greatly.

People would stare anyway. Tonight, she'd show them her truest beauty.

She cracked the door and peered cautiously out to be sure no one was watching. The coachman who had brought them tonight was a stranger, as they usually were, and wouldn't dare ask questions. Still, less observation was better. She waited until the drivers were distracted by something they saw through the window before she stepped out.

When she was well away from the carriage she shook out her

skirts and hurried around the side of the house toward the kitchen door.

With any luck, no one would notice her entering and would only remember Eamon saying she was around somewhere if they'd asked about her earlier.

The scents of roasting meat and spices wafted out from the kitchen door, and Aster stepped into the organized chaos of cooks and servers moving through their paces as they prepared fresh food and dealt with platters the guests had already emptied. Aster stuck close to the wall, trying not to interrupt their coordinated movements.

"Aster!"

Aster held back a wince. "Kalleigh!" She tried to inject enthusiasm into her voice and forced a bright smile. She'd hoped to make it to a more appropriate setting before anyone spotted her, but she'd make do.

The red-haired girl made her way through the kitchen, emerald skirt held up in one hand as she wove her way past the black-clad kitchen staff, light from the gas lamps glinting off the cascade of rubies that dripped from her throat and drew attention to her modest décolletage. The servants made a wide path for Kalleigh and her dress, which was twice as wide as Aster's and trailed behind her, stalling the progress of a plate of roast venison and drawing a scowl from the fellow who carried it. "What are you doing in here?"

Aster nodded toward the door, which the staff had left open to release the heat from the kitchen. "I needed some air and got a little turned around in the garden. Decided to come back in this way. Where have you been? I haven't seen you all night."

Kalleigh's laugh reminded Aster of a cascade of pleasant bells. "I was just thinking the same. Too many people here, I say." She took Aster by the arm and led her toward the doorway leading into the museum. "I saw your father, of course."

Guardian, Aster thought, but felt no need to correct her. He was her father in every sense but biological and legal. "Tell me he's behaving himself."

Kalleigh laughed again. It seemed practiced, but not insincere. "Same as he always is at these events. Interesting, charming, but no one leaves a conversation with him without pledging at least a little more to the cause. I think a few of the old skinflints are avoiding him out of sheer terror."

Aster's smile came more naturally at that. Even without using magic, Eamon knew how to make things happen, always for the benefit of someone else.

She thought he probably did use his magic in subtle ways to increase his own fortunes, but even that was for the good of all in the end. Better him than those who would hoard their wealth until someone like Eamon pried it from their stingy, grasping fingers.

They stepped into a hallway papered in a subtle floral pattern and made their way to the museum's entryway. Two floors high with a grand, sweeping staircase, it was as much a part of the party's setting as the dining room or ballroom. Aster looked around, but Eamon was nowhere to be seen.

"You look stunning, by the way," Kalleigh said, and touched a finger to her rubies. "Makes a girl feel overdone when you show up looking like an absolute treasure in something so simple and perfect."

Aster's cheeks warmed. "You're too kind. I had Bonita Bonnifog do the dress for me. It's all in the fit and fabric."

Kalleigh smoothed a hand over her own voluminous skirt. "Hmm. Perhaps a change in my style is overdue. Anyway, I wanted to tell you that a few of us are getting together on Solvar Eve. It's going to be quiet, but fun. We'll wait until our family obligations are finished, then meet up at Horace's place. Did you know his attic is haunted?"

Aster was only half-listening, still scanning the crowd for Eamon, but she arched an eyebrow at that. "You don't say?"

"I do." Kalleigh squeezed her arm tighter and shivered. "It'll be fantastic. Ghost stories in a haunted attic on the longest night of the year, and you know their cook makes the most decadent cocoa."

"It does sound lovely." Ghost stories had been a Solvar tradition for as long as anyone could remember, and though she and Eamon didn't celebrate any particular religious or cultural holidays, joining in on things for once sounded quite nice. Ghosts themselves were a lot of poppycock, but she'd picked up a few stories about them on her travels that might rattle her peers. "I'll try to make it."

"Please do." Kalleigh turned to her and clasped both of Aster's hands in hers, brow furrowed. "I know you don't often like to come out with us, but I really think you'd fit in. You're sort of mysterious. I envy that."

Aster was glad she didn't have a drink in her mouth. She'd have spit it out.

If only you knew.

"I'll see what I can do," she said. "Would you excuse me?"

"Of course." Kalleigh released her, and Aster drew away slowly.

It would be good to have friends, to socialize with people instead of spending her days and nights training, studying, and stalking her prey, to do something just for fun every once in a while. But it wouldn't happen until her work was done, until everything that made her *sort of mysterious* was in her past and she didn't have so many secrets to keep.

But maybe, if all went well tomorrow, she'd take a break and drink some cocoa before she set out after the last wolf. She wasn't friends with the rich young people who moved in Kalleigh's circles, but surely some of them would be interesting if she got to know them.

Aster made her way across the room, nodding polite greetings to everyone she passed, fixing her presence in their minds. The odds of Ilcone's disappearance ever being connected to her were vanishingly slim, but a strong alibi never hurt anyone.

The people here tonight had overpaid for tickets to attend the party, which featured a string quartet in the ballroom for those who wished to dance, a dazzling buffet of fragrant meat, vegetable, and dessert dishes from around the world, and a chance to show off fine clothes and generous gestures in front of other high society folks. There would be dozens of parties happening all across the city every night from now until the solstice, but tickets for this event had sold out quickly.

Eamon had been pleased. He never chaired committees or drew attention to his involvement in charities, but Aster had no doubt he'd pulled plenty of strings behind the scenes to make the night perfect.

She spotted him in the ballroom. Not dancing, but tapping his fingers against the glass ball in the head of his cane, his ever-present gold rings dancing in the lamplight as he belly-laughed with a handsome bearded fellow in a green turban and white suit.

Aster struggled to remember the other man's name. Such things often slipped away from her, but she knew they'd met before, and she felt that she liked him. Only truly painful memories vanished entirely.

Eamon wore a midnight-black suit that offset his pale complexion and complemented his full, black beard and hair that had long since gone grey at the temples. His suit was cut from fine imported wool, which had felt more like silk when Aster helped him into his jacket earlier, and tailored to stylish perfection. Eamon cared deeply about his appearance and presentation but preferred to let others show off their vibrant plumage while he hung back and watched.

Eamon wiped a tear away and gave his perfectly waxed moustache a twist as he calmed his laughter, then he turned and raised his glass to Aster as though he'd known all along that she was there.

"My dear," he said as she approached. "You remember Lord Dashthi?"

"Of course." Aster held out a hand, and Lord Dashthi bent to kiss it.

"A daring choice," he said, nodding approvingly to her scar and the gold makeup she'd applied to it. "Battles fought and won must be celebrated."

"Well said," Eamon murmured, but his smile was strained. It always was when her scars reminded him of what his magic hadn't fixed on the day he saved her.

When Lord Dashthi excused himself, Eamon looked out over the dancing couples on the floor. "Having a good time, dear?"

"I am." A server passed with a tray of sparkling white wine, and Aster took a glass. "Remind me what we're fundraising tonight?"

Eamon's moustache twitched as he smiled. "Society to Improve the Treatment of Working Children. Changing laws regarding factories, funding inspections, that sort of thing."

"Certainly." Aster sipped her wine. The bubbles tickled pleasantly. "Though one would think the children would be treated best by not making them work in factories at all."

Eamon downed the rest of his drink in one gulp. "Quite. But one step at a time. Slow progress is better than none, and no one can fix the world overnight." He leaned in closer and dropped his voice. "And how has your evening been?"

"The deed is done."

"Good."

They walked to the dining room, Eamon leaning heavily on his cane with every step. Aster knew better than to hurt his pride by offering her arm, but it pained her to watch. Eamon had cut off a toe as his sacrifice to magic when he became a witch, but that wouldn't have caused this much trouble. He'd been injured in that long-ago fight with the wolves and had then sacrificed all his magic to save Aster. By the time he'd replenished it enough to heal his own wounds, the damage was done. He treated his pain with magic, but he'd never recovered his natural gait.

He couldn't pursue justice himself. Aster was happy to do it for both of them.

"I'm going after the daughter tomorrow," she said, speaking quietly.

Eamon frowned. "You need rest, my dear. And I suspect healing. It's been weeks, and you've been working hard."

They approached the buffet. The party had been going on for hours, but the cooks and servers had kept the table filled. Aster took a plate and piled on the most generous servings of decadent finger foods she could take without drawing attention, then glanced around to make sure no one was listening.

"I want to end it with her before she catches wind of what happened to her uncle and decides to make things difficult for me. I have a plan."

"I trust you." Eamon took a tiny cake and popped it into his mouth. "I'm working on finding the last one."

"I have an address."

"We're almost there, then."

Aster shivered. She couldn't imagine what life would be like without her quest for justice.

Lady Nallsthorpe stepped into the room, and Eamon straightened his shoulders. "Back to work for me."

"I'll fill you in on the details later," Aster said. She'd have to. Once Eamon used his magic to shore up the enchantments he'd placed on her body all those years ago, she'd forget everything about tonight's kill and the hours surrounding it, if not more. Sometimes she lost days, or even weeks.

She flashed a friendly grin at Lady Nallsthorpe. The older woman had dressed in red and had large candy twists sticking out of her hair, and she looked like the picture of holiday cheer. It was a little silly, but thoroughly delightful.

"I also have things to tell you," Eamon said. He, too, smiled as

Lady Nallsthorpe approached, and spoke through his teeth. "I have something in the works that will improve things for you—for both of us. I'll tell you more when I know more."

He stepped away and greeted his wealthy acquaintance with a kiss on each cheek. Aster found a seat and picked at her meal, but she barely tasted anything.

Better. It could mean altering her enchantment, which he'd been loath to experiment with before this. If he'd found a way to fix it, that might mean no more lost memories, or no more healings at all.

And then the possibilities for her life would be endless after the last wolf lay dead. Not just fitting into a life here in Queen's Run with Eamon, but travelling on her own. Studying abroad while he took care of things at home. Finding new ways to use her skills that didn't involve murdering people.

Eamon was deep in his conversation and would be seeking out more of his peers for the rest of the night. It would be a miracle if he made it home before she left in the morning. Details and Aster's questions would have to wait.

Enough people had seen her. She set her plate aside and made her way through the party, saying quick goodbyes, then went out to find the hired coachman.

She'd want an early start on tomorrow's hunt.

CHAPTER THREE
GALE

The gold-trimmed clock on the wall read five minutes to seven.

Gale had been stealing glances at it since midnight. The hands had seemed to slow gradually, teasing her as the night drew out longer and thinner with each passing hour and each party guest who came to sit at her little table in Archibald Poncifer's library.

The night-long party and most of the house seemed to belong to his wife, but the library had the masculine air of a wealthy man's retreat. Gale had given in to temptation and taken a peek at some of the books between readings, but the handsome leather-bound volumes on the wall-to-wall and floor-to-ceiling oak shelves were either dull tomes on business or history told in the least interesting way possible. It was just as well—neither of the Poncifers would have been pleased if their guests had entered to find the hired entertainment perusing the pages of his personal library instead of sitting in knowing readiness at the table she'd set up in the centre of the room. Displeased hosts led to fewer recommendations, fewer jobs in the future, and...

Well, Gale wasn't quite sure what. Jes wouldn't see her sent to the poor house. At the same time, she didn't want to find out what her boss might have in mind for her if fortune telling didn't work out.

Three minutes. Gale reached for her crystal ball and the deck of artfully decorated cards she'd brought with her, eager to stuff them into her bag and be on her way.

The door cracked open, and she set them down, forcing a smile as a thin-faced woman poked her head into the room.

"Am I too late?"

Yes, Gale thought, but forced herself to gesture for the woman to sit in the leather-upholstered armchair on the other side of the table. "Of course not."

The guest's red gown rustled as she entered and took in the transformed space. Mrs Poncifer had gone all out with the decorations in every part of the house visible to guests. Even Gale, who had worked at three parties already this holiday season, had been impressed by the massive pine tree in the entryway lit with candles and hung with hard candies and gifts, the boughs of beribboned cedar that hugged the bannisters and mantels, and the towering sugar castle she'd caught a glimpse of in the dining room on her way by.

Only a glimpse, though. She'd been stuck in this room all night, save for two stolen trips to the servants' toilet and one quick journey to the kitchen to beg a sandwich. She'd eaten it in the library, which was decorated not with holiday cheer, but with a sombre, mysterious atmosphere of low lights, dusky fabrics, and silence that seemed to set people's nerves on edge when the door closed and dulled the music and laughter from the party downstairs.

"Gosh," said the woman, and tucked a loose strand of brown hair behind one ear. "Bit spooky, isn't it?"

She closed the door and took her seat.

Gale smiled mysteriously. She didn't look past the guest at the ghost who floated through the door and glanced at the woman's dress and face.

"Chauncen," Madrigal said. She didn't keep her voice down—no one but Gale could hear her. "Didn't catch her first name. Not the subject of much gossip that I overheard, but her husband's downstairs drooling over one of the poor young maids. Third one I've seen him flirting with tonight, if you can call it flirting. Not sure he's sober enough to tell the difference between any of them." The ghost crossed her legs and hovered at table height, her simple green dress and bare feet in stark contrast with Mrs Chauncen's elaborate puffed sleeves and the ridiculous purple costume dress Gale wore in an attempt to look the part of the seer. Madrigal hadn't aged since the first time they'd met, and as far as Gale knew she hadn't changed her clothes since the day she died.

At least she looked better than she had that day, lack of corporeal form notwithstanding. No gash to her throat left by the children she'd taken in when their parents abandoned them to starve in the woods, no blood soaked into her golden hair.

"Mrs..." Gale paused, squinting, as though drawing the knowledge from the air. "Chauncen, is it?"

"It is." She didn't seem impressed. They didn't usually, at first. Only the most gullible didn't assume the hostess had provided a list and perhaps some guidance. "I didn't come with any specific questions. My husband's not quite ready for the party to end and suggested I come up to see you."

Madrigal let out a *hrmph* that only Gale could hear.

"A general reading, then," Gale said. She let some of the natural warmth return to her voice, sensing that this woman would be put off by any theatrically mysterious behaviour. A small blessing. Jes had taught her to play a number of parts, and most of them were exhausting. She was barely keeping her eyes open as it was. "Your palms, please."

Mrs Chauncen smiled nervously and set her hands on the table, palms up. Gale pretended to look them over before selecting the right one and holding it in her left hand. Hands were only useful to the sort of palm reading Jes had taught her if there was a scar or the ghost of a missing ring. It was the rest of a person that told her what she needed to know, and she took careful note of all of it.

Gaudy jewellery. Big gems, flashy but not artfully set or well-coordinated. Spear of Ghallais on one of her pendants. A wine stain on her cuff.

No, not wine. Jelly.

"The past year has been good to you," she said, tracing a finger over Mrs Chauncen's palm. She glanced up and caught a faint tightening of her brow. "It hasn't been without its trials and sorrows, but you've emerged stronger for them."

The frown disappeared. "That's true."

True for anyone else I said it to tonight, too, Gale thought.

"You've enjoyed the party, though you celebrate Solvar yourself, not Langnaak as your hosts do."

"Hmm."

Gale held back a sigh. This woman was sober as a stone. If she'd been tipsy, she might've been open, offering more information Gale could build on to make it look like mind reading. If she'd been flat-out drunk, it wouldn't have mattered much, as she wouldn't have remembered it in the morning.

Nothing risky for her, then. Something simple and straightforward.

"You have a dream," Gale told her. "Something that burns in your heart, something you want to accomplish, but you've held yourself back because you fear the consequences."

"Do I?"

Of course she'd be boring, too.

"You do," Gale said. "I see it clear as sunlight." She tapped a random spot near the base of Mrs Chauncen's thumb. "It may be hidden deep within you, something your heart once treasured and now keeps safe even from your mind. Something that would be a frightening adventure, requiring risks and uncertainties, something you know deep down is tied to your purpose." Gale rubbed the bridge of her nose and closed her eyes as though the knowledge had exhausted her. "I can't tell you what it is. But it's there."

It was always there. Everyone had something they thought made them more interesting than everyone around them.

Mrs Chauncen nodded slowly. "I was thinking of having a dress made of that pink striped silk. My friends said it would be terrible with my complexion, but I don't know. It calls to me."

Madrigal, who had been listening without comment, turned her back in disgust.

"Maybe," Gale said. "Perhaps dig a little deeper, but that does sound lovely." She bent over and gave the hand one last look. "As for your future, I see troubles to come in the year ahead, but you'll find prosperity and great joy on the other side."

"And a pink dress," Madrigal added. Gale ignored her.

Mrs Chauncen examined her palm. "You really see that?"

"I do. Stay strong. You have no idea how good things will be."

Mrs Chauncen smiled and pressed a silver coin into Gale's hand. No one but the hostess was required to pay her that night, but many had. "I needed to hear that. Thank you."

Gale waited until she'd closed the door behind her, then packed her things into her old satchel before anyone else could come in.

"You didn't tell her about her husband," Madrigal said. "I'm not sure what the point is of me spying if you're not going to use what I give you."

"Bad news doesn't put a thank-you coin in my hand." Gale wrapped a pale pink wool scarf around her neck and slipped into her long wool coat. It buttoned to the neck and covered the foolish purple gown to her knees. It was one thing to be seen in something flashy and a little revealing when she played a part for a job, but quite another to wear such things out on the street.

"Besides, I can't imagine she doesn't suspect. If she'd wanted to know for sure, she'd have asked me about it."

Bad news also didn't make regular customers out of the people she met at these parties, who had come for a good time. She didn't expect to see Mrs Chauncen again but only had one business card left in her coat pocket of the twenty she'd brought with her. Even if only a few ever became regular clients or recommended her to a friend, it would make tonight worthwhile.

Good news, a dire warning to give weight to the reading and make it memorable, assurances of fair weather to come, end on a positive note. Be ready to pivot if a guess didn't land, be ready to pounce if it did, observe, observe, observe. After nine months working for Jes, it was routine, something she could do half-asleep.

And thank God for that.

Gale took her bag and plodded down the back staircase into the kitchen, followed by Madrigal. A few servants were scrubbing pots, looking well past worn out after the long night. Delia Poncifer was still wearing her party dress, white swirled with green paisley, as she quietly lectured the head cook on something.

"All done, dear?" she asked, turning to Gale.

"I am. If there's nothing else…" Gale let the sentence trail off, praying there was nothing else. She'd made sure to collect payment at the beginning of the night. Taking her leave was a formality.

"No, not at all." She turned away. "Now, as I was saying, the roast was lovely, but the gravy? Lumps, Ophelia. *Lumps.*"

Gale left them to it and added Ophelia to the list of folks she'd pray for when she had the energy to do any such thing.

The sky outside was still mostly dark and covered in thick clouds, and the frosty air bit at Gale's cheeks and nose as she closed the garden gate and stepped onto the street. A few cabs passed, out trawling for tired folks needing a ride home after the night-long parties that were so common during this week before the solstice, when so many cultures and religions celebrated the coming of longer days.

Gale reached into her pocket for the roll of bills and the handful of assorted coins she'd collected over the course of the evening—payment for her presence, tips and gifts from folks pleased by her readings or who seemed to think they were buying a look down her dress as they passed it to her.

But there were better uses for that money than a cab ride to ease the ache in her feet and get her home to bed more quickly. A good portion of it would go to Jes, who'd created this dubious position for Gale after she first came to the city and continued to offer leads, advice, and training. Gale would save the rest for new boots and maybe a dress made just for her instead of the serviceable but plain ones she'd bought at an estate sale she'd attended with Jes. Something colourful, but not as gaudy as what she wore now.

She considered spending a little and finding a way to send a gift to Bright Hollow for her nephew, Fox, but he'd never see it if she did. Her name had been stricken from public records and official memory, and any toy she sent would be burned.

In the time since she'd left home, she'd learned to distract herself from thoughts of her home and family, knowing they could only hurt her. During the holidays, though, even the kindest smiles from jolly strangers and the most interesting traditions celebrated in the city couldn't outweigh the ache in her heart. Hovering at the edges of other people's elaborate parties left her hollow and empty when she thought of how people at home would be busy preparing special recipes and making gifts to be given at a town-wide celebration where no one was a stranger, where everyone was both a servant and guest of honour, where—

She trudged through a puddle, and the shock of icy water

seeping into her old boot jolted her out of her thoughts of music and candlelight.

You left for a reason, she reminded herself. Even if they'd let her go back, the price would be too high.

But it still hurt to wonder whether they missed her in spite of the Luminary's orders.

She pulled her hood up against the cold, cutting off her peripheral vision. It would have been a foolish mistake for most folks walking alone in a city where pickpockets or worse might be watching, but for a young witch with a ghost keeping an eye on every movement in every shadow it was no concern at all.

"Talk to me, please," she said, keeping her voice low even though there weren't any people about to hear her talking to what they'd see as thin air. They'd reached a broad thoroughfare that separated the fine residential neighbourhood of Avlon from the shops and flats of upper midtown. A cab stopped to let them cross, and the piebald mare pulling it snorted and pawed at the cobblestones as Madrigal passed in front of her nose.

"Love to." Madrigal was as bright and fresh as always. Gale had the impression the ghost never needed to sleep—not here in this world, probably not even when she visited the borderlands between life and death. She walked backward in front of Gale, her feet a few inches above the snowy sidewalk that would neither wet nor chill her even if she tried to touch it. "We should discuss the lesson plan for today."

Gale groaned, and Madrigal scowled at her.

"After you rest, of course." Madrigal said this as though sleep were an inconvenience rather than, at least for the moment, Gale's fondest wish. "You're wasting too much time on work for that woman, and it's leaving you too dull and lifeless for your studies."

A painful pang of regret shot through Gale's chest, and she winced. "I know. I'm surprised you didn't mention it sooner." She glanced down and found Madrigal's fists clenched at her sides, betraying emotion the ghost had schooled out of her voice.

"I've wanted to. I know you're only working for that woman to keep spirit and body together, but it's holding you back. Too much time with clients, with learning how to keep them hooked so they'll keep paying. Too much focus on trying to learn enchantments so you can get good enough for her to sell the items in her shop."

"You specialized in enchantments," Gale reminded her.

"I did, and you show great promise with them." Madrigal's brow furrowed. "It's the balance that's wrong, and your reasons for doing any of it. Your potions are coming along better than anything else, which is fine, but you're not connecting with the language of magic as you should be, and you're letting your worldly needs guide your journey."

Instead of letting you guide it? Gale thought, but bit her tongue. Madrigal had every right to be angry. She was the reason Gale was a witch at all, and Gale's lack of mastery was, at least in theory, the unfulfilled purpose tying her to this world. Gale owed it to her to devote herself to her lessons.

But against every expectation Gale had when she became a witch, those lessons had become a chore. Wonder had turned to work, discovery to drudgery as she pushed herself to perform false magic for Jes's sake and the real thing for Madrigal's.

"Perhaps it's time to consider other options." Madrigal drifted higher, skirting a snowbank. "You could leave. Go back to my cabin. Repairs would be a lot of work, but it would be quiet there. We could make it what it once was, a place of magic that provides everything you need."

Gale's stomach twisted uncomfortably at the idea of going back. It had been a wonderful place when she was a child, and now that she'd sorted out the truth of her time there from the lies she'd believed about Madrigal, she cherished the memories. But Madrigal had been there then, a living, breathing presence. As had Hawk, even if he'd been a horrid, churlish boy during their time with her.

To go back now, to live with a few chickens and maybe a goat, studying magic and tending the garden all day long, would be to step into the life Madrigal had been living before her death. It had been perfect for her, but to Gale it seemed like a terribly lonely existence, having only one ghostly person to talk to.

It would be a less distracting setting, but it wouldn't fix whatever was wrong in her heart. A beautiful dream, but it wasn't Gale's.

Though it would have the added benefit of never having to wear ridiculous purple dresses again.

"It's too dangerous," she said, grasping at the only answer that came to mind that wouldn't hurt Madrigal's feelings. "Do you remember when we went back there for your books and your enchanted shelf?"

Madrigal sniffed derisively. "It was a lovely journey, aside from when you almost drove that poor cart-pony into the stream."

"Of course it was lovely for you. You weren't looking over your shoulder every other moment to be sure your family wasn't lurking about waiting to kill you."

"No," Madrigal said softly. "That's not a danger for me these days."

Gale sighed. "I really couldn't live there even if I fixed it up. Hawk is probably watching for exactly that." Her heart ached again at the thought of her brother. He'd made himself her personal villain, but she couldn't help longing for what might have been. "We don't need to leave the city. I'll try harder, really."

Madrigal nodded. "I know."

They turned a corner and entered a neighbourhood that was more familiar to Gale, its rows of buildings packed so tight against the streets they seemed to lean in overhead. The lower levels of the half-timbered structures tended to house shops and offices, while the upper levels were occupied by flats topped with steeply pitched slate roofs. It wasn't the best neighbourhood in the city, and the police at their station six blocks away from Gale's home kept plenty busy. But it wasn't the worst, either, and Gale thought she did well enough living there even if the cold did come in around the windows now that winter had arrived.

A large public courtyard between a barber's shop and a place specializing in cheap meat pies provided a shortcut, and Gale crossed the street to make her way through. Even at this early hour, and in the darkest part of winter, a handful of merchants had hauled their carts in to ply their trade and to try to catch the eye of anyone shopping for Solvar or Daybreak gifts, depending on the patrons' inclinations. Gale passed one with racks of brightly coloured scarves that her fingers itched to touch, one selling bottles of wine from around the world, and an elderly man selling wheeled wooden pull-toys in the shape of animals. Folks were coming out now that the sky had brightened, and Gale wove her way through the thin crowd.

Her steps slowed as she approached another cart, this one staffed by a tall, thin man with dark hair poking out from beneath his battered top hat. His nose leaned a bit toward the squashed tomato side of things, but his voice was smooth and confident as he called out to a broad-shouldered woman in black who had paused several paces from his cart.

"Genuine curatives!" he called. "Madam, are doctors failing you?"

The woman laughed bitterly, and Gale stopped to listen.

"Doctors aren't doing anything," the woman said. Gale noted the fallen hem of her threadbare coat and ratty boots that made Gale's look like glass slippers by comparison. "They need money before they'll try, don't they?"

The fellow at the cart snapped his fingers. "Exactly! Cash for a visit, cash for a cure, and what do you get?" He didn't wait for her to answer. "Sick again in a month, that's what. I don't say it myself, but some folks claim doctors make things worse just to keep getting that coin."

Gale gritted her teeth.

"It's not worth it," Madrigal said. "And for all we know that false healer is another pie your boss has her fingers in."

"No," Gale said, speaking more quietly than Madrigal had. "Jes might have him selling to the folks who were at that party last night, but not here. Not to these people."

Madrigal answered with a non-committal huff. She'd disliked Jes from the start, insisting that no good could come of Gale working for her, but Gale suspected she'd warmed to the young swindler personally, even if she still maintained professional objections. The fact that Jes only stole from those who could afford it had helped Gale get past her own discomfort at stepping into the periphery of a nascent criminal empire.

Two more people gathered to listen to the man in the top hat. "Halts aging like that!" he cried, snapping his fingers again. "Or look here, just for you, as you seem like a trustworthy bunch." His voice dropped to a conspiratorial but clearly audible pitch as he produced a dark bottle with a brown label covered in fancy lettering. "A genuine magical potion guaranteed to cure most any ill, and still—still!—I offer a dose for less than the cost of a visit to a doctor who will do less."

The two who had stopped wandered away, but the woman in black was still listening. "What of the croup?" she asked. "Or the winter cough that's going around stealing babies' breath?"

The seller noticed Gale listening and frowned before resting his full attention on his target. "Madam, I swear to you, this is true magic that will aid any respiratory illness your child might suffer."

Gale's cheeks warmed. She'd learned to control the temper that so often got her in trouble as a child, but sometimes it still lit a fire in her.

"Nightingale," Madrigal said, a warning in her tone.

"I should be helping," Gale whispered, casting a quick glance around her to be sure no one was listening. "I'm learning magic, using magic, and what is it good for but lining pockets? If my life had gone differently, I'd have become a healer in Bright Hollow. I already took my oath during training to help and heal when it was within my power, without judgement or hesitation. Now I'm doing nothing to help anyone."

"If you'd stayed in that place," Madrigal said, "you'd have no magic to help anyone with, anyway."

"But now—"

Madrigal gave her a sharp look. "But now? Now you're a promising apprentice who's dabbled in healing potions and enchantments but still lacks the knowledge to help this woman. And even if you could, you know the risks."

"You don't need to remind me," Gale murmured, when it seemed Madrigal was about to do just that.

Two months ago, a woman from a village outside the city had been beheaded over witchcraft. Gale hadn't strayed from her flat save to visit the toilets in the yard until Jes sent Cas to tell her the king's mages had left the area.

"The more people you help, the greater the risk of exposure," Madrigal said. "Besides, people get in the way of proper study. They complicate things when we get close to them. Distract us."

Gale didn't answer. She'd accepted that greatness in magic meant a mostly solitary life like the one Madrigal had chosen for herself, and the ghost was proof of the harm that could come to a witch if she let people in.

But as incredible as magic was all on its own, she wanted more. As she watched the poor woman and thought of what it would be like to offer her real help, a glimmer of something she hadn't felt in months warmed her. Interest. Hope. Maybe even passion.

Madrigal sighed. "It's hard, I know. Keep up with your studies. Then someday, when you've mastered your craft, you'll help these people. And when that time comes you can have a clear conscience as you wait for the mages to come lop off your head. By then my unfinished work will be done, Lord Death will have taken me to what lies beyond the veil, and I won't have to witness what becomes of my apprentice."

Gale glared at her but didn't argue. Madrigal wasn't wrong, much as Gale might want her to be.

The woman stepped closer to the seller, reaching into her pocket.

Gale stepped forward. "Madam, don't." She counted out several of the bills her patrons had offered so generously at the party. "Take your baby to a real doctor. I heard the teachers at the medical college have their students applying themselves to that infant sickness now that it's affecting wealthier households." She glared at the seller. "No magic, but specific, researched cures. I'll pay for the visit if you'll go now and not come back here."

The woman's eyes widened, and she took the money. "Thank you."

Gale didn't watch her leave. She was too busy keeping an eye on the seller as she backed away. He glared at her until another potential customer caught his attention and he spun into his pitch again. His voice seemed to follow Gale down the road.

Gale's anger cooled as she walked on.

Ought to call the cops, she thought, and dismissed the idea. Satisfying as it would be to see him taken in and questioned over his potion, she knew from personal experience that faking magic wasn't enough to get more than a night in jail and perhaps a token fine. It wasn't worth risking police attention on herself or her employer.

The encounter had helped awaken her mind, though, and there was no risk of dozing off as she walked on toward home.

"Waste of money," Madrigal said. "You need savings. A way out."

"Perhaps," Gale said, but privately she thought that feeling a little like her old self for a moment was well worth the cost.

The familiar scent of bread and sugary spices drifted from the bakery below Gale's third-floor flat. She passed by, though her stomach growled. Sleep seemed far more important.

"Things aren't so bad for now," she said as she stepped into the alley, trying to convince herself as much as Madrigal. "I'm learning. Growing in my craft, if more slowly than either of us would like. I have food and a home. I'll help others someday, and Jes will help me figure out how to stay safe."

"Long as it doesn't come back on her, anyway." Madrigal paused, frowning. "Wait," she said, and drifted down the long alley and to the top of the stairs near its far end, as far as she could go from Gale's magic without disappearing into the borderlands.

She returned, scowling. "You've got company."

Before Gale could ask more, a pair of policemen in black uniforms came down the rickety wooden staircase to meet her halfway to the street.

"Constables Podix and Altwell," Gale said. "I don't suppose you've come to wish me a happy Daybreak? A merry Langnaakk? A joyful Solvar?"

They exchanged a look. "Miss Alcorini," said Podix, the taller of the two, with a moustache so tidy and dark that it looked like it had been carefully drawn on with boot polish.

"*Lady Orianna*," added Altwell, with sarcastic reverence that lacked the energy needed to sting. "Had a report that there was a fortune teller giving..." He pulled a leather-covered notebook from his breast pocket and flipped it open. "'Suspiciously accurate prophesying' at a party last night, thought it might be real magic."

Gale bit the inside of her cheek to keep tears from coming to her eyes. "How many times have we been through this? You know it isn't."

Podix shrugged. "Not up to us. I'm afraid you're under arrest, m'dear."

Gale considered running and decided against it. Podix and Altwell patrolled the neighbourhood regularly. Podix played hoops and sticks with the children in the park in the summer—strictly when off-duty—and Altwell had taken Gale's recommendation to find Duronian ginger tea for his wife when she'd had morning sickness several months back. They were known. Familiar, thanks to previous complaints from clients. Unthreatening as long as they thought Gale was faking everything.

"I didn't do anything illegal," she said, knowing it would do no good. If the finer folks of the city had complained, the cops would play their part. "It was clearly stated that I was the entertainment, no promises of anything more."

"They might've mentioned something about missing cash, too," Podix said, and visions of new boots fluttered from Gale's mind as she considered her income being taken as evidence. Every forin had been freely given, but it was her word against theirs.

No money for boots, no money for Jes, no money to replenish her potions supplies for her studies, and the prospect of a day in a cold, stinking cell... Suddenly a lonely life in the woods didn't seem so terrible, after all.

"Come on, now," Altwell said, taking her gently by the arm and motioning toward the end of the alley. "It's a lovely morning for a little walk. We won't cuff you if you swear not to make a fuss, and I promise I won't let Podix sing any holiday songs at you along the way."

Podix shot him an offended look. "She should be so lucky."

Madrigal glared daggers at the cops behind their backs, but there was nothing more a ghost could do.

"Fine." Gale tried not to think about her cozy bed upstairs as they led her away.

CHAPTER FOUR
ASTER

It was one thing to kill a wolf in the darkest part of the night and in the privacy of his own home. It was quite another to go hunting in a public park in the heart of the city and the bright light of morning. But Aster was prepared, and this wouldn't be the first time she'd been forced to act in less-than-ideal circumstances.

She pulled her moth-eaten fur stole tighter around her shoulders, lowered her gaze, and made her way through the fenced-in park near the centre of the city. She'd taken care with every aspect of her disguise, from the worn boots to the faded brown dress to the floppy wool hat that shadowed her face. It wasn't as comfortable or familiar as her red cloak, but it blended in better.

She couldn't afford to be recognized, and dressing as a beggar had the advantage of not only not drawing attention, but of actively repelling it as folks avoided eye contact that might have led to conversation and requests for coin.

When she touched her face, she felt the scar that cut down its left side, but thanks to a small illusion spell Eamon had placed on her, no one else would see it.

He'd once offered to try to find a longer-lasting form of the illusion that would hide her scars when she went out in public. She'd refused, only allowing him to apply his spell when she needed to be someone other than herself. Her scars were a part of her, one that spoke of her unremembered past and couldn't be taken away, for better or worse, by Eamon's healings. The scars were her truth, and the enchantment a lie.

But today that lie was a tool, and it would serve her for several hours before it began to wear off.

She wouldn't need hours.

As she passed through the park, focusing on the pain that lingered in her scars so she could take on a convincing limp, she watched for her prey. A young cop wandered the paths around the duck pond. She'd keep an eye on him. He looked fresh out of training, wearing his stern gaze like a mask, the copper buttons on his black uniform shining as though they'd just come from the factory. He'd be a threat if anything went wrong.

The other people in the park didn't worry her. The quartet of musicians playing merry songs in the big whitewashed gazebo, a young couple edging closer to a bough of lover's thorn growing on an oak tree, a businessman checking his watch as he strode from one end of the park to the other... not one of them glanced her way.

Aster turned when she reached the gazebo and walked a short way down the path, stopping to sit when she reached the wood-and-iron bench she'd chosen days before.

Jesamyn Windram—better known as Jes, among other names—had hidden herself well, and it had taken years for Aster and Eamon to track her down. She and her mother had split from the rest of their sorry crew after they met Eamon and things went so disastrously wrong for them, and then they'd vanished. There would be stories here and there about a mother and daughter fitting their description swindling the poor out of money at a factory or a false witch and her assistant selling fake magical cures, but the trails were always cold before Eamon could confirm anything.

But a criminal couldn't pass through the world unnoticed, and certainly not without leaving an ocean of grudges in her wake. In the end, all it had taken was a little targeted bribery for Eamon to find out that Jes was running a second-hand store in Queen's Run.

They'd assumed Jes would run the sort of pawn shop that profited off human misery as she and her family had always done. Instead, Aster found Jes calling herself Delian Carraway and running a respectable little shop, charging too much for old books and jewellery, fine furniture from estate sales, fake unicorn horns, and the occasional real enchanted item sold legally on the antiques market.

Aster hadn't risked going into the shop or getting close enough to be spotted, but she'd spoken to customers who'd noticed that the shopkeeper had one brown eye and one gold. She'd watched Jes's comings and goings from a distance, freezing her bones overnight on the rooftop across the street when she wasn't watching her other prey, ignoring the aches in her scars that demanded she return home to Eamon for healing.

She couldn't, though, when remembering every moment of her surveillance was so important. She could tell Eamon every-thing before the memories were washed away and he'd give it all back faithfully, but learning about a thing was never the same as experiencing it. Any seemingly insignificant, half-remembered detail might become essential.

Pain flared up her right leg, and she rubbed it through her thin dress before she readjusted the skirt to hide the shape of the dagger strapped to her thigh.

Healing tonight, she promised herself. *Then one more hunt.*

She looked up, searched for a moment, and spotted her prey stepping into the park. Aster held back a smile.

Jesamyn was clever, occasionally leaving her shop and the

apartment above at night but never on a regular schedule and always accompanied by the young man who lived with her, one who Aster had only seen in silhouette behind the curtains or hidden in nighttime shadows. Had Aster been less reluctant to harm folks who hadn't hurt her, she might have tried to break in while they slept. As it was, there was never any time she could catch the so-called wolf unguarded in her home.

There was nothing in Jes's routine or appearance that suggested criminal activity.

But they don't change, Aster reminded herself. Whatever had come between them in the end, Jes had worked faithfully with her mother since childhood and had become quite an accomplished criminal. She wouldn't have given it up. More likely she was hiding in plain sight as Aster was now.

But there was this, every day. The solitary walk in the park across from her shop, cocoa in a paper cup from the cart near the gazebo, and nodded greetings to folks she seemed to stand apart from, in the crowd but not of it.

A wolf among sheep.

Aster's plan was risky but simple. Wait for Jes to approach, visually confirm her identity based on Eamon's description, and follow until Aster saw her chance to slip her dagger between the shopkeeper's ribs from behind. Heavy layers of clothing would be no obstacle for Eamon's enchanted blade, and she would be gone before Jes realized she was dying. There would be no time to confront Jes with *why* she'd been killed, and that didn't sit well with Aster. But it would be done.

Aster put those thoughts aside and watched Jes from beneath the wide brim of her hat. Jes's complexion was a little lighter than Aster's, her smile genuine as she waved down at a baby in a pram, her posture relaxed but perfect.

Aster's stomach dropped as she realized one other fact she'd missed when she'd been keeping her distance—Jesamyn

Windram couldn't be more than a few years older than Aster herself.

It wasn't that it was wrong to kill a woman in her twenties, only that the others had been older. She had been picturing a young woman there that day at her grandmother's cabin, not a girl like herself. The gap in her understanding made her stomach drop as it did when she missed a step going down the stairs.

But it was her, no doubt.

Jes walked with her head held high, looking every inch the upstanding citizen she now claimed to be. Her thick, dark hair was pulled into a tidy bun at the back of her neck, and she wore a full skirt of chocolate brown wool and a matching waistcoat with a white blouse underneath. As she came closer, Aster noted the fine leather gloves she wore.

She was doing well for herself, whatever she was really up to.

Aster looked down at the ground, preparing herself to stand once Jes had passed. But Jes's feet—clad in brown leather boots with sensible heels—stopped and turned to face her.

The brim of her hat kept Aster's face shadowed as she took a closer look at her enemy's clothing. The blouse was simple, lacking the excess fabric in the sleeves that would have made it truly fashionable, and though the waistcoat was cut to fit her, the heavy fabric was unusual in its lack of feminine flourish, and the watch chain hanging from her pocket was heavier than it should have been. But then, a slightly odd appearance probably served her well as the proprietor of a shop that dealt in unusual items.

Costumes. Lies. Tricks.

Jes reached into her pocket and pulled out three copper coins. "Here," she said, holding them out toward Aster. "You look cold. The cocoa is good today."

Aster hesitated, then decided that a beggar refusing good coin would seem suspicious. "Thank you," she muttered, and pocketed the money.

When Jes didn't leave, Aster looked up higher, meeting Jes's eyes. They were as Eamon had said, one deep brown, one more golden. It was subtle but striking.

And in spite of everything, memorable.

Something moved deep in Aster's mind, a sort of doubling, the image of a laughing girl with those same eyes overlying the young woman now looking down at her.

Aster reached desperately for the memory, heart racing, but it vanished.

At least I know it's her, anyway.

"Bless you, ma'am," Aster added, hoping it would be enough to send Jes on her way. It worked. Aster lowered her gaze, and Jes walked on.

Aster waited for a few moments. It wouldn't do to follow too closely now that she'd been properly noticed. But she stood and stretched, trying to ignore the cutting pain that radiated out from the scars on her face, her chest, her right forearm, her left thigh, and a dozen smaller spots on her body. Jes had stopped to listen to the band.

Perfect. She'd give her a minute to relax into it, then make her move.

A flash of bright pink caught Aster's eye near one of the entrances to the fenced-in park—a young woman with pale blonde hair, her rose-coloured dress cut low enough to catch anyone's attention. It had certainly worked its magic on the middle-aged gentleman she was speaking to, though he appeared to be making a valiant effort to keep his eyes respectfully raised. They were too far off for Aster to hear them, but the man's keen attention and the way the young woman's gaze searched for more desirable company even as she kept smiling brought up painful empathy in Aster. She knew the feeling well, having conversed with far too many dull rich folk at the fundraisers Eamon asked her to attend, forcing smiles until her cheeks ached.

Another figure approached the awkward pair, noticeable only for the quick clip of her determined strides. A girl, much younger than the one in pink, with mud-coloured hair and a pale, pinched face, the skirt of her grey dress fluttering behind as she held her weathered black coat close around her. Aster watched with sharp interest as she collided with the gentleman, appeared to apologize, and went on her way.

The gentleman, who was now checking to make sure the lady in pink hadn't suffered any harm, would likely find himself missing his wallet later. Aster hoped someone would catch the thief, but random criminals weren't her business. Only the ones who had hurt her so deeply, and who had all evaded the law until she'd come for them.

Aster checked that the cop was on the other side of the park, rubbed the stiffness from her left leg, and moved slowly through the crowd toward the band and her prey. She reached into the slit she'd cut into the side of her skirt and drew her dagger, keeping it hidden beneath her long stole.

Approach. Slide the blade home. Pull it out. Retreat. She'd run if she had to. It wouldn't take long to escape if someone started screaming about blood on the snow. Her reflexes and movements would be slowed by her pain, but she knew how to use crowds to her advantage, and she knew the city well. As soon as she left the park, she'd vanish.

Aster's heart raced even as a sense of steady, focused calm settled over her mind. *Peace at last. Justice done. A new life around the corner.*

Four paces, now. Three. Two. The dagger vibrated in her hand, ready to kill.

Aster focused on Jes, anticipating any movement, any sign that she'd spotted her death approaching.

Something moved to her left, but Aster saw it too late to brace properly against the man who charged from the crowd and collided with her. They hit the ground with a thud that sent sharp pain blazing through Aster's scars. The dagger spun out of her hand, narrowly missing several people's feet before it skittered into a clump of thick bushes in the shadow of the gazebo.

If she'd let Eamon heal her after he'd come home from the party, if she'd been at her strongest and the impact hadn't made her feel like her body might fall to pieces right there in the park, she might have broken free of the grip her attacker had on her arms. Instead, she twisted to glare at him as the people around them shouted and hurried away.

Aster blinked hard as the sight of his face connected with something in her memory. For a second, he reminded her of a bearded version of one of the princes of Andonia—she'd seen a few of them at a ball years ago, an event that remained largely intact in her mind if a little foggy around the edges. But he was dressed like any other lower-level gentleman, and royals certainly didn't spend their afternoons tackling beggars in Queen's Run.

He hauled her to her feet. Aster fought back, acting indignant and as innocent as she could.

She scanned the area. Jes had vanished.

The cop ran toward them. He was thinner than he'd seemed from a distance, his crisp new uniform hanging loose on his shoulders.

"What's the ruckus?" he huffed, winded from the short run.

Aster prepared to defend herself. She'd kept the dagger concealed, but this fellow must have seen it somehow before he attacked her. No one else could have, though. It was his word against hers.

"This woman picked Lord Farthing's pocket."

Aster stopped struggling and stared at the young man who still held her by the arm. "Are you mad?" she asked, almost laughing. He hadn't seen the dagger at all. The only mystery was how he'd mistaken Aster in her old fur stole for the younger and smaller pickpocket in her black coat. She turned to the cop.

"Officer, I was just on my way to buy a cocoa, not harming anyone. I swear."

The young man released her, and Aster stood before the cop, eyes wide and innocent, doubly glad for the spell that hid her scars and her identity.

"Then you won't mind if I search you," the cop said.

Aster stiffened but knew better than to object. If she'd been dressed normally, if she'd been recognized as related to one of Queen's Run's most celebrated philanthropists, the cop wouldn't have dared to lay a hand on her. But she wouldn't trade on Eamon's name when it would cause him so much embarrassment and lead to so many questions. She would remain a beggar for now, and the cop would do as he pleased.

The dagger was gone. He wouldn't find anything on her.

The cop reached into the pocket of her dress and pulled out a leather wallet and a set of keys.

Aster gaped at him. "That's not—I didn't—"

"Save it for the courts," he said, and pulled her arms roughly behind her. Cold metal clamped down on her wrists, tight enough to bite her skin.

The fellow she'd seen getting his pocket picked earlier sauntered over, chest puffed out importantly. "Ah, yes," he said. "I saw that one skulking about."

Liar, Aster thought. He'd been too busy noticing pretty girls in pink dresses.

"We'll need to keep these things as evidence, Lord Farthing," the cop said, holding up the wallet and the jingling keys. "Not for long, though. You'll be able to claim them at the station tomorrow."

Lord Farthing nodded and waved them away. "Of course, of course. Thank you, Constable."

The cop gave Aster a shove, pushing her ahead of him down the path. She looked frantically for the young woman who'd actually stolen the wallet, but she was nowhere to be seen.

She did, however, spot Jesamyn Windram standing with the young man who had tackled her. She was frowning, but when he leaned in and whispered something in her ear, she smiled. Then she lifted one hand and waved with her fingers as the cop hauled Aster away.

CHAPTER FIVE
ASTER

Aster kept her head down and her eyes open as the skinny young constable, who'd turned out to be significantly stronger than she'd expected, guided her through a police station a half-dozen blocks from the park. She noted every window, the direct route to a back door past an open area filled with oak desks set atop green carpet, the uniformed police who cast stern glares in her direction as she passed.

Escape routes. Obstacles. Opportunities. It wasn't the stickiest situation she'd ever been in, and Eamon would start looking for her once he realized she wasn't coming home. Still, it never hurt to have a back-up plan.

Her stomach sank as the cop steered her by her handcuffs toward an open doorway at the top of a set of enclosed wooden stairs. He gave her a little push at the top, and Aster stepped into air that grew less pleasant with every downward step, heavy and damp and touched with the scents of vomit and the vinegar likely used to clean it up, human filth, and something else she couldn't place.

Misery, maybe.

After a sharp turn at a landing, the stairs ended in the basement beneath the station. Aster took everything in at a glance, feeling less optimistic than she had upstairs.

No windows, and the stone walls lit only by flickering gas lamps that did nothing to dispel the chill already threatening to seep into Aster's bones. They illuminated a series of posters on one wall, black ink sketches depicting wanted criminals and a number of missing persons. No other exits, either.

A wooden desk strewn with papers sat at the near end of the long room, its wooden chair occupied by a balding officer with a fine belly swelling beneath a pressed black uniform that hadn't yet been altered to accommodate it. He glanced up and sighed.

Beyond him, two rows of cells made of iron bars allowed a clear view from the desk into every corner. The bars and low light at that end of the room confused Aster's eyes, but it looked like four cells on each side, with the doors facing each other on either side of a narrow passage. Only the first and last cells on the right were occupied, and neither prisoner took any apparent interest in Aster's arrival. One sat on the floor facing the far wall, muttering in barely audible tones. The other wasn't moving at all.

Aster stopped when she reached the desk and tried to read the papers that littered its surface, but the cop placed a massive ledger on top of them and drew a pen and inkwell from a drawer. He tapped his ragged fingernails on the edge of the desk and waited, then sighed again.

"Who's this, then?"

The arresting officer gave her another shove.

"Elissa Gregory," Aster said, using the name Eamon would search for her by.

"Pickpocketing," the officer added, and handed over the wallet and keys. "For evidence."

"Ah." The bald cop seemed a little more interested in this, but returned to his previous state of apparent ennui once he'd shut the items in his drawer and handed over a set of keys. "Number six."

"It's a misunderstanding," Aster said, hoping this great lump of a man would prove more sympathetic than his sprightly young co-worker.

"It always is," he said. Aster waited for another sigh, but he only nodded toward the cells.

A low groan rose from the body on the floor of the closest one as they passed, a lanky fellow who lay in a jumbled lump like a scarecrow that had been tossed into the cell for storage at the end of the harvest.

"Shaddup, Charlie," the cop muttered to the scarecrow, and banged his night stick against the bars.

They passed one of the empty cells and he unlocked the door of the next, one hand still holding onto Aster's cuffed arm. The person in the last cell, who sat on the floor with their back turned to Aster, fell silent.

"In you go," the cop said, unlocking the handcuffs. "Nice and quiet."

Aster stretched her hands out in front of her, cursing the stiffness in her shoulders and herself for refusing Eamon's healing between kills. He was always telling her she needed to be more conscious of her limits. One day, she'd learn to listen.

The door clanged shut behind her, and Aster surveyed her temporary home. It didn't have much to offer save for a wide wooden bench next to the wall that would serve as a bed, a flat pillow she didn't dare touch for fear of lice and bedbugs, and a bucket in the corner she hoped had been washed recently.

She sat heavily on the bench and shoved the pillow to the floor, then rested her aching head against the wall and closed her eyes.

The cop's boots clumped away over the hard floor, and the gentle muttering in the next cell resumed, along with the sounds of shuffling movement.

"Well, what else was I to do?" A feminine voice. Soft, but a bit peevish. "Yes, I have faith in it, but I still don't want anyone thinking they have reason to search my flat."

Aster cracked one eye open and looked over. Her next-door jail-mate's cell was in the corner at the end of the row, and she'd turned so her back was pressed against the far wall, her legs crossed beneath a voluminous bright purple skirt. She wore a patched wool coat over top and had pulled her hands inside the sleeves for warmth.

Aster didn't recognize her. Not from conscious memory, not from any deeper place like how she'd known Jesamyn when she saw her in the park. She was just a girl, if a pretty one, somewhere close to Aster's age. Brown hair tucked beneath the collar of her coat, full cheeks with a rosy flush to them... but her eyes were the most striking detail. Not for their summer-sky hue, but the way they looked ahead and to her right, focused intently on the centre of the empty space in her cell.

"I know that," she said, as though responding to another part of a conversation. "Honestly, I've been doing this for the better part of a year now, and..."

Aster tuned her out, leaving her to her imaginary conversation as well as she could. It was a shame, really. The girl was clearly suffering some disconnect from reality, but on first glance she seemed harmless enough. Too many folks like her ended up in jail when what they needed was a hospital.

It might be a cause Eamon would like to contribute to.

Aster shivered and pulled her stole closer around her shoulders, but it did little good. As the chill set itself deep into her, her muscles stiffened and the ache in her scars deepened.

Scars.

The scar on her face felt no different when she touched it, but that meant nothing. The officers hadn't said anything about sudden changes, though. The spell was holding, at least for now.

She stood and paced the cell, two steps in each direction. It wasn't enough to warm herself, so she banged her forearm against the bars. "Hey!" she hollered at the cop at the desk, who was now reading a magazine. "Excuse me, do you have any blankets out there?" Aster glanced at the grimy pillow. "Laundered ones?"

The cop licked his thumb and turned the page.

"They don't listen," the girl in the other cell said. "Would you like a turn with my coat? It's much warmer than what you've got, and I think it'll fit through the bars."

Aster turned to find her already shrugging out of the coat, revealing the rest of a ridiculous purple gown with long, fitted sleeves and a pink scarf around her neck that barely disguised the dramatic neckline of her dress.

"You don't have to—" Aster began, but the girl shoved the coat between the bars. As she did, Aster caught sight of her right hand, where the index finger was completely missing.

Not an unusual thing on its own. People lost whole limbs in the factories sometimes. But they weren't the only ones who suffered losses.

Eamon had cut off a toe as his sacrifice, but each witch made their own choice of what they'd give up to gain power. He'd then studied well and properly, intending at first to become a legally sanctioned king's mage and choosing otherwise when he learned how restrictive their ways were. He'd selected his teachers carefully, and his control had grown along with his power. But he'd spoken to Aster of the dangers of magic, of how those who were careless or ignorant as they played with it could be harmed in mind and body.

If this girl had lost her finger in an attempt to take magic into herself, if she hadn't been as careful as he'd been, perhaps that explained her current mental state.

It was not a power to be trifled with lightly, and Aster had always been satisfied to leave it in Eamon's hands.

But as Aster accepted the coat and muttered her thanks, the girl's eyes and expression were as clear and lucid as anyone's

Aster had met. Sharp, even. Clever, but not wolf-like, more curious than cunning. She looked Aster over, lingering on her eyes.

"Been here long, then?" Aster asked as she slipped into the coat. It was a little big, but plenty warm, and it smelled pleasantly of lavender and pine needles. "Or frequently?"

The girl laughed and held her hand through the bars. "Why not both? Name's Gale. Nightingale, actually, but I hardly bother with that anymore."

Aster shook it, then let go. Gale's hand was warm, her grip pleasantly strong. If there was magic in her, it was nothing Aster could feel. "Elissa."

"Hey!" The cop, finally distracted from his reading, strode down the hallway toward them. "No touching."

Gale rolled her eyes and pulled her hand back through the bars. "Just making friends, Tom. Nothing to get pissy about."

Aster smiled to herself. Gale sounded like a child who'd recently learned a naughty word testing it out on her parents.

Tom shook his head as though mourning a great burden. "Save the handshakes for when you get out, yeah? I've got a job to do here." He turned and stalked back toward the desk, ignoring the drunk's half-conscious groans as he passed.

When Aster turned back, Gale was looking at nothing again. She frowned and shook her head.

Then Gale turned her attention back to Aster and smiled. It was a nice one, mischievous and sweet at the same time. "So, what are you in for?"

Aster supposed this was one advantage to being introduced in jail—no shortage of topics for small talk. She didn't usually care for idle conversation, but Gale seemed interesting, if odd, and Aster supposed she could do worse than talk to a pretty stranger to keep her mind off her pain.

"Pickpocketing," she said. "It's all a misunderstanding, though. My father will be along shortly to sort it out. How about you?"

"Fortune telling." The pink in Gale's cheeks deepened. "Did business with the wrong people, I suppose."

"You're being charged with magic?"

"Oh, no. There's no magic to fortune telling. Not the way I do it."

Aster glanced down at her missing finger. "That a coincidence, then?"

Gale hid her hands behind her back. "Must be. Anyway, I've been in and out of here a few times over this sort of thing. It's not so bad, really."

A moustached fellow in a dark-brown suit clomped down the stairs and crossed the room without glancing at the prisoners. Gale nodded toward him. "And sometimes it's downright interesting."

The newcomer leaned over the desk and spoke to Tom.

"He's the detective investigating the disappearances," Gale said, her voice low and conspiratorial. "You've seen the missing persons posters around town?"

"Sure. Nothing unusual in a city this size, though."

"He thinks some of them are connected. Abductions or murders."

"How can you hear anything they're saying from here?" Aster's own hearing was particularly acute, and she hadn't picked up anything.

Gale only smiled. Then she glanced back at Aster's face, and her eyes widened.

The spell. Aster turned her face away, and they watched as the detective signed something and left.

She might be able to bluff her way through explaining the appearance of her scar with the cops, but not with a witch. And if that witch reported anything...

"Busy man," Gale said, as though the strange moment hadn't happened. "I wish him luck. Nice to see the police doing something other than persecuting harmless witches and fortune-tellers."

Aster turned back to her, gauging her reaction carefully.

"Funny, isn't it?" Gale asked, looking at Aster's scar without flinching. "How even the best makeup comes right off in these damp conditions."

Aster relaxed, willing to follow her lead if Gale wanted to give her an out. "Quite."

"Forgive my boldness in saying so, but you look nicer without it," Gale continued. "Scars tell so much about a person."

Aster glanced at her hand again, and this time Gale didn't hide it. "I've always thought so, myself."

As she slipped her hands into the coat's pockets to warm them, her fingers brushed something in the right-hand pocket—a small rectangle of cardboard. A business card, perhaps.

Another set of footsteps descended the stairs, quieter than the detective's, and Aster and Gale both turned to watch. Jesamyn Windram stepped into the room looking as comfortable as she'd been strolling the park. She glanced at the cells, setting Aster's teeth on edge, then strode toward the desk as Tom rose to meet her. Jes pulled a paper envelope from the pocket of her jacket and handed it to him, then stepped around the desk so her body blocked Aster's view. They spoke, but too quietly for the prisoners to hear.

Aster had no conscious memory of most fights or dangers she'd faced before, but the cold calm that came over her as she watched them felt deeply familiar and strangely comforting. There was nowhere to run or hide and her weapon was gone, but that didn't make her helpless. If the wolf meant to buy her way into the cell or pay Tom to harm her, they'd both find a few surprises waiting.

She forced her hands to rest, relaxed and ready, at her sides as Tom escorted Jes closer, keys in hand. The hairs on her arms and neck stood up.

But they passed by her cell, and Tom opened Gale's.

The sense of icy certainty drained from Aster's body, leaving her feeling off balance. "She's bailing you out?"

Gale gave her a strange look, as though Aster might be the one whose brain was disconnected from reality. "Of course. It's been lovely meeting you, but I wasn't planning to stay longer than I needed to." She looked to Jes. "Thanks."

She seemed like she wanted to say more but glanced at Tom and fell silent.

She belongs to the wolves, Aster thought. *Either she's not who she seems to be, or she's in trouble.*

Aster palmed the business card and hid it as she shrugged out of the coat and passed it through the bars, then held her hands behind her back and tucked the card into her sleeve. "Thanks for the warmth."

"You're welcome." Gale glanced uncertainly between Aster and Jes.

"Why don't you go with Tom and get your paperwork signed," Jes suggested. A moment later she stood alone at the bars, looking in on Aster like she was a caged animal, all the warmth and humour gone from her strange eyes.

"I'm not interested in speaking to you," Aster said.

"And I don't particularly care what interests you." Jes looked down her nose at her, though she wasn't much taller than Aster. "I'd like to know what brought you to me this morning with a dagger in your hand and murder in your heart."

"Poetic." Aster approached the bars and forced herself to look into Jes's eyes. There again—the tantalizing hint of memory, though not as strong as before, something moving deep within the black waters of her mind. A connection, if a small one, to a time that had been erased the day they first met.

"I saw you skulking around earlier this week," Jes said, "then again this morning—saw you before you saw me, I'd wager."

Aster flashed her a threatening smile. "You should worry more about the times you didn't see me."

Jes's gaze didn't waver. "I want to know why you were in the park, why you wanted me dead."

There was something in her eyes that betrayed emotion deeper than anger or the pride suggested by her verbal posturing. Not fear, Aster thought, though she'd have understood that. Not quite curiosity, but that was closer.

"Your uncle asked me the same thing before I slit his throat," she said, her voice barely rising above a whisper so even the drunk two cells down wouldn't hear. If Jes tried to use the confession against her she'd deny every word.

The blood drained from Jes's cheeks, but she didn't flinch. "Which one?"

"All of them." Aster wrapped her hands around the bars. "You're nearly the only one left of your sad little pack of wolves."

Jes swallowed hard. "Why?"

"We've met before." Aster broke eye contact for long enough to make sure no one was listening. "Years ago, during the time of the curse. Your family took my grandmother's home, and then her life. I'm collecting the debt your family owes to mine."

Jes looked away. The sense of victory that warmed Aster faded, though, when Jes looked back to her with steel in her gaze and her chin held high. "You said I'm nearly the last. What of Mavolia?"

"I'd have expected you to know."

Jes smiled at that, though without any joy or humour. "Haven't done your homework as well as I thought, then. I haven't seen her in almost two years, or the rest of them for longer."

Aster gripped the bars tighter. "That doesn't make you innocent. You're still one of them. Still a criminal."

"Of course I am. But I'm a better class of criminal now." Jes looked Aster over, disdain written on every line of her face. "You're one to talk, skulking about and murdering people."

"My victims deserve it."

Jes's lips twitched in a hint of a smile. "So do mine. But you're not one of them."

The cold was creeping back into Aster's muscles now that Gale had taken her coat, and the backs of her eyes ached. "If you've got something to say, say it. This is getting tedious."

"Very well." Jes paused, clearly thinking something through. "What you're saying doesn't line up with what Mav told me about the day we left the family, which I remember very little of. She didn't say anything about killing any old ladies or children."

"Would she have told you?"

"No." Jes leaned in, almost close enough that Aster could have flattened her fingers and struck her through the bars. "She didn't share plans with me then. None of them did. Not because I was stupid or useless, but because I was a child. I grew up in that family, that world. I did what I was told. I didn't choose my family, or to be there that day, or..." She trailed off, and her jaw muscles clenched. "If this is really about a debt or punishing those responsible for your grandmother's death, you might consider removing me from your list. I was there, but I wasn't much older than you. If you kill me for this, you're killing a child who had no choice and a woman who regrets much of what she did before she knew better. Call off your hunt. At least for me."

"And your mother?"

Jes shrugged. "Her sins are her own to deal with."

Tom and Gale were watching. Jes motioned for them to wait.

Aster turned away. She couldn't think with Jes's eyes on her.

Deceivers, Eamon had called them. Snakes with forked tongues who could whisper lies that felt like truth. He'd said they all needed to die, that every one of them deserved this. But if Jes were speaking the truth, punishing her for her mother's crimes would be no better than killing that guard dog would have been. Aster squeezed her eyes closed, willing herself to remember anything about that day, but there was only liquid darkness.

I'll ask Eamon, she decided. *Confirm what she's said, decide then.* Maybe he hadn't realized how young the girl had been if she hadn't been in the grandmother's cottage during the fight. He might only have known that she'd become partner to the woman who had planned the whole thing.

And I'd have killed her without knowing.

A wave of dizziness washed over Aster, and it took all her focus to keep from stumbling or grabbing onto the bars to hold herself up.

Or she's lying.

Either way, it would do no good to let Jes leave with her guard up. If what she said was true, Aster would have no part in whatever justice she deserved for her other crimes. If she was lying, still better that she think Aster had moved on to another target.

"Should I expect another visit from you?" Jes asked.

"No." Aster held her right hand through the bars, ready to shake on it. "I'll let bygones be bygones if you will. I'd go so far as to call you a friend if you'd bail me out, too."

Jes chuckled. "You're funny. I think I like you better in here, though." She walked away, her footsteps quiet as a cat's, and spoke to Tom. His eyes widened and he looked to Aster, nodded, and leaned in closer to speak. Jes shook her head, then left without another look at her enemy.

But Gale looked down the row of cells, brow furrowed, her expression otherwise unreadable, before she followed Jes up the stairs.

Figures the only interesting person I've met in ages is wrapped up in all that, Aster thought.

She sat on the bench and pulled the card from her pocket, hiding it in her cupped hands as she looked it over, though Tom had already gone back to his magazine. The cardstock was thick and cream-coloured, with fancy type in brown ink and decorative flourishes in the corners.

> *Orianna Alcorini, Seer of Fates.*
> *Fortunes Told, Tea Leaves Read, Futures Revealed.*

She turned the card over.

> *324C Givens Street*
> *(above Grimmbal's Bakery)*

Not the name Gale had given her, but the odds of her carrying another fortune teller's card around seemed slim.

The card and Aster's dress carried the faint scent of Gale's coat, lavender and pine, a shadow of the kind of person Aster might like to spend more time with when her quest for revenge was over. Meeting her reminded Aster that ending the hunt would change her life, opening up room for friendships she might find outside of Eamon's circles, with odder and more interesting people.

Maybe more than friendship, if she ever met the right person.

Not Gale herself, of course. Not when she was so tight with the enemy. If Aster used the information on the card, it would be as a connection to Jes.

She tucked the card securely into the top of one of her thick wool stockings.

Best to keep that door open, she told herself. *Just in case.*

CHAPTER SIX
GALE

Gale raised a hand to block her eyes against the late morning sun as she followed Jes out of the police station. She'd only been in the basement for a few hours, but her eyes had grown accustomed to the dim light, and with every step into the fresher air outside, she became more aware of how the unpleasantness of the dank cell clung to her hair and clothing. Now the need for a bath battled with her empty stomach and her desperate desire for sleep, leaving her as utterly miserable as she'd been since the first time she'd come to the city.

But Jes walked quickly, and Gale tried to keep up. Madrigal walked beside her, casting dark looks at Gale's employer that went completely unnoticed.

Gale hoped Jes would say something about what had happened—the obviously heated conversation with Elissa, the quick, hushed words she'd exchanged with Tom afterward. Madrigal had eavesdropped on all of it and would tell her later, but it would have been good to hear it from the boss herself, to feel like a part of things for once.

Jes slowed as they passed a Duronian restaurant that had made itself at home on this street of timber buildings in the

Jatlish style, with ornate, sharply peaked roofs designed to shed snow that didn't fall as heavily in Andonia as it did there. Gale didn't notice Cas until he stood from where he'd been seated at one of the round iron tables set out on the sidewalk, folded his napkin, and fell in beside them. He wore his customary suit, well-cut but not fancy enough to draw attention, and had grown in a handsome beard since she'd last seen him.

"Good morning, Gale," he said, and passed her a paper packet that warmed her fingers. When she opened it, the airy egg and cheese bun inside released scents of garlic and onion. "Long night?"

"The longest." She paused, noting the pine boughs hanging in the restaurant windows and the unlit candles resting on the sills, decorations for holidays that were still a few days off. "For me, if not by the calendar."

Cas smiled faintly, then looked past her. "Good morning, Madrigal."

He hadn't gotten her location quite right, but the ghost nodded back. "Tell him I wish him a good morning, as well."

Gale did so, speaking around a mouthful of breakfast that was gone too quickly.

Jes turned. "Good morning, Madrigal."

Madrigal scowled. "Tell her I wish her the day she deserves."

Gale held back a sigh. Having people around who believed her when she said she saw and heard a ghost was wonderful, but acting as go-between in conversations had quickly become dull at best and awkward at worst.

"She wishes you the day you deserve," she said, expecting Jes to laugh as she usually did at Madrigal's barbs, but she only nodded.

"I'm afraid I just might be," she said, and rubbed the back of her neck. "Off to a fine start, anyway." She reached into her pocket and, in a movement so subtle Gale would have missed it if she hadn't been watching for it, passed something off to Cas. He made it disappear, though Gale couldn't tell where it had gone.

"What's that?" she asked, knowing there wasn't much point in asking but unable to help herself.

"Nothing important," Jes said, and handed her a roll of cash. "That's yours. Everything they took when they arrested you. You earned it."

Gale stopped and looked down at the money. Jes had never given up her share of a fee before or rewarded her for time spent in jail.

"You had me arrested," she said. Not an accusation, exactly, but a statement of obvious fact.

Cas and Jes exchanged a look, then stopped and turned back to her.

"May every god damn her to every imaginable torment," Madrigal said, drifting close enough to look into Jes's eyes and turning away, disgusted. "Those were my hours with you. Now we'll lose the whole day."

"As I said, you earned every forin," Jes said, then waited until a group of laughing women walked by before speaking again. "I needed a reason to see Tom today that didn't connect me to any other events. Bailing you out didn't raise eyebrows."

Gale slipped the money into her pocket and ran her thumb over the edges of the bills. She'd expected to feel angry, but it was embarrassment that warmed her. "I'd appreciate a warning next time. I thought that after almost a year of loyalty you'd at least offer me that much courtesy."

Jes sighed. "You're right, you do deserve more courtesy. More trust. More responsibility, maybe. You've earned it, and I'm sorry."

Madrigal crossed her arms. "Didn't know she knew those words."

They walked again, sticking to the shadowed side of the street to avoid the pedestrians who soaked in what little warmth the thin winter sun offered on the other.

"Did getting me arrested have something to do with the girl in the cell next to me?" Gale asked. "You seemed to be having quite the conversation."

"Not directly."

When Jes didn't say more, Cas picked up the thread. "We needed a particular set of keys carried by a certain gentleman." He glanced at Jes as though confirming Gale should be allowed to know this, and Jes nodded. "You've met Agnes?"

"Almost." Gale didn't know how many people Jes had working for her these days and hadn't met many, but she'd seen the girl coming and going from the back door of the shop.

"She's really coming along as a pickpocket," Cas said. "But that certain gentleman would have noticed his keys missing and been on his guard, and probably changed some locks before we could make use of them. By having a pickpocket caught with them, we leave him thinking they're safely in police custody while I get copies made."

A creeping sense of unease turned Gale's stomach. "So you framed her. I'm guessing there was a reason."

"What did you think of her?" Jes asked. "You seemed to be having a good time. Sharing coats and such."

There was more to the question than Jes's casual, conversational tone revealed.

"If you'd meant for me to spy on her," Gale said, "you should have told me what you wanted to find out."

"Don't sulk." Jes smiled, taking the edge out of her words. "You were only meant to be there for a little while so I could bail you out. The two of you being neighbours was a stroke of good luck if you learned anything useful. If not, no harm done."

Madrigal's face reddened and she vanished into the borderlands for a moment. When she returned, she was calmer, but still looked angrier than a wet cat.

Gale started down the street again. "She said her name was Elissa, that she was in for pickpocketing, that it was a false charge."

"And?" Cas prompted.

Gale thought back to the short time she'd spent with Elissa. Jes wasn't wrong to expect her to have information. This was part of her job now, too—not only telling fortunes, but observing and reporting on her clients. "I don't believe she's as poor as her clothes wanted to claim she was. She stood too straight and protested too loudly when she was treated as anyone who's spent time on the lower end of society would be accustomed to."

"True," Jes said. "Now tell me what I couldn't see for myself."

"She was using magic to hide that scar on her face before you got there."

"That's not her business," Madrigal said, sounding more disappointed than angry. "You as good as told that girl you wouldn't tattle on her."

"Not to the police," Gale said. "Jes isn't a threat to magic users."

"But they could be to me," Jes said. "Is she a witch?"

"No," Gale said at the same time as Madrigal. "I didn't feel magic in her."

Cas frowned. "You're learning to hide yours, though. Could she be doing the same?"

"Madrigal would have recognized a witch. But there was something, wasn't there?"

"There was." Madrigal floated backward in front of Gale, passing through objects Gale herself had to step around. "A strangeness. It felt wrong somehow."

Gale nodded. "She was strange," she said to Jes and Cas, though she hadn't felt the same unease at it that Madrigal apparently had. "Even when the illusion hiding her scar wore off, there was something…" She paused, unsure of how to say it. Odd, yes, but compelling. Elissa had paced her cell like the poor tigers in the zoological garden that were pampered and kept in the most natural surroundings but still carried the wild in them. It was frightening and beautiful.

"You asked for my impressions," Gale said, "but they're hard to pin down. She carried herself like a lady, but I'd bet money on that scar coming from battle rather than an accident. I could imagine her as a warrior or a hunter as well as I could taking tea with the queen. She seemed strong, maybe dangerous, but…"

"Beautiful?" Cas asked.

"That, too," Gale said, remembering Elissa's dark eyes and full lips. "I may have let my guard slip over it."

Cas did a poor job of holding back a smile. "You wouldn't be the first."

"So why did you have her arrested?" Gale asked, and turned right at a corner where an Ignatite temple of ornately carved white stone held court over the plainer buildings that surrounded it. They'd be back to her flat in a few blocks, and she intended to learn as much as she could before then.

Jes hesitated before she spoke. "I'd seen her around over the past few weeks. She was watching me, stalking me like a cat after a mouse. I thought my mother had sent her to murder me. This was our little way of killing two birds with one stone—get the keys, get the would-be assassin out of the way. We had another fellow lined up to take the fall and spend a night in jail if she hadn't shown up."

Gale shivered. She'd heard a few stories about Jes's mother, mostly from Cas, and none of them pleasant.

She felt the money in her pocket again, not because it comforted her, but because it gave her hand something to do. The other hand traced the smooth lining of the empty pocket, searching for something Gale vaguely felt should have been there.

"It wasn't Mav?" Cas asked.

"Not directly. Apparently this girl has an old vendetta against my family, something to do with Mav's plan that tore us all apart. It's Mav's fault, but not her doing. This fine young lady claimed to have killed my uncle, so I ran it by Tom. He said he'd look into it but hadn't heard anything. I believe her, though."

A chill gripped Gale, slowing her steps. "She *was* trying to kill you?"

"Got within a few steps. Don't worry about being friendly with her, though. She wasn't after you, and she can't find you even if she cares that you work for me."

Gale's fingers searched again. *I had one left. I know I did.*

Jes narrowed her eyes at Gale. "You look like you're about to vomit."

"My business card." Gale dug through her pockets one more time but felt only the rolled cash. Her stomach turned. "She must have taken it when I gave her my coat. She has my address."

"Gods," Madrigal whispered.

Jes folded her hands behind her back and looked up, watching a flock of pigeons that nested in the temple's eaves fly past, then started walking again.

"Jes?"

"I'm thinking."

Gale gave it another block before she spoke again. "Maybe I lost it."

"Let's assume you didn't," Cas said, and ran his hand down his face. He looked nearly as tired as Gale felt.

"Should I be looking for a new home?"

Jes glanced around, making sure there was no one listening, and turned to her. "You could. There are safe places you can go if need be. But you're not the person she wants dead. And she said she wasn't going to come after me again."

"You think she'll keep her word?" Cas asked, clearly not believing it.

"She seemed sincerely surprised when she realized I wasn't one of the hardened old criminals she thinks hurt her, but I wouldn't be alive now if I trusted folks that easily." They continued on, and Jes stopped at the bakery under Gale's flat to study the tempting display of holiday cakes and treats in the window. "You want more trust, more responsibility?"

Gale felt the blood drain from her cheeks. "Maybe not."

Jes's expression softened slightly. It did nothing to put Gale at ease. "I've only kept things from you in the past because you were safer not knowing," Jes said. "That's no longer true, and you deserve a choice in this. I'm going to make myself scarce for a while, and you won't know where I am if anyone asks. If you want to leave home, I'll understand. If you choose to stay, though, it might be our chance to learn something useful—who she really is, whether there's someone else behind all this that I should watch out for."

The witch who created her illusion, maybe, Gale thought. It was strange to think there could be another in Queen's Run that neither she nor Madrigal knew about.

"Don't even consider it," Madrigal said.

Gale didn't need to wait for her to explain why before she spoke. "That's not my job." It pained her to not preface it with an apology, but she'd learned a few things from Jes over recent months about maintaining the upper hand in negotiations. "Our deal is that I do readings, I give you your share of the profit, I learn magic that will be mutually beneficial. I make money, you keep me safe."

Jes's customary mask of confidence and certainty fell, leaving her looking as vulnerable as Gale had ever seen her. "True. But I'm not asking as your employer. I'm asking as a friend."

Madrigal clicked her tongue.

"I've spent the past few years watching over my shoulder for Mav," Jes said, "assuming she'd come after me for revenge or to take whatever she thinks I owe her. I thought anyone else we'd hurt in the past would be too weak for revenge to be an option— that was usually her approach to things. But clearly this is something different. Another enemy, possibly one with magic in their pocket…" Jes stepped closer and took Gale's hands in hers. "You're the only one who might have a chance to learn anything useful given your skills and experience in that area. I'm not asking you to seek her out. Your God willing, she won't ever come to your door. I only ask that if she does, you tell me what you learn."

Gale watched a pair of young mothers walking down the street, one pushing a rickety pram, the other with a baby in her arms and a toddler clinging to her legs. Not a life Gale wished for herself, but the way they leaned in close to look into a shop window and then laughed together made her ache for home and the family she'd left behind.

She looked to Cas, then back to Jes. These people had been strangers when she'd come to Queen's Run, then helpers and obstacles, sometimes all at once. But they'd become more than that since then, and Gale couldn't help thinking they were the closest thing she had to living family anymore.

God help me.

"If she comes, I'll see what I can find out," she said. "Madrigal, would it be all right if we did some more work on magical protections?"

"Of course."

"Good." Gale hesitated, then steeled herself and turned back to Jes. She might be helping a friend, but that didn't mean she'd let opportunity pass her by. "You'll need to cancel any other parties I'm booked for until this is all over, of course."

Jes smiled. It made her look more like her usual self. "And the income you'll lose?"

"I suppose the person who needed my help and made the cancellations necessary might cover at least a portion of it. Boss."

Cas turned away and coughed. Gale suspected he was trying not to laugh.

Madrigal let out a frustrated sigh. "Should've asked for all of it."

"I suppose we could make that work," Jes said. Gale couldn't be sure, but she thought she detected a hint of pride in her employer's voice. "Promise me you'll do what you can to stay safe."

"And if you need anything," Cas said, "contact me at the shop."

A cold gust of wind blew down the alley, and Gale pulled her coat tighter around her. "You're not going into hiding, too?"

"Not if you might need us," he said. "I'll keep my distance from you until then. We don't want to give that murderer any reason to think you're more closely associated with us than she needs to."

"Thank you."

Jes and Cas left her, and Gale stepped into the alley's shadows and climbed the stairs to her flat.

"She probably won't come," she said to Madrigal. "I'm sure it'll be fine."

The ghost didn't answer.

CHAPTER SEVEN
ASTER

Aster held back a wince every time the carriage hit a bump or jostled particularly hard over the cobblestone streets. Eamon sat across from her, watching every expression. He knew how bad it was, and the creases in his brow told her how terrible he felt for not being able to help her more.

She wouldn't make it worse by complaining.

"I waited too long to come for you," he said.

"I shouldn't have been caught." Aster rested her head against the wall, but it only made the carriage's movements hurt more, sending sharp pains through her skull that felt like they might split it open.

She glanced out the window. It was only a little past supper time, but night had cloaked the streets with inky blackness held back only by gas lamps and the bright warmth shining from behind windows along the way. Candles, lamps, fires blazing in hearths, all fighting to carry the light until days grew longer again.

The inside of the carriage was dark, though, and soothing in its lack of holiday cheer.

Eamon leaned forward, resting his hands on the glass ball in the head of his cane. It was a unique piece, hand-blown in greenish glass dotted with tiny air bubbles, reflecting gold when it caught the right light. The cane wasn't made to be sturdy, created as a fashion statement more than to serve as a crutch, but he refused to concede more to his injuries than was absolutely necessary. As they passed another lamp, the light caught on his beard, making it shine blue-black before the shadows returned.

Aster had been fascinated by his beard when she was a child and had sometimes stolen a little of the fancy oils Eamon used on it to comb through her own hair, only stopping when he'd agreed to concoct a lighter formula especially for her. It was one of few memories she held from her childhood, at least in a vague, distant way. Not like the harder things that inevitably became formless gaps in her story when Eamon healed her more physical woes.

It's worth it, she told herself. Memories would do her no good if the pain killed her.

Still, her throat closed and her chest tightened when she thought of the coming loss, and she clawed through her recent memories, trying to burn each moment into her mind, knowing it would do no good in the end.

It was all a muddle already. Her brain seemed to be made of damp wool, musty and heavy and useless. It always came to this if she went too long without letting Eamon heal her. First the phys-ical pain, then the mental jumble, a sense that her streams of thought were becoming lost in fog. She didn't remember it, but she knew.

There was no winning, and there hadn't been since the wolves.

Eamon cleared his throat. "We'll be home soon. Is there anything else you need to tell me?"

Aster tried to think. She'd told him every humiliating detail of her failure in the park, and her talk with Jes.

Almost everything.

"I told her I'd call off the hunt," she said. Her tongue felt heavier than it had just a few minutes ago. "Not for her mother. Only for her, and only if what she said was true. Was she a child that day?"

She watched Eamon's reaction carefully as he leaned back and smoothed the expensive wool of his trousers over his thighs. "I suppose she may well have been. I didn't see that girl or her mother in the cabin, you understand. Only those I fought. They were there, though."

Aster nodded slowly so as not to jostle her brain. "Jesamyn said as much. She also didn't deny that Mavolia was the mastermind behind the whole thing. I get the feeling there was a true falling out there. I might be doing her a favour if I killed her mother."

"Didn't point you in her direction, though, did she?" Eamon rested his elbow against the window and curled his fist beneath his chin, watching as they turned onto a street of fine houses. A moment later he looked back to Aster. "Does it really change anything for you? That girl no doubt lured you in so you wouldn't flee from the strangers at your grandmother's house. And even if they're not together now, my sources have shown that she and her mother were tight as twins in the years after, swindling the poor in cities from Beardbranch to Greenhaven over the course of a decade." He looked deep into Aster's eyes. "It's what she was raised for, and she hasn't changed. The police won't bring her the justice she deserves any more than they will the others you've taken care of."

"I know." Aster leaned forward, resting her aching head in her hands. Its weight only made the pain in the scar that circled her right forearm complain louder, and she forced herself to sit up again. It was hard to think, but something she thought she'd understood earlier came back to her. "Her later crimes aren't mine to punish, though—if I took it upon myself to punish every person who'd ever wronged another, it would never end. What I do is about bringing justice to those who harmed you and me, who killed my grandmother. She was there that day, but she wasn't responsible for what happened as the adults were. She was a tool, not a…"

Aster trailed off. The word she'd wanted was gone.

Eamon pursed his lips, thinking, then nodded. "Very well. If that is your judgement, I suppose that puts us one step closer to the end of it all." He smiled. "I'm proud of you, Aster."

She held back a laugh. "For failing?"

"For your wisdom."

He didn't apologize for sending her after someone she might have regretted killing, but Aster supposed that was all right. He'd known only as much as she had.

And if she'd succeeded, the world might have been better off anyway.

"We should go back to the park," she said, and shifted to try to find a position that didn't put pressure on any of her scars. "I lost the dagger under the gazebo. I'd hate for anyone to find it."

Eamon frowned. "Let me worry about that after we get you taken care of. You're in no shape to be wandering around out there."

Aster didn't argue. It pained her to admit it, even to herself, but she didn't want to.

The hired carriage stopped in front of 465 Greybaud Avenue. If Eamon had called on someone to drive his own carriage they'd have taken the narrow path that separated the house from its neighbour and led to the carriage house out back, where the vehicle would have been stowed before the hired driver took the horses away. There had been no question of Eamon taking his distinctive personal carriage to the police station tonight, though. It was bad enough he'd needed to show his face there.

Gossip was the last thing they wanted.

Aster let Eamon leave first, aided by the driver, then eased herself to the ground with the same assistance. She waved off his offer to walk her to the door and waited as Eamon paid him for his time.

The house loomed over them, its wooden siding painted black as funeral garb, every window dark, the door undecorated by the wreaths and ribbons that adorned most on the street. It had been Aster's home since she was six years old, and she wondered whether she'd been frightened of it the first time she'd seen its sharply peaked roof, its tightly drawn curtains, and the unwelcoming box hedges that enclosed the little front yard. An imposing structure for those who didn't belong there, but all she wanted to do was run inside and hide herself away.

There would be no running, but she followed with shuffling steps as Eamon made his way past the iron gate that broke the hedge, mindful of icy patches. At her strongest, she could have held her balance on a skating rink wearing stilts. Now, at her weakest, she babied her body as though it might shatter if she fell on the flagstone path.

Eamon unlocked the front door and pocketed his heavy keyring, then made his way down the narrow house's long central hallway, flicking his hand at the lamps on the walls as he passed, setting them ablaze and illuminating the mahogany-panelled walls and the few paintings that hung on them. The fire in the front parlour's hearth came next, just as easily, burning so hot they'd need to crack a window before long. Aster was tempted to rest on the settee under the window or sink into Eamon's chair next to the fire, but knew she'd have little hope of getting back up if she did.

There was no butler to greet them, no maid to keep the fires burning while they'd been gone, no cook to have a hot supper on the table. It was the two of them against the world, and their home was their fortress against wolves, against the king's mages who would see Eamon's head roll if they learned of his illegal magic, and against circumstances that had stolen too much from them both.

"Shall I draw you a bath?" Eamon asked.

Aster assessed her situation more closely than she'd dared in jail or on the ride home, isolating each area of pain and measuring it. Everything from the skull-splitting headache to the burning scar on her face and scalp, from her arm feeling as though it had been sliced through to her heart threatening to shatter with every beat, was as bad as it had been since...

Well, she couldn't truly remember the experience of pain before this, but it might have been the worst it had ever been.

"If it's all the same, I'd like to skip to the healing and get some sleep. I'll bathe in the morning." She forced herself up the narrow staircase to the second floor, where her bedroom awaited. "Give me a few minutes to change?"

"Of course."

Her room was cold and dark, with only a little moonlight coming in through the big window on the wall that overlooked the yard behind the house. The oak bookcases on either side of it stood in deep shadow, and the silvery light picked out only the edges of Aster's dressing table, writing desk, wardrobe, and the large bed. All the furniture had been there longer than she had, and the familiarity of it eased some of the tension she carried. In the morning when she woke with little knowledge of what had happened for days or weeks, she would at least know she was safe at home.

Aster lit the lamp on her dressing table and slowly removed her hat, her fur stole, and the threadbare dress that had done such a poor job of keeping her warm in jail. Her hands and feet still felt cold as a corpse's, and she left her knee-high wool socks on when she shed her undergarments and changed into her red flannel nightgown.

She glanced at the writing desk and considered leaving herself a note, but the bed beckoned.

I already told Eamon. He'll remind me of everything.

Except she hadn't mentioned the witch to him. Hardly the most important thing, but—

Eamon knocked at the door.

"Come in."

He carried a small tray with two cups on it, and Aster took one and inhaled the steam.

"Beef-bone broth," he said, as though the delicious aroma wouldn't give it away. "Good for the joints."

Aster drank it all down, willing its warmth to infuse her body. Eamon sipped his more slowly and lit the fire in her bedroom's modest fireplace as she climbed into bed.

"I feel like a child," she grumbled, "needing to be tucked in." She pulled up the colourful quilt she'd bought from a down-on-her-luck grandmother in one of the local markets and lay back against her heavy feather pillow. The mattress sank beneath her, and she let her muscles relax into it.

Still, a strange sort of apprehension trailed over her skin.

She knew the good that came from healing. She remembered the last time she'd wakened, how she'd later stalked her prey and attended a tedious luncheon and bought a new dress without the pain that now plagued her. She believed it would be the same when she woke.

But she couldn't remember any past healings. Those memories were gone, washed away with everything else. She had the sense that it was good, but at the same time it felt like this was the first time she'd faced it. It wasn't like fighting, where her instincts and muscle memory told her all would be well if only she trusted them.

With healing, there was nothing.

Eamon set his cane down, pulled the stool over from the dressing table, and sat beside the bed. "Perhaps you won't need to be tucked in so often once things quiet down," he said. "You've been under extraordinary strain these past few years, even for someone without your special circumstances. And if all goes well, maybe I'll find that permanent fix for you."

Aster smiled up at him. His voice chased her fear away, and sleep began to cloud her thoughts. "Then you'll be able to turn some of your attention to finding a way to fix yourself."

Eamon chuckled, low and quiet. "From your mouth to every conceivable god's ears. Now, are you ready?"

Aster steeled herself. "I think so."

Then she remembered the witch—the detail she hadn't shared, that she'd forget if she said nothing. She opened her mouth to speak again, but something held her back. Not the vague sense of unease that surrounded healing, but something more familiar. It was the voice that came not from reason, but some place deeper in her mind, offering wisdom and counsel when memory failed her.

It said not to speak of the witch.

A foolish thought. It was true the girl seemed unlikely to tell anyone about the magic Aster had been using, but surely there was no harm in mentioning her to Eamon.

"Are there other witches in Queen's Run?" she asked. Her heart clenched tight, but her mind offered no reason for it.

She had a vague sense that Eamon had told her irrationality, along with muddled emotions and reactions, came when she was long past needing a healing. She promised herself she wouldn't leave it this long again, though she knew she'd forget.

"None that I know of at the moment." Eamon stood and held his palms out a hand's breadth above the blankets, moving his fingers slowly, feeling out old points of pain without touching her. "Why?"

His magic stirred the air, cold and sharp as the stars Aster pictured dotting the sky beyond the roof. For a moment she saw them and imagined them watching.

It doesn't matter. She probably wasn't a witch, anyway.

With that thought, her needless anxiety eased.

"There was a girl in jail," she said. "Not a real witch, a fortune teller. I only wondered about the real thing. Whether you were the only one."

Her thoughts became heavier again, but her body relaxed and the tension flowed from her muscles as the magic intensified. As Eamon moved, the light from the fire caught a hint of gold at his throat—the chain of a locket that contained tiny paintings of his wife Winifred and daughter Claudia, who had died before Aster came into his life. Aster closed her eyes and pictured them. Winifred with her black hair swept up, a few loose curls framing her rounded features. Claudia, a serious-faced toddler who looked at the viewer knowingly, as though aware that this was about it for her.

The thoughts drifted through Aster's addled mind, twisting together with other faces.

Jes, keen as a knife, and a fellow who had seemed strangely familiar. Gale offering her coat, where Aster had found the card that she'd forgotten slipping into her stocking.

Balls.

She'd meant to hand that over to Eamon. Even if the girl wasn't a witch, they might still need that connection to Jes, and therefore the final enemy on Aster's list.

She tried to get up, to speak, but her body had grown heavy and everything felt like a dream.

"I have to remember," she murmured. Her voice sounded like it was coming from blocks away even as it echoed strangely through her head.

"I know, dear," Eamon said, his voice gentle but strained with effort. "I'll remind you of everything in the morning. Hush, now. I need to focus."

His magic passed over her again, cold and prickling, familiar and yet fearsome in its strength.

Some people believed magic was harmful, corrupting the spirit. Aster was living proof of the good it could do, but in that moment she understood why folks might believe such terrible things. The power was cold, as deep and dark as the ocean. Waves of pain washed over her, sinking into her scars and the bones beneath, ebbing and returning.

She gasped and held back a cry.

The room spun, twisting and tilting until Aster gripped the blankets to keep from falling out of bed. Images of the past few days flashed through her mind, bright and clear as if they were happening in that moment.

She was on a rooftop, crouched uncomfortably and watching the back door of Bellawick's Curiosity Shop to see whether Jes would slip out during the night.

Waiting for a drugged dog to collapse.

The sun was in her eyes, the scent of hot cocoa was in the air, and her dagger was in her hand.

She was in a dank jail cell, listening to a moaning drunk and a kind girl who spoke to the air.

Aster tried to reach for Eamon's hand to tell him to stop, but he pulled away.

"It's all right, child," he said. A light film of sweat shone on his brow as he controlled the magic that swirled in invisible currents through the room, but he smiled down at her. "It's always this way as the pain draws out and the enchantment is strengthened. You won't remember this part in the morning."

Jes's eyes now, again, looking curiously into her own, and then they were gone. Aster grabbed at the thought, trying to hold on to it, and found she couldn't remember what she was reaching for.

Jail, I was in jail, there was... someone.

And then she couldn't think at all. A hurricane of magic blew through her, tossing her thoughts and memories into chaos as her awareness of her body vanished entirely.

She thought she screamed, but couldn't be sure.

CHAPTER EIGHT
ASTER

ster rolled out of bed at sunrise the next morning and moved straight into her habitual stretching routine, moving her body through its gentle paces like a cat working out the kinks after a long nap in the sun. Everything felt new. Good.

Freshly healed.

She strained to remember a healing, or anything that had happened before it, and a disorienting sense of loss touched her mind. She tried to remember what day it was and couldn't quite decide.

Something happened.

The calendar on her writing desk was turned to the eighteenth of Winternight. That marked several weeks since she knew anything for certain. Aster closed her eyes, ignored the seasick pitching the disorientation brought to her stomach, and searched her memories. All that came were vague ideas and bright shadows.

An event of some kind—she'd worn her gold dress. With that, she remembered picking it up from the shop, though that, too, felt like something that had happened to someone else. More would come back, but for now each scrap floated in empty space, unanchored to herself or any other events, with no sense of order or causality.

Massive gaps. Whatever had happened had been big.

What else? Aster opened her eyes and grounded herself in her body, her room, anything familiar, then searched for what might feel out of place.

She still wore her wool stockings, which wasn't her habit when she slept. It had been cold last night, then, but there would be more to it. The fire had gone out overnight, and she left them on as she slipped into her robe and turned to her dressing table.

A little white box tied with a blood-red satin ribbon sat beneath the mirror, and Aster grinned as she snatched it up.

One more down.

A silver charm shaped like a wedding ring sat in the box on top of a smooth, white cushion. Aster held it up to the light, then added it to the chain of the bracelet Eamon had given her after her first kill. The other charms glittered as she slipped it onto her left wrist. A horse's head with the tiniest diamond eyes imaginable, a miniature dagger perfect in every detail, a medicine bottle… each represented the wolf she'd brought down to earn it in some subtle way. There was no other evidence, no trophies, no memories, but there was always this.

How it had happened would remain a mystery until she spoke to Eamon, but he'd be awake soon.

Aster descended the stairs with light steps and relished the strength of her body. Even without the memory of weakness, she knew to be grateful.

The sun streamed bright through the kitchen windows at the side of the house, bathing the countertops, the iron stove, and the high table in the centre of the room with warm light that echoed the buttery yellow paint on the walls. A thin coating of fresh snow had fallen while she slept, leaving the yard crisp and white. Blackcaps twittered in the bare bushes beneath the window, and Aster opened it to toss them a bit of seed.

There was no sign Eamon was up yet, so Aster lit the stove the old-fashioned way and warmed the cast iron pan on it. A basket of eggs sat on the counter. No bread, and she'd have to scrape the bottom of the sugar bowl for enough to sweeten the tea as much as they both liked, but it would do.

It was only when she had six eggs sizzling in the pan and tea steeping on the sideboard that Aster realized she was quietly humming one of the jolly carols folks sang in the streets during the winter festivals.

I'm happy, she realized, and wished she knew why it felt like a weight had been lifted from her shoulders.

It couldn't be because her task was finished. If it had been, she'd have had three new charms on her wrist. Still, it felt something like that. Like the home stretch of a race she was sure to win.

The eggs were finishing in the pan and the tea steeping on the table when Eamon thumped his way into the kitchen, leaning hard on his cane. He never wore his nightclothes around the house and was already dressed in one of his less-than-best suits. The materials were quite fine. It was the cut that made it less than best—an idea Aster accepted even if she didn't care quite enough to keep track of men's fashions like Eamon did.

"I thought I smelled breakfast," he said, and inhaled deeply as he sat on a stool at the table. The house had a fine dining room, but they only used it when they had guests.

To the best of Aster's knowledge, it had been unused for at least four years.

Aster slid three eggs onto each plate and seasoned them with salt and pepper, passed one to Eamon, then stood opposite him and dug in. Orange yolk spilled over the plate, and she scooped as much up as she could with her fork. She felt like she hadn't eaten in days.

"You have questions, I suppose," Eamon said, smiling a little. "Care to take any guesses?"

"Ilcone is dead," she said. The name hadn't come to her upstairs when she'd tried to remember it, but when she spoke aloud without trying to think, it came. She held up her bracelet. "Wedding ring. Some kind of marriage racket?"

Eamon poured two cups of tea and scraped the last of the sugar into them. "Very good. Not only fraud, but murder. It was a quick and clean kill, body gone before anyone showed up."

"The resurrection man?" She couldn't recall speaking to him, but it was an idea she'd had before, and as she suggested it there was a sense of it fitting like a puzzle piece into one of the gaps in her experience. She knew it was right before Eamon answered.

"Indeed. Unpleasant but efficient. You were right."

Aster's skin crawled. "Anything else?"

Eamon talked her through the past few weeks—the plans she'd made, the charity event and the holiday parties she'd been required to attend, and what he knew of her long hours observing not one wolf, but two.

Aster set her fork on her empty plate and leaned on the table, aching to head back out on the hunt. "Am I to go after Jesamyn next?"

"No." Eamon poured them each a fresh cup of tea and frowned at the empty sugar bowl. "You did, yesterday. It didn't go well."

Aster gripped the edge of the table tighter as shame crept over her, twisting her stomach into tight knots, coming from a place deeper than memory. "Tell me."

"You planned to kill her quietly in the park, the only place you'd found to catch her unguarded. The long and short of it is that she and an accomplice framed you for pickpocketing before you could make your move, and you ended up imprisoned for most of the day."

"Not for attempted murder?"

Eamon arched one dark eyebrow. "Interesting, isn't it? I suppose it would've raised too many questions. In any case,

Mavolia is your next target, in Embercliffe—you found a recent address last night. But not yet."

Aster scowled. She'd probably put a lot of work into that plan, but Eamon was right. If Jesamyn knew someone was after her, she'd become even more guarded and cautious, at least for a while. Better to come back to her later.

She searched again, hoping Eamon's reminders would trigger a memory, but there was nothing. It was as though someone had come into her mind and tidied up, folding her memories and stowing them away in a locked cabinet so they couldn't trouble her anymore.

Eamon reached out and patted her hand. "I know that look. Shall I apologize again?"

Aster made herself smile. "You know that's never necessary."

Eamon had done his best with his healing spells and enchantments, but he'd been a less experienced witch when he saved her, working with more intention than skill. The memory loss was a flaw in an otherwise miraculous event. An oversight.

Better to let it go and move on. Aster poured hot water from the kettle into the basin and put the plates in to soak. "Why can't I go now? Please tell me it's not because we have more parties to attend this week."

"No. I'm going on a little trip, and I think it's best if you stay at home while I'm gone." Eamon twisted the plain gold ring he always wore on his left hand, one he said Winifred had given him. Aster never saw him without it. "Do you remember anything of our conversation at the party the other night?"

Aster tried again to recall anything specific and shook her head.

Eamon leaned forward. "I believe I've found someone who can help me fix the flaws in your enchantments. He used to be one of the king's mages and now carries knowledge not available to most witches. We'll rebuild everything from the ground up and set it right at last."

Aster pulled in a sharp breath. "Fix my memory? Or take my pain away for good? Or…" She trailed off, waiting for him to fill in the blanks before her hopes soared too high. There were other questions—how a fully trained mage could be allowed to leave the king's service alive, for one—but they paled in comparison to her own concerns.

"To make everything perfect." Eamon grinned. They'd never indulged in the custom of giving each other presents for any winter holidays, but Aster imagined this was what he'd look like if he watched her unwrapping the perfect gift—excited, proud, happy. "To ease your pain forever, my dear. Erase your scars as though they never existed. And as for the memories, we'll see what can be done. Certainly you'll keep them as they come in the future, good and bad. We might even recover what was lost."

Aster braced herself against the counter. She wasn't the fainting type, but the unexpected notion made her head swim.

"It's about time, too," Eamon said. "I won't be around forever to work magic and ease your pain."

Aster glared at him. "Don't be silly, of course you will."

Eamon raised his teacup, but didn't drink. "Here's hoping. This has been a long time coming, and I'll know more once I've spoken to my contact. It would have been fitting if you'd finished with the wolves first so you could have a truly fresh start, but it doesn't matter." He set his cup down. "Speaking of which, you lost your dagger in the park. I retrieved it last night, but I've left it in my workshop. Give me a moment and I'll fetch it for you."

"Don't trouble yourself," Aster said, eager to give something back in return for the hope he'd just offered. "Give me your keys and I'll get it, and then we can talk about this contact of yours."

She felt like she had a flock of birds trapped in her stomach.

Eamon reached into his pocket, hesitated, and pulled out his keyring. He held it out of sight under the lip of the table, then handed only two of its many keys to Aster.

"You can trust me," she said. "I know the rules."

Eamon chuckled and shook his head. "I know you know. Be quick, though."

"I will."

Aster unlocked the heavy oak door and started down the stairs, thinking of what it might mean to not rely on Eamon to keep her pain in check, to remember everything that made her herself. To wander the world without fear of staying away from home for too long, to choose a new purpose that was all her own.

It sounded too good to be true, and Aster decided to allow herself hope on a strictly provisional basis.

The lamps were usually lit in the basement, not that Aster saw them much. The basement storage room rarely held anything important, and the only other room was what Eamon called his workshop. More like an office, with a desk, a lot of papers, a few books, and some dusty, old equipment—scales and beakers and such. Aster was strictly forbidden to touch any of it, and rarely even allowed to come down to bring Eamon his meals when he was hard at work. He kept a full tea service and an icebox of food in his workshop so he wouldn't starve.

As she descended the enclosed staircase, Aster felt proud he'd trusted her to not only enter the basement, but to come down alone.

Now that she knew the dagger had been missing, her fingers itched to hold it again. She turned right at the bottom of the staircase and hurried toward Eamon's office, key in hand, but stopped short in the hallway outside.

Office door. Storage room door across from it, set into the stone wall as it always had been.

But there was another door at the end of the hall.

Aster squeezed her eyes closed.

Eamon's workshop. Storage room. She could picture them easily, twin wooden doors, rectangular, made of oak planks with iron fittings and knobs. But when she remembered the end of the hallway there was only a blank wall.

The hairs on her arms stood on end as she opened her eyes and looked again.

Memory was a tricky thing. She forgot events, experiences, even people if they were associated with anything dark and dangerous. Recollections of unfamiliar places and even non-threatening people could be fuzzy, but they didn't just vanish, and they tended to seem familiar when she encountered them again. She'd been to the basement before.

There should be *something*.

But this felt new, though the door at the end of the hall looked as old as either of the others.

Aster stepped closer, and the prickling of her skin became something more like blind fear that ran like ice water through her veins.

"Aster!" Eamon called from the kitchen.

"Coming!" Aster backed up, unlocked Eamon's workshop, and stepped inside. The strangeness eased as soon as the…

She frowned. Something had been strange in the hallway, but she wasn't sure what.

The enchanted dagger sat on Eamon's desk, clean and sharp, its jewelled hilt shimmering in the lamplight. She grabbed it and hurried out, not taking time to look around at anything else. Her stomach felt like a ball of ice, and for some reason she wanted to run from the basement.

She locked the workshop door and glanced to her left.

"Odd," she whispered.

There was a door at the end of the hall, one she swore she'd never seen before. She stepped toward it, but hesitated as something deep within her said not to. Dread pooled in her belly.

She decided she'd ask Eamon when she got upstairs. There had to be an explanation.

But by the time she'd reached the third step, she'd forgotten what she'd meant to say, and as she stepped into the kitchen the idea of asking anything at all vanished.

CHAPTER NINE
ASTER

Aster shed her nightgown in the steam-filled warmth of the bathroom, ready to slip into the deep claw-footed tub. She lifted her arm and wrinkled her nose. The pain last night must have been unbearable for her to have skipped bathing and go straight to bed. The long hunt hadn't left her feeling or smelling her most ladylike, and it seemed a miracle that her stockings didn't have visible stink lines rising from them like in a newspaper cartoon when she bent to roll them down.

A heavy business card fell to the white tile floor with a soft *plap*, and she frowned at it for a moment before picking it up to examine it.

"A fortune teller?" Aster wasn't one for speaking aloud to herself, but sometimes the questions needed to be asked. There was no answer from the depths of her mind, though, no stirring of recollection or reason offered for why a clairvoyant's card would have been stowing away in her sock.

The odds of there being a witch in Queen's Run who could do such things were vanishingly slim, and to openly advertise such talents would be to invite a swift death sentence when the king's mages found out. If there were witches besides Eamon in the city, they were keeping themselves as well hidden as he did.

Fraudulent, then, which made it even more of a mystery why she'd have kept such a thing.

She read it over again, then tucked it into the gold frame of the mirror above the basin and stepped into the hot, rose-oil-scented water in the tub.

Stockings were on overnight, so the card must have been in there yesterday. But why?

She cursed herself for not leaving a note before the healing.

Aster held her breath and dunked her head beneath the water, then ruffled her fingers through her hair, which floated in front of her eyes to block out the light. She waited there, still as a sunken stone, and willed memories to come.

There was something there now that Eamon had explained things, as though he'd cracked the door on her memory vault enough to almost see inside. She caught a vague recollection of the jail, though there'd been no trace of it in her mind before. The ill-defined shape of an officer at a desk, a dank cell, a drunk curled up on the floor. She held ideas of being in the park and in a stranger's house, and she knew things about them even if she couldn't place herself there or see them in her mind. A guard dog, a hidden weapon, holiday songs played by a brass quartet.

But that was all they were. Ideas, not experiences. Knowledge, not memories.

She remained in the silent darkness of the water until her lungs burned, but nothing else came back no matter how desperately she tried to grab on to the spider's-silk-thin notions. No fortune teller, no words exchanged with the wolf before his death, no memory of what the kill had been like, though the idea that she'd done it felt satisfyingly correct.

There was no point trying harder. There was always the danger of imagining memories into being to fill the empty spaces, and that would do no one any good.

She surfaced and glanced at the white paper rectangle on the mirror.

I'll ask Eamon. I must have said something about it.

She took her time washing, soaping every bit of herself, examining her body for signs of newly healed injuries. Every part comforted her with its familiarity—every smooth expanse of lean muscle, every modest curve, and every scar. The pale line on her face was the least of it, a technical, cosmetic flaw to many folks, but one she'd grown attached to over the years. It marked her as a survivor and a warrior even if no one was supposed to know about the latter.

The scar on her chest was the worst of them, a twisted mass of tissue between her breasts and extending down her stomach that made her wonder how she'd survived the injury that caused it. She placed a hand over it and felt her heart beating beneath solid bone, strong and certain.

Then there were the other scars—one encircling her right forearm like a seam on a ragdoll, one trailing up her leg and branching out into a starburst across her thigh, a dozen slashing across her ribs, her back, and the palms of her hands.

Damaged, thanks to a pack of soulless swindlers, but alive in spite of their efforts. Strong. Honed into the weapon that had brought nearly all of them to justice.

She dried off and treated her hair with the light potion that would tame her curls as they dried, then smoothed a concoction of oils and botanicals over her skin from her face to her toes. Her favourite wool dress, deep blue with white snowflakes embroidered on the hem and cuffs, hung in the corner with her undergarments, and she quickly had herself dressed and presentable.

With the business card in hand, she headed downstairs.

"Eamon?" she called, but there was no answer.

No sign of him in his bedroom on the ground floor, nor in the parlour or the kitchen. The basement door was locked tight again.

Aster stood before the door, flicking the business card against her thumb. He was probably doing something to get ready for his trip, setting protections to keep him safe on the road and gathering information he'd need to pass along to his contact if this person was to offer any help. She could bang on the door and hope he'd hear her even with his workshop door closed, but he likely wouldn't.

What, then? Physical training in the attic, perhaps, but there would be plenty of time for that while he was away. And besides, she'd already dressed in proper going-out clothes.

She sat at the kitchen table and picked up the empty sugar bowl.

Someone needs to go out for sugar and bread, she thought. *And a walk would do me good.*

The fortune teller's address would take her a good distance off the usual route she took when she ran errands, but what of it? The sun shone outside, people in the streets would be glowing with the good cheer that came with the holidays, and that was always pleasant even if Aster herself had no plans to celebrate any of them.

She reasoned that the fortune teller likely wasn't dangerous if she hadn't bothered to warn herself about it. She'd wear the fine coat she'd modified to hide a dagger in the sleeve, just in case, and have a little adventure before Eamon went away. Her body was healthy, free of pain, and pulsing with energy.

Might as well use it.

She considered the address on the card, slipped it into her pocket, and went to fetch her coat and boots.

Givens Street was located a short distance beyond Midtown Meet, one of the many open squares that dotted the city and created space in the midst of its otherwise crowded streets. The square, which was surrounded by brick buildings housing shops, offices, and a fine old hotel on one corner, was snow-dusted and nearly empty today, but during summer festivals it would be packed with stalls, carts, and buskers plying their trades, hoping to relieve the wealthier citizens of Queen's Run of some of their gold. Such noisy, messy events were never allowed in their neighbourhood parks, of course—not near Aster's house, and certainly not out in Gorwood, where the lords and ladies kept their city homes. But well-off folks loved to come down for a taste of what they thought was real life for the common folks, and the festivals provided a fun, interesting, and mostly safe place to enjoy it.

Aster cut diagonally across the square. The massive stone fountain at the centre had been shut off for the winter, leaving its four stone gryphons looking more shocked than fierce with their rounded mouths open and empty of the water that usually flowed from them. A rumpled brown tabby cat lay on the fountain's edge, washing its face. It watched with narrowed eyes as Aster passed, then resumed its bathing. Other than the two of them, the centre of the square was empty. The other pedestrians who were out enjoying the fine weather stuck to the sidewalks next to the buildings.

At the far side of the square Aster paused to look over the patchwork of Missing Persons posters pasted to the stone wall on the side of a tailor's shop. She wasn't quite sure why she stopped. The posters were no different from those found across the city. They occasionally changed when the old ones rotted away or new ones went up, but they weren't her concern.

Still, something tugged at her mind. Not quite a recollection, but the idea that these posters had been brought to her attention recently.

A newer poster caught her eye. Fresh black ink on pale cream paper showed a detailed drawing of a young man with dark, floppy hair, ears so large they stuck out from beneath that ragged mop, a heavy brow, and a pleasant look to him.

According to the poster he'd been missing for just over a week.

Nothing newer. Nothing about her recent kill. If anyone missed him, they weren't going to the cops about it. It was as Aster expected and how she wanted it, but it still sent a prickling sensation up her spine to think how easily a person could be erased from the world.

A few more blocks over, after wetting her boots on the slush-covered sidewalks of unfamiliar streets, Aster found the bakery mentioned on the fortune teller's card.

The twin plate-glass windows that framed the bakery's inset door displayed a dizzying array of treats—a massive cake with rose-pink frosting dotted with delicate sugar crystals, dainty little cookies with creamy filling sandwiched in the middle, breads and rolls and sweet buns. A well-dressed lady exited carrying a white box with blue string, and the scents of jam and yeast and sweet goodness chased after her.

Aster's mouth watered despite her recent breakfast, and she promised herself she'd stop on her way out for a few treats to take home.

The only access to the two floors above the bakery appeared to be a wooden staircase accessible by way of the alley beside it. Aster climbed past the second floor and the door marked with a discreet "B". Apartment C was tucked beneath the roof on the top level, and its door had a fresh coat of midnight-blue paint. There was no nameplate, no sign that someone might be running a business here, but that was to be expected for someone offering legally questionable services.

Aster checked in with herself, feeling out her body's reactions now that she'd reached her destination. There was nothing strange, no instinctive warning of danger based on details her conscious mind had missed. Just the usual awkward feeling that came when she faced a social interaction her lack of memories left her ill-prepared for. It was always unpleasant, but if she walked away every time she felt that sort of anxiety, she'd never accomplish anything at all.

She knocked.

Shuffling noises beyond, someone speaking. Aster touched a finger to the tip of the dagger in her sleeve, reassuring herself of its presence. If she didn't pause to think, if she let her body take the lead when danger arose, she could have it in her hand in a second.

She'd timed herself.

The door swung open, revealing a young woman with waves of chestnut brown hair, pale porcelain skin, and rosy cheeks. Her eyes were the blue of a cloudless sky, but warmer, and seemed to be focused on something just past Aster's left shoulder.

A wave of vertigo hit Aster, accompanied by the feeling that she knew this girl even as she was certain she'd never set eyes on her before. There was no fear, though, and nothing that told her to flee. The dizziness settled quickly, leaving behind a warmth that made Aster think of running into an old friend she hadn't expected to meet today.

At least, she assumed that was what it felt like. Aside from Eamon, she didn't have anyone she'd call a true friend. But when she tried to find a memory associated with the pretty young woman, there was nothing there at all.

The rose colour of the girl's cheeks deepened.

"You came," she said. Her voice, too, was familiar for a strange, brief moment. The girl wore a thick button-front sweater over a blue dress. She pulled it tighter against the cold, hugging it to her eye-catching curves. Her feet were bare.

There was something forced about her tone. Apprehensive, perhaps.

Aster's stomach sank. She often forgot events, but she rarely forgot a person entirely unless they were connected so intimately with a painful event that Eamon's healing washed them away. She had no memory of the wolves, but also none of the boy who had apparently broken her heart after a brief weekend fling a few years back.

She hoped she hadn't done anything silly that had embarrassed her so terribly she'd forgotten it. Actual danger would be far more comfortable to deal with, but she sensed nothing of that here.

She took a deep breath, laughed in a nervous way that she hated, and pressed on.

"This is awkward," she said. "I found your business card on my person and—" She hesitated.

The fortune teller frowned. "Is something wrong?"

Aster rubbed her throat as though it might loosen and release the right words. It was as if her mind were split in two. The trained, cold-blooded killer side knew should be cautious, or perhaps demand answers. But the natural, instinctive, emotional part of her wanted nothing more than to avoid embarrassment in front of this wide-eyed stranger.

"I apologize if this seems strange," she said. "I have no recollection of meeting you. I hoped you might clue me in."

The girl tilted her head to one side as though listening to something. Aster listened, too, but heard nothing except a pigeon cooing on the roof and the distant clatter of carriage wheels on the street. Then the girl nodded.

"We did meet. Yesterday. In jail, actually. I was in the cell next to you."

Warm relief flowed through Aster's veins, and she relaxed slightly. It was strange that even this prompting didn't bring a whisper of memory to confirm it, but it did explain a few things. If she didn't remember being in jail, it only followed that she wouldn't remember anyone she'd met there.

The young woman, who Aster decided didn't fit the name Orianna Alcorini at all, tilted her head to one side. "Does this happen to you often? The memory loss?"

No judgement in her voice, no morbid curiosity. Only genuine concern.

"More than I'd like," Aster admitted. "I'm sorry to have bothered you."

"Not at all."

A sharp gust of wind cut down the alley, and the fortune teller shivered.

"I don't suppose you'd like to come in?" She sounded uncertain. "There isn't much to tell about the card, but I've got water on for tea if you'd like to warm up."

"Thank you."

Aster reached into her pocket and touched the card. It would be a bad idea to lower her defences, but she let herself hope that her former self had kept the information because she'd found a friend.

Or more.

Aster shushed that thought. Even a friend would be a difficult thing until her work with the wolves was finished, and surely anyone she'd flirted with to any degree of success would have been happier to see her.

Again the girl seemed to be listening. Then she turned and entered the flat, leaving the door open. Aster followed and closed it tight behind her.

The room beyond should have been open, taking up most of the top floor of the long building, but was divided across its width by a series of mismatched silk folding panels that blocked any view of the other side except for the raftered ceiling. Every surface in the makeshift room they created near the door was draped with layers of silk and cotton fabric in an array of rich colours and patterns that should have clashed with each other. Instead they gave the room a sense of exotic mystery, even if Aster couldn't decide exactly which culture the decor was trying to emulate. A pair of well-stuffed armchairs flanked a round table decorated with a glass ball set on an iron stand and a few burnt-down candles.

The space smelled of dry herbs and soap, candle wax, and pine needles.

"Don't mind all this," the girl said, and vanished through an opening between the dividing panels and the far wall. "This is my professional life, not the place for guests. Leave your boots on, I need to wash the floors anyway."

Aster stepped between the table and one of the chairs and followed. The other side of the room seemed to belong to a different person entirely. It was still colourful, but the hues came from the quilts piled on a bed in the corner, the bright glow of a fire in the hearth, and a range of flowering potted plants at the windows that made Aster feel she had not only stepped out of the cold, but into another season entirely.

A plain wooden bookshelf with cabinets at the bottom stood against the wall opposite the fireplace, accompanied by a heavy oak wardrobe, more ornate but propped up at one corner on a pair of books where a leg was missing. Two mismatched armchairs sat by the fire, settled cozily on a braided rug in hues of faded purple, blue, and orange. This was home, then, a cozy and welcoming room that at first glance suited its occupant better than her professional life seemed to.

The girl turned back to Aster and stuck out her hand. "I guess I should introduce myself again, shouldn't I? I'm Gale. Short for Nightingale."

Aster smiled and shook her hand. Her touch was warm, her skin soft and smooth against Aster's callused palm. "Let me guess, only your mother calls you that, and only if you're in trouble?"

Gale smiled sadly. "She used to. Please, have a seat. Tea will only be a moment."

"I'm Elissa," she called after Gale as she went through an open doorway into another room at the front of the building. "But I suppose you knew that."

No answer. Aster sat in one of the chairs and crossed her right ankle over her left, sitting like a proper lady. As she did, she caught a hint of something on the air. Not a scent, but… Something. An energy, almost.

Restlessness overtook her, and she stood to look around the room.

Nothing interesting on the shelf—a few books, some of them impressively old. One of children's stories, one of Andonian history, and several that looked to be notebooks. She glanced at the kitchen, listened to the sound of water being poured into a pot, and slowly opened one of the cupboard doors.

Nothing there, either, save for a few folded sweaters. Aster closed it.

Gale said something in the kitchen, speaking so softly Aster almost didn't hear it. She turned and crept closer, her footsteps silent on the worn wood floor. Gale whispered again, and Aster tensed.

It sounded like one side of a conversation.

"Need a hand in there?" she called. She braced herself, ready for a fight if there should be anyone in the kitchen waiting to ambush her, and flipped the catch that would allow her to shake the dagger into her waiting hand.

"All's well," Gale answered, and emerged carrying a tray precariously stacked with a teapot, cups, milk and sugar, and a plate of chocolate biscuits. "I'm afraid my table is in use for other purposes. Just let me set this on the bed."

Aster stood aside, then peered into the kitchen. There was no one there, and nowhere to hide. Just a stove, a tiny square of counter and a sink, and a table covered in more potted plants drinking in the sun from a south-facing window.

Gale set the tray down with a sigh and busied herself preparing cups of tea, her back turned to her guest.

Trusting, Aster thought, and secured her blade again. She hoped that meant Gale didn't see her as an enemy.

"Milk? Sugar?"

"Sugar, thank you. Who were you talking to in the kitchen?"

Gale glanced over her shoulder and wrinkled her nose. "Oh, that. Don't mind me. I've lived alone for a while now. I suppose I've picked up some odd habits."

She seemed genuinely uncomfortable, and Aster smiled to put her at ease. "As long as talking to yourself makes for good conversation, why not?"

Gale offered a shy smile and nodded. "I suppose. Here you go." She held out two identical earthenware mugs filled with steaming tea. "Take your pick. I'll read your leaves after."

Aster took the one from Gale's right hand. Her nails were short and tidy, her fingers long and graceful save for the first, which was conspicuously absent. Aster's stomach tightened.

Magic. I caught a hint of magic. It seemed possible. Eamon had carefully chosen his sacrifice to make it easy to conceal from the authorities, but not all witches were so wise or cautious. He'd said some held superstitions about extra powers granted or intentions set by the loss of various body parts, but that it was a lot of nonsense—a powerful witch would bend magic to suit them.

She didn't drink until Gale had taken a long gulp from her cup. When she tasted the tea, it carried a hint of spices that echoed the scents from the bakery downstairs.

"When we met—" Aster said, at the same time as Gale spoke.

"Your memory loss," she said. "Is that from..." She let the words trail off and gestured to her own face, tracing a mirror image of Aster's scar.

"It is." Aster supposed it wasn't a lie, strictly speaking.

The tea warmed her, sending a faint prickling heat over her arms and back.

Gale's brow furrowed, then smoothed. "Nothing to do with the magic?"

The heat increased, becoming uncomfortable. "Excuse me?"

Gale swallowed nervously. "When we met your scar was hidden by magic. The spell faded as we were speaking. I suppose you explained it away later if the cops could be bothered to notice, but I knew what it was."

"That was temporary. Something I got from a witch in another town."

"I see. Well, I suppose I could fill in some blanks for you, if nothing else."

"I'd appreciate that." Aster kept her tone polite. The last thing she needed was for this girl to think she was hiding something.

Bad enough she'd seen evidence of a spell. No one could ever know about the enchantments, not even a witch who had as much to lose as Eamon if her own secrets came out.

"What do you remember?" Gale asked. "Anything at all?"

"No. I know I was brought in on charges of pickpocketing. My father bailed me out yesterday evening."

Gale's eyes widened. "Long day for you."

"I suppose."

Gale sat, and Aster did the same, though the prickling had sunk beneath her skin, leaving her agitated and wanting to pace. The chairs both faced the fire but were tilted toward each other in a friendly arrangement. Gale sipped her tea again. Aster didn't follow suit. "Let's see," Gale said. "I was there before you. Basement cells. Cold. Damp. The only other person being held was a drunk fellow, but he wasn't exactly up for conversation."

Aster focused on the fire, unwilling to close her eyes and let her guard down, and tried to remember. There was something there. Flickering lamps. A desk. Not much more than before, but what Gale said about a drunk fellow felt right, and for a second Aster could almost smell sour old vomit on musty air.

"You were dressed strangely," Gale said. "Ragged dress, a terribly unflattering hat. Fur stole with glass eyes that stared at me."

Aster knew the items from her costume wardrobe. It made

sense that she would have worn them if she wanted to go unnoticed in the park.

Gale tilted her head slightly to one side. "I lent you my coat."

Something squirmed in Aster's memory, then vanished. "Did we speak?"

"A little." Gale looked off into the distance. "Let's see... a detective came in and we speculated about what he was up to. Tom, the cop on duty, yelled at me for sharing my coat." Her gaze sharpened, and she turned it on Aster. Not threatening, Aster thought, but analyzing.

"Something wrong?"

"No. It's only that I didn't expect to have to tell you all this if I saw you again. You and I, we were friendly. You seemed quite hilariously out of place there, but not afraid, and I liked you for that."

Invisible fingers of ice trailed over Aster's back. "But then?"

Gale tapped her fingers against the arm of her chair. "You had another conversation. With the woman you'd tried to murder that morning."

Aster's breath caught in her throat, and she cursed herself for coming without asking Eamon about the card.

Gale nodded as though Aster had spoken. "It's all right. Jes didn't tell the cops anything about that, or about you claiming you'd killed most of her family. That's her own personal business, I guess, and she has no reason to turn you in as long as you stick to the agreement you made."

"Which was?"

"That you would strike her name from the list of people you owed justice to. Those weren't your exact words, but—"

Aster laughed. It sounded rough and unfamiliar. "Are you joking?"

Gale tensed, and again Aster caught the feeling of magic in the air—not like Eamon's but undeniably present. Her skin tingled as though in response to it. "I'm not. You realized Jes was a child back then and not responsible for what the adults in her family did to you."

Aster opened her mouth to tell her the idea was ridiculous, then paused.

It *was* ridiculous. But when she let the idea settle for a moment, something clicked into place. There was an inexplicable rightness to the thought that she'd had such a conversation. It felt like the answer to the question of the peculiar lightness she'd felt that morning.

Not one enemy crossed off, but two, even if only one had earned her a new charm on her bracelet.

But it's not right.

"You're lying," she said, and set her mug on the floor. Her voice came out tight and hard. "I might not remember much, but I have a person I tell everything to so he can remember for me. He'd have told me anything that important this morning."

Gale gripped the arm of her chair, but it didn't hide the tremble in her hands. "Would this person have any reason to hide such information from you? So you'd try to kill Jes again, perhaps?"

"No."

She wanted to stay calm and ask questions of her own, but her stomach turned, and she tasted tea and her breakfast at the back of her throat. Something moved in her, setting her on edge. It felt wrong—not like when her deeper self warned her of danger, exactly, but like the creeping unease that came before a thunderstorm. Something not of herself. Something that grew more terrible with each second that passed.

"What did you put in the tea?"

"Nothing I didn't also drink. I didn't poison you." Gale's voice remained warm and soothing. "Why, what's wrong?"

There are bugs crawling under my skin. Lightning in my veins. My teeth are falling out.

Aster pushed the irrational thoughts aside.

"I'm fine." The lie made her feel a little better.

"I don't think you are." Gale's skin had paled. "I feel it in you. The magic. You have nothing to fear from me."

"Then why do you look so afraid?"

"Because I remember what it's like. I had magic in me once, too, before I became a witch. Placed there by someone else to harm me."

Aster's chest tightened painfully. It took her a moment to recognize the feeling as panic, a thing she'd trained out of herself long ago.

"It hurt me." Gale looked deep into her eyes, searching for something. "It hurt a lot of people. A curse on my village. Blood magic, born of pain, death, and the theft of human souls. It almost killed me. So when I feel magic in you, harming you—"

"No one is cursing me or harming me. It's healing magic. It's —" The back of her throat closed, cutting off her defence.

Gale leaned in. "Who did this to you?"

Aster wouldn't have answered if she could. She looked toward the door, filled with sudden desperation to run.

Gale still looked terrified, but she pressed on. "I know you have no reason to trust me, but I am concerned. I'm guessing the witch responsible for this healing magic is also the one who withheld the information about Jes and could be keeping other secrets from you as well. You're in trouble. I'd like to help you. I haven't been working with magic for long, but my mentor has. Maybe we could figure out what's been done to you."

Aster stood. Her boot bumped the mug, knocking it over and spilling tea across the floor, but she barely noticed. "I know what's been done to me."

"Do you?" Gale rose and blocked Aster's path toward the door. "My mentor feels what I do. Darkness. Wrongness in this magic."

Aster glanced toward the kitchen. "Is that who you were speaking to in there? You said you were alone."

Gale nodded. "Technically. She's a ghost, but you don't need to fear her, either."

"You're mad." The thought should have made everything better. It didn't.

"I'm not." Gale squared her shoulders. "Please. I've bungled this, I know. But I haven't lied to you. You did speak with Jes. You did agree to call off the hunt."

"Enough!" Aster clenched her jaw hard enough to bring pain to her temples. It sharpened her thoughts. "You don't know what you're talking about. Why do you care so much about Jes, anyway?" She frowned. "You're familiar with her. Close. Like…" She tried to focus on a connection that hovered just outside of reach. "A relative? Employee?"

Gale's magic crackled through the air. It didn't feel threatening, or like she was about to attack. More like she thought Aster might and wanted to be ready.

"I work for her," she said. "That doesn't mean I lied to you, only that I have reason to want to know you won't go after her again. The questions about magic are my own, not hers, and I swear I don't mean any harm."

"There's nothing wrong with any magic that may or may not be in me." Aster fought to keep from screaming the words as her thoughts were screaming through her head, out of control in a way that felt terrifyingly foreign to her.

Gale stepped closer. "I could be wrong about what I feel. If we could speak calmly about this, I'm sure we can figure out what's going on."

"Nothing is going on except that you're mad and a liar and a crook." The words spilled out without thought. The only thing Aster knew was that she needed to get out. The strangeness inside her was building, and the walls seemed to be closing in.

But Gale still stood in her way.

A new urge rose in Aster, not to flee, but to fight. She resisted, but clenched her hands at her sides. "Move."

"I will, once you promise not to tell your witch about me or about this conversation." Gale's voice trembled. "Swear on... on their life."

"Fine." Aster thought she might promise anything if it got her out of there. Her heart slammed in her chest. "As long as you stay away from me. The second you cause trouble, the second you come sniffing around in my business again, I tell him everything."

Gale stepped aside. Aster stumbled past her on legs that felt like they were made of wood, knocking over a section of silk panels as she passed. All she cared about was getting out. She rushed through the fortune teller's studio with none of her usual care and grace, knocking the table with her hip and sending the heavy glass ball crashing to the floor. The door seemed leagues away, but she reached it in four steps, threw it open, and took the stairs two at a time as she gasped in frigid outdoor air.

The panic faded, and by the time she got near the end of the alley, she was able to slow her steps and catch her breath.

"You're in danger!" Gale called.

Aster stopped and turned. Gale leaned over the edge of her balcony, hands gripping the railing tightly. "Not from me. Not from Jes. If we could speak calmly—"

Aster imagined what could come from such a conversation. More talk of memory loss and its causes. Talk of enchantments.

Questions about Eamon and his magic.

An icy hand gripped her heart, and she hurried toward the safety of home like death was following.

CHAPTER TEN
GALE

Gale closed the door more gently than it had been opened. It seemed a miracle the hinges hadn't broken when it hit the wall.

"That went well," Madrigal said, looking over the wreckage.

Gale leaned against the door and willed her heart to stop pounding. "We learned a few things, anyway."

Madrigal floated to Gale's chair—or rather, to the fictional Lady Orianna's chair—and sat. She didn't look as flustered and undone as Gale herself felt, but her piercing eyes were shadowed with concern.

"I hope the most prominent lesson you learned was how dangerous she is," Madrigal said. She leaned down as though to pick up the crystal ball from the floor, but her fingers passed through it. She sighed.

"She certainly is that." Gale took the other chair, stretching her legs toward the door. It was strange to look at the room and the table from this side, but it felt good to sit. Now that the storm had blown itself out the door, whatever foolish courage had allowed her to stand up to her guest was draining from her. "We already knew she was dangerous, though. Unless she was lying, she's killed most of Jes's old family. Jes certainly didn't consider those people anyone to be trifled with."

"But?"

Gale picked up the crystal ball from the floor and held it before her eyes, as though it were anything other than a lump of glass enchanted to cloud up mysteriously when she spoke the right words over it. A pretty trick and nothing more. She set it down in its iron cradle.

"But I'm not convinced the danger is all her." Her breath trembled as she remembered the strange force that had surrounded Elissa when Gale had spoken of Jes and the missing memories. It had brought an odd shift in her demeanour. Not a person dropping a mask of civility when it wasn't getting her what she wanted, but more like a spirit entering her and taking control.

Gale's people didn't believe in such things, but since she'd opened her eyes to magic and its mysteries, she'd learned to consider ideas she never would have before.

"You felt the magic, didn't you?" she asked, more to make sure she hadn't imagined it than out of concern her mentor might have missed anything.

"Of course I did. The migglewort you put in the tea did its job." Madrigal rested her elbows on the table and her head in her hands. "It revealed something truly powerful."

Gale's mouth went dry. "Blood magic?"

She'd suspected it when the magic in Elissa had revealed itself. It felt cold, dark, and unthinkably powerful.

But it hadn't felt like being cursed, which hadn't felt like anything magical at all.

"I don't know," Madrigal said, her voice soft. "I recognized it in you because your wound was caused by a curse, and the only curses I know of come from blood magic. This is different."

That's not a no.

It wasn't the time to press the issue. It *never* seemed to be time to talk about that curse or the fact that the blood witch who had done it was still out there somewhere, torturing and killing people to access power so corrupted it destroyed a witch's ability to hold it in their body.

And it was certainly never a good time to talk about the ember that burned deep in Gale's belly, a smouldering desire to see that particular witch's power removed from the world. The healer's oath she'd taken forbade killing a human for any reason, but there were other ways.

Maybe this wasn't blood magic, but it might be the closest thing she'd had to a warm trail since she'd been banished from her home.

"If weren't a curse, could it be an enchantment?" Gale didn't like to ask. It was more comfortable to think of her sort of magic as good and blood magic as evil, but she'd read accounts of true witches like herself enchanting people's minds.

As far as she could tell, robbing someone of their free will never ended well.

Madrigal rested her head on the back of the chair, eyes closed. She could have passed through the furniture, the floor, and the ground that supported them if she'd wished, but made a convincing show of solidity when she wanted to. "That would be my best guess. I'm not sure what sort, though. She seemed lucid, if awkward about her memory loss. In control of herself until your special tea revealed her magic to you."

"And to herself?"

"Maybe. It's well hidden from the world, why not from her? In any case, she seemed aware of its presence, as if it were a necessary thing she wanted to explain."

"And couldn't. Like the enchantment was defending itself."

"Perhaps."

Gale stood and left her workspace behind. The other side of the room was a mess, with Elissa's chair knocked over and tea spilled everywhere. The mug was chipped where it had hit the floor, and Gale sighed as she set it aside to be used for rooting plants.

"Think out loud, please," Madrigal said, and sat on the bed as Gale collected rags from the kitchen.

Gale had found that request irritating when she began proper training, preferring to perfect her ideas before presenting them and feeling embarrassed when she exposed her flawed thought processes. She'd grown accustomed to it, though.

"I'm thinking a few things." Her rags made quick work of the tea, and she piled them beside her on the floor. "I'm thinking Jes was right to go into hiding, and she won't be pleased that I didn't find out more about who Elissa really is. If that's her real name, at least it's a start."

Madrigal nodded. "Do you think it is?"

"I doubt it."

"What else, then?"

"I'm thinking that there probably is someone else behind all this," Gale said, speaking slowly. "A partner, at least, probably the person holding her memories. They might be the source of the magic. That girl's not a witch."

"What makes you say that?" Madrigal obviously knew the answer, but wouldn't hand it over.

"I just know."

Madrigal narrowed her eyes. "You can do better than that."

Gale reminded herself that she wanted this, even if having a teacher present nearly every waking moment was trying at times. "The power didn't feel like her. When I became aware of your magic, it felt like you in a way I can't quite define. I believe another witch would say mine feels like me."

"It does." Madrigal smiled sadly. "I wish there were more here for you to meet."

"That's it, then. The magic didn't feel like it was of her, only in her. Like the curse was in me." Gale paused, thinking back. "Did you see her face when it happened? She acted angry, but she looked terrified. Confused. I don't think she'd ever felt it that clearly."

"True. And there's no predator more dangerous than a frightened one." Madrigal came closer, kneeling before Gale, placing herself at eye level. "I hope the next words to come out of your mouth aren't going to be *she's in trouble and needs help* or *if this is blood magic, I need to stop it.* None of this is your concern."

Gale didn't answer. Both thoughts had crossed her mind.

"Nightingale. Look at me."

Gale met Madrigal's eyes expecting a stern reprimand for foolish thoughts. Instead she found concern. "You're not ready to face that. Not for anyone, no matter how interesting you may find them."

Gale looked away. "I don't like her. I barely know her."

Madrigal shook her head. "You think I didn't see how you two were in jail, looking and assessing and wondering? I haven't been dead so long I've forgotten what it's like."

Gale's cheeks warmed. "Was it that obvious?"

Madrigal drummed her fingers silently against her leg. "You've grown up a lot since you left your sheltered past behind, but you're still a child in so many ways. This isn't a storybook where the brave-but-naïve young woman tames the dark and damaged object of her affection and finds the goodness that was inside them all along. Such foolish ideas will get you killed before they'll lead you to true love."

"I know. And yet I do wonder."

Madrigal glared at her. "Don't wonder."

"Not about that sort of thing, but the fact that we met at all." Gale rubbed the spot where her right index finger had once been. It had become an unconscious habit since the wound had healed. "The odds of me being arrested at the same time as someone who might be connected to blood magic must be impossibly slim. What if I was in jail at the same time she was for a reason?"

"You're not clinging to notions of God's will, are you?" Madrigal's tone was sharp, and Gale couldn't blame her for it. The old beliefs Gale had been raised with had led directly to the witch's death.

Gale pulled her knees to her chest. "I left behind a specific set of beliefs. I think they're wrong about what God's will is concerning magic and witches, but that doesn't mean God's will doesn't exist. You've seen Lord Death yourself. You know there are beings higher than us and powers beyond magic that we can't understand. Who's to say there isn't a reason I should be brought together with a person who needs help, even if she doesn't know she needs it?"

Or with a person who might lead me to the witch who cursed Bright Hollow, she added but didn't dare say out loud. Madrigal would only tell her again that she wasn't ready to face any such thing, and she'd be right.

But still.

"What I wouldn't give to have corporeal form long enough to slap you up the side of your head," Madrigal muttered, scowling. "I understand that you miss your old life and your old purpose, but you're asking for trouble with that one. Some people can't be helped, and she clearly doesn't want to be."

"Or the enchantment doesn't want her to be. Could it be broken?" Gale didn't look at her mentor, not wanting to see her disappointment or irritation. "If it were affecting her memory, hypothetically, and someone who's not me could break it, she'd remember the conversation with Jes and leave her alone. That *is* my concern."

Madrigal didn't say anything.

Gale collected the rags and carried them to the laundry basket in the corner beside the bed. "I'm supposed to be focusing on enchantments, am I not? I should know these things, at least in theory."

"True, and you're behind in your studies." Madrigal floated

toward the shelf Gale had brought from the cellar beneath her cabin.

Gale knelt before the shelf and whispered *"Alhamadra,"* then opened the cupboard at the bottom.

The sweaters that had been inside had vanished. In their place sat Madrigal's books from her cabin, a few from the secret library of witches in Queen's Run, and Gale's notes from the past nine months.

The earliest volumes of Gale's notes were written in a mix of old and new Andonian. Everything she wrote now was in the old language, which came more easily than it once had even as she continued to struggle with its complications. One word could mean different things depending on context, different words could mean the same, and a complicated idea could often be contained in a simple symbol if only one had the knowledge to figure out how to connect it to magic. Gale had come far, but Madrigal said she had a long way to go, that understanding the language wasn't the same as thinking in it or knowing its true nature.

She still needed to follow established spells and instructions to make anything happen, a fact that seemed to be a great disappointment to her teacher.

She selected *Enchantments and Effects*, a thick volume of notes and observations from a witch called Ardonette LeRoi. It was old enough that Gale had to be careful not to break the pages, but it had been an excellent supplement to Madrigal's teachings.

"Not that," Madrigal said. "I think we'll study illusions today."

Gale scowled, but chose a slimmer, newer work by an unnamed witch. "I'll never use this," she said. "You just want to take my mind off other things."

Madrigal leaned against the bookcase and gave her a grim smile. "Sometimes I think the true reason Lord Death hasn't taken me past the veil yet is that you need someone to keep you safe from yourself."

"And sometimes I wonder whether you're concerned about me for my sake or because I'm your ticket away from this world." Gale muttered the words, but Madrigal's hearing was impeccable.

The ghost leaned in closer, her eyes hard as flint. "Do you wish to go back on our agreement?"

"No." Gale swallowed back her frustration. "You helped me end the curse. I'll do whatever it takes to fulfil your purpose here. I only wonder what happens if we're wrong, or if I'm never good enough to please you. When does this end? When does my magic become mine?"

Madrigal's expression softened. "When you've earned it. I told you magic was a hard road, especially if you aim for greatness. You made your choice, and you have so much potential. It would be a crime to let you waste it."

"I understand."

She didn't like it, but in her heart Gale knew Madrigal was right. Even if it were God's will that she should help people, there were battles she was nowhere near ready to fight. It was better to stay safe, become stronger, fight the battles she *could* win. She didn't doubt that if she'd tried to detain Elissa, it could have come to a physical fight. The memory of the look in the strange girl's dark eyes, which could have been rage, fear, or uncertainty, gave Gale a chill. They hadn't been the eyes of the person she'd met in jail, or even the pleasant, slightly awkward young lady who had entered the flat with no apparent ill intentions.

And Elissa couldn't be half as dangerous as whoever was responsible for her current state—someone who might have connections to the kind of dark power that had cost Gale so much even as it opened the door to her new life.

The time to deal with that would come someday.

In the meantime, studying illusions seemed like cruel and unusual punishment for minor sins of curiosity and speculation. Whether it was tricking people's minds or objectively changing reality, illusion spells weren't something Gale felt drawn toward.

Still, she sat by the fire and opened the book.

Build your knowledge, she told herself. *Learn it all. Someday it will matter.*

But two hours later, when she'd managed to send a convincing, if shockingly pink, mouse scurrying silently across the floor, she felt as far from her old purpose as she ever had.

CHAPTER ELEVEN
ASTER

Streets, shops, pubs, and offices went by in a blur as Aster strode down the street. She tried to be mindful of the situation, of her fine clothes marking her as worthy of greeting, of the whispers that would follow if anyone she knew saw her plunging through the crowds, acknowledging no one, looking distraught and overwhelmed.

It was a valiant effort, and she managed to keep her steps slow and a vague smile on her lips despite the storm raging within her. The worst of it had passed. The bleak, black thing that had arisen from nowhere and caused her to lose control of herself had vanished as though it had never existed. It had left chaos in its wake, though, and Aster struggled to pick up and sort through the pieces of herself that had been left in disarray.

"Happy Solvar, Miss Islington!"

Aster looked around, more than a little ashamed by her lack of awareness of her surroundings, and smiled at Mrs Pinnagle. Aster had met her enough times that her name came easily to mind. She was the head of the Faithful Workers Welfare Fund, of which none of the members were actual workers. A gentle-looking woman, soft and round, with silver-streaked black hair and laugh-lines around her eyes, she was nevertheless a bit of a bulldog when it came to fighting for what she thought the poor of the city wanted.

"Happy Solvar to you, too," Aster said.

Mrs Pinnagle frowned. "Are you quite well, dear?"

"Oh… yes, quite." Aster tried to mind her manners and focus on the conversation, but she couldn't help worrying she might lose track of the rest of her fluttering thoughts if she let go of them. "I hope you are, as well. I really must be going."

She didn't wait for an answer before she walked away. Terribly rude. She added Mrs Pinnagle to the growing list of people she owed an apology to.

Not that I owe one to Gale, she thought, though she knew quite well that she did.

If nothing else, speaking to Mrs. Pinnagle had extracted her from the worst of her mental chaos, and in that bit of space she found she could imagine how things had looked to Gale, who had seemed so sincere in her wrong-headed attempts to help someone who didn't want or need it. She'd offered some information, which may or may not have been correct, and she'd asked a few ridiculous questions. In return Aster had made a mess of her flat, questioned her sanity, and stormed out.

Shame pooled in Aster's belly as she remembered it. Maybe a person employed by a swindler didn't deserve better, but that wasn't the point. What mattered was how out of character it had been for Aster to lose her temper and panic over nothing.

So think it through, she told herself. *What went wrong?*

She said I spoke to Jes. That was a problem. Eamon had said no such thing this morning, either about talking to her or deciding to call off that portion of the hunt. It seemed most likely that Gale was lying about all of it, but it wasn't a plan that made much sense when Aster could easily confirm the facts, either with Eamon or the cop who guarded the cells.

If it was a lie, it was a foolish one. Gale seemed a little out of touch with reality, but she hadn't struck Aster as stupid.

She felt magic in me. Very well. The young witch wouldn't tell anyone for fear of her own secrets being found out, so that was nothing to be upset about. Only cautious.

She said it was dangerous and causing me trouble. Perhaps it did seem that way from the outside. She wasn't wrong to suspect Aster's memory troubles came from the enchantment. She was mistaking side effects for intentions, but on a normal day, Aster would simply have set her straight, or at the very least thanked her for the tea and left with her dignity intact.

After all her training to keep her head when under pressure, it simply wasn't like her to lose control. It was like someone—some*thing*—else had pulled the reins from her hands and steered her emotions and behaviour into unfamiliar territory.

And even now, with those feelings vanished like morning mist, the conversation troubled her.

Blood magic. Eamon had never mentioned any such thing. He'd had no reason to when Aster didn't take an interest in magic, and it had never been necessary for her to learn. If Gale thought that was what was in her, she'd need to be corrected before she caused trouble.

Aster stopped to buy a crisp paper bag of roasted chestnuts from a cart on the corner and slipped them into her pocket. They were Eamon's favourite, and he'd be pleased to have them.

A block later she paused to look up at the columned marble facade of the Royal Bank. Pigeons fluttered and cooed under the eaves, and she leaned against a low stone wall, watching them without really seeing them.

She popped a chestnut into her mouth. She didn't really care for them, but it gave her body something to do as her mind chewed on the problem of Gale's accusations.

It should have been easy to dismiss them. Gale had seemed painfully sincere in everything from the guilty confession of her relationship with Jes to her awkward attempt to tell Aster she needed help. But beliefs could be sincere without being true.

The problem was that parts of it had *felt* true. When Gale said Aster and Jes had spoken, it had made a strange sort of sense even when Aster knew it hadn't happened. And when Gale said Jes had been a child on that day and Aster had agreed to call off the hunt...

A pigeon landed on the wall to Aster's left and cocked its iridescent purple and green head at her.

"It felt right," Aster told the bird, and crushed a nut in one hand before setting the crumbs out before it. The flock descended on her offering, and Aster walked away.

The idea had fit perfectly into the deep place of knowing that lay beneath conscious thought, even as her mind said Eamon wouldn't have omitted such an important fact this morning.

Thought or feeling. Knowledge or instinct. Life was so much easier when they had the common courtesy to agree with each other.

Aster continued toward home.

All the shops in this part of town were familiar, upscale, and expensive. Aster looked in the window of Brederick's Books, considering the display of new and used volumes of ghost stories. The tradition of telling tales about haunted homes, lost loves returning to remind the living of the value of life, and more frightening spirits had originated in Jatlind, an ice-bound nation across the sea. Those who fled its long winter nights had brought the custom to Andonia, and even those who celebrated other holidays had made it part of their traditions.

But they were fiction, stories told to impart a lesson or heighten the emotions of the season. Ghosts weren't real, though Gale clearly believed she was haunted by one. Perhaps she meant well, but she obviously wasn't in complete touch with reality.

I shouldn't have said it, but she is mad. And misguided. I should have pitied her, not yelled at her.

Aster considered stopping to buy something to read while Eamon was away, but decided a ghost story might not be the thing for a dark night alone in an old, empty house. She left the store behind and made her way home.

The only thing to do was to ask Eamon. He'd explain everything.

Pain like a punch to her lower gut hit her halfway across the street, drawing a gasp. She pushed on until she stood within the safe confines of her front yard, then closed her eyes.

Not illness. Not injury. Her body was trying to get her attention in the only way it could, but she didn't know why the thought of speaking to Eamon should feel so wrong. It wasn't until she thought back to Gale with her frightened eyes and strong words that she realized what it was.

I know I promised not to tell anyone about her magic or our little chat, she told her deeper self, *but Eamon won't harm her.*

I know, her instincts whispered back. *But still...*

A promise was a promise. Aster had murdered people, true, but with good cause, and without integrity what did she have left? And besides, if she revealed a troubling experience like the loss of control that had come with the conversation, Eamon might decide to postpone his trip to keep an eye on her.

No trip meant no imminent fix for her enchantment. No freedom from pain, no chance of recovering memories.

And that, especially given the way her mind had slipped out of her control this morning, simply wouldn't do. The revelation would ruin everything and hurt Eamon if he thought she believed even a shred of what Gale had said about dark magic.

Perhaps her gut wasn't being completely unreasonable. Still, Aster tossed the chestnuts in the gutter on the off chance they were the true cause of her intestinal distress.

She'd tell Eamon only what she needed to. She hadn't revealed anything to Gale about who was responsible for the magic she carried in her, or her own identity. Gale might track her down based on her appearance, but by then Eamon would be back and they'd have sorted things out.

For now she'd only ask enough to prove to herself that Gale was wrong, no matter how disturbingly true some of her lies had felt.

A wave of warmth greeted her as she entered the house. The fire in the parlour was burning hot, and she shed her coat and boots as quickly as she could.

"Eamon?"

"Packing, dear." His voice came from behind the closed door of his bedroom, which had once been the first-floor study at the front of the house. The desk and books had been moved upstairs and the bed brought down so Eamon wouldn't have to climb the stairs more than he wished to.

Two suitcases sat open on top of the bed's heavy green blanket, and three small wooden crates were stacked on the white-carpeted floor. Eamon stood next to one of the two wardrobes that faced his bed, assessing his warmest, down-filled coat.

"Packing light for your trip?" Aster looked toward the suitcases, both of which were nearly full.

Eamon set the coat aside and turned to her. "One never knows what will be needed far from home. Or a day's journey away, for that matter."

Aster perched on the only free space at the bottom corner of the bed, facing large portraits of Winifred and Claudia that matched the ones Eamon wore in his locket. Aster had asked him to move them from the hallway to his bedroom years ago. Something about having Eamon's deceased wife and daughter observing her every day had made her skin crawl.

She looked over the crates, each small enough to be carried by a single person but likely heavy enough that he'd struggle on his own. "You're sure it's just for one night?"

"That's the plan," Eamon said. "Up to Hampstead to meet with my contact and deliver some potions he requested. If all goes well, I'll bring him here to work on your enchantment. Will you prepare the guest room?"

"Of course."

"Good. I'll know more when we get back, after he meets you, and—" Eamon frowned at her. "Is something wrong?"

Aster hesitated. Something was twisting again deep in her gut.

There was a time when she wouldn't have considered lying to him. They were a team, the feral mage and the teenaged vigilante, both on the wrong side of the law for the right reasons. Aster owed him everything, from her life to her education to the position in society she'd shortly be stepping into.

But it's only for now, she told herself. *Spare him some worry while he's away, talk it over later if it still seems like it matters by then.*

"I found a note I left myself last night," she said.

"Oh?" Eamon continued packing.

"Did I mention anything to you about speaking to Jesamyn at the jail?"

Eamon hung a robe on the bedpost and turned to her. "You did. You decided you didn't wish to pursue her. We didn't know she was a child back then. I argued that she was still morally responsible for her actions at the time, and you disagreed."

Aster hated how relief flooded her, how it only proved how deep Gale's suggestions had gotten beneath her skin.

"Why didn't you mention it before?"

Eamon sighed and closed the first suitcase, and Aster leaned on it while he tightened its leather straps. "It didn't seem immediately relevant, and I had quite a lot on my mind at the time. This meeting, this journey, your future. I believe I did mention you planned to pursue Mavolia next?"

Aster thought back to their conversation that morning. He'd never mentioned why Jesamyn wasn't her next target. Aster herself had made assumptions and filled in those blanks.

"You did. I'm sorry if it sounded like I was accusing you of anything."

Eamon added a handkerchief to the second suitcase, paused, and added three more. "I planned to discuss it with you again, when we had more time."

That's that, then, Aster thought, and relaxed. Not a lie, but an error that would have been rectified when he was less distracted. Eamon was a good man, but no more perfect than Aster herself.

She had to sit on the suitcase before it would close.

It didn't really matter, but a part of her wished Gale could hear this conversation. The poor girl was obviously deeply troubled by the dark places her imagination had led her when she felt magic in her guest and saw its unfortunate effects. It might ease her mind to know the truth, but Eamon's magic wasn't Aster's to speak to strangers about.

"A note, you say?" Eamon asked. "I didn't see one when I left your gift."

"Under my pillow."

"Ah."

She watched him fussing with his suitcases and checking his pockets. The idea that he might be harming people for the sake of magic was ludicrous, but Aster stiffened when she remembered the strangeness that had crept beneath her skin while Gale spoke of blood and lost souls.

Winifred and Claudia gazed down from their portraits, and Aster couldn't help feeling the weight of their judgement. Eamon had lost both of them in the same magical turmoil that might have taken Aster's parents. Andonia had been a cursed patchwork of plagues and blights in those days, and Aster didn't mind not being able to remember that part of her story.

You're all he has left, the portraits' eyes said. *His only family, his chosen daughter who he's sacrificed so much for, and you keep secrets from him.*

I know, Aster answered without speaking, as though their ghosts could hear her.

And with that thought she realized there was at least one way she could assure herself she'd been foolish to let any of Gale's strange accusations get to her, no matter how sane she'd seemed.

"Are ghosts real?"

Eamon followed her gaze to the portraits. "Aster, what are you—"

"Not them!" Aster looked away. "I know they're at peace, of course. But when someone dies, is there any reason they wouldn't leave this world? And that they'd be able to speak to the living?" She felt silly asking.

Eamon considered for a moment. "Generally, no."

Aster let out a long breath. *I knew it.*

"At least, not like you hear in stories." Eamon picked up his cane and sat next to Aster, looking up at the portraits of his lost family. "I tried to speak to Winnie after she died, but she was gone. Most people are, straight away. But there are souls who stay in this world, whether they want to or not. Most of them go unnoticed because they can't speak directly to the living—some say it feels cold when a ghost touches you, but that's not the sort of thing that's easily tested or proved. Once in a while, one will manage to make itself heard. That's exceedingly rare, though."

A chill passed over Aster like a breath from the grave. "How would they do that?"

"Magic on the part of the deceased," he said. "A deep, pre-existing connection with the living person they're communicating with. Sometimes dreams will open a doorway for far less powerful spirits, but I'd guess the living don't remember those dreams often. Magic makes a powerful spirit, and sometimes a tenacious one."

Aster told herself it didn't matter. All this meant was that there was a small chance Gale wasn't the victim of an overactive imagination and her brain might not have been addled by magical experiments.

It didn't mean she was right about anything else.

Still, Aster shivered at the thought that there might have been a deceased person in jail with them. She thought of Gale's whispered conversation in her kitchen and felt a little ill.

Eamon sighed. "If I'd died before Winnie, I might have spoken to her."

"And I wouldn't be here." Aster placed a hand on Eamon's. "I'm sorry for bringing it up. It was on my mind what with the stories people tell."

"The holidays, yes." Eamon said it as though he'd forgotten they existed. "I'll be back before Solvar and Langnaak and all that." He frowned and looked into her eyes. "Are you sure you're all right? You look as if you've seen a ghost." He said it like a joke, but there was real concern there, too. He'd always been good at reading her. "Shall I take another run at healing you before I go?"

"No," Aster said, ignoring the strange way the thought made her want to pull away from him. "You don't need to take time to do that. I just feel unsettled with the holes in my recollection, and I think I might have dreamed of hauntings last night." She forced a smile she hoped would reassure him.

"I hope that's all it is." Eamon's frown deepened. "You sometimes struggle after healings that take large portions of memory with them. Strange thoughts. Paranoia. Even confusing dreams with reality as your mind struggles to fill in the emptiness."

"This isn't that," Aster said. She remembered no such thing in her past, but it would make sense for her to have forgotten it. "I feel fantastic, really."

"I see," Eamon said. "I could—"

The bell at the front door rang, and Aster hurried to look out the window. "Your carriage." Without waiting she carried the first of the crates from the room and set it on the steps with a nod of thanks to the unfamiliar driver.

Eamon stood aside and watched as the driver carried the other boxes and suitcases out. "I'd like for you to stay at home while I'm away," he told Aster when the last of them were gone.

"Don't go to the shops or the library or out to tea. There's enough food here to last you."

"Eamon, I'm fine."

He held up one hand. "Promise me, please. I've worried for some time that I've waited too long to make this trip, that your enchantments were taking an unexpected toll on your mind." He took both her hands in his. "The road may be dangerous, and my negotiations difficult. I'd prefer to not have to worry about you while I'm away."

Aster kissed him on the cheek. Two days at home wasn't a high price for his peace of mind, and it would give her time to sort things out and calm her nerves before his return. "I'll stay home. Plenty to do here, anyway. Be safe."

Aster stood at the door and waved until the carriage was out of sight, then stepped into the house and locked the door behind her. She made her way up the stairs, telling herself that the odds of this house being haunted were exceedingly slim, and that surely Gale's ghost couldn't be watching her now. There was no need to think of it. She found Gale's card in her coat pocket and tucked it into her desk drawer, far at the back.

It almost helped her feel better.

CHAPTER TWELVE
ASTER

Aster awoke in darkness to the sound of the wind howling and rattling the windows, utterly confused about where, when, and who she was.

My bed, she thought. *Aster. I'm Aster and Eamon has left for a few days. I was reading. The lamp was running low on oil, I was thinking I should refill it, and then—*

Rational thoughts. Right thoughts, but they seemed distant and far away compared to the dream she'd been having. In the darkness of her room, the dream seemed more real than the blankets beneath her or the leather-bound volume on the history of criminal punishments in Andonia that she could feel when she reached out her fingers.

She'd been cold in the dream, as she was now. And she'd been in darkness there, too, but it hadn't been complete. There had been a box, and it had glowed with an eerie sort of light.

Not a box, she thought. *A chest. And I didn't know what was in it, but I was afraid.*

She pressed the heels of her hands against her eyes, making bright white light appear, but it didn't chase the visions away.

I was afraid, but I wanted nothing more than to open it, even though I knew that what was inside would destroy me.

She forced herself to sit up. Her heart was pounding like she'd run from one end of the city to the other.

God, but it's cold in here.

She reached for the drawer in her nightstand and fumbled for matches and a candle. The bright, warm light illuminated the space around her and brought her back to true, blessed reality.

Still, the feeling of the dream clung to her like scraps of spider's silk on bare skin. The fear, the uncertainty of what was in the chest, and the knowledge that she would open it, that nothing could stop her, that—

"Enough," she told herself, and swung her feet off the bed and onto the floor. Her heart still raced, but she stood and carried her candle to the window. The curtains were open, but sheets of blowing snow obscured the light from the lamps on the street.

Her stomach growled, and she checked the clock on the dressing table. Three o'clock. Too early to start the day, but she had no urge to go back to sleep. So, though the irrational terror from her dream held her tight, she headed to the kitchen.

Hiding beneath the blankets would only get a person so far. If she faced her fear, she could find out whether it was real and meet it head-on—or more likely she'd find it vanished like so much morning mist when confronted.

Her talk with Gale had obviously brought the dream on. The supposed truth about Eamon's magic was inside the box, or some nonsense like that.

Dreams, in Aster's opinion, were foolish things, and only fools lived by their counsel.

She lit a lamp in the hallway as she passed. Dream fear might be a silly thing, but she would keep the shadows at bay until she'd had a bath and scrubbed the sleep sweat from her body and the eerie sense of knowing-unknowing from her mind.

Maybe longer.

The fire Eamon had lit in the parlour before he left had gone out, which explained the chill that had crept into the house and her dreams while she slept. She re-lit it and warmed her hands over the flames.

Tea next, to calm her nerves and finish the job of waking her up. She'd lit the stove, boiled the kettle, and poured her tea before she remembered the sugar bowl was empty.

She mentally kicked herself for not picking up more when she was out. She'd intended to, if things had gone as planned. At least it was a normal memory lapse this time, the kind that could happen to any person when she was distracted and distraught, but still. Sweet tea would go down so much better.

Nothing in the cupboard except a bit of honey. Eamon hadn't been to the shop while she was out this morning, then. He liked his tea as sweet as she did.

Even when he was locked away in his workshop.

Aster drummed her fingers against the countertop as she thought it over.

There would be a full bowl there on the shelf by the back wall. Aster could picture it perfectly, white porcelain with yellow roses around the edge to match the pot and cups sitting next to it.

It would mean going into the basement without permission. But the tea was getting cold, and Aster had no intention of disturbing whatever he was working on down there. Not a page nor a quill would be out of place when he returned. Through the door, grab the sugar bowl, and leave.

Her skin tingled with the fear from her dream. She ignored it. Instinct was one thing. This was quite another, born of imagination and lies, and she wouldn't be ruled by it.

There was, however, the matter of getting in. She padded down the thickly carpeted hallway to Eamon's bedroom, kitchen lamp in hand, and eased the door open. Everything was as he liked it, neat and orderly, marred only by the dents in the carpet where the crates had rested earlier.

He kept his keys in the top drawer of his tall bureau, returning them to the same spot every time he came up from working on his magic.

She slid the drawer open. For a second she thought maybe he'd taken them with him, that there would be no sugar for her tea after all, but she found them beneath a stack of handkerchiefs folded into tight squares. The key ring was heavier than she'd expected, and fuller than she'd realized. Here was the front door key, its top inset with red glass to match Aster's copy. Here were the keys to the basement storage room, the basement door, and Eamon's workshop. A fourth key would open the carriage house out back. She'd borrowed that one before, too.

But it was always one or two keys removed and handed over, never the full ring, and Aster had never properly noticed the other key.

Or at least, she didn't remember noticing it.

It was an ornate skeleton key, large and heavy, its surface scratched and pitted with age. There was nothing else strange about it, but it gave her an odd feeling, like when she'd seen Gale and somehow knew she should recognize her. But this feeling was far less pleasant.

It's the key to the chest in my dream, she thought, and pushed the idea aside before it could work her into a real fright.

It's a key. Just a key. And I'll have it and the others back here in half a twitch of a horse's tail.

She unlocked the basement door and hurried down the dark staircase, turning at the end to head for Eamon's office. The flickering light of her lamp against the darkness made goosebumps rise on her arms.

Definitely a good thing I decided against ghost stories, she thought. *Foolishness.*

She stopped as the lamp's unsteady light picked out the shape of a door at the end of the hall that shouldn't have been there.

Ice flooded Aster's veins, and the keys jingled in her trembling hand. She found the workshop key and slipped it into the lock, pushed the door open, and entered feeling like she had a wolf at her heels. She closed the door tight behind her, not quite sure why she felt the need to shut herself in, and the strangeness flowed out from her body, leaving her with only the unease of disobeying Eamon by entering this forbidden room.

She knew exactly where the sugar bowl would be and found it quickly. But she couldn't resist the urge to hold the lamp high and look around, curious about what exactly he didn't want her to see, wondering whether she might find signs of whatever natural potions he used to bring magic into himself. Gale had said his magic felt strange. Perhaps the answer to that lay in different approaches taught by different masters.

Everything was as Aster remembered. Desk, tables, papers and ink and quills. Piles of books. A few jars on the shelves. Innocent. Boring, even.

She fetched the sugar bowl, touched nothing else, and made her way back into the hall.

And stood staring at a door she was sure hadn't been there a minute ago.

Go upstairs, her mind whispered.

But she couldn't turn her back on that door. It wasn't only the wrongness of it being there. It was something else. Something dreadful that she couldn't name.

It wasn't a chest in my dream. It was a door. This door.

Two desires battled within her. One told her to leave. Eamon asked so little of her and did so much. It was bad enough she'd entered the basement against his wishes. To poke around in matters that clearly didn't concern her would be even worse. If he was keeping a secret from her, there was a reason for it.

But there was the other, too. Gale's voice suggesting Eamon's magic could be harming her through more than a flaw in the healing enchantment, and her own temper flaring irrationally at the suggestion that there might be a dark side to it. That he might be keeping secrets from her.

Gale's wrong, she thought.

If she's wrong, Eamon has nothing to hide.

So why don't I remember this door?

She stood still as a post, thinking.

To unlock the door would be a betrayal. She'd feel guilty, especially when she found there was nothing wicked behind it.

But then, what would it mean if she didn't look? That she believed there was something she was afraid to see?

That Gale had, in fact, planted doubt in her mind?

"He'll never know I opened it," she whispered, and slipped the sugar bowl carefully into the pocket of her robe. "It'll be a broom closet and some weird flaw in my memory. Everything will be all right, and I'll laugh about it later."

But as she approached, there was a shift in the air. Something strange, deep, and unthinkably vast.

And dark.

And cold.

She placed a hand against the door. It vibrated beneath the skin of her palm—not like the enchanted dagger, which was a tool she used to suit her will, but like the hide of a wild animal that was allowing her to touch it before it turned to bite her hand off.

It was locked.

I shouldn't look. I don't want to know.

I have to know.

She slipped Eamon's iron key into the lock before she could change her mind. The vibration intensified, irritating as a swarm of hornets trapped in her skull.

The lock clicked open, and the key turned to dust and vanished completely as the noise faded.

"Shit!" she cried, and grabbed at the air beside the lock as though she might snatch the key back into existence. But it was gone, and with it any chance of lying to Eamon about what she'd been up to while he was away.

Aster's breath caught in her throat.

It's not all right. It won't ever be all right.

But the door was unlocked now, anyway.

Better to know.

She tugged at the handle, and the door swung open.

The darkness beyond the doorway pressed in on Aster like a living thing, suffocating in its grasping heaviness. The light from the lamp in her hand seemed reduced, leaving the walls of the room in black shadow, barely illuminating the edges of a table with rough, thick legs ahead and to Aster's left. The air was colder here, too, but strangely dry and lifeless. A cloying scent hung in the air like long-dead roses or ancient perfume. And though the vibrations of magic she'd felt in the door had disappeared, there was still a sense of power in this place.

She licked her lips and stepped forward, willing her eyes to adjust to the darkness. Slowly, more shadowy shapes began to appear at the edge of her lamplight.

The room was significantly larger than Eamon's workshop, likely extending out beneath the bit of yard between the house and the street. She took a few more steps, following the curved wall to her right, testing the smooth stone beneath her feet. The room was solid. Real. But it didn't feel like a part of her home.

There was a workbench not far from the door, built of plain, heavy wood unlike any of the fine pieces in the house above, shaped to fit the wall of what seemed to be a circular room. Dried flowers and herbs were scattered over it, along with a small stack of leather-bound books. Above it, shelves held glass jars and opaque canisters, more books, and loose papers. A white-enamel basin sat on the table beside the books. It looked clean, but when she lifted it to examine it, she came away with flakes of rust dusting the ends of her fingers.

Aster's heart beat hard and steady, but a numbing fog overcame her mind, dampening the fear, leaving her feeling like a spectator within her own body. She wiped her fingers against the side of her robe and moved on.

Another few steps along the workbench and the books and the bowl were left in darkness. At this end she found a pile of steel sewing needles, large and sharp, and a set of silver knives in a cherrywood box. She picked one up. It looked like the throwing knives she trained with in the attic, but the balance was wrong.

And it buzzed faintly in her hand. Magic, like her dagger. The familiarity of the sensation in such a dark place turned her stomach, and she set the knife carefully back in its place.

She turned, and the light illuminated the edge of the table she'd spotted before, set out from the walls in the centre of the room five long paces away from the workbench. It, too, was made of wood, worn smooth in the middle. Dark stains covered its pale surface in horrific patterns that spoke of blood spattered and spent in a great struggle. Heavy leather straps were bolted to its surface.

Something broke in her, chasing away the numbness. Terror colder than the howling winds outside tore through her, stealing her breath.

Aster's hands trembled, and she nearly dropped the lamp as she backed away. She bumped into the wall and spun, startled. The light illuminated a pair of small cells set into the stone wall opposite the door, each a little larger than a casket set on its end, empty. The doors stood open, each made from solid wood with only a small, barred window set into it.

She froze, wishing her heart would cease its pounding so she could slow down and figure out how this couldn't be what it looked like.

Enchanted key, she thought frantically, though she wasn't sure such a thing existed. This wasn't her basement at all. It was the dungeon of some far-off castle. In Embercliffe, perhaps, or somewhere farther. There were old stories of goblins in the northern mountains with magic and underground palaces and…

She squeezed her eyes closed and forced herself to breathe.

Slow down. Figure it out. And go home before whoever owns this place comes and finds you.

Once she'd slowed her breath and stopped moving, the thoughts came smoothly, like the gears in her brain had been oiled. *Prove it. Prove where you are and figure out later why Eamon would need to visit such a dark and terrible place.*

He could be fighting against dark magic. Visiting these places when he says he's down here working, locking the door so I won't follow.

Of course he'd keep this a secret.

She forced her body into motion, giving the cells a wide berth as she made her way back to the worktable and the papers on the shelf above. The parchment was smooth, thick, and vaguely oily as she pulled a sheet down. But the writing on it was familiar—strange symbols, messy script.

Eamon's handwriting.

Her mouth went dry and she dropped the page. It fell to the floor and vanished into the darkness beneath the table, and she hurried to pick it up and put it back just where she'd found it.

His place. His notes. His magic.

She scanned the jars on the shelf, hoping for an innocent explanation. There were herbs there. Maybe this was where he mixed potions to increase his magic or aid in his spells. And as for the table…

Animals, she thought. Herbs could be used for magic potions, but so could animal parts. Eamon might be bringing animals here to do his work because…

"Because he needs them fresh," she said, her voice barely disturbing the heavy silence.

It was an answer, and one she knew she could accept for now. When Eamon healed her again this memory would be tidied away as so many others had, relieving her of the burden of uncertainty.

But it wasn't the right answer, and she knew it down to her bones.

She might wish she hadn't found the door, but to wish to un-see it now was pure cowardice.

Gale had spoken of dark magic from dark sources. Of blood, murder, and lost souls.

Walk away now. Nothing good can come from looking further.

But she stepped again toward the bloodstained table. The straps she'd noted earlier were set out in a clear pattern, ready to hold a human torso, arms, and legs.

If powerful magic can come from using animals, from their body parts and their blood...

Her mind shied away from the thought before she'd finished it.

He wouldn't. He's a philanthropist. A humanitarian. One of few wealthy people in this city who actually care.

A drop of thick, dark fluid hit the table with a dull splash.

Aster's throat closed, and the room began to grey out around her before she remembered to breathe again.

She held the lamp higher, its light shaking with the tremors in her arm, catching the forms and shadows of a trio of naked human bodies suspended by their feet from the room's ceiling, the tips of their dangling fingers reaching for her head.

Aster held back a scream and forced herself to look into the places where their eyes should have been. Those were gone now. So were their genitals, their fingernails, and some portion of their entrails—each of the three had been sliced from sternum to groin and left open, drained of blood.

Most of their blood, anyway. Another shining drop waited on the tip of a finger on the freshest looking corpse.

Aster clapped her free hand over her mouth, trapping the low moan that rose in her throat. Her thoughts left her. All but one.

I know him.

She didn't really. But she'd seen his wide lips and prominent ears on a poster. He hadn't had those cuts down both cheeks in the poster, though, or the deep bruises covering his face and body, or any of the multitude of other injuries and insults she hoped had come after his spirit had left his body.

The other two were too dried out and old to be remotely recognizable even if she remembered more faces from the posters. It didn't matter. She had no doubt that these were the missing citizens of Queen's Run, their mutilated corpses being held and used for gods only knew what in a secret room beneath her own home.

It can't be, though. I'd have seen something, heard something. He wouldn't, he'd never—

Her stomach heaved, threatening to spill bile from its otherwise empty depths over the floor. With a sob, Aster turned and ran without looking into the shadows beyond the table.

The hallway was as she'd left it, a normal part of her home, off limits but in no way unfamiliar, calling her back from the dark new world she'd so thoughtlessly stepped into.

She slammed the door behind her and turned to look at it as she backed down the hallway. She expected it to turn invisible, as surely it must have been all this time for her to have never seen it. But there it was, standing slightly ajar, as real as anything else around her.

Aster stepped toward it on shaking legs that threatened to give out beneath her. Now that she'd seen the corpses, she imagined she could smell them beneath the rose perfume scent that drifted out, making her retch violently. She forced herself to touch the door and pushed it closed more gently.

It opened again, leaving a thin line of maddening blackness between its edge and the wall.

The lock.

She fumbled for the key ring and remembered the key was gone.

The dungeon would remain open. There would be no hiding what she'd done.

Aster groaned and ran, her footsteps uncharacteristically clumsy, thoughts churning as she raced for the stairs.

Gale hadn't been wrong.

Eamon's magic came from a dark place, indeed, from the blood of humans stolen off the streets and carved up in his true workshop—not the one she'd been allowed to visit, but one that had somehow been hidden from her all these years.

The magic that flowed through her, that eased her pain when it got to be too much to bear, that had saved her life all those years ago…

Think about it upstairs, where it's safe. For now, just get away.

With every step up the stairs, her heartbeat slowed. Her thoughts drifted. She tried to grab on to them, but it was like chasing dandelion seeds scattered by the breeze.

Magic, she thought on the first step. *Dark magic.*

On the third step, she paused and wondered why she'd been thinking about such a thing when all she'd been doing in the basement was fetching the sugar bowl.

The skin on the back of her neck tensed like someone was watching her from below. She didn't let herself turn around.

It's only because I wasn't supposed to be down there, she thought, and chided herself for acting like a spooked child afraid of being caught with her hand in the cookie jar. *Eamon won't mind. He'll never even know.*

Because there had been nothing to fear in Eamon's workshop.

Nothing dark or strange, or even anything magical. Just his boring papers and a weird smell of perfume.

By the time she reached the top of the stairs, even the memory of stale roses scenting the air was gone. But the feeling of unease followed her back to the kitchen, and she lit every lamp in the house before she finished making her tea.

The next afternoon Aster woke feeling like she'd been out at the pubs, drinking herself into oblivion. At least, she assumed that was what she felt like. Aside from a few sips of wine at dinner and punch at parties, she'd never been a drinker. She'd never understood how anyone would choose to have their mind altered, and she was in no way tempted by anything that might threaten to steal more of her memories than she was apt to lose anyway.

Yet here she was, her mouth dry and sour-tasting as if she'd thrown up a day's worth of meals, her muscles aching and her scars burning like her body was trying to tear itself apart, having slept far later than she'd normally allow. Her thoughts were muddled and hazy, and her brain felt like so much wet cotton packed into her skull.

Worse, she was afraid. And she had no idea why.

She kicked the covers back and lay on her bed, trying to remember.

There had been a nightmare, she was sure of that much, and she'd gotten up after to make tea. Her gaze landed on a book on the nightstand—*Common Crimes and the Punishments Thereof, 3rd edition*. She'd been reading it last night and must have fallen asleep. It might have set off the dream, though why she'd have nightmares about anything as mundane as beheadings and light dismemberment was beyond her.

It wasn't that. It was Gale. Something about what she'd said about Eamon.

It wasn't the dream that concerned her, though. It was its aftermath, and the fact she only remembered it vaguely, as though waking from the nightmare had only been another part of the dream. Going downstairs, lighting a lamp, having a cup of tea. Nothing there at all to explain why she felt a panicked flutter in her chest even now, or why she wanted to crawl not only back under the covers, but under the bed itself to hide from…

Something.

She stood and slipped into her bathrobe and the thick wool socks Eamon had knit for her and went downstairs, dousing lamps as she went. It seemed odd that she'd have left them all burning.

Stranger still was the unease that continued to nip at her heels as she went. This house had been her home for as much of her life as she could remember, but today it felt different, like she'd awakened in a mirror realm that looked like her own but was wrong somehow. The world had tilted slightly to one side, but she had no idea how or why.

She stepped into the kitchen and found a plate and a teacup in the sink. She vaguely remembered using them. Then she spotted the sugar bowl on the counter. She froze, every hair on her body standing on end.

Eamon's sugar bowl, white with yellow roses, the one that belonged to the set in his workshop. She picked it up and studied it.

She remembered nothing save for feeling its weight in her pocket as she walked up the stairs from the basement. If something had happened down there to make her feel so strange, it was all a black void in her mind.

Aster carried the sugar bowl to the island in the centre of the kitchen and set it down carefully, then took a seat on one of the stools.

Eamon wasn't here. He hadn't healed her, so her mind hadn't gone through its process of putting things away. This was something different, maybe the thing Eamon had mentioned about her mind desperately trying to fill gaps, confusing dreams and imagination with reality. There were so many blank spaces in the days and weeks before her last healing.

Maybe this did happen sometimes and she'd forgotten each episode with her next healing. The thought made a horrible kind of sense, but rationalizing her fear did nothing to ease it.

The other sugar bowl, the one that belonged in the kitchen, was out and empty. The memory of deciding to go down to get Eamon's surfaced as though it had never been missing, but brought nothing else with it.

But why would she have forgotten that in the first place? And why did the sight of a sugar bowl make her body break out in a cold sweat?

I disobeyed the rules, that's why. I went to the basement without permission.

That didn't explain the shivers like she was coming down with a fever, or the feeling that she had an invisible blade pressed to her throat. Eamon might be displeased if he knew she'd disobeyed him, but he wouldn't be cruel or unfair if he decided to punish her for it.

He'd never hurt me.

The strangest thought came to her then, that she'd hurt Eamon somehow. She couldn't say why, or how it could have happened when he was so far away, but it seemed right.

She had the distinct feeling that someone was watching her. Her shoulders tensed and she spun to look, but there was no one. She was alone in the house.

Unless there are ghosts, she thought, forcing the joke to lighten the mood. It landed heavy in her mind, though, like the idea was closer to the truth than she knew.

She gritted her teeth.

No ghosts. Even if they do exist, they'd have no business here and no reason to speak to me.

But thinking of ghosts made her think again of Gale—the young witch who might or might not be truly haunted, who had claimed to know things about the magic that flowed in her. The ideas had angered Aster, and what was stranger, had made her afraid.

A new surge of energy filled her, and a desire to move.

Gale was wrong about Eamon, she thought, but her legs carried her back up to her bedroom as though her body were disagreeing with her mind.

I embarrassed myself. She won't want to see me again, and she certainly won't agree to help me. But her hands made quick work of dressing in a burgundy skirt with a clean white blouse and matching jacket, then slipping her jingling bracelet onto her left wrist.

She decided she'd allow it to happen. Her body was following her instincts, not her thoughts, and in the face of the loss of her memories and the unending sense of unease that had plagued her since she woke, it seemed somehow rational to follow the irrational urges.

She couldn't trust her conscious mind when it was behaving so erratically, so why not trust what lay beneath the surface to guide her?

Maybe it was only because she'd felt welcomed and safe at Gale's flat—at least, until she'd started asking those questions— that her deepest self seemed to be pulling her back there now that her own home suddenly felt so dangerous.

But maybe it was more. With Eamon gone, there was only one person in the city who might have an idea of what was happening to her. Gale had said she knew about enchantments, that she wanted to help. *If I spoke to her, explained why she's wrong without giving anything away...*

She laced her boots and tucked a dagger into the one on the

right. She had no sense that she was walking into danger, but that she was running away from it. Still, it was only good sense to be prepared.

Eamon said to stay in the house.

She ignored that thought. The pull toward the door and the world outside was too strong, and the thought of sitting alone in her home for another minute made her feel like screaming until her voice gave out.

Besides, she'd already disobeyed one of his orders. Maybe going against another would help set things right if Gale could assure her she wouldn't go mad before he returned to fix everything.

Her heart lightened as she padded down the stairs.

She pulled the door open. Heavy snow had drifted against it overnight, but the sky was bright and clear, the previous night's blizzard having blown itself out. The three children who lived across the street had toted out their sled and were dragging it past the gate. The smallest, a blonde girl in a powder-blue coat, waved to her.

Aster waved back, and as she closed the door behind her, she found she could add a smile to the greeting.

She trudged through the snow, which had come down unusually heavy, and walked through empty streets. It would be hard to get carriages out in such weather, and the odds of many businesses being closed for the day were good.

Not the factories, and not the homes where servants worked. The poor of the city rarely got a day to rest. But the quiet streets of her neighbourhood were lovely with the clean, white snow sparkling in the afternoon sun, and as she crossed Midtown Meet she spotted a few folks out enjoying its warmth.

Her good mood faded as she caught sight of the missing persons posters on the side of the tailor's shop. Something told her to keep walking, but she didn't listen. If there was a problem she couldn't remember, it was better to know.

She looked over the notices, and her eyes were immediately drawn to the poster she'd looked so closely at the day before, the young man with big ears and bright eyes. For no reason Aster could imagine, she pictured the drawing with his eyes gouged out and deep gashes cut into his skin.

Invisible hands closed around her throat, cutting off her breath and leaving her faint. Aster was glad there was no one nearby to see when she turned and vomited into the gutter.

By the time she reached Gale's door, Aster's stomach had settled.

Her nerves had not. The urge to leave and try to figure things out on her own battled with the knowledge that Gale was apparently the only person she knew besides Eamon who might have some inkling of what was happening to her. A person working for her enemy, a person she'd yelled at for no good reason, but a person she desperately needed to speak to, if only to ease her mind.

She raised her fist to knock, but the sound of voices from the other side of the door interrupted her. Two voices, Gale's and a man's. Aster couldn't hear what they were saying, but the man let out a burst of excited laughter.

Aster's stomach twisted, though she couldn't say why. If she'd had any immediate interest in Gale the day before, she'd let it go when she realized the reality of the young witch's employment situation. There was no reason to mind about Gale entertaining anyone.

She stepped aside and crouched on the balcony with her back against the wall next to the door. She didn't want to listen, and she knew her fingers and toes would quickly freeze if she didn't keep moving, but she also didn't want to miss Gale when the door opened.

Her stomach knotted as she went over her apology, as she

imagined Gale's bright eyes filled with anger and the door slammed in her face before she got a chance to say a word. She'd become good at hunting people, serving justice, forcing her will on them. This gentle approach, this raw honesty that she'd decided would be required, felt like foreign territory. Much more challenging than holding a knife to a person's throat.

The door opened a few minutes later, and Aster leapt to her feet and brushed the snow off her skirt. A middle-aged man with a lean frame and iron streaks at the temples of his dark hair emerged. He gave Aster a pleasant nod, then descended the stairs with a light bounce to his step.

Aster turned to the open door to find Gale standing with her arms crossed, blocking the entrance. Her appearance left Aster unable to speak for a moment. She was dressed in what was almost a parody of a fortune teller's costume, in a poison-green dress that clung to her body and crossed daringly low in the front. Her neck dripped with jewels Aster assumed were made of glass, and her brown hair was curled and accented with gold combs and a small peacock feather that trailed down over the front of her shoulder. She'd lined her pale eyes with black, intensifying their sharpness and the sense that she might actually see into other worlds.

She didn't look at all surprised to see Aster, and somehow even less pleased. She didn't say anything, but also didn't immediately slam the door.

"Hello," Aster said when she found her voice, wishing for the confidence and certainty she'd have felt if she'd had a dagger in her hand and an enemy in front of her. "You look... well."

Gale arched an eyebrow. "You remember me?"

"I do. And I remember everything that happened last time we met. I've come to apologize."

"Fine. Done." Gale started to close the door, and Aster put out a hand to stop it.

"And I need the help you offered yesterday. Please."

They watched each other for a moment, Gale warily searching Aster's eyes.

"What's your real name?"

Aster swallowed hard. "Aster."

"Hmm." Gale looked over her shoulder, then back to Aster. "I won't invite you in, but if you give me a moment to change out of these ridiculous rags, I do feel I need a bit of air. You can buy me a tea and a cinnamon roll, and I'll listen."

"Thank you, I—"

Gale closed the door before Aster could finish. Sounds of cupboard doors slamming followed, along with what sounded like one side of a heated conversation, though Aster still couldn't make out the words.

The ghost. Aster told herself she wasn't afraid. *Even if it's real, it's harmless.*

I think.

She wished for a moment she were the praying sort so she could ask someone for protection, but she wasn't. With nothing left to do, she settled back in to wait.

CHAPTER FOURTEEN
GALE

Gale shed her green dress and stood in her undergarments before her wardrobe, considering its meagre contents.

"You can't be considering this." Madrigal sat on the floor next to the fire and watched as Gale tossed all three of her not-for-costume dresses onto the bed.

"We're just going to talk. You saw her. She's distraught and might be ready to listen now." Gale scowled at the dresses. Though all of them were nicer and significantly more proper than what she'd answered the door in, not one was as fashionable as what Aster wore.

At least my hair looks better.

Aster had clearly rushed from the house, and her curls were wilder than they'd been on her last visit. The fact that this careless version of her was as fascinating as the more polished one Gale had seen the day before was irrelevant, but the lack of attention said something about her mental state, and that was worth noting.

She slipped into her blue dress with the high, square neckline, which was at least five years out of fashion but in excellent condition, then washed her face in the basin, scrubbing away the darkness from around her eyes. Once her hair was pulled back from her face and fastened with a pair of plain combs, she pulled her heavy black shawl around her shoulders and slipped into her old boots.

"Not going to dab on a bit of perfume while you're at it?" Madrigal asked without a hint of humour in her voice.

Gale glared at her. "It's not like that, and you know it."

"Does she?" Madrigal moved closer. "Her eyes nearly popped out of her head when she saw you."

Gale straightened her shoulders. "Well, that's the idea of that costume, isn't it? Distracts the eye and the mind. It works." She motioned to the dress she now wore. "No distractions here. I'll see what I can find out. Something more for Jes, maybe, or a lead on whoever created the curse on Bright Hollow."

"*Lead.*" Madrigal rolled her eyes. "You've been reading detective novels again, haven't you?"

Gale shrugged. "I can't read about magic all the time."

Madrigal looked as though she thought her student should, in fact, think of nothing but studying. Gale decided not to push it further.

"I did as you wanted, I didn't go after her. But she's here now. Jes wants to know who besides this girl she needs to watch out for, and I intend to find out. If offering her advice on whatever's got her shaken is how I get there, what's the harm?"

Madrigal stood, eyes narrowed. "What's the harm? You felt the power in her. Even if she can't use it to hurt you, someone else could. We don't know what level of control the witch has over her. The enchantment only made her lose her temper before, but it might make her snap and kill you if you keep prodding."

Gale's heart picked up its pace, and her cheeks burned. She'd never liked being scolded, but she tried to hold her temper.

"Is it about the danger?" she asked. "Or the distraction? I know you want me here studying at every possible moment, but you also showed me how to choose my own path, to do what feels right for me even when it's dangerous." She thought of Aster's troubled eyes, of dark magic she didn't know enough to fear. "Maybe I can help her. If this is blood magic, maybe I can save people from dying for it."

And maybe I can find out who cursed Bright Hollow, she added to herself. The argument would hold no weight with Madrigal, but she couldn't deny how it pulled her toward one more talk with Aster.

Madrigal's nostrils flared as she took a sharp breath. "Of course I'm concerned about the distraction, and about your education. I'm stuck here until you master your power."

Tears pricked at Gale's eyes, surprising her. There had been a change between her and Madrigal in recent months, frustration and irritation replacing the excitement and joy of the early days of Gale's schooling, but it had never come this close to a true fight. "Is it so horrible, being here with me?"

Madrigal looked away. "My existence isn't one I'd wish on anyone."

"I see." Gale took her coat from its hook and slipped it on.

"It's not—" Madrigal said, and stopped herself. She walked closer and rested her weightless hands on Gale's shoulders, chilling them. The gesture was gentle, but her eyes burned. "I won't help you. This can only lead to trouble."

Gale turned away, and her flesh froze as Madrigal's hands passed through. "I'm just going to speak to her."

Madrigal let out a bitter chuckle. "You don't know yourself at all, do you?"

And she vanished.

Gale waited for a moment to see whether she'd reappear, then took her gloves from the chest at the end of the bed and slipped them on. She found a blue glass bottle of pain potion on the shelf and slipped it into her pocket—she'd meant what she'd said about going to the bakery, and it only made sense to make a personal delivery while she was there.

I'll handle this myself, then, she thought. It would have been better to have Madrigal in her ear to offer her thoughts on any magic-related information Aster had to offer, but she'd make do.

"I'll have to do things on my own when she's gone, anyway," she said out loud. There was a good chance Madrigal would be listening from the shadows of the borderlands, invisible but ready to appear if there was trouble.

For now.

The thought of facing the world without Madrigal left Gale feeling cold and empty, but it was a fact she'd have to face sooner or later, whether she gave in and stayed home now or did as she wished.

Aster was still standing by the door when Gale left the flat. Gale turned to lock up, then headed down the stairs. "Are you coming?"

There was a time when she would have tried to be as welcoming as possible, forgiving Aster's outburst and moving on. It was how she'd been brought up. But that had been in Bright Hollow, a town where everyone was as close as family. This was the city, and Aster was a stranger who had insulted and frightened her.

And the harder Aster had to work for Gale's help, the more grateful she'd be to receive it. In this moment Gale had the upper hand, and Jes had taught her how valuable that was.

Aster followed.

The sleighbell hung over the bakery door chimed as Gale entered. Aster followed close behind, pausing to carefully wipe her boots on the mat inside the door before she stepped onto the white tile floor. Gale decided not to like her better for that small courtesy, though it was tempting. She watched for a moment as Aster took everything in from the back side of the window display to the single table and twin chairs by the wall and the glass case beside the register. Today the case was stuffed with loaves of fresh bread, tiny cakes piled high with decadent frosting, and little squares covered in smooth, green icing.

"Good morning, Pria," Gale called, though there was no one in sight. The door behind the counter swung open, and the baker's daughter stepped out from the kitchen, wiping her hands on a clean towel. She was only sixteen, two years younger than Gale, but already the backbone of the business.

"Morning," she said. "What'll you have?"

"Two sweet teas, please. And two cinnamon rolls. How's your mum?"

"Good days and bad," Pria said. "That medicine you gave her is helping with the pain."

"Does she need more?" Gale reached into her pocket, ready to hand the bottle over.

Pria shook her head. "Still got half left, thanks. Potent stuff." She turned to make the tea, and Aster stepped closer.

"I don't actually need food," she said, speaking to Gale. The subtle roughness of her voice was as pleasant as Gale had found it on their previous meetings.

"But you do," Gale told her. "Anya is an amazing baker, and she's taught Pria all the tricks of the trade. They import spices from Kardav and Ellendal, and they blend them in the most wonderful ways. You'll regret it if you don't try something." She looked Aster over, taking in her bloodshot eyes and the ashen tone of her skin. "Besides, you look like you could use something to pick you up."

Aster didn't argue, and when Pria set two paper cups of milky spiced tea on the counter and slipped two buns covered in glistening icing into a white paper bag, Aster laid down more than enough money and waved away the change.

Gale let Aster carry the bag but took her own tea and led the way out the door. "There's a spot where we can sit over here," she said.

Aster walked by her side, her boots crunching softly over the snow, matching Gale step for step. "I'm not sure how to ask this," she said. "Is your… that teacher you mentioned. Is she with us?"

"Not today. She had other things to do." Gale paused. "But she could be here in a moment if I were in danger."

"Noted." Gale had expected Aster to laugh off the threat, but she didn't. "I'm not here to hurt you. Really."

"So you believe in ghosts now?"

Aster smiled nervously, and Gale told herself it wasn't at all charming. There was no palpable magic in her now, none of the unhinged emotion from the day before. Whatever had been there had hidden itself again. "I think so. I learned yesterday that it's possible she exists. You can't prove it to me, but I'm willing to take your word. And I'm sorry for calling you mad."

Gale sipped her tea and thought it over. "Don't worry about that. I've been called worse. Here we are."

She led the way into the empty lot on the corner. The windowless walls of the adjoining buildings said there had been something there once, but now a little park stood in its place. It wasn't much, just a bench, a small tree, a rubbish bin that was rarely emptied, and a frozen-over bird bath, but to Gale it felt like a tiny breath of fresh air in the claustrophobic crush of the city. She sat on the bench and motioned for Aster to join her.

Aster sat obediently and set the bag from the bakery down between them. It wasn't like yesterday, when she'd seemed awkward about forgetting their first meeting but confident in herself. She looked haunted now. Empty.

"I'm also sorry for everything else," she said, looking into her tea. "I don't know what happened. I remember it, but I don't understand. It's not like me to panic or fly into a rage, to yell at a stranger who I think was trying to help me. It felt like something that wasn't me. But that's no excuse for how I behaved, and I apologize most sincerely for it."

Gale removed her gloves and took a roll from the bag,

plucked a bit off, and popped it into her mouth, taking a moment to savour how the cinnamon and a spice with a sharper bite perfectly balanced the sweet icing. "Fancy apology. You must really need my help."

Aster looked up. A hint of a smile pulled at the corners of her lips. "You're good at reading people, aren't you?"

"I am, and I'll tell you more so we can finish this conversation before my nose freezes and falls off." Gale let her mind relax as her gaze sharpened, taking in every detail of Aster's appearance, posture, and presence. She'd become good enough at this to impress clients even without Madrigal's help, and it might finally be useful for more than a bit of cash in her pocket. "Something in what I said yesterday hit a sore spot for you, maybe one you didn't know existed. It angered you, frightened you, whatever it was." This much was only her repeating back what Aster herself had said, but such things spoken in the right tone sounded like revelations. "You fled. Fine. But now you're back with your tail firmly between your legs." She narrowed her eyes and held Aster's gaze. "Something has happened to confirm that I was at least partly right."

Aster took a long sip of her tea. "Well done."

"I'm not finished." Gale didn't look away, and Aster shifted uncomfortably. "You can't trust me because of who I work for. That tells me there's no one else you can go to about this. I'm your last resort. You wouldn't be here otherwise." She ate another bite of her roll and washed it down with tea.

"Mostly correct," Aster said. "Maybe all correct, but I can't be sure. If something happened to prove you right—and I'm not saying it did—I don't know what it was."

Gale frowned. "You've forgotten again?"

"All I know is that I woke up this morning feeling like I had my head on a block and an axe hovering over my neck, and I don't know why. And I felt certain I needed to speak to you again."

"I see. How often does this sort of thing happen?"

Aster bit into her roll, chewed, and swallowed. No reaction to the flavour. Gale decided she really must be in a dire state if something so sublime could go unnoticed. "I've never spoken to anyone about this."

"I can't help if you don't."

"But you still want to?"

Gale made herself wait before she answered. She wanted to say yes. Her nature, her upbringing, and the oath she'd sworn when she'd hoped to become a healer all demanded she help when she could, regardless of whether the suffering party was a friend or an enemy.

But there were other considerations now.

"I'll try, on the condition that you swear you meant what you said the first time we met, that you won't go after Jes again."

"Agreed."

Gale narrowed her eyes. "That was too easy."

"I spoke to the person who holds my memories for me and he confirmed what you said about that. He just forgot to mention it."

Gale wondered whether *forgot* was the word for it, but decided not to push it yet.

"Good. Now, about your memory troubles?"

Aster didn't answer. Gale decided to take a different approach.

"Tell me a story, then, about someone whose situation might be like yours, but who we'll agree is unquestionably not you. We'll see whether I'd have any advice to offer her."

Aster chuckled under her breath and relaxed visibly. "All right. Let's say that once there was probably a little girl who lost her family during the great curse. She went to live with her grandmother but ran into trouble with some very bad people along the way. They attacked and injured her terribly, and it took a great deal of magic to save her life."

Odd.

Gale had been disappointed to learn how difficult it was to heal bodies with magic. It could greatly speed up the natural process, but to repair life-threatening injuries would require skill that would have been beyond even Madrigal when she lived. It wasn't a question of the amount of magic a witch could wield, but of its natural laws. And as far as she knew, corrupted blood magic couldn't heal at all. Maybe this was a dead end as far as that was concerned.

She wished Madrigal would come to voice an opinion, even if it was offered grudgingly.

"Healing spell, or enchantment?" she asked.

"Enchantment," Aster said. It sounded like she had to force the word out. "It requires constant upkeep. I—rather, this girl needs frequent treatment by magic because she still feels pain in her scars. Nothing else helps. But when she's healed of physical pain, a flaw in the enchantment means she loses memories of painful and troubling things."

Gale raised an eyebrow. "Like pleasant conversations in one of Queen's Run's finest incarceratory establishments?"

Aster didn't smile at that. "Usually bad things, though the good ones surrounding them often get muddled as well. They're like gaps in her memory. But this morning she—" Her shoulders slumped. "*I* woke up with a gap like that. But no one healed me last night. And I felt strange. Frightened out of all proportion to anything I might have done to bring it on, desperate to escape my own home. I'm scared the flaws in the enchantment are getting worse, that I'm losing not only my memories, but my mind. My grip on reality."

Gale sensed there was more, but Aster fell silent and drained her cup to the dregs.

"Why can't you ask the person who heals you about all this?"

"That person isn't here." Aster's voice fell to a harsh whisper. "And I think… I think that person is what I'm scared of, or maybe for, but I don't know why."

Gale shivered and stood. "Come on. Put the rest of that roll in your pocket for later." She took Aster's cup and tossed the trash into the rubbish bin. "We need to walk and warm up."

Gale let Aster take the lead, and they headed up the street. There were people out and about, but no large crowds. Avoiding anyone who might take an interest in their conversation was simple enough.

"What would your advice be?" Aster asked.

Gale folded her hands behind her back and thought it over, doing her best to project an air of competence she didn't feel. She'd studied, but only what Madrigal had directed. She'd worked magic and solved problems, but only with guidance.

For the first time since she'd begun proper schooling, she was on her own.

Madrigal is right, she thought. *If I can't handle this, I can't hope to face anything harder.*

No choice but to handle it, then.

If nothing else, she could at least do the job Jes had assigned.

"I'd need more details before I could tell you anything useful," she said. "Who placed the enchantment, who was doing the healing, that sort of thing."

Aster shot her a sharp look. "Why?"

"So I'd know their background and training. Speaking to them would be the smartest thing, but if I could do that you wouldn't be here. Do you know anything about the nature of your enchantment?"

Aster pressed her lips together and shook her head. "I've never been encouraged to learn about magic. I don't even remember what the healing is like. It's gone when I wake up."

Gale's skin crawled. There was a chance Aster was right, of course. It wouldn't do to let her own excitement over finding a potential connection to blood magic overshadow reason, and perhaps an inexperienced witch forced to use enchantments to save a life could create one with such a tragic flaw.

But the detectives in the stories she enjoyed wouldn't let it go at that. Not when it seemed equally possible that someone didn't want Aster to understand how it all worked, especially if it were blood magic. They could be intentionally stealing her memories and hiding the true nature of their work.

Maybe because they were close to her and wanted to keep her respect. It was certainly a secret worth keeping.

"Is it your father?" Gale asked. "The one you said came to bail you out?"

Again, Aster didn't respond.

Always leave them thinking they need you more than you need them. Jes's advice.

"You came to me for help." Gale put a hard edge to her voice. "This is a waste of my time and yours if you don't really want it. I thank you for the tea, but I must be getting home."

She turned to walk away, though everything in her screamed to not let go when she was so close to learning something useful.

"He's a good man," Aster said. Gale stopped and turned to find her looking defeated. "He wouldn't have placed a harmful enchantment on me. Not intentionally. It's just this one mistake he made with it. That's why he's away now—he's gone to get help to fix it. I'm sure this won't be a problem then. I shouldn't have bothered you."

Gale stepped closer. The sun was at her back, and Aster squinted against light that picked up the warmth in the depths of her dark brown eyes.

"I know you have suspicions," Aster said. "They might make sense to you, but they're wrong. I feel torn between keeping his secrets and explaining everything so you can understand."

"I know how dangerous exposing them can be. I only want to help."

Gale tried to imagine what it must be like for Aster to have grown up believing one thing about the goodness of her father and the nature of her own life, only to be faced with the idea it could all be wrong.

She understood that pain quite well.

"I felt the magic of your enchantment yesterday," she said. "It was terrifying."

"You still think it's this blood magic thing?"

"Yes." Gale waited to feel a storm brewing in Aster, but there was nothing. "I can't prove it, though, any more than I can prove Madrigal exists when you can't see or hear her."

"Is that your ghost's name?"

Gale shrugged. "She's very much her own ghost. The idea that the magic that's hurting you comes from a dark place fits with what I felt and what I know, but I could be wrong."

Aster turned and walked away, and Gale kept pace beside her.

"What is it?"

Aster cleared her throat and brushed a hand across her eyes. "I feel so strange. When you said these things yesterday, I was angry and confused, and felt like I'd lost control of myself. I feel the stirrings of that again, but my fear is so much greater."

"Fear of what?"

"Of how your words feel right. Like when you're working on an equation for a while and nothing makes sense..."

"And then suddenly the answer is there, and you know you've got it." Gale hadn't studied mathematics in years, but knew the feeling well from studying potions and spells. It was all nonsense, and then suddenly it wasn't.

"But it's not," Aster said. "I know it's wrong. I feel it's..." she hesitated. "Possible. Hypothetically. For that other girl. I just don't know why."

Gale rested a hand on her arm. "It's frightening to question ideas you've been raised with. To realize there might be more to your story than you knew, to consider the idea of heroes being human." *Or worse,* she added to herself, but that knife hardly needed to be driven deeper. "But it's important to seek the truth, even if it might be ugly. At least then you know, and you can make a true choice. May I speak freely?"

Aster nodded. "I'll warn you if I feel that strangeness coming up in me again. No destruction of property today, I promise."

"Good." Gale believed her, but it was still hard to walk close beside Aster knowing she might lose control. "The enchantment could be helping you, but it's causing you more harm than you know, and I wonder whether the harm is a flaw or an intended effect. I can't feel the magic clearly today, and I can't tell you its origins for certain, but I do think that, whatever happened last night to make you feel frightened, there's a very good reason your instincts told you to come to me today. Even if your mind doesn't know what that reason is."

Aster looked away and took a long breath, and Gale suspected she'd gone too far, that another blow-up was on the way. But when Aster looked back to her, her eyes were clear and focused, if troubled. "I appreciate your concern. But you're wrong. He does work magic, but it's got nothing to do with blood or murder. He heals me. That can't be bad."

She's resisting it, Gale thought. If the enchantment was rising to protect itself, it had taken Aster by surprise before. Now she'd seen the enemy and was fighting back.

Gale wondered how much strength that took.

"Healing is good," Gale agreed. "I hope I'm wrong, but I suppose ideas are all I can offer until we know more."

And she did want to know more, but they'd reached the end of what Aster could offer. Even if Gale won her trust, there was too much lost to blank spaces in her memory and knowledge of magic.

Aster seemed satisfied with her answer. "If we set aside this idea of blood magic, is there anything you can do to help me with the strangeness in my mind? Just until he gets back tonight. Or could you at least tell me I won't go mad from it before then?"

"Let me think."

They walked a few more blocks in silence, past shops and barristers' offices and several small hotels. They passed the street where Gale had told fortunes a few nights before and stopped on the corner across from a tall black house with a steeply pitched roof. It glowered down at the street, daring anyone to pass through its gate.

"Is that your home?" Gale asked.

Aster looked to her, surprised. "How did you know?"

"Call it a hunch."

Aster turned back to the house, observing it without any apparent desire to go inside.

"How do you feel about it now?" Gale asked. "You said you felt afraid in there before, like you wanted to escape."

Aster flashed her a sheepish smile. "Fine, actually. It's been getting better since I left earlier. Maybe it was nothing more than a lingering nightmare, and the fresh air has dispelled it."

Gale considered her options. She could try to push for more information on Aster's father's work, but that would likely drive her away.

Or she could give up.

I promised Madrigal we'd only talk. She'd tell me to leave it at this. But if I'm careful...

"I want to help you," she said, and walked away as quickly as she could without jogging. "But not here."

Aster followed, and in a few minutes they were back at the shops, in an alley behind a furniture store, standing in the shadow of a stack of large wooden crates that perfumed the air with the scent of freshly cut pine.

The brick walls facing them didn't have windows, and there was no one around.

Uncertainty and self-doubt ran circles through Gale's mind as she tried to think through what she needed to do.

Protect Aster's memories. That was the most important thing. If her father's enchantment was intentionally stealing them, Gale wanted to know what he was hiding. All would be lost, including this conversation and the tiny cracks it had produced in Aster's certainty of his goodness, if he healed her when he returned home.

Aster might remember things when she went back into the house, but they would only be of use if she could hold onto them long enough to tell Gale later.

It's for Aster's benefit, she told herself. *Either we'll learn that I'm wrong, or she'll be protected long enough to learn the truth. Then she'll want the enchantment broken.*

And that would certainly happen if her father was beheaded as a witch. The blood magic enchantment would vanish without him there to maintain it.

But it was more than that. It was about Bright Hollow, about the curse that had almost taken Gale's life, about the people who were dying for the sake of that kind of power.

Forgive me if my anger makes me a selfish fool, she prayed. She no longer felt as certain as she once had that God was listening, but it felt right.

Aster was watching her closely.

Act or walk away. Now.

"First," Gale said. "Do you ever make notes to yourself about things you're worried about forgetting?"

"I…" Aster paused, her brow furrowed. "It seems strange that I wouldn't keep a diary, doesn't it? I think I write things down sometimes, but I usually rely on my father to tell me what I've forgotten."

"Time to start keeping strict, private records." Gale made sure her tone left no room for argument. "If you must go back into that house, make use of your time. Walk around, see whether anything comes back to you that might explain how you felt this morning, and write it down as you go."

"Easy enough," Aster said.

Gale chose her next words carefully, trying to avoid anything that sounded like an accusation. "You say your enchantment isn't from blood magic, and we can agree to set that aside for now, but if there is something wrong, I might be able to offer protection from unwanted effects of this flaw you mentioned."

Aster crossed her arms, defensive. "Another enchantment?"

"Not on you." Gale looked her over. "Do you have an object? A piece of jewellery, maybe, that won't seem odd if you wear it around the house?"

Still eyeing her warily, Aster slipped a bracelet off her wrist. It tinkled merrily as the gold and silver charms hanging from it brushed against each other. "Will this do?"

Gale took the bracelet in both hands and loosed her magic, just a little, to see whether it would react to any enchantments. It seemed to be nothing more than bits of metal fashioned into delicate shapes—a gold horseshoe, a ship, a heart, and more.

She looked around, hoping Madrigal would appear and offer advice. Even if she only materialized to offer a reprimand, that might be long enough to ask for help. Nothing happened.

I've managed simple enchantments before, she reminded herself. *I know the theory. I know the words.*

I have to try.

The idea behind the enchantment was simple enough, but the execution would be complicated. Protective charms sold in markets and shops were useless, even on rare occasions when there was real magic involved. Specificity was the key, and Gale felt she knew enough to do something. The question was what words to use. A new and uniquely tailored enchantment was far more of a challenge than using proven spells from books.

"I can enchant one of the charms," she said. "It won't affect you directly. Won't change your mind or your thoughts, won't affect your perceptions."

"All right." Aster sounded uncertain.

Gale thought through the complicated paths she'd have to follow with her spells for the enchantment to work—and not only to work, but to hide itself well enough that another witch wouldn't feel the bracelet pulsing with magic the moment he entered the room.

"I can't protect you against your father's enchantment as a whole," she said, thinking aloud for Aster's benefit and to avoid another awkward silence. "We don't want to disrupt its healing benefits. But I believe I can protect against specific harm."

"Memory loss?"

"Precisely." Gale tightened her hands into fists to keep them from shaking. The idea was frightening, but also wonderfully exciting. "I can only work with the idea of the enchantment as I've felt it in you, which means there'll be no protection against anything else that might be going on in that house. But if your father heals you when he comes home, perhaps this will allow you to hold on to something."

Aster raised her eyebrows. "You really think you can do that?"

Gale drew herself up to her full height, which matched Aster's, and straightened her shoulders. "Of course. I'm a witch, and studying under an excellent mentor."

"I believe that." Aster's brow creased, just for a moment. "I might suppose that if such protection were possible, Eamon would have managed it by now, but I'm willing to give it a go if you are."

"Eamon is your father?"

"My guardian, actually, but he's the closest thing I have to it." Aster shrugged. "I took his name because I didn't have my own. It's complicated."

A shred more honesty, another minor secret shared.

Jes would be proud.

"How much?" Aster asked.

It took Gale a moment to understand that she was talking about money and not how much magic it would take to do the enchantment.

"Nothing for now." It hurt to pass up a bit of cash when she was so strapped for it, but her other goals were more important —building trust, proving herself capable, getting closer to answers to her own questions. Taking money now would feel greedy. "Let's see whether it's worth paying for, first."

She stripped her gloves off and pinched the gold horseshoe charm between the thumb and middle finger of her right hand, next to the place where she'd sacrificed her index finger to become a witch. Common wisdom said it wasn't any more powerful than any other spot on her magic-inhabited body, but it always felt right to her.

"Give me your hand." She held out the one not holding the bracelet, and Aster laid hers on top of it, palm to palm. She kept her glove on, but the weight of her hand and the intensity of her eyes sent sparks through Gale's body.

Focus.

Aster's enchantment was well hidden today, but Gale remembered it clearly and imagined it as a mountain lion defending its young, teeth bared and claws ready to strike. She wouldn't prod it directly, but she needed to focus on its nature to create anything useful.

Madrigal would call even this a stupid risk. Gale called it terrifying but thrilling.

"*Inglats, rourain, glosphais,*" she murmured, translating each word carefully in her mind. Spells and enchantments relied heavily on intention, but she'd quickly learned that imprecise phrasing could ruin everything. She kept her eyes on Aster's as she spoke, weaving her own words with existing spells to build the enchantment. She focused her thoughts on what little she knew of the magic in Aster, and her intentions on protecting this misguided warrior from any way it might be harming her. It was a balancing act between thought, emotion, translation, speech, and controlling the flow of magic.

Magic poured from her, leaving her physically exhausted, weak-kneed and sweating as she finished. She felt like she'd come out of a week with a bad stomach bug, and she wished she was at home so she could crawl straight into bed.

But it was done. The bracelet didn't feel more enchanted than it had before, but something had happened. Only time would tell whether the magic had obeyed her intentions and instructions.

She handed the bracelet to Aster and sat on a crate. "All done."

"Just like that?" Aster's voice was quiet and a little awed. "Are you all right?"

"Of course." Gale couldn't muster the energy to try to look competent and impressive. She rested her head in her hands. "Just give me a moment and this will pass."

The effort of attempting something new always left her in a sorry state, but there was still plenty of magic in her, and it would restore her soon enough.

The crate creaked as Aster sat beside her. "That was incredible. Your magic felt…"

Gale lifted her head. "Felt what?"

"Warm. Welcoming. I felt like…" Aster looked down at her hands. "It was most impressive."

Gale laughed. "I'm glad you think so. My mentor isn't always so free with praise."

"Ah." Aster stretched her legs out and crossed them at the ankles, and Gale did the same. "I know how that is. I had a weapons master who could watch me take down three men and would only tell me I should have done it twenty seconds faster." She smiled. "I learned to praise myself. What choice do we have?"

She spoke kindly, but the words hit like a crashing wave, stealing Gale's breath.

She watched as Aster put the bracelet back on.

I worked real magic. Alone. Improvising.

I've learned so much.

She owed it all to Madrigal, of course, but it felt good to think of how far she'd come instead of how far she still had to go.

"Can you meet me again tomorrow?" Gale asked. "Let me know how it goes?"

If Aster didn't show up, she'd have her answer.

"It might be difficult to get out if Eamon comes back tonight. I assume you still don't want me to tell him you exist?"

Gale shuddered, but tried not to show it. "No. I know you think I have no reason to be afraid—"

"It's all right," Aster said. "I'll come up with some other reason to slip out."

"Please do." Gale rubbed a hand over her face, which seemed a more socially acceptable action than the slap she was tempted to give herself to chase away her sleepiness. "And don't let him heal you if you can avoid it. My enchantment should help with peripheral effects of his, but I can't say whether it'll hold up against—" She paused. She'd almost said *a direct attack.* "Against a fresh renewal of the magic that might be inadvertently harming your mind. Here." She reached into her pocket and pulled out the bottle she'd planned to deliver to the baker. "For the pain, so you don't need healing. Just a drop at a time to start."

Aster took the bottle and looked down at it. "Thank you. But the druggist's medicines don't help, nor anything magical we've tried. Or if they do, they dull my senses and put me to sleep."

"This won't," Gale assured her. "Worst that could happen is it won't do anything at all."

Aster reached into her pocket and pulled out three bank notes. "Take this, then. If you won't take payment for the enchantment, you should for this."

Gale didn't have the energy to argue. She slipped the money into her pocket without checking the denominations. "Good luck," she said. "I hope you'll forgive me if I don't walk you back to your door."

She thought again of the house, which in her memory looked ready to come alive and swallow her whole, and held back another shiver.

"Thank you," Aster said as she stood, then turned and offered Gale a hand up. "It feels strange to be asking for help from a stranger, and to be trusting you."

Gale took her hand and stood, then held on for a few seconds as a wave of dizziness passed. "Bad strange?"

Aster considered for a moment. "Not as bad as I thought it would be. You're sure you're all right getting home?"

"I am. Thank you."

Aster took a few steps backward, gave Gale a tight smile, and left the alley.

Gale waited for Madrigal to appear to give her a piece of advice or a larger slice of her mind, but nothing happened. She started home, walking slowly at first, then picking up her pace as she recovered from the enchantment and began to feel more like herself.

She decided she'd brew up a strong tea to wake herself up when she got home, no matter how much better she felt by then.

She had research to do. It was going to be another long night.

CHAPTER FIFTEEN
ASTER

Silver daggers flew through the air, one after another, and hit the target dummy at the far end of the attic with dull thuds, burying themselves deep in the straw-stuffed canvas. One to the shoulder, one to the chest, one to the throat.

Aster hung upside-down from the rafters, her head cocked to one side, assessing the damage. She dropped to the floor, landing in a crouch, making hardly a sound, and stalked toward the dummy through a flurry of dust motes that danced in the sunset light from the round window at the end of the room.

The attic had everything she needed, or at least as much as could be packed into the space under the peaked roof. The vertical walls at each end were too short to make for decent climbing walls, so she'd attached bars and knobs to the underside of the roof itself, learning to cling and climb like a housefly. Ropes and a sturdy net attached at all four corners hung from its upper reaches, providing more climbing opportunities—and in the case of the net, a place to rest. The room was long enough to allow for short-range archery practice. For anything more challenging, she headed out to the country to hunt rabbits and shoot apples off trees on windy days.

This was her armoury, her classroom, her sanctuary. It was the place where she felt the most grounded and comfortable, honing skills the loss of memories couldn't take from her, where she did her work while Eamon locked himself in the basement to do his. On days when she felt like she couldn't rely on her mind, it had always been helpful to come here, find certainty in the strength of her body, and focus on things she had complete control over.

But not today.

Today everything was wrong. She still couldn't remember the events of the previous night, not even catching hints of what she'd forgotten, and the gap in her memory left a painful sense that a part of herself was missing. It was one thing to agree to such losses when Eamon healed her. To have it stolen without warning was quite another.

She pulled the daggers free from the dummies and wiped them clean on the hem of the loose tunic she wore for training, then set them back in their places on the wall next to the swords, the axes, the rope, the heavy silver candlesticks, and all the other potential weapons she trained with. Eamon had taken her abroad to learn from masters who could be paid to forget her name and her face, who taught her to make use of every object and weapon available to her in a fight. But when it came time to kill, Eamon insisted his dagger be used whenever possible.

A magically sharp blade made for clean kills and minimal suffering. Aster had never objected.

She glanced at it, then turned away, for the first time having no desire to feel its familiar weight in her hand.

Aster rubbed her shoulder where the old pain was digging its claws into a particularly deep section of scar tissue. It was a hazard of training, nothing she couldn't handle.

Still, it would be a good test for Gale's potion. Less pain might mean a clearer head.

And she certainly had thinking to do.

She still wore her bracelet with its charms, hoping that by some miracle Gale's enchantment was helping, and carried the potion along with a folded piece of paper and the nub of a charcoal pencil in the pocket of her trousers. She opened the little vial and sniffed, then wrinkled her nose. It smelled like the woods in autumn, all rotting leaves and mushrooms, damp pine wood and heavy rain. Not an unpleasant smell, but nothing she wanted to swallow.

The drop she placed onto her tongue tasted exactly as it smelled. She fought back a gag and waited.

There was no sense of magic, but it was only a few minutes before the pain in her shoulder had pulled into itself, the ache growing smaller and fainter until it vanished almost completely. And nothing else came with it, no fatigue like she'd had from the druggist's concoctions she'd tried or the potions Eamon had made for her.

And no forgetting.

"Remarkable," Aster said, looking down at the vial. Common witches were turning out to be far more talented and useful than Eamon had ever suggested when he spoke of his own advanced training. He'd be pleased to know about this if Gale ever agreed to let Aster mention her to him.

Aster stood and paced the room. She'd have to go back downstairs soon. Training wasn't helping her get any closer to answers.

She'd searched, though, after she came back from her walk with Gale.

She clearly remembered the time since she'd come home and now walked through it step by step in her mind—her memory was remarkably clear when it was allowed to be. She'd come in and immediately started searching for any hint of why she'd felt so strange that morning. She'd found nothing in Eamon's room. Some of his clothes and other items were missing because he'd taken them on the trip. His keys had been in his top drawer, his coat missing from its hook. Front hallway, basement, storage room, workshop, carriage house. She'd been through the parlour, the dining room, the study, the bathrooms, and the guest bedroom...

And then I came upstairs to change my clothes.

She frowned and closed her eyes, picturing her circuit of the ground floor again.

Kitchen, Eamon's room, hallway, parlour...

Back to the hallway.

And there it was—another gap in her memory. She could remember every room she'd passed through on her search, picture every painting on the wall and ornament on the shelves. But she couldn't remember seeing the basement door when she'd passed by it or thinking about going down.

But Eamon's workshop would be the most logical place to look for answers to questions about the nature of his magic, even if she only wanted to prove Gale wrong.

So why didn't I?

She focused harder, knowing she must have wanted to go down. She'd only have needed to borrow the keys from his room.

All she got from that thought was tight flutter in her chest and a desire to stay in the attic, as far away from the basement as she could be.

Very well, she thought. If something didn't want her to go to the basement, the only thing to do was ignore the fear and face whatever was down there.

She touched the paper in her pocket again.

I didn't write anything down. She told me to, and I forgot.

Aster pulled the page and the charcoal out and held them in her hand. It would be impossible to forget them there.

She climbed down the ladder from the attic and closed the trapdoor behind her. Then she paused, unable to remember where she'd been going.

Again she retraced her steps. Again she realized what was missing.

Gale was right. Eamon's magic was here with her, and it wanted her to forget the basement existed. Her sense of unease deepened as she considered what he might be hiding, and she tested out the idea that Gale might be a little bit right after all.

She looked down at her bracelet. The enchantment had been a good idea, but it didn't seem to be working.

The morning's fear crept back, and she felt she should pack a bag and flee before Eamon returned. But the pain was already returning to her shoulder—even the best potions couldn't keep it at bay like his magic could.

And running would be foolish. Eamon had warned her of these problems. Fear, confusion, her mind making up stories to fill the gaps. Reason said she should stay and wait for the cure he'd gone to find. Her instincts had served her well in the past, but at heart they were only feelings.

Loud feelings, though, that made her heart thunder and her blood freeze when she came back around to the thought of going into the basement.

So she'd prove them wrong.

She unfolded the paper, pressed it to the wall, and wrote across the top.

I am going to the basement.

Her script was clear and neat, recognizable as her own. She added another line to it.

Aster, this is you. You might forget writing this or forget whatever you see written below. Please believe yourself, even if it feels like madness.

Then, for good measure, she signed it.

Satisfied, she made her way to the ground floor. At the bottom of the stairs, she turned toward the kitchen to get her customary post-training snack. Then she felt the paper in her hand, read it, and remembered.

Her throat tightened as reason conceded that this did feel suspicious.

Maybe Gale's enchantment had failed. Or maybe this was something else, something apart from the magic in Aster that the witch didn't know to protect her against.

She turned and went to Eamon's room to get his keys, then fetched a lamp from the kitchen. He wouldn't have left the lamps burning while he was away.

Through the basement door and down the steps then, feeling like she was creeping into a den of enemies. She'd done it before and survived. That knowledge was enough to get her to the bottom of the stairs, even if she had to force every step.

A memory surfaced, flashing like a fish leaping from a lake before disappearing again and leaving barely a ripple behind. A strange smell. Dark flakes of something beneath her fingernails. Terror, pure and shining.

Something happened here.

She turned down the hallway and her lamp picked out the shape of an unfamiliar wooden door at its end.

Nothing but trouble there, spoke a little voice in her mind. *Turn back now. It's not too late. Eamon told you to stay away. He wants what's best for you.*

But as she moved closer, she saw that the door stood slightly ajar. Whatever was behind it had already been set loose.

She'd been here. She'd done this.

And she dearly wished she hadn't.

Aster crept toward the door, one hand held out in front of her, feeling like she was walking in a dream where every step was a slog through waist-deep mud. She laid her hand against the door, pushing it closed, and it was as though another door within her mind opened.

Memories spilled out—coming down for the blasted sugar bowl, finding the door and being surprised by it as she had been just now. A dungeon, a bloodstained table, desecrated bodies strung from the ceiling.

The face on the wanted poster.

A key crumbling in her hand.

She cried out and sank to the floor, pressing her back against the door to keep it closed. She hated being there, hated being so close to the horrors behind it, but it was obvious that the moment she stepped away from the door, she'd forget.

There was no need to look to confirm anything. The memories were clear, sharp, and wholly real in a way few others were.

She still held the paper and charcoal crumpled tight in her hand. She set her lamp down close beside her, as comforting and useless as a child's nightlight, then smoothed the paper against her leg.

Beneath her neat handwriting, she began:

There's a door in the basement. You won't remember it, but it's there. And behind it—

As she wrote, her arm grew heavy. Something seemed to be pulling at it from behind the door so that the line of her writing scrawled down across the page and the letters drew out long and messy. By the time she wrote the word *bodies* it was barely legible. The hallway spun around her, and the letters she'd already written became scrambled before her eyes as she fought to remember how to write more.

Bodies behind door. E killing for bloooooooo

She paused and forced herself to breathe.

blud magic missing peple in basmnt notes in Es handritin trust insinkts not him nevr him

She mustered her focus and read the note over, then did her best to sign it again at the bottom. It would have to do.

She stood, bracing herself against the door, caught between wanting to flee and not wanting to let it open behind her again, even a crack.

In a way, she told herself, this was good. She wasn't losing her grip on reality. There had been a proper reason for her to wake this morning feeling frightened and apprehensive of Eamon's return. Her missing memories were still there, locked away but still a part of her.

There was no need to feel guilty about disobeying Eamon, even if every terrified beat of her heart told her to regret it. He had good reason to want to hide what he was doing down here.

And it _was_ him. She might doubt it again later, when her memories were gone, but she knew it now. The magic she felt in the door was too familiar. Not a part of her personal enchantment, but his work nonetheless.

Gale was right. Blood magic. Not just blood, but suffering. Death.

Her entire body trembled, and she swallowed back the acid that rose in her throat.

And I've been benefitting from it for as long as I've been in his care.

Eamon would be home soon. He'd find the door unlocked and realize that Aster knew he was the man responsible for the disappearances of so many folks in Queen's Run.

He'd erase these memories as surely as he had the others she'd lost.

She smoothed the paper out again and added a note at the bottom in the clearest print she could manage.

RUN

CHAPTER SIXTEEN
ASTER

Aster stood in the centre of her bedroom and stared in disbelief at the paper in her hands. She remembered returning Eamon's keys to his bureau, coming upstairs… but not this.

The first part of the note was clearly her handwriting and sounded like her own thoughts and phrasing, though she couldn't recall writing it.

The rest was the ravings of a mad stranger, and reading it made her want to scream until the noise drowned out the disjointed terror that rose in her when she looked at it.

She'd told herself to believe that there were bodies in the basement, that Eamon was a murderer, that every good thing his magic had brought into her life was bought with the suffering of others.

And, clearest of all, that she was to leave the house at once. Good advice if her beloved guardian were, in fact, a prolific murderer. Ridiculous and harmful otherwise.

I am losing my mind, she thought, *just like he said.* Nothing about this felt sane or rational.

The note said to trust her instincts. Her mind said to wait for help, but what felt right was packing up and running, consequences be damned.

The worst that happens if I believe it is that Eamon comes back and I'm not here and we sort it out later. The worst that happens if I don't and I turn out to be wrong...

She took a knapsack from her wardrobe and pulled on a warm grey sweater over her tunic, then braided her hair behind her neck and tucked it down the back. With the addition of a hat, folks might dismiss her as a boy until she'd made her escape from the city.

Eamon had said he'd only be away for one night. If things had gone well, he could be back in Queen's Run at this very moment. The less visible she made herself, the better.

Her bracelet caught on her sweater. She worked it free, then looked over Gale's enchanted charm.

"A little help would be lovely," she told the tiny horseshoe, and went back to packing.

Trousers, a skirt, an extra sweater, and underthings went into the knapsack. Hairbrush in the bag, a dagger on her belt. Now that she'd made her decision, her heart raced and her muscles tensed, ready to move as soon as her mind would let them.

She looked at the note again, then went to her desk and pulled an unused diary from the top drawer, wondering again why she'd never made a habit of writing things down when she knew there was such a good chance of forgetting them. Carefully, she tore a page out and wrote a new message—in ink this time, and in her own clear handwriting.

Eamon Islington took the missing people and killed them. Bodies in the basement at 465 Greybaud Avenue.

Her stomach flipped as she wrote the words. *I am the worst daughter in creation,* she thought. Who else would believe the theories of a haunted witch and a scribbled note in a stranger's print over the words of the man who had raised and protected her?

But when she looked at what she'd written earlier, her resolve stiffened. The writing was hers, but it looked like she'd written it drunk. Something was fighting her as she tried to expose Eamon. And whether it was the magic in the basement or the enchantment in her own mind, she had a duty to figure it out.

Bodies or not, he's hiding something.

The front door slammed, and Aster froze where she stood, her heart trying to leap from her chest, finally understanding what it felt like for her prey when they turned and saw her standing with her dagger poised, waiting to take their lives.

She eased the bedroom door closed.

Steps ascending the stairs. A solid thump, then the drag of Eamon's bad leg behind it.

She looked frantically around the room, her gaze landing on the window. There was an oak tree in the yard with a branch she could reach if she jumped. Eamon would never be able to follow with his bad leg. By the time he'd found her escape route and made it back downstairs to the door, she'd have disappeared into the early night and be well on her way to freedom. The plan formed in her mind even as she opened the window and judged the drop if she fell.

"Aster?" Eamon called. He was halfway up now.

"I'm getting changed!" she called. Her voice trembled, and the false cheer she'd injected into it sounded entirely wrong. "I wasn't expecting you! I'll be down as soon as I'm presentable!"

The sound of two voices speaking low and quick followed, then Eamon's steps descending the stairs and the familiar creak of his bedroom door.

Aster finished stuffing her knapsack and went to get the cash she kept for emergencies.

"Aster!" Eamon bellowed, this time with his voice a roar of

rage and indignation. As far as Aster could remember, she'd never heard him so angry.

I put the keys back, she thought. *He shouldn't know yet. I should have time.*

Footsteps again, this time thundering up the stairs, heavy and even.

Guess he found the fellow he was looking for.

Aster's gaze fell on the desk, where the sheet she'd torn out of her diary sat, doing no one any good if she escaped and forgot everything again. She lunged back across the room and grabbed it, then ran for the open window, hauling her knapsack onto her shoulders as she went.

The door flew open, leaving a deep dent in the plaster of the wall behind it. A stranger stood in its place—a true stranger, one she had no sense of ever having met before. He was completely bald and unusually tall and had lips that reminded Aster of freshly cut bits of raw chicken. Everything he wore was black, from his shoes to his badly fitted suit and the shirt collar that strained against his muscular neck. The only spot of brightness was the gold watch chain that hung from the pocket of his waistcoat.

She recalled her conversation with Eamon.

I believe I've found someone who can help me fix the flaws in your enchantments. He used to be one of the king's mages and now carries knowledge not available to most witches. We'll rebuild everything from the ground up and set it right at last.

She'd believed him when he said he meant to fix her memory problems as well as her pain. Now she wondered why this mage was really here.

The stranger buttoned his jacket and stood in the doorway, composed and calm. "Miss Aster?" His voice was like gravel beneath carriage wheels, but he spoke pleasantly. "Glad to see you're all right. Eamon was concerned you might be having another bout of your unpleasantness."

Aster stood with her hand on the ledge of the open window, caught between the certainty that she needed to leave and the desire to be wrong about all of it.

"What do you mean?"

The stranger bowed. "My name is Roderick Bates. You can call me Roddy, since we're to be friends and all. I have some skill with magic, being fully trained as a mage before I elected to leave the king's service, and Eamon's asked me to come and see if I can help you with your problems." His brow furrowed with concern. "Have you been experiencing trouble while he was away?"

Aster set her jaw and forced herself to meet his eyes. "What sort of trouble?"

"Nightmares. Frightening thoughts that creep up on you during the day, dark fantasies so real you believe they're true. Death and decay. Pain and blood. Holes in your memory that your mind fills in with the most disturbing ideas." He clucked his tongue gently. "Poor dear. You knew, I think, that there were flaws in your healing enchantments, and that Eamon was seeking help? This is all to be expected, and I'm sorry it's gone this far."

Aster took a step back. "I was fine before he left. I need to go."

Roddy looked her over, his expression dripping with pity. "Were you fine? Or have you only forgotten the badness, as you always do?" He didn't wait for her to answer. "I'm here to make all those troubling thoughts go away forever so you can have a better life. No more pain. No more dark thoughts. Won't that be good?"

A sob caught in Aster's throat.

"It's not safe for you to leave in your current condition, Aster. That's why Eamon ordered you to stay at home while he fetched me." Roddy took a step into the room, closing the space between them. "Do you remember that?"

It sounded so plausible. She *did* have memory problems. And she certainly had nightmares. If things were getting worse, why shouldn't waking nightmares come to fill in the gaps in her memory?

More than that, she wanted it to be true. The past few days had been terrible. Things had been so good before. And they could be good again if Roddy was speaking the truth.

But that was what her mind wanted. The other part of her—the instinct, the animal, the thing that remembered what she herself could not—screamed for her to run.

There is danger here, it whispered. *The fact that you can't remember what it is should be proof enough that this is wrong, wrong, wrong.*

Gale had thought Eamon was against her.

But if Roddy was right, maybe she'd imagined Gale, too, and her promise to help. Maybe she'd never left the house at all and had dreamed every bit of it.

There was only one way to find out.

She stepped onto the window ledge and leapt out the open window. Roddy hollered, and she felt the brush of his fingers against her boot as she caught the rough bark of the oak branch and hauled herself up onto it.

He said something then, harsh words in a language Aster couldn't wrap her mind around. The world shifted around her, and suddenly the snow-covered ground was above her and the evening sky opened like an ocean below. She clung to the branch, shaking.

He's coming. Move.

She closed her eyes and let her body take the lead. Without the visual confusion, she made her way forward, slowly feeling out every movement.

Faster.

A gust of winter wind pushed at her, and she held tight as she crawled, the note crumpled in her clenched fist, the weight of her knapsack threatening to throw off her balance and pull her to the ground.

Then the rougher bark of the trunk was under her fingers. When she opened her eyes the world had righted itself. She shinnied down the trunk, barely feeling the bark scraping her palms and knuckles. This was what she'd trained for. Her fear shifted to focus.

Next steps. Go.

She dropped and hit the ground running, headed for the back fence and the alley beyond. The dizziness lingered, leaving her feeling like she was running across the deck of a ship in a storm.

She'd reached the top of the fence when strong hands grabbed her knapsack, hauled her backward, and threw her to the ground.

Her hand opened as she prepared to turn and fight, and the wind caught the slip of paper that held her memories.

Aster twisted and scratched, but Roddy was unnaturally strong and seemed to predict every move. He held her tight against his chest and clapped a hand over her mouth, holding back her screams.

She reached for the knife on her belt. A backward kick to his knee distracted him just long enough. She twisted, arched her back, and plunged the blade into his forearm.

Roddy snarled and held her with the other arm while he shook the knife free, sending bright blood spattering across the snow. Aster watched the blade fall and disappear into a deep drift.

"Quiet, girl," he grunted as he hauled her toward the house, using both arms again. "Stop fighting. This is for your own good."

Roddy muttered something in the language of magic, and the strength drained from Aster's muscles. She slumped to the ground, and Roddy left her lying there as he examined the wound on his arm. Her heart still raced, but she couldn't move.

Aster watched the note fluttering against the wooden planks of the fence. She'd never been the praying type, but she sent one up now, almost without thinking.

Let someone find it, she thought. *Let them find it before I become one more body in the dungeon.*

Roddy stalked toward the fence and plucked the note up. He read it, then tore it into tiny pieces that he tucked into his pocket.

Aster tried to scream, but nothing happened.

Without another word Roddy picked her up under one arm and carried her back into the house.

CHAPTER SEVENTEEN
ASTER

Roddy hauled Aster down the basement stairs. She fought him every step of the way, struggling as well as she could with muscles that felt like they were made from bread dough. Eamon followed close behind.

"Stop, Aster!" he called, his tone somewhere between annoyed and frantic. "Neither Roddy nor I have any desire to hurt you!"

"Speak for yourself," Roddy grunted. He held Aster to his chest, his arms like iron bars. The front of her sweater was smeared with his blood. "If you'd let me use a stronger spell…"

"No," Eamon said. "I need her awake."

As Roddy carried her toward the door at the end of the hall it felt as though someone had conjured a pit of snakes into Aster's stomach. They grew fangs and started biting as they entered the dungeon chamber.

Memories returned like they'd never been gone at all. Discovering the gruesome room, her return such a short time ago… and the key that had disintegrated in her hand that first night, announcing her disobedience the moment Eamon had picked up his keyring.

Dark fantasies? she thought, and kicked back, catching Roddy's shin with a weak, glancing blow. He squeezed tighter, stealing her breath, and she stopped struggling. One of his arms held her tight as the other hand patted her down and pulled the vial of pain relief potion from her pocket.

The lights in the dungeon were lit, a series of oil lamps hung from the wall at regular intervals that cast warm light over the otherwise grim space. Aster saw details she'd missed in the dark —bloodstains on the floor to match the ones on the table, manacles hanging from the far wall. A shallow wooden cupboard hung near the cells with its door opened wide to display more knives, needles, thumbscrews, and other assorted dark items than she could count in a glance. There was a dagger on the table that hadn't been there before, too. It looked like hers, with a line of gold running up the blade, but was bigger and heavier looking.

Two wooden chairs had been set out next to the table. Roddy dumped her into one and held her arms to her sides. Eamon sat in the other and plucked at his trousers to smooth the wrinkles. He was still dressed for travel in his less-than-best suit and wore the flat cap he seemed to think made him look like a common man, but his moustache was waxed and curled above his well-kept beard, and his boots had cost more than some families in Queen's Run saw in a year.

He rested both hands on the head of his cane and shook his head. "I told you to never enter my workshop without permission," he said. "I trusted you. Imagine my displeasure when I returned and found my key missing. Were my instructions not clear? Did you not trust me in return?"

He sounded so wounded that Aster almost laughed at the absurdity of it.

"Your instructions were clear," she said. Her tongue felt as heavy as any other part of her, but her strength was returning. "I came down looking for nothing more than a way to sweeten my tea. But I saw the door, and I had the key. I had reason to believe you hadn't been entirely truthful with me about the kind of magic you'd been using on me."

Eamon frowned. "What reason?"

Aster pressed her lips together. Even if she hadn't promised Gale that she would never speak of her in this house, she wouldn't have dragged her into this mess for anything in the world.

Eamon gestured upward. Aster refused to look at the bodies. She'd seen enough of them to last her ten lifetimes. "Yes, Aster. I am a practitioner of blood magic, as is Roderick. It is an ancient art and the most powerful source of magic known to humanity. It's also one that few are brave enough to use."

"Brave?" Aster jerked her chin toward the mutilated bodies. "You call this bravery? I wonder what they'd have called it." Tears burned her eyes, and she blinked them back. "I thought better of you."

He sighed and looked down at his hands. "This is exactly why I never told you. Your sense of justice is admirable, and you've made so much of yourself. I feared learning the truth too soon would be your downfall."

"Or yours," Aster whispered.

Memories and ideas were at war now—Eamon tucking her into bed when she was a child, then those same hands opening the flesh of an innocent person and letting the blood flow as they begged for mercy. Eamon gently encouraging her in her Kardavi and Duronian language lessons, Eamon speaking dark incantations that would allow him to steal the spirit and power of those he murdered.

He searched her eyes. Aster wanted to turn away, but couldn't.

"You have no idea how much I've done for you, Aster. How much I continue to do."

The room was cold despite the lamps, and its chill clung to Aster like a second skin. Now pain like slow fire blazed along her scars, searing deep into her. She gasped, and Eamon smiled sadly.

"How much you do for me?" Aster renewed her struggle against Roddy's grip. Moving would ease the pain, or at least give her body a distraction from it, but he held her tight against the chair. "Like hiding memories you don't want me to keep?"

Eamon paled. "I hoped you'd never know about that."

Aster drew in a sharp breath as another thought came to her. "Is this the first time? Have I figured all of this out before and you made me forget?"

"This is the first time you've opened the door." Eamon tapped his cane against the floor in a slow rhythm Aster suspected would drive her mad if it went on too long.

He's deciding what to do with me.

Running was out of the question. Even if she broke free, no surprise or trick would get her out of range before Roddy could knock her down again with his magic. If there was a way out, it wasn't through force.

"Why?" she asked. Roddy's grip tightened, and she ignored it. "Please, Eamon. I thought we were a team. I thought we had no secrets. Help me understand."

"There's no point," Roddy said. "She's going to forget anything you say."

"Then why not try?" Aster spoke to Eamon, not Roddy. "If your magic is brave and worthwhile, if everything you've done has been for my own good, why should I not be able to see that?"

She tried to sound humble and compliant, but failed. It came out as a challenge.

Still, Eamon seemed to be considering it.

"Confession is good for the soul," Aster said. "Please. Give me a moment of understanding before you steal it away from me again. Unless you're afraid you won't be able to justify your actions."

"I have little hope you'll see things my way," he said. "At least, not yet." He looked to Roddy. "It would be interesting to see whether things change."

A tight knot of fear twisted Aster's stomach. "What?"

"Up to you," Roddy said. He didn't seem to be weakening from the wound she'd given him. Either she hadn't struck well, or he was using magic to sustain himself.

Aster wondered who had died for that.

Eamon looked into Aster's eyes. "I've curated your memories and kept you ignorant of my magic so you could do the work that was so important to both of us. There was too much pain. Too much potential for guilt and doubt. But I've always wished it could be otherwise."

"I'd have been fine if I'd remembered killing the wolves. Those were my victories. I wish I remembered them."

Eamon nodded. "Necessary omissions, I'm afraid. You spoke to them too often once you were close enough to kill. I couldn't risk it."

"Couldn't risk what?"

Eamon rubbed his bad leg and winced. "That wasn't all, though," he went on, as though she hadn't spoken. He looked up at the bodies hanging from the ceiling. "I had to erase the memories of you helping me find these people."

Aster looked up in spite of herself, taking in the pathetic forms of the tortured souls he'd left hanging there. Cold hands tightened around her throat.

"I would never."

"Not knowingly, but you've helped me. You thought you were searching for people I might offer aid to. Once you gave me their names, I couldn't let you remember them. You'd have seen their faces on posters and put the pieces together. Once or twice I convinced you to bring them here to me. Other times I hired outside help for that part. Either way, you made it so much easier to get what I needed to fuel my magic."

Aster's mouth had gone dry. "How many?"

"Since you've been old enough to find lonely, unwanted souls few people would miss when I took them? Twenty, I suppose. I haven't kept a close count."

Aster felt like Roddy was squeezing the breath from her again, but his hands remained firmly clamped on her arms. It was Eamon's words that were stealing the air from her lungs.

Twenty people dead, plus the wolves. And I remember none of them.

Aster glanced at the knife on the table that looked so much like the one Eamon had given her. "The enchanted blade I used on the wolves... is that part of your dark rituals?"

"Oh, yes," Eamon said, as though it didn't matter. As though it wasn't a fact that might tear Aster's soul apart. "It draws in the power of their blood and their life. You kill far too mercifully for me to get the full benefit, but it's plenty." He smiled, delighted by his own cleverness. "They stole from us. Why should we not take their blood, their pain?"

"Their souls?"

Eamon leaned in closer. Aster could have kicked him in the jaw, but she held back. Her need to understand was stronger than her need to hurt him, at least for the moment.

"You're as guilty as I am, Aster," he said. "And you benefit as much as I do. But I'm the only one who bears the burden of knowing our crimes, and that's a sacrifice I make out of love for you. That is my confession."

Hot tears spilled over Aster's cheeks as she imagined herself luring people to the house, then forgetting they existed as they suffered for the sake of her pain. "I never would have done any of that if I'd known."

"And that's why I never wanted you to find out. I'm only telling you now because I want you to understand, just once, even if you'll forget all of this tomorrow."

"I will never understand." She glared at him. "There are ways of working magic without hurting innocent people."

"Innocent?" Eamon chuckled sadly. "My dear, no one in this world is innocent. And if you think they wouldn't do the same to you or me to protect themselves or their loved ones, you're more naïve than I thought." He looked to Roddy. "This is what I was saying last night. Removing the memories isn't enough. A deeper change is needed, and more permanent."

"A reinvention." Roddy sighed. "It's possible, but it won't be easy. We'll need more magic. Better magic."

"We'll find it," Eamon said. "One thing at a time, though. Once I perform the healing, she'll forget all this and we can move ahead as we planned."

Eamon stood and held his hands out toward Aster. His magic began to flow, familiar and newly terrible, cold and dark as it drew the pain from her. But at the same time as she feared it, Aster couldn't help wanting it in some dark, craven part of herself.

It would be so much easier to give in and return to ignorance.

No, she thought, and kicked out at him.

Eamon frowned. "Come now, Aster. It's been a hard few days, but you'll wake up tomorrow refreshed and ready to take on the world, just like always. And then, soon enough, Roddy and I will fix the flaws in your mind that make the truth so hard to bear. You'll be able to keep doing the work that sustains us both with no more guilt. No more burden. No more painful scars."

Aster's stomach clenched. "You said you were going to make everything better."

"And I will." Eamon frowned down at her. "Once the enchantment is perfected, there will be no reason to hide your new memories from you. You'll delight in every hunt, every kill, every drawn-out bit of pain that will strengthen my power. We'll have no need for secrets between us because you will be my perfect weapon."

A perfect monster. Aster trembled with a mix of fear and rage that came wholly from herself, not from Eamon's enchantment as he raised his hands again to heal her. "I don't want your blood magic."

His power flowed, and Aster imagined her skin as armour, defending her from him. Where the pain tried to leave, she clung to it, fighting with everything in her to shut him out.

"You wouldn't resist me if you knew—"

Roddy dug his fingers into the muscle of her arms, and Aster's gasp cut Eamon off.

"Seems to me she deserves to know that part, too," Roddy said. "If you want her to willingly accept your generous gifts, I'd say a demonstration would have more impact than a discussion."

Aster twisted her neck to look up at him. "What are you talking about?"

Eamon frowned. "Perhaps you're right. But I won't risk it until I'm sure I have the power to restore everything properly. Fresh blood. A strong life. We'll have to keep her safe until then."

"What risk? Why—" Aster's questions were cut off as Roddy hauled her out of the chair and toward one of the cells set into the wall.

She pulled an arm free and reached for the dagger on the table, but he caught her wrist and twisted it, sending a sharp, agonizing flare up her arm. He pushed her into a cell and slammed it closed before she could turn. The bolt on the outside slid home, leaving Aster with only the light that came in through the bars of the small window to see by. She tried to snake an arm through to reach the bolt, but the bars were too closely spaced for her to get more than her forearm out.

The chairs scraped across the floor as Eamon set them back in their place against the wall. "I had her researching one for me," he said. "We'll need a better supply for the final enchantment, but it'll do for now. He won't be missed."

Aster remembered no such thing, but she believed him. There were blank spots in her memories of the past few months that might have had nothing to do with hunting wolves.

He was going to resupply his dark power.

Aster bit back a frustrated scream and kicked at the door. "Eamon, don't! I'll be good! I'll listen!"

They ignored her.

Eamon lifted the heavy dagger from the table and admired the liquid play of light over its blade. "We'll give this a try, see if it's really so much better than my old one."

"If Delgrade claimed it was, it is," Roddy said. He rubbed his wounded arm and scowled at Aster.

She pressed her face to the bars and glared right back at him.

"I'll need to repair this first," Roddy said, "and then we'll be off. Perhaps you could explain the mechanism of—" The door closed, cutting him off, leaving Aster alone with the bodies of people she had no memory of helping to kill.

CHAPTER EIGHTEEN
GALE

Gale had made it back from the library just after sunset, loaded down with books. She'd carried the most delicate and least discreet in her bag, and only a pair of nondescript tomes bound in brown leather in her arms. Still, every step of the walk had felt steeped in danger, and she'd been glad to return to the safety of her flat.

Nothing from the regular library would have had her scuttling home like a frightened mouse. But these books, from a collection the dusty old librarians knew nothing about, could get a person killed.

Now she sat with a cup of tea at hand and the half-dozen books she'd taken from the library open in front of her, surrounded by untidy piles of papers covered in scrawled notes.

Six books out of a library overflowing with the knowings and musings of generations of Andonian witches seemed like far too few, but they were the only ones she'd found clearly cross-referenced with mentions of any practical information on blood magic.

It had been her first visit alone. Madrigal's absence was

starting to feel less like a fit of anger and more like a lesson she was supposed to learn.

Still, she wasn't surprised when Madrigal appeared before her and sat on the carpet on the other side of the books. She looked over them, reading upside down.

"Truly impressive," she said, leaning back to take in the scope of the clutter that surrounded her student. "It would take most witches a week to make a mess like this, and you've done it in less than a day."

Gale glanced up from the thick volume that lay cradled on her crossed legs. "Thank you, I take great pride in it."

Neither of them spoke for several minutes. Gale kept paging through the collected diaries of Voltana of Bristnea and sipped her tea.

"What is all this?" Madrigal asked.

"Researching blood magic. I'm more convinced than ever that Aster is a victim of it, but the fact that it healed her makes that seem impossible." She looked up at her mentor. "Did you really need to ask?"

"No." Madrigal drew a finger across a page of another book, though Gale knew she couldn't feel it. "I was watching from the borderlands. I was angry and thought if I made you go it alone you'd see how foolish you were being. But I couldn't abandon you with someone so dangerous. Even if I couldn't have done much, I'd have been there to try to save you if things went wrong."

Gale set the book aside, afraid she'd harm it if she clenched her hands in anger. "For my sake, or yours?"

Madrigal didn't take the bait. If anything, she seemed to deflate a little. "I shouldn't have said those things earlier."

"But you meant them." Gale didn't phrase it as a question.

"I did, but I spoke in anger and said things that should have come out otherwise, and sooner." She looked up to meet Gale's gaze, and her eyes were wet. "The truth is that it *is* hard to be the way I am. I feel trapped in your life, going where you go and speaking to your acquaintances, and then only through you. Teaching you would be a joy if my freedom didn't depend on it, but as it is there's too much pressure. I feel like a cruel schoolmistress when I wanted to be your friend and your guide." She cleared her throat. "You're right. I am pushing you for selfish reasons. I don't know how much longer I can stand to be trapped here, isolated and feeling like a burden on you. But I also care about you and want to see you prepared for life after I'm gone. It's frightening to care so much. I should have told you that part."

"You're not a burden." Gale's anger cooled, and she spoke respectfully. "I'm grateful for everything you're teaching me. And I care for you, too. I want you to be happy."

"I know. But it's not easy being my mouthpiece, is it? Or having me over your shoulder all the time?"

Gale didn't want to answer. Madrigal was right, but what would be the point of admitting it? To ask for time alone was to banish her to the borderlands, or perhaps to the ruins of the life she'd left behind—Gale had never asked whether she could still go back to the cabin on her own now that her assumed purpose for lingering among the living was rooted firmly in her student.

"We're both in situations we didn't intend to find ourselves in," she said, when it became clear Madrigal was willing to wait forever for her to turn this into a proper, honest conversation. She tried to imagine herself in Madrigal's situation, chained to one person who held the key to her freedom. "It is hard, in spite of all the goodness. I feel bound to your purpose instead of my own, and then I feel selfish when I rebel because you have so much more at stake in this than I have." She traced a finger over the page before her, feeling the roughness of the handmade paper that she'd barely noticed while she was reading minutes before. To feel, taste, and smell fully were miracles Madrigal had been denied since her death, and she couldn't escape into anything better.

And all I can do is complain that she sometimes makes me learn about illusions.

A hard lump formed in Gale's throat. "I'll try harder. For both our sakes."

Her hand went cold as Madrigal laid hers on top of it. "Me, too. I don't know what will make you a true enough witch that I'll be free to leave you. I thought teaching you as I was taught must be the best way, but perhaps letting you follow your whims occasionally will help inspire you." Madrigal folded both hands on her lap and looked over the books again. "Blood magic isn't what I'd choose as a suitable subject for anything but dire warnings and cautionary tales, but at least you're studying on your own for once. I'd be interested to know what you've learned."

Gale smiled, and any lingering hard feelings melted away. As far as she knew, their relationship was unique in the history of Andonian witches, maybe in the world. It might never be an easy one, but they'd make it work.

"And I'd be interested to know what you thought of my protection enchantment." The fact that Madrigal hadn't stepped in to instruct her in it was the only thing that had made Gale wonder whether she'd actually been watching.

"I'd have gone with a base Dorsaline enchantment," Madrigal said. The advice had obviously been on the tip of her tongue. "But you did well with your workarounds. You shielded it well, which was my primary concern."

"Will it work?"

Madrigal looked past Gale's shoulder, lost in thought. "I don't know. It's tricky business, and she didn't give you much to work with. You did better than I anticipated, though."

"You knew I'd try it?"

Madrigal scowled, but not without humour. Now that the air had cleared, she seemed more content than she'd been in months. "Did I expect you to get involved even after you swore you wouldn't? Obviously. You're not asking all of this because you want instruction, are you? You're worried about her."

Gale winced. "Will you be angry if I say yes?"

"No." Madrigal sighed. "I have good reason for advising you against letting your compassion drag you into other people's dangerous affairs—look where it got me. And, even setting aside my own stake in all this, I'd hate to see your potential wasted by having your focus stray from magic. But I think we're both better served by you telling me what's true instead of what I want to hear."

"I do care." Gale thought back to Aster's gloved hand on hers, the fear and confusion that melted into gratitude when Gale tried to help her, the cautious hope in her eyes. "I feel for her. I don't know what her life is like, but I know what it is to be afraid of losing everything if I questioned the truth as I knew it. I think she's being controlled, by magic and by circumstance. She only has her father, like I only had Bright Hollow and the Path. I knew there was something outside my cage but wasn't brave enough to escape until I had no choice. I don't think she even knows she's trapped. Or didn't, until this morning. She deserves better."

Someone knocked at the door. Gale leapt to her feet, certain it was Aster, that she'd remembered everything and hurried back. But when Madrigal passed through the wall and returned, she didn't appear anywhere near wary enough for that to be the case.

"It's those two wolves," she said, without her usual bitterness.

Gale hurried to open the door and Jes and Cas stepped into her workspace, knocking the snow off their boots on the side of the doorway. They followed Gale into her living area.

"Any news?" Jes asked as she removed her coat and laid it over the back of one of the chairs. She wore a sage-green dress with a full skirt, and her dark hair was coiled into an efficient bun at the top of her neck, dressed to blend in with the other women of the city.

Cas kept his coat on in spite of the warmth from the fire.

"Her real name is Aster, and she's not working alone," Gale said. Whatever she felt about or toward Aster, there was no question of not sharing everything. "Her father's responsible for the magic I felt in her at the jail and when she visited me yesterday. And when I saw her today."

Jes raised one dark eyebrow. "You've been busy."

"I have. It's more complicated than I thought. The long and short of it is that I got her to swear you're not in danger from her, and in exchange I'm helping her..." Gale struggled to think of how to describe it all quickly. "Her dad's enchanted her, and I think he's stealing her memories to control her, and you're going to be in a lot of trouble if she forgets making that promise because I strongly suspect he wants you dead even if she doesn't."

Jes and Cas looked at each other, then back to Gale.

"What's his name?" Cas asked. A cold, sharp edge Gale had never heard from him before had come into his voice.

"Eamon. That's all I got from her, but the address is 465 Greybaud."

"I'll see what I can find out," he said, and left without another word.

Jes sat and moved her coat to her lap. "Sounds like you're up to your nose in all this. What's the plan?"

Gale blinked at her, startled.

"Speak up, girl," Madrigal muttered.

"I... sorry," Gale said. "I do have thoughts. It's just that I'm used to you giving orders, not asking for ideas."

Jes smiled, looking uncertain in a way that shook Gale. "Enchantments are your territory, not mine. I'd feel better if you helped me to understand, but I know when I'm out of my depth."

Gale looked to Madrigal, who shrugged. "Witch business isn't for her kind to understand," she said, "but it is her neck on the line. I'll leave it up to you."

Gale didn't have to think about it. "I suspect he uses blood magic," she said. "He's probably responsible for more than a few of the missing people here in town, and more elsewhere if he's trying to cover his tracks. Killing them, fuelling his magic with blood and pain and whatever souls are made of."

"I see." Jes looked as though she already regretted asking. "And you think she'll forget her agreement with you?"

"I don't know. I've done all I can to protect her for the moment, but nothing is certain."

Jes thought for a moment, then drew in a long breath and stood. "Thank you. You've done well, and you've done enough. It's time for us to leave."

Gale was about to ask what she'd do without them, then understood. "*We* including me?"

"Obviously." Jes took her by the hand, squeezed tight, and released her. "Like it or not, you're one of us."

One of us. Not a grand, impressive, or morally sound family, and nothing like the one she'd left behind in Bright Hollow, but Gale knew without question it was the one she wanted.

Jes looked around Gale's little apartment. "I know this city is your home now. It's mine, too, but it's too dangerous to stay. We'll start over somewhere new and let the mages handle this Eamon fellow."

Gale didn't like to think about the mages, about their dark building in Embercliffe and the cells beneath it, or their grand room full of magical weapons. The mention of them made her shudder. "I'd rather not bring them here if we can avoid it. In this case, the enemy of my enemy is not my friend."

"We'd hide you far from here," Jes said. She spoke gently. "And we wouldn't contact them ourselves, so there would be no connection to you."

More memories came. A headless body on a stage, a robed mage standing over it, axe in hand.

And another mage without eyes who might see anything if he knew to turn his attention to it.

"No," Gale whispered. "No mages. If my protection works and

Aster sees the truth, I think she could be the key to bringing him down without them."

She wasn't sure Aster would agree to any such thing, but it sounded good.

"And if it doesn't work?" Jes asked. Madrigal looked to Gale, seconding the question.

"If she doesn't show up here tomorrow, we'll assume the worst. We'll run before her father can send her after you again, and then I suppose we'll have no choice but to report him." The thought of helping the mages turned Gale's stomach, but the alternative was worse. "But I can't abandon her until I know I have no other choice. If you want to go without me, I'll understand."

"I'll wait until tomorrow." Jes collected her coat and turned to leave. Gale followed her past the panels that divided the room. "In the meantime, I'll see what Cas has found out and remind him not to do anything foolish before we hear from you." She reached the door, then glanced over her shoulder. "Promise you'll be careful."

"I will."

When she was gone, Gale locked the door and sat on the edge of her bed, suddenly exhausted.

"You should have taken her up on that offer," Madrigal said. "Nothing good can come of staying here."

Gale rested her head in her hands. "I know."

CHAPTER NINETEEN
ASTER

Aster banged on the door until her knuckles were bloody and screamed until her throat went raw, though she knew no one would hear. She'd never heard the other victims, and gods only knew how long Eamon had held them down here before he'd finally let them die. But it felt good to vent her rage.

At least a little of it. She held some in reserve.

I think I didn't hear them, she amended as she crouched against the wall of a cell too small for her to sit comfortably. *But maybe not all my nightmares were dreams.*

He certainly wouldn't have let me remember if I had heard anything.

The blazing anger that had fed her screams now burned low and hot, and she directed her thoughts toward what would come next.

There might be hope of holding on to her memories. The charm hadn't worked against the door, but that hadn't been its purpose. She'd simply have to ask for something more if Gale offered to try again. Broader. Find an enchantment that would protect her not only from the magic within her, but from whatever else Eamon might throw her way. But first Aster needed to escape. And her first stop after she did would be the police station.

The fire in her heart warmed her pleasantly as she imagined it. She'd let Eamon heal her, let him think he'd won, that she'd lost her memories and was his ignorant, loving daughter again. Then she'd pack a bag, make her way to the local precinct, and spill everything. Eamon would be arrested, someone would find a way back into this room, and no matter what happened, Aster would be free.

Free and gone without a trace before he could pour any poison into the cops' ears about her role in the whole thing.

Gale had proven herself more than capable and would help her deal with the pain Eamon had been using blood magic to treat for so long—if that were even true. She supposed the pain might have been his doing, too, used to keep her coming back so he could erase her memories.

And if the pain were real and Gale couldn't fix it… well, better that Aster suffer for the rest of her life than allow more people to die for Eamon's power. She'd simply have to find a way to survive it.

Her stomach tightened at the thought of what would happen when they executed Eamon, as they surely would once the truth came out. Would his enchantment be broken, releasing all her lost memories in an overwhelming surge that threatened to carry her sanity away with it?

Or would they remain locked away forever?

Not appealing either way, but better than allowing him to continue as he had been.

Eamon was right. She'd grown up with a sharply defined sense of justice, knowing the people who had harmed her would eventually pay for their crimes. She'd acted on that belief, knowing the legal system would never punish them as they deserved. She'd trained, hunted, and killed, just as he'd wanted.

Eamon had created a monster with a conscience, and now it

was time for the creation to turn on her master before he could strip her of what humanity she had left.

Her throat tightened and tears burned her eyes.

Even in her anger, there was still a part of her that cared for the man she thought of as her father. What she'd learned over the past few days didn't erase the love he'd shown her. The patience. The laughter that had filled this big house. The games. The lessons. The sacrifices he'd made to see her brought up well, the daughter he'd found after his first one was lost.

But she couldn't love evil. And if everything else in him had to die to see that evil removed from the world, so be it.

Hours later, the door opened again.

It had been closed tight, and she heard a key turn in the lock. That would make things more difficult when the police came, but that was a problem for later. She stood and winced. Her thighs had cramped in the cold as she'd crouched in her cell, and the pain in her scars had crept back so slowly that she'd barely noticed its familiar presence until she moved again. She wished Roddy hadn't stolen the potion Gale had given her. It would have made whatever came next so much easier.

Eamon entered first, checking the room to see that Aster was still in her cell and everything else was in its place. Aster smiled. He might think of her as a child, but he knew her well enough to suspect she might escape, claim a weapon, and return to her cell to wait for her chance.

But the pleasure faded quickly as muffled grunts floated in from the hallway beyond the door. Roddy appeared a moment later, pushing a thin man in front of him. The stranger seemed drunk but had more likely been the victim of another of Roddy's spells.

Aster tried to remember if she'd seen him before and came up blank.

Eamon closed the door behind them, and the lock clicked into place. Roddy shoved the man onto the table on his back and held him down with one hand pressed hard to his narrow chest while Eamon tightened leather straps around his torso. The stranger screamed and flailed, but one by one his arms and legs were fastened to the surface beneath him.

"Hey!" Aster banged on the door in an attempt to distract them, but neither Eamon nor Roddy so much as glanced at her. The high panic in her voice frightened her, and she fell silent.

Roddy's shoulders rose and fell as he took a deep breath and glared down at the stranger. He'd obviously come here expecting to be more than Eamon's hired muscle, and Aster hoped he was hating every second of this.

At least he had a choice in it, she thought. *Lucky bastard.*

He opened the cell, and Aster bolted, forcing her body to move even as it felt like her stiffened and aching muscles might be pulling away from her bones. Roddy caught her by the back of her sweater and swung her around, sending her flying into the open cupboard of knives and torture implements. She crouched and sheltered herself under her arms as the items rained down on her, no doubt leaving cuts and bruises she'd only feel later, and scooped up a knife that she held behind her back as she prepared to run again.

"Careful there!" Eamon called.

Roddy grabbed her wrist and clapped a cold steel manacle around it. As he reached for the other, Aster swung the knife at his throat.

He grunted out a spell. The weapon flew from her hand, leaving behind a sensation that felt like numbness and burning at the same time.

She screamed and threw a punch, and Roddy shoved her against the wall, knocking her head hard enough that he got the second manacle around her weakened hand before she could recover.

The man was a fighter, whether by magic or by physical force.

And Eamon had never taught her to fight magic.

She'd never felt so helpless, so betrayed by her own body. The chains, which were too short to allow her to reach the weapons that lay scattered over the floor at her feet, betrayed her emotions as they shook with her fear and rage.

Roddy picked up a razor-thin dagger from the floor and walked toward the table. "Where shall we begin?"

"Soon, Roddy." Eamon looked at Aster as he spoke. "I need a moment with my daughter first. Would you excuse us?"

"You're paying the bills," Roddy muttered, and carried the knife into the hallway, leaving the door ajar.

Aster pulled against the chains, but they were set deep in the stone above her head.

"Roderick and I have been discussing matters," Eamon said. "Oh, do stop struggling. You're making everything so much harder than it has to be."

Aster leaned against the wall and scowled at him. "Better?"

Eamon tapped his cane once against the floor. Deep creases formed between his eyebrows. "I've decided Roderick right. It's best you gain a full understanding of what I do for you so you can truly comprehend the necessity of this." He gestured toward the man on the table, whose shouts had faded to terrified whimpers.

"Please," the stranger whispered. He had a thick accent. Jatlish, maybe.

Aster's pulse pounded in her ears.

Roddy knows more about me than I know about myself. My secrets aren't even mine.

Eamon reached out and tucked her dark curls behind one ear —a familiar gesture, and one that had comforted her many times over the years.

Aster jerked her head away, and Eamon sighed.

"You are my only living child," he said. "I love you."

His touch left Aster's skin crawling. "Do you? Or am I a possession? A doll to dress and pose how you please, or a dog to train as you see fit?"

He drew one of the chairs closer and sat in it, wincing. "I never told you the full extent of what happened the night your grandmother died—the night you became my daughter. You'll forget again soon enough, but you're right. You deserve to know at least once.

"I've told you that I saved your life, and that it took magic to do it. So much that I had little left to use for my own healing while the wound was still fresh enough to do any good." He rubbed his leg. "I've never regretted that decision. I would bear this and more to see you whole and healthy."

Aster glared at him. "I'm surprised no religion has named you a saint yet."

"You were dead, Aster." He looked at her, his eyes shining with something that looked like true grief. "Your body had been shattered. Tortured by so-called wolves who took pleasure from cruelty, crushed beneath the portion of the building that fell. I knew I should bury you, but you reminded me of my little Claudia. So young, so innocent, so fragile. I'd have done anything to bring her back if I'd had the chance. I could do no less for you."

White spots appeared at the edges of Aster's vision as she pictured a younger version of her body, too broken to hold her spirit in it. Eamon digging it out from beneath the rubble, horrified by his accidental role in her death. Cradling her, speaking words of dark magic. Bringing her back.

Not a memory, but easily imagined. Acid rose in her throat.

"No regrets about bringing you back to life," he said, leaning heavily on his cane as he stood and went to the workbench to pick up his new dagger. "But you have no idea what it costs to sustain someone like you." He carried the dagger to the table and the man strapped to it.

"What are you talking about?"

Eamon smiled sadly and closed his eyes. "*Vranth'i reoul,*" he murmured, his voice cold and crisp as winter air. "*Corailu vargrel.*"

"Please, no!" The stranger's words were a trapped animal's cry.

Eamon didn't seem to hear. He plunged the dagger into his victim's thigh. The man cried out and Eamon twisted the blade, then leaned his head back and gasped. He stood straighter, barely leaning on his cane at all, stronger than Aster had ever seen him.

"You'll learn to do this soon enough," he told her. "Once your mind is corrected, once you're less concerned with the mercy of a quick death, you'll bring me so much more power. Enough to shape the world to our liking in time."

Roddy entered and stood leaning against the wall by the door, watching with keen interest. Aster wondered when he had last killed, when he'd need to do so again to replenish the power he'd just used to fight her.

A hundred questions flooded her mind, all things she'd have asked Gale if she'd taken the idea of blood magic seriously instead of choosing to defend Eamon's honour.

Stupid.

Eamon pulled the dagger free. Blood covered the blade, but disappeared as though the metal were drinking it in. He dragged it across his victim's cheek, and the man whimpered as a dark spot appeared at the front of his trousers.

"It's best if I show you rather than trying to explain," Eamon said, turning to Aster. "You think me a liar now, and I want to be sure you understand."

"I don't think you're lying," Aster said. Her voice came out a rasping whisper. "I believe you."

The man on the table turned to her, words spilling from his

mouth in a flood that likely would have sounded like incoherent babble even if she'd spoken the language, and his terror and pain echoed through her.

Eamon buried the knife in the man's chest below his heart and twisted, carving deep. Blood flowed, quickly soaking through the victim's shirt, flowing over the edge of the table, pattering to the stone floor. The man screamed again, but Aster's attention was on Eamon. The expression written on his face was pure bliss as his sacrifice's cries faded.

He released the dagger, leaving it buried in ruined flesh as the hapless fellow's skin turned pale and the life left his eyes.

Eamon turned to her. "I'm sorry for this, my dear. I truly am." He held out his hands as though he was about to heal her.

Aster opened her mouth to ask exactly what he was sorry for, but the sudden sense of physical loss that overcame her made her gasp. It took her a moment to realize what was being stolen—not the breath from her lungs or the blood from her veins, but something just as familiar that she'd never fully recognized was in her.

Instead of offering his magic, Eamon was slowly draining it from her. Aster leaned forward without thinking, trying to hold onto the power.

The slow loss left her cold and weak as the pain worsened, searing and slashing and shrieking through her scars.

She knew, at least in theory, that in the past it had been terrible. Though she couldn't remember it, she *knew* it, and had imagined the pain he saved her from as burning, as cutting, as feeling like she was going to split open, but she couldn't imagine that those ideas had ever felt so true. Agonizing pain erupted within her skin and muscle, driving down to her bones, so complete it threatened to eclipse thought, memory, and her deepest self.

"Stop," she begged, but the enchantment still drained away.

"You have to see," Eamon said. He sounded like he was in pain, too, and Aster didn't care at all. "I won't have you fighting me when I heal you. For once, you will fully understand and embrace this gift I've given you, as I've always wished you would."

In each moment, Aster thought she'd reached the limit of her torment. And in each moment that followed, she discovered she'd been wrong.

Her left femur snapped, and she lost herself to the pain. When the darkness receded, she found herself slumped on her knees, held up only by the manacles that dug into her wrists. She struggled to get her intact leg back underneath her to ease the pressure in her shoulders. Thick, hot wetness flowed into her eye as the scar on her head tore into a fresh, blinding hit of agony. More blood dripped beneath her loose sweater as the old scars on her arms opened into fresh wounds.

Roddy crossed the room. Aster braced for an attack, but he only released her from the manacles, letting her fall.

She tried to crawl toward Eamon. She wasn't thinking. All she knew was the magic was leaving her, she needed it back, and he had it.

Her right arm went out from under her as another bone snapped, and she collapsed face-first to the floor.

"Show her," Eamon ordered.

Roddy rolled Aster onto her back and pulled her sweater and the shirt beneath it over her head. She screamed—it felt like his tugging would pull her arms off. She wanted to close her eyes but couldn't. Not when he grabbed her wrists, lifting her arms toward the ceiling, and she saw what Eamon was doing to her.

Without his enchantment, she was falling apart.

His blood magic had stitched her together like a ruined ragdoll, and now the threads he'd carefully maintained for more than a decade were unravelling. Deep gashes had opened on her arms, cutting down to the bone, and she felt the same happening to her legs. Blood flowed, muscle parted beneath skin, and bones crumbled as the magic holding them together left her body.

Her right arm came apart between the elbow and wrist,

leaving Roddy holding her twitching hand as her upper arm thumped to the floor.

She could barely hear her own screams over the roar of agony and terror in her brain.

Her chest felt as though it were on fire and being crushed, both at once. Her screams stopped. She couldn't draw a breath. She managed to lift her head long enough to see blood spreading across the fitted white undershirt she'd worn for training. Roddy, stone-faced and silent, stood over her with a knife and looked to Eamon, who nodded.

He had tears in his eyes.

Roddy slipped the blade beneath the shirt and sliced upward. It opened, revealing the gory mess her chest had become, splintered ribs, ruptured skin, and more blood than seemed possible.

She'd seen people die from losing far less blood, but Eamon's control was perfect, holding her to life and consciousness no matter how she wished to slip away.

Roddy stepped aside and Eamon took his place. His strength and power were palpable. So much flowing through him, and none of it for her.

"This is how I found you," Eamon said. "This is what you would be without my despicable, hateful magic holding you together. I knitted your bones, pulled together the shattered scraps of muscle that had been your heart, put the broken pieces of you back together, and gave you life. If I were not constantly renewing your supply of my power, you would return to this. I could withdraw my magic any time I wished, and you'd be lost if I died, but I've never used that fact to control you. A labour of love, Aster." He leaned over her. "As I said, you're very expensive."

Aster tried to mouth words, but couldn't make her lips move. Her jaw had broken, too, but the rest of her body had been such a bright well of pain that she'd hardly noticed.

"Do you want it back?" he asked. "I'm strong now. You can be whole again, and all of this can be over in an instant. You won't even remember when you wake. All you need do is ask, to accept what I do for you, to know and be grateful, just this once."

Aster stared up at the bodies hanging from the ceiling.

A strong person would say no. A strong person would gladly die instead of living by such dark and terrible magic. Her life was worth no more than that of the man on the table.

A fresh wave of pain tore through her chest and her heartbeat stilled. Darkness closed in from all sides until all she could see was Eamon and the corpses that had fed his power and her life.

The darkness was so cold. So unbearably final.

With the last of her strength she jerked her chin upward.

Yes. Save me.

The shadows closed in, and there was nothing.

CHAPTER TWENTY
ASTER

Aster came slowly back to herself.

No pain. None at all.

She had to open her eyes to be sure she wasn't dead. The familiar ceiling of her bedroom came into view, and, when she turned her head, the rest of the room. The clock said she'd slept most of the day away.

The window was closed, and anything she'd strewn about while packing was gone. It was just her room, fastidiously tidy, nothing disturbed.

Just as my memories should be.

She sat upright and nearly toppled over as clouds of vertigo beat her about the head.

Blood loss.

I should be dead.

I was dead once.

Her stomach turned, and she took five long, measured breaths, waiting for her heart to stop pounding.

I'm alive.

And I remember.

As she thought back over the previous day, she found no blank spaces in her experiences. Every pain, every revelation, every conversation was still there. Even the dungeon she'd forgotten before was there, now inextricably and unforgettably tied to her own bodily experience.

Every familiar scar was still intact when she sat up and examined her body, but she was whole again. No broken bones, no open wounds. She tugged at the neckline of her nightgown, nauseated by the thought of Eamon or Roddy changing her into it, and rubbed a hand over the centre of her chest. The scars were back, just as they'd been before, thick and pale, twisting between her breasts. Her heart beat strong and certain under the palm of her hand, and the lines of her ribs beneath the spiderwebbed surface of her skin were smooth and unbroken.

He knit me together again.

The knowledge should have comforted her, but she couldn't stop shaking as she thought of what had been.

Aster held her arms out and pushed back the sleeves of her nightgown, then cradled her right arm against her chest, rubbing the scar that encircled her forearm. It had come apart so cleanly, as though sliced through by an invisible blade.

She forced her eyes closed until her guts stopped rolling.

But I remember.

The charms on the bracelet around her left wrist jingled faintly when she moved. She touched the horseshoe-shaped charm and decided she'd pay Gale any price she thought reasonable when the time came to settle her debt.

Aster pulled her feet up onto the bed and leaned against the headboard, knees to her chest, eyes squeezed closed.

I only live because he says I live. I only breathe because his dark magic makes it so.

But damned if it didn't feel good to pull in those breaths. She wanted to shout, to run, to climb, maybe even to dance, just because she could.

Her chest tightened, and her next breath came with more difficulty.

She'd known the price when she begged for her life, and it hadn't mattered. All she'd cared about was saving herself.

I really am a monster.

A quiet knock at the door made her jump.

"Aster, my dear?" Eamon's voice, soft enough that it wouldn't wake her if she were still sleeping. "Are you awake?"

"I am!" she called, forcing something like cheer into her voice. She considered the situation quickly and let her instincts take over, focusing only on becoming what Eamon should think her to be now. He'd seemed certain she'd forget everything he said to her, and every moment from the second he'd arrived home had been a disaster. He'd have taken that from her, too, along with the days he'd been gone.

Probably. Anything she said now was a gamble.

"When did you get back?"

Eamon paused long enough that Aster thought she'd assumed wrong, that she was supposed to remember something about his arrival. She looked to the window, wondering whether she'd have time to try for another escape.

"Late last night."

Aster relaxed, though only slightly. "I'm sorry I wasn't up earlier. Just need a moment to get moving. Be down in a few."

The doorknob turned.

"Getting dressed!" she added.

"Very good. We'll have a very late breakfast when you're ready."

He step-thumped back down the hall and the stairs.

She dressed quickly in a grey skirt, a white blouse with a high lace neck, and the fitted jacket that matched the skirt, wishing to expose as little of herself as possible. She pulled her curls back in a low, modest bun. Eamon liked for her to look presentable, and a good and faithful daughter with no suspicions would want to look her best when her father returned.

And that was what she had to be. Grateful as she was for the preservation of her memories, they only made the situation more dangerous.

If I can convince him I remember nothing, he'll let me go out. If I can get out, I can—

She sat heavily on the little stool at her dressing table and stared at her reflection.

"I can what?" she asked the girl in the mirror.

Her plan had been to escape and go to the police. They'd find evidence, convict Eamon, and...

"And behead him." She rested her forehead in her hands.

With Eamon dead there would be no one to maintain the enchantment. She'd entertained the idea of withstanding the pain when he wasn't there to relieve it, but hadn't understood the true price of losing his magic.

If he died, so would she. Maybe not right away, but the pain would return, and would only get worse. Her flesh would tear itself apart again as the magic degenerated, and this time there would be no stopping it.

But it was unquestionably the right thing to do. With him gone, the people of Queen's Run would be safe from him. She'd chosen selfishly when she'd asked him to save her, but that would be made right if she used her freedom to bring him to justice.

Her eyes were bloodshot when she looked back up at the mirror.

Her life should have ended years ago. Every breath since then had been drawn from blood and pain and death, a gift given by dark magic. She'd harmed innocent people to keep his magic fed, whether she'd intended to or not. Seeing Eamon executed and letting herself go to the grave would be...

"Justice." The word tasted bitter on her tongue for the first time.

But it was true. It would be a return to balance, a righting of wrongs. It didn't matter that she hadn't asked for any of this. Now that she knew the truth, continuing to benefit from Eamon's power would make her as guilty as he was.

Aster supposed it was funny, in a way. Eamon had saved her so she could deliver justice by death to those who had harmed them. Now the same would come for her.

But she couldn't laugh about it. Not when her heart felt like it was coming apart again.

She went to the basin and splashed cold water on her face to take the heat from her cheeks. Her reddened eyes could surely be explained by a bad sleep, maybe even strange nightmares she'd say she couldn't remember.

It wouldn't be easy. She'd trained to fight, to track, to hunt, to dance, to make polite conversation, but she'd never had much practice in lying to Eamon.

I can face him. And then I'll go back to Gale. If there's a way I can be saved when he dies, she'll help me find it.

Either way, she promised herself the police station would be her next stop after she spoke to Gale.

Aster pulled on her stockings and boots and headed for the kitchen, ready to pretend nothing had changed.

Eamon was seated on a stool at the table when Aster entered the kitchen. He wasn't wearing a tie, but his white shirt was freshly pressed and spotless, gold cufflinks gleaming at his wrists. He'd made tea and was sipping from his cup, creamer and sugar bowl set out beside the pot.

The usual bowl. He'd refilled it and hidden the other away. No reminders about what had happened during his time away, no questions.

On any other day, the morning sun would have been coming

in through the window, warming the room. She'd have welcomed the sight of the only person in the world she loved and trusted. Now most of the day was gone, lost to her body's recovery. The sun had moved to the west, leaving only cold grey sky outside to light the kitchen, mirroring the dank chill in Aster's chest as she looked at the only father she could remember knowing.

He hadn't cooked breakfast, but the pan was out and the basket holding four eggs sat on the counter along with a bouquet of blush-pink roses in a heavy glass vase.

Aster shut away all thoughts of dark magic.

What would I do if none of that had happened?

She smiled as though a little confused and crossed the room, leaned over the flowers, and sniffed. The scent was clean and natural, but it reminded her of the strange perfume of the dungeon. Cold sweat broke out on her forehead, and she wiped it away before she turned back to Eamon.

"Where in the world did you find these in winter?"

He beamed. "You'd be amazed what you can get when you travel to visit mages."

She almost asked where Roddy was, then remembered that she shouldn't know he'd been in the house. "So you were success-ful? You found him?"

She turned away and busied herself at the stove. She could make her voice behave, but her eyes would give her away.

"I did. And I'm feeling more hopeful than ever before." He paused. "Aster? You haven't greeted me yet."

She swallowed hard and carefully set down the egg she'd been holding, afraid she'd crush it in her clenching fist.

"I'm sorry." She hurried over and placed a kiss on Eamon's cheek. His skin felt clammier than she recalled it being. She forced herself to look into his eyes. "I'm a little out of sorts today. Breakfast will help."

She caught his frown before she turned away and went back to her work.

"What's wrong?"

"Oh, the usual. A little pain, but mostly it's just a headache. Might've had a nightmare or something. I'll be fine as soon as I've eaten. I can't believe I slept so late." She cracked three eggs into the pan, then fumbled and dropped the fourth. It cracked on the counter, and its innards plopped against the tile at her feet.

Eamon's stool scraped across the floor.

"No need," Aster said, and reached for a cloth. She dropped it over the mess. "I'll clean it up after."

"Must be quite the headache," Eamon said.

He sounded genuinely concerned. Aster knew it was because he was worried something had gone wrong with the healing, but she smiled at him as though she appreciated his interest. When she flipped the eggs it was with practiced ease. She hoped he couldn't see the effort it took to keep her hands from shaking.

"I suspect it's from being stuck in the house," she said. "I'm used to getting out, stretching my muscles, taking the air. You said not to go out while you were gone. I may have taken that a little too seriously." She frowned. "At least, I think I did. I can't quite recall what I did with myself while you were away. Did you heal me last night?"

"I did." Eamon held out two plates for her to slide the eggs onto. "You'd deteriorated while I was gone."

"What do you mean?"

"You decided to do some training and pushed too hard, and it took a physical toll. You told me you'd had trouble sleeping, as well. Nightmares, as you just said. You really remember nothing?"

Aster fought the urge to swallow the lump in her throat. "No. Probably just as well if it was that bad."

She'd expected him to lie to her, but the ease with which he did it was shocking.

Of course it's easy, she thought. *He's had plenty of practice over the years.*

She looked down at the plates. "We're one egg short."

Eamon offered her the plate with two on it, but she took the other and ate her breakfast in three bites.

"I'll go and get more," she said. "And pick up some bread. I must have finished what we had while you were gone. We'll have toast and tea later. Or cakes! And we can discuss your trip!" She was blabbering, and she knew it. She pressed her lips together and smiled. "Sorry."

"No need to be." Eamon sat and picked up a fork, ready to eat in a more proper fashion. "I do wonder whether you should be going out in such a state, though."

"It'll help, really. There's nothing like a walk in the sunshine to put things right."

Eamon narrowed his eyes, but only for a moment. "Good. Perhaps over tea we can make plans for dealing with the remaining wolves, too. Talk of good hunt always puts you in better spirits. And we'll discuss how we'll proceed with a fresh enchantment."

Of course Jes was back on the list. He'd never intended to remove her. He'd only agreed as a means to placate her until he could deal with Aster's inconvenient memory.

Eamon sipped his tea and wiped his mouth on a napkin. "Everything's going to change for the better, my dear. I brought the mage back with me, and you'll be right as rain soon enough."

"Change how, exactly?" Aster hoped the tremble in her voice sounded hopeful, not as fearful as she felt. She remembered what he'd said—no more pain, no more guilt.

No more free will, she supposed, or conscience to keep her from doing his work.

But he'd expect her to ask.

Eamon's smile didn't falter, but something dark came into his eyes. "Patience, my dear. We'll discuss it later. Roderick will be able to explain things better than I can."

"Excellent." She tried to sound enthusiastic. "I'll go get my purse and be off. Back before you know it."

She went to her room and grabbed the things she'd need most if she never came home—only what she could fit into a small bag, which meant there was much she'd have to leave behind. No extra clothes. Just a knife in her boot, all the cash she'd saved in the little box she kept beneath her sweaters, and the clothes she wore.

She hesitated before she closed the wardrobe, looking at the deep red cloak she'd worn on all her hunts, its hem stained with the blood of her slain enemies. It should have seemed a dark and dangerous thing given what she now knew about how Eamon had used power taken from those kills, but it wasn't. Her cloak was the shadow that had hidden her from her enemies, the warmth that had protected her when she hunted in snow and rain. It was her identity—the assassin of wolves, the victim who had come back to finish them off.

Leaving it felt like leaving a piece of herself behind, but there was nothing for it. It would look too suspicious if Eamon saw her wearing it out of the house in broad daylight.

She glanced at the closed guest room door, then headed down the stairs to escape the house.

"Aster?"

She froze with her hand on the doorknob, shoulders hunched nearly to her ears like a dog caught with its nose in the roasting pan. She turned, hoping Eamon couldn't tell how her heart was pounding.

"You almost forgot the market basket, dear." He held it out to her. "You're sure you're all right?"

Aster laughed and shook her head. "I'm fine, I swear. Just a little ruffled up here." She knocked a fist against her skull.

"Don't worry," Eamon said, and smiled. "A better life is waiting just around the corner."

Aster made herself kiss his cheek again. It felt like kissing the corpse in the basement, and it was all she could do not to gag. She hurried out of the house, pulling the door closed tight behind her.

~

The grocer's shop wasn't more than five blocks away, but Aster made her way slowly, first past the fine houses on her street and the next, and then past the shops. She held her head high and walked with her shoulders back, taking the air as she'd told Eamon she would and pretending to enjoy the bright sunlight, denying herself when the urge to grab on to her freedom and run came over her.

Someone would be watching.

She stopped every few shops and looked in the windows. She didn't really see the hats, the candies, the toys, or the books. She was too busy watching reflections and casting quick glances from the sides of her eyes.

It was only when she was a block away from the grocer's, turning to greet an acquaintance of Eamon's, that she spotted Roddy not twenty paces behind her. He looked away and pretended to be searching for something in his pockets. Aster didn't watch him, save for in her peripheral vision. She was never supposed to have seen him before, and she'd have no reason to take special notice of one more stranger on the busy street.

But now that she'd spotted him, she could get on with her plans.

She lifted a hand to wave to a non-existent friend across the street, who was conveniently situated on the far side of a dense group of well-dressed folks that had gathered to listen to a violinist. Aster crossed the street a few paces in front of a plodding horse-drawn omnibus that would hold Roddy back from following directly behind her and disappeared into the crowd.

The musician was truly gifted. Heartbreakingly sweet strains cut through the frigid air and vibrated against the newly repaired fibres of her heart, the notes somehow carrying a sense of longing and absence that echoed things she herself had felt but couldn't quite remember. Her steps slowed, and she had to force herself to move on.

She brushed past a lady in a mint-green coat who held a matching handkerchief to one eye. The woman was so enraptured that she didn't seem to notice the disturbance.

The open violin case on the ground was overflowing with bank notes and coins, and Aster wondered whether the instrument was enchanted or whether the musician himself was the source of what seemed likely to be magic.

But the odds of Roddy being enraptured by music were slim, and time was short. Aster reached the far side of the crowd and slipped into the narrow alley beyond, then broke into a run. Her flat boots slapped against pavement and through puddles of slush until she reached the end of the alley, which opened onto the backs of another row of shops on the next street. She assessed the buildings on either side. No ladders, but there was a drainpipe, and no one around...

Without taking another moment to think it over, she tied her skirt around her waist and scaled the building. She used every hand and foothold available—the drainpipe, the window ledges, the tiny balcony of a second-floor flat. When she reached the top, she rolled onto the flat roof and rested a moment, catching her breath.

Then she risked a peek over the edge.

Her disappearance into the alley hadn't fooled Roddy. He stood in the narrow passage below, looking suspiciously at the backs of shops, checking the ground for fresh footprints. Aster ducked back, afraid he might look up. A moment later she heard him running south, toward a main street.

She lay on her back for a few more minutes, looking up into

the uniformly grey sky, until she was sure he wasn't coming back. Then she stood and walked north across the roofs until she found a building with a ladder and climbed back down.

She made her way across town, on full alert with every step, watching for her newest enemy.

CHAPTER TWENTY-ONE
GALE

"What if she were right about him, though?" Gale searched through pages of notes until she came to one she'd written early in her investigation. "If it wasn't blood magic, the enchantment would last even if she ran away, even if he were dead. We'd have plenty of time to figure out how to break it without hurting her."

"*Could* last," Madrigal said. "Not *would*. The kind of person who would manipulate her through memory loss would also have failsafes built in so she can't leave or harm him."

Gale set her notes aside. "But she could be right about that, too." It didn't seem likely, but it was still possible that the magic only felt strange because it was unfamiliar, that the memory loss really was an unfortunate effect of a difficult enchantment. For her own sake, Gale wanted Aster to be wrong, for them to have found out a blood witch who could be stopped before he hurt Aster or anyone else further—maybe even the one responsible for the curse that had changed Gale's life forever.

For Aster's sake, though, she hoped this was all a great misunderstanding.

"Either way—"

"Hush." Madrigal stood and walked to the other end of the room, disappearing through the divider. She returned a moment later. "Speak of evil, and it shall arise."

A knock followed her statement.

Gale rose quickly, then forced herself to slow down and walk with appropriate speed to the door. Madrigal would still be watching to see whether there were signs of non-professional interest in her, and Gale intended to prove herself capable of ignoring any irrational feelings her body might throw at her.

But when she opened the door and looked into Aster's eyes, taking in the snow caught in her eyelashes and the wisps of hair that had come free and framed her face, it was hard to pretend her interest was entirely practical.

"You came," she said, trying to tell herself she was pleased only because something had gone right to have brought her back—the enchantment had worked, or she'd remembered something before the father could heal her. It was that victory that made her breath catch and her heart beat faster.

Nothing else.

Aster stepped sideways past her into the flat and closed the door hard behind her.

"What's wrong?" Gale asked.

"Nothing." Aster paused, then laughed. It was cold and humourless and a little unhinged. "Everything, actually. But specifically, there was someone following me. I lost him, but don't want to be caught standing outside if I can help it."

Madrigal frowned and drifted through the door. She couldn't go far, but she'd get a sense of any immediate danger.

"Your father?"

"No. His new friend." Aster's voice dripped with bitterness.

Gale stepped aside and motioned toward the other side of the room. "Better come in and sit down."

She watched as Aster picked her way through the mess,

cautious as a cat in a room full of rat traps, and settled herself in one of the chairs. Madrigal reappeared and took the other.

"Tell me what happened," Gale said.

Aster cleared her throat and clasped her trembling hands tight in her lap. "There are bodies in a secret room in the basement of my house. Eamon has been using blood magic to treat my pain, control my memories, presumably to maintain his own strength… oh, and to keep me alive because I was dead when he met me."

"Gods," Madrigal muttered.

Gale took a long breath. "Could we try again, but maybe with a little more detail?"

Aster's leg jiggled as she tapped her heel against the floor. Gale suspected that if there'd been room for it amid the clutter, she'd have stood and paced. "There's a room—a dungeon, really— under my house, and I never knew because it's enchanted and I couldn't remember its door existed when I looked away from it. Not until today, anyway. Eamon and his new goon took me down there last night, and he showed me exactly how everything … how *I* fall apart when he doesn't use his magic to hold me together. Literally."

Gale sank onto the edge of the bed. Her legs suddenly seemed reluctant to hold her up. "Your scars are…"

"Without Eamon's magic, they go back to the wounds they were before the enchantments." Aster's voice came out flat, but there was still that wildness in her eyes that said she was teetering on the edge of chaos. She gripped the arms of the chair tight, leaving her knuckles bloodless. "I was dead. He brought me back and fixed me up with his blood magic, and for all these years he's been feeding it into me to maintain the enchantments."

"Of course," Madrigal said. "Blood magic doesn't heal. He made it look convincing, but it was never real. It still isn't."

"I'm sorry I doubted you," Aster added, and made a sound that was somewhere between a hiccup and a held-back sob. "You were right. About everything. He's been taking my memories to control me and to keep me from figuring things out."

Gale closed her eyes and willed her thoughts to form something like a coherent pattern.

"How many bodies did he have down there?" Madrigal asked, and Gale repeated the question to Aster.

"Three hanging from the ceiling." Aster stared into the fire. "They mostly looked like they'd been there a while. Oh, and the one he killed in front of me last night. So four all together. He said I'd helped him find about twenty of them over the years. I, um…" She paused, still not looking at Gale. "I don't remember that. I swear I can't have known what he wanted them for. If I had, I'd never have helped."

"Of course not." Gale crossed the room and waited for Madrigal to vacate the chair so she could sit. She wanted to take Aster's hands in hers to offer comfort but was unsure of whether her touch would be welcome.

"It's got to be more than that over the years, though," Madrigal said. She drifted back and forth in front of the fireplace, clenching and unclenching her fists. "Look at her. Scars, yes, but functioning incredibly well. Mentally sharp, physically strong in spite of what happened, grown into an otherwise healthy young lady. And the memory enchantment…" She shook her head slowly. "Please don't mistake this for admiration, but it's fantastic work. I can't fathom how much energy it takes to maintain it without the ability to truly heal her."

Gale leaned closer to Aster. "Did he say anything about other deaths? About Jes's family?"

"Only that I fed his power when I killed with his blade. He only said as much as he did because he wanted me to know how responsible I was for all of this, to make me understand how good it was that he'd let me forget. He didn't offer more than that." Aster rested her forehead in her hands and took a shuddering breath. "He has to be stopped. I'm only alive because other people are suffering and dying. I…" She looked to Gale, her eyes bloodshot. "He showed me what would happen to me without his magic and I agreed to being healed, but that's the last time it will happen. Your enchantment is the only reason I remember any of this, and I can't tell you how grateful I am, but it's not a solution. I can't let him kill again. I have to go to the police while I still can."

There was a hint of a question at the end, a door left open in case a scrap of hope wished to enter. Gale searched frantically through every bit of knowledge she'd gained in her research and came up empty.

"She's right," Madrigal said. She didn't sound pleased, but there was also no regret in her tone. "I don't know how he brought her back to life. Even blood magic isn't strong enough to do that on its own. But her being alive is—"

"Don't say it," Gale whispered, and was surprised at the force behind the soft words. Aster looked up, surprised, then seemed to realize Gale wasn't talking to her. "It's not wrong for a person to live. And even if it is, she didn't choose this."

"No. But she knows now." Madrigal looked to Aster, then back to Gale, her expression gentle. "Isn't this what you wanted? For her to know the truth and choose her path? She's obviously a better person than I assumed and doesn't want more blood on her hands than she already has."

"Then we find a way to stop the blood without killing her." Gale stood, putting herself face to face with her teacher. "You're brilliant. I'm willing to do the work. We can figure this out."

Madrigal placed her hands on Gale's shoulders, sending a wave of goosebumps down her arms. "Tell me why it's so important to you. Why you're willing to further upset the balance of life and death for this girl."

Gale glanced back at Aster. She'd drawn her feet up onto the chair, her boots wetting her skirt, and looked more like a child than a trained killer.

"If I deserved a second chance, she does, too," she said, and turned back to Madrigal. "She's had even less of a choice in any of this than I had. It isn't fair that she should die for what he did to her."

"Life isn't fair," Madrigal said, her voice as cold as her touch. "Nor is death. I should know."

"Fine." Gale held her gaze steady. "Then I want to do this because I refuse to believe blood magic can do more good than we can with our power and knowledge. If he could save her, so can we. And if I can, I must. My oath says so."

"Your oath," Madrigal grumbled. She looked away. "I suppose I can't stop you. And if I can't stop you, there's nothing for it but to at least see that you learn something along the way and don't destroy yourself in the process. I assume your oath doesn't demand self-sacrifice?"

"No." Tension flowed out of Gale's muscles. "Thank you."

"Don't thank me yet." Madrigal's stony expression melted, exposing something more frightening—something like pity or grief. "There are lessons here, but I doubt you'll be pleased to learn them."

Gale turned back to Aster. "Madrigal says she'll help me look for some way to fix this."

Aster blinked slowly at her. "Fix it? Don't take this the wrong way, I believe you're both competent witches, but I did mention that I quite literally came apart at the seams?"

"You did. But I'm going to look into healing."

"You can't heal that," Madrigal said. "Magical healing of living tissue only speeds up what was already possible. It's not as simple as enchanting an inanimate object. Lord Death will not be cheated by spells."

Gale ignored her. "Healing," she repeated. "And with true healing might come less pain. Or something more manageable. The important thing is that we control how the curse is broken. Your father has to live long enough for us to do it slowly, so I can fill in the gaps as we go. If he dies and his magic disappears, I can't help."

Madrigal raised an eyebrow but didn't correct her.

A flame kindled in Gale's chest, a mixture of magic, excitement, and hope. "We have to try," she said. "But you need to give me time to research this form of enchantment and come up with some way to save you."

Aster sat up straighter. "I won't see anyone else die for me."

"No, of course not. Madrigal, how long do you think we have?"

Madrigal's brow furrowed. "He killed yesterday, but he'll have used an incredible amount of energy to piece her back together after his little demonstration. And because he's not a vessel like you are, he won't replenish naturally."

"What did she say?" Aster asked.

"He'll need to fill his vessel soon."

Aster took a deep breath. "I suppose I could wait, at least for a few days. It seemed like it would take some time to prepare the new enchantment he wants to try on me."

"What enchantment?" Madrigal asked, and Gale repeated the question.

"He told me it would fix everything—my pain, my scars, the memory problems. I think he plans to do it by turning me into a mindless killing machine to power his magic." Aster blinked, and a tear slipped from her left eye. "He doesn't want me to suffer, so instead of stopping the killing, he'll remove my guilt and my loyalty to anyone but him."

Gale's skin prickled. "So if he did this, you'd kill anyone he wanted?"

"Sounded like it. In any case, I expect he's already looking for his next victim. If we don't figure this out soon, I go to the police." She looked up at Gale with a strange expression on her face.

"What?" Gale asked.

Aster smiled. "I don't know. It's odd. We're talking about me dying, about slim odds and maybes, but I'm glad to have found this before I go. Someone who'll fight for me, whatever her reason. Who thinks I deserve a chance."

"A friend?" Gale asked, and reached out her hand. "I think that might be the word you're looking for."

Aster took it, a half-smile on her lips, and held it for a moment before she let Gale pull her up. "That must be it."

Madrigal let out a huff of breath and vanished into the borderlands.

"So," Aster said. "How do we start?"

"We assess the enchantment," Gale said, and offered her other hand. Aster rested her hands on Gale's, palm to palm, and the fire in the hearth seemed to burn warmer.

Aster's hands were callused, but her touch soft. Gale focused on her magic and on sending it forth, not directing it to do anything, but simply allowing it to feel. The strangeness she'd felt in Aster the first day they met was there, the freshly renewed enchantment not quite hiding itself. Gale opened herself to it. Like her own magic, it seemed to have physical properties without affecting the senses, but this was cold where true magic was warm, dark instead of shining, heavy and deep.

Gale shivered.

"May I touch one of your scars?" she asked.

Aster removed her jacket and rolled up the right sleeve of her blouse, exposing one that cut a ring around her arm. "Goes all the way through," she said, looking ill.

Gale met her eyes. "You must have been terrified when he—" She didn't let herself finish, afraid her anger would come out and ruin everything. "I'm sorry all of this is happening."

Aster smiled sadly. "Better to know and deal with the pain than to go on in ignorance and let others suffer for it. What do you feel?"

Gale moved one hand up to the scar. The magic was stronger,

somehow tense, like a coiled spring. "There's a lot of energy here, and it's working hard. I'd guess you feel pain when things get a little loose, and when your father—"

"Eamon," Aster said. "I'd prefer we not call him anything else."

"Eamon," Gale repeated, tasting his name like poison. "May I ask you something about him?"

Aster laughed under her breath. "I don't think I owe it to him to keep his secrets now."

"I mentioned a curse on my hometown last spring. It was caused by blood magic that was purchased in Queen's Run. Is there any chance he was responsible?"

Her heart pounded as Aster thought it over.

"I don't know." Aster shrugged one shoulder. "I'm sorry. Yesterday I'd have said it was impossible, but now I don't know anything."

"All right. Thank you."

Even if it wasn't him, what he was doing was more of the same. Gale decided he could suffer the weight of her hatred for what had happened to Bright Hollow, at least for now.

"I wish I'd asked you more yesterday," Aster said. "About this enchantment, about all of it. I don't even know what you mean when you say *vessel*."

Gale traced her fingers over the scar on Aster's arm, and Aster shivered.

"They're objects that hold a reserve of magic, that amplify and strengthen the magic that's put into them. Most witches are vessels, carrying magic in our bodies, but blood magic is such a corrupting force that it atrophies the channels our power normally passes through." She remained focused on the enchantment as she spoke, but the words came easily after the reading she'd been doing. "I have one to amplify power from potions and to use as a generous well to draw from if I drain myself, but my own magic replenishes naturally, if slowly. In a blood witch, it flows through the body from a vessel or a more direct source, but it can't linger. If Eamon were to break his vessel, he'd have nothing. At least, not until he started over from scratch."

"And that would be the end of the enchantment?"

Gale thought back over her recent lessons. "I believe so. A natural witch's enchantments can outlive her by a thousand years if she sets them up properly, but again, blood magic comes with costs. Yours deteriorates quickly because of its corruption." She hated that word, which had been used to scare her away from magic for most of her life, but it was the only one that truly fit. "When he heals you, he's shoring up weak spots. Blood magic is strong, but fragile. Powerful, but easily shattered. Without him or his magic…"

"That's the end for me." Aster looked down at Gale's hand resting on her arm.

"Which means we need to work quickly. I don't suppose he told you anything else useful? Explained the enchantment, showed off his vessel?"

"Neither." Aster's full lips pursed slightly. "It's all a bit of a mess in my mind. There was something about putting together the pieces of my shattered heart. The rest was all blood and broken bones."

Gale's heartbeat quickened, and she reminded herself to be professional. She'd examined patients before, back at the clinic. This was no different, save for the magic involved. "Might I feel your heart?"

Aster hesitated, then reached for the buttons beneath the lace at her throat. "Whatever you need." She opened her blouse, revealing a fitted undergarment of cream-coloured cotton that laced up the front. It cut low between her breasts, revealing a mass of scar tissue that covered her breastbone and branched into the flesh above, paler than the skin that surrounded it.

How could anyone survive this? Gale wondered, then remembered the unthinkable truth.

She hadn't.

God help me.

Gale rested a hand against Aster's breastbone, trying to keep her breath slow and praying she wouldn't blush. Aster's skin was warm, and her heart beat hard and fast.

"Don't be nervous," Gale said, and closed her eyes.

"I'm not," Aster answered. In spite of everything, there was a smile in her voice. Gale's own heart picked up in response, matching Aster's beat for beat.

Focus, Gale.

The magic in Aster's chest was overwhelming. Gale squeezed her eyes tighter and willed her magic to go deeper to feel it out. There was a distinct shape to it, almost as though—

The hairs on her arms stood on end. "It's not just scars," she said. Her voice sounded cold and distant. "Parts of your heart must have been destroyed. He's replaced them with something else. It feels like pure magic."

"Can you heal that?"

Gale didn't answer. She didn't want to until she had some answer other than *no.*

She drew her magic back from Aster's body, willing it to hide itself within her again, but it wouldn't come.

A dark, fathoms-deep chill crept up through her magic like a climbing vine, making its way into Gale's body, flowing up her arms and toward her heart. Her skin turned cold, and panic rang through her like pealing bells.

"No," she whispered. She didn't know how to defend herself from a blood enchantment, but her next words came easily, in the cadence of a spell. "May this darkness be cast out of me," she murmured, her voice low and her breath hitching, "and let the armour of true magic protect me from its poison. Let my power be sheltered behind impenetrable walls and cast out the enemy."

She didn't realize until the words stopped that she'd been speaking them in old Andonian. Not praying, but commanding magic with her own words instead of an established spell.

The dark power flowed back out through her hands, and her own familiar magic returned to her. But a portion of the dark power lingered, moving more slowly now that it was cut off from its source, making her want to tear her skin off to release it.

She bolted, knocking a chair over and toppling a stack of books as she ran to the kitchen. Aster called out behind her, but Gale barely heard as she searched through the cupboards until she found a tonic of hagerwort. She poured it onto her hands, mindless of how expensive the aquatic herb was and how difficult it had been to come by, and rubbed it over her skin from fingertips to elbows. It smelled like a mixture of vanilla and slightly rotten fish, but the last traces of dark magic left her as she repeated her spell. She collapsed into the chair beside the kitchen table and touched the leaves of one of the plants that covered it, trying to ground herself in something alive and good.

Aster stood in the doorway, looking as terrified as Gale felt. "What happened?"

"Exactly what I'd like to know," Madrigal said, appearing as though from nowhere. "I felt that."

Gale drew a long, shaking breath, feeling like she'd outrun a pack of hungry wolves. "It knew I was there. It was trying to protect itself."

"Excellent," Madrigal said. She leaned back against the stove. "Another complication was exactly what this situation needed."

Aster sat on the floor, her back against the doorframe, and buttoned her blouse. "It's bad, right?"

Gale nodded. "Can you leave home now? Run away?"

Aster looked down at her hands. "He's expecting me home soon, and he already mistrusts me enough that he sent Roddy to keep an eye on me. He made it clear he could revoke the enchantment at any time, but didn't say whether there was a limit to the distance he could do it from. If he thinks I've gone to turn him in…"

"Right. We won't chance it." Gale took a moment to observe

her body. Everything felt normal, except she couldn't shake the repugnant sense that she'd been invaded. "If you go home now, can you get away again? Tonight?"

"I can't sneak out," Aster said. "He'll figure things out as soon as he finds me missing, and we'll be no better off than we are now. Better for me to make up a reason to disappear for a few days to buy a little more time."

"How about a week? If he knows he won't need it right away he might hold off on replenishing his magic for that long."

"I can try."

"Good. We need to get you out of that house, and I'll need your help." A plan was forming in Gale's mind. It was vague and tenuous, fragile as a spider's web and twice as thin, but it was something. "In the meantime, I'm going to ask Jes for help."

Aster laughed. "There's no way."

Gale smiled back, though without feeling at all amused. "Eamon wants her dead, doesn't he? If I know Jes, that will give us a foot in the door as long as our plan ends with him disappearing."

"And as for keeping me alive?"

"Your money will have to make up for her lack of motivation there."

Madrigal cocked her head to one side, observing Gale. "What are you thinking?"

"I'm not quite sure yet," she said. "We'll need the knowledge of a hundred witches, which we can get from the library, but I think those books will tell me I can't heal a heart that's missing large pieces."

"Good guess," Madrigal said, but she sounded interested rather than dismissive.

Aster leaned forward. "You're going to ask Jes for a heart?"

Gale shrugged. "Why not?"

When Roddy found her, Aster was two blocks from the house, walking with her basket filled with bread from the bakery below Gale's flat and eggs she'd purchased at a shop closer to home. She walked past him, barely glancing his way.

"Miss?"

Though she'd expected it, Aster's shoulders hunched defensively at the sound of Roddy's voice behind her. She mustered a smile and turned.

"Do I know you, sir?"

"Your father sent me." Roddy stood with his legs slightly spread, hands at his sides, relaxed but ready for a fight if it came. "You've been gone longer than expected. He's worried."

Aster took a step back. Not because it was Roddy, but because she would have under normal circumstances if any strange man offered to escort her somewhere. It would seem strange if she let her guard down, and for that she was grateful.

"I'm quite capable of escorting myself," she said, aiming for a soft tone fit for a cautious young lady and not one in fear for her life. "Thank you for your concern."

Roddy smiled, warm and genuine. He wasn't a handsome

man, but if Aster hadn't known better, she'd have thought he seemed quite pleasant. "He told you he was going to bring a friend home, right? I'm the friend. Roderick Bates at your service." He bowed slightly, but didn't offer to let her call him Roddy this time.

"Of course, Mister Bates. How nice to meet you. I suppose we could walk together?"

He offered his arm, but she pretended not to notice.

They walked the rest of the way without speaking, Aster maintaining her awareness of his movements with every step. Roddy kept a sharp eye on her, and Aster was careful not to give even a hint that she wanted to be going anywhere but home.

Necessary, she reminded herself, and she wouldn't be there long.

As long as Eamon believed he'd stolen her memories, there was one sure way to get him to let her out of the house again. Jes would be helping in more ways than she realized.

Eamon was waiting at the door when they arrived. Aster handed him the basket.

"I think I've found her," she said, and waited for Roddy to leave them to their conversation, but it seemed he had nowhere else to be.

Eamon raised his eyebrows. "The wolf?"

"The wolf." Aster kept her tone cool and businesslike. "I decided to extend my walk and visit a lovely bakery I'd heard about, and I ran into a contact. It seems Jesamyn, or whatever she's calling herself these days, is heading out of the city tonight. She's been hiding here in town, but she's leaving for Farvale. I plan to be there to meet her."

"Hmm." Eamon frowned. "That'd take you away for a week."

Aster forced her expression to remain as he'd expect—eager for the hunt, not terrified of being denied a chance to leave home again. "Not quite. I'm feeling well, I don't think healing would be an issue."

Eamon and Roddy exchanged a look, and Aster hoped her heart wouldn't stop dead in her chest, crushed under the silence in the hallway.

"You've done well," Eamon said, and Aster forced herself to breathe. "Didn't I tell you she was exceptional, Roddy?"

"You did." Roddy looked down at Aster. "I wonder whether it mightn't be prudent to let someone else finish up that bit of work, though."

Aster's heart skipped. "This is my job. My revenge." She looked to Eamon. "You said so."

"I wanted it to be," Eamon said. "But I suppose, now that we're so close, there would be no harm in accepting help."

"I think not," Aster said, putting on her haughtiest tone and throwing in a hint of wounded pride. "I've done this myself every step of the way. Do you think me incapable?"

"Not at all." He stroked his beard as he thought it over. "But remember what happened last time, when you ended up in jail. She'll be ready for you this time, as well."

"Not as ready as I'll be." Aster returned Roddy's brooding glare, then focused on Eamon. "I have not run this race only to let someone else step in and cross the finish line for me."

Eamon set the market basket down and took Aster's hands in his. "You're right, of course. You've proven yourself so many times. It's a shame you have to be away for Solvar Eve, but perhaps this timing is appropriate."

"New beginnings," Aster agreed, though she hoped they would be nothing like what he intended.

Eamon didn't speak for a moment, lost again in thought. "Farvale won't do," he said. "She'll have defences planned at her destination as she does at home, so you'll do better to catch her before then. There are a limited number of inns along the way, and only so much she can do to keep herself safe. Or take her on the road if you can. If you can't do it in two nights, I want you to return so we can finish our work on your enchantments. The kill can wait."

Objections came to mind, but died on Aster's lips. Her usual self might point out that he'd never told her how to do her job before, but he wasn't wrong. Fighting for more time would raise suspicion.

She lowered her gaze. "I'll do my best."

"Good. Be quick, and be careful."

Aster buzzed with irritation and excitement but was careful to show none of it. She had less than half the time she'd asked for, but at least it was something.

It had come too easily, and she had no doubt she'd be followed again, but she'd deal with that in its own time.

"I will, as always." She squeezed his hands tight and climbed the stairs, stopping to look back only when she'd reached the top. "I'll need to pack and prepare. Would you arrange a carriage for this evening?"

"Of course." Eamon smiled up at her. Nothing seemed odd or out of place, but having his eyes on her made Aster feel as though she'd touched a dead fish. "Enjoy your quest for justice, my dear. When you return, everything will change for the better."

Aster forced a smile and turned away, considering who, exactly, it would be better for.

She went to her room, took her cloak from the closet, and laid it on the bed. Only when she heard Eamon and Roddy's voices disappear into the basement did she leave her room and climb into the attic to collect her weapons.

She hoped she wouldn't need them once she left the house, but it never hurt to be prepared.

CHAPTER TWENTY-THREE
ASTER

A black carriage rolled up the street four hours after a spectacular winter sunset. Days would be getting longer soon, leaving the wolves and vigilantes of the world with less night to cloak themselves in.

But tonight it was perfect.

Aster wore a brown wool dress with dull black buttons up the front of the bodice, plain and sturdy for travel, under a matching coat. She carried only an overstuffed satchel and refused the driver's offer to take it as she climbed into the carriage. Eamon had already given him his instructions when he ordered the service. He was to take Aster outside the city, heading toward the inn at the Onderbil crossroads where the fictional Jes would likely be spending the night.

Aster didn't plan to make it that far.

The carriage rocked and bumped gently as it made its way down the street. Aster removed her coat, opened her satchel, and pulled out her red cloak. She kept her dress on beneath it, but with the cloak's dark folds surrounding her and the addition of a belt holding six throwing knives, the dagger in her boot, and a coil of wire with flat wooden handles at each end in her dress pocket, she felt ready for the night's work. Aside from those, all she carried was a spare dress, her full supply of cash, and Eamon's dagger.

He'd have thought it odd if she hadn't taken it, but she hated the weight of it in her bag, and she shuddered when her fingers brushed against it and she imagined it delivering the souls of her prey to Eamon.

She'd wanted them dead, removed from her world and delivered to whatever awaited them beyond this life. But that—to be destroyed entirely, burned up as fuel for magic—was an unthinkable punishment.

Aster knelt on the seat and opened the curtains covering the back window. There were plenty of carriages out, full of people heading to holiday parties or to visit family, to sing songs by candlelight and feast on roast goose and heaping piles of sweets. But after a few blocks, she picked out the one that was following her, identifiable only by the perfect white star on the forehead of the big bay horse pulling it. They were staying nearly a block back. Not much, but a clear attempt to not be too obvious.

Good evening, Roddy.

Aster closed her satchel, slung its long strap across her chest beneath her cloak, fastened the buckle, and waited until her carriage reached Alderbury Road. The shipping yards by the river had gone dark when workers were sent home to spend the night with their families. Lamps still burned in places, but the darkness between them was going to be the best chance she'd have to slip away before the carriage left the city.

Massive, hulking buildings blotted out sections of the star-filled sky above, providing a multitude of hiding places if only she could get to them.

She ordered herself to be patient, and waited.

Her driver made the turn around the corner of a large brick building that butted against the street, momentarily cutting off the view of the carriage behind.

In one smooth motion, Aster opened the door, quiet as a breeze, and stepped out onto the running board, careful to hold her cloak close so it wouldn't be caught in the door as it clicked shut.

Then down to the ground, hitting the road running, and disappearing into the shadows of a broad, flat yard, empty save for a few carts loaded with crates. She crouched in the shadows behind its crumbling stone wall and watched until her carriage was gone, and Roddy's after it. Then she felt along the wall until she found a loose stone in the corner near the ground, pulled it free, and wedged Eamon's dagger into the empty space before she jammed the stone back into a rough semblance of its proper place.

It would have to do. She couldn't bear its weight anymore and had no desire to carry it into Gale's home.

No more carriages came down the road, and neither hers nor Roddy's returned.

By the time he realized she'd vanished, he'd be three hours outside the city, and if Eamon ever had a chance to confront her about it, she'd tell him she'd suspected she was being followed by Jes's people.

What mattered now was that he couldn't know for sure what had happened. She hoped that sliver of uncertainty would be enough to stay his hand if he considered withdrawing the enchantment and killing her.

But if all went well, Eamon would never have a chance to ask.

The journey to Gale's neighbourhood progressed uneventfully, with Aster sticking close to the shadows, hood pulled up to shield her face from anyone who might recognize her. Plenty of folks were about, but all seemed wrapped up in their own cheerful business and disinclined to stare at cloaked strangers on dark streets.

It was only when the bakery came into view that Aster's stomach tightened and her steps slowed.

She stood at the entrance to the alley, knowing she shouldn't linger in the street but needing to sort out why she felt so strange. It wasn't fear, exactly. Gale was largely still a mystery, but nothing in Aster said she was a threat. She was a friend. Kind. Lovely. Intriguing. A bit too earnest, perhaps, and the moments when she acted tough fit her like a badly sized glove, but…

Aster scuffed one boot against the ground.

Nervous. That's the word I'm looking for. A silly way to feel when there were life-and-death decisions to be made and no room for distraction, but there it was. She liked Gale, and part of her desperately wanted to be liked in return, not just seen as a project or the tragic victim of a dark enchantment.

And not just as a friend, either.

A foolish notion, but she decided that under any circumstances it would be rude to show up empty-handed, especially when Gale had done so much for her and tried so hard to refuse payment for most of it.

The bakery was busier tonight, and Aster had to wait for three other customers to be served before Pria was free to attend to her.

The young baker smiled. "Friend of the lady upstairs, right? Bought bread earlier. What can I get for you?"

Pria clearly knew Gale went by a few names and wasn't willing to make assumptions about which she'd given to Aster. "I am. Actually, I was wondering whether you could tell me what she likes here."

Pria's lips quirked to one side as she thought it over. "The sweet tea, obviously. Did you enjoy it?"

"It was delicious. And the bun, too." In truth, Aster had been too distracted to really appreciate the tea and had given most of the bun to the pigeons on the way home because of the knots in her stomach, but she wasn't about to say so.

"She does like those. And the honey cakes. And the cherry pinwheels."

Aster looked into the glass case. It was less full than it had been earlier, with only a smattering of each baked good left, but she spotted dark, dense fruitcake, frosted strawberry tarts, and slices of raisin bread along with Gale's favourites. "I'll take two of whatever you've got, and two cups of that same tea."

Pria beamed.

A few minutes later Aster stood at Gale's door, her purse a little lighter but her hands full as she carried three white cake boxes tied with pink string and two cups of tea precariously balanced on top. She gave the door two gentle kicks, though she assumed Madrigal had already announced her arrival.

It felt strange to have accepted the existence of a ghost. Her natural inclination was to cling to a sliver of doubt so she could claim to have known all along when it was revealed as a clever trick, but there that was too. She believed.

Gale opened the door and stepped aside to let Aster in. The flat was pleasantly warm, the smell of soil and plants and drying herbs as welcoming as the nervous smile Gale flashed her. She wore her thick hair piled on her head in a loose bun, and the errant strands that brushed her shoulders gave her a soft, undone look that made Aster feel like the floor had gone out from under her.

"You made it!" Gale said. "Did he suspect anything?"

"Maybe. Not enough to chain me in the basement."

"We'll call that a victory, then. What in the world is all this?" Gale took the boxes and the tea, freeing Aster to lock the door behind her and remove her boots and cloak, which she left in the dark side of the room with the trappings of Gale's professional life.

"Sustenance." Aster thought back on the contents of the boxes.

"Not the most nutritious, but I thought necessary." She followed Gale through her cheerful living space, which had been cleared of books and papers, and into the little kitchen. Gale set the boxes on the counter next to a plate piled high with sandwiches and opened them.

"Definitely necessary," she said, and leaned in to sniff at the sweet, spice, and fruit scents. "I made food for our bodies. Yours will feed our souls."

She spoke as though completely enraptured, and something warm and strange flowed through Aster from her heart to her toes.

Only it's not entirely my *heart*, she thought, remembering what Gale had said about dark magic filling the gaps. It was enough to put a damper on the good feelings, but not to erase them. The enchantment was a problem. Eamon was a problem. They'd be dealt with soon. But for now, in this tiny sliver of time and space, all was well. The fire was burning, the flat warm. There was food and tea and excellent company.

She wished she could pretend nothing else mattered.

"Is Madrigal here?" she asked.

"Not at the moment. I asked for privacy." Gale cleared her throat and busied herself with placing pastries and sandwiches on a set of weathered plates she took from the shelf. "You seemed to prefer it that way before, and she wanted time to do some thinking about the difficulties of your physical condition."

"Such as?"

Gale turned to her, her smile too bright. Aster's stomach sank. "Nothing we can't overcome given enough time and the right help. I spoke to Jes and have a meeting tomorrow with a friend of hers. Long shot, but I'm hopeful."

"Two days would be plenty of time, I suppose?" Aster tried to make it sound like a joke, but it was useless. "I couldn't get more. I almost didn't get any."

Gale pressed her lips together and nodded slowly. "If that's what we have, we'll make it work. Come on, I'm starving."

As the table in the kitchen was covered in a jungle of thriving garden plants, they spread a quilt out on the floor by the fire and laid out all the food. Gale had made a variety of sandwiches filled with egg, vegetables, cheese, and potted meat. Between them and the bakery goodies, there wasn't much room for human bodies on the blanket. Still, they both ignored the armchairs and sat on the floor, their backs to the fire, and dug into the feast without any care for proper courses.

"Phenomenal," Gale said, her mouth full of flaky cherry pinwheel. She brushed the crumbs from the front of her dress. "I needed this."

"Me, too." Aster set aside her cinnamon bun, which she was quite enjoying now that she was relaxed enough to do so, and took another bite of the cucumber-and-cheese sandwich she'd set down a moment before. "Food and sleep."

She had slept most of a day away after Eamon's demonstration, but its benefits felt false and thin. With good food and warm drink in her belly, the exhaustion of the past weeks and months were catching up with her.

"I love sleep," Gale agreed.

Aster raised her nearly empty cup. "To common interests."

"Indeed." Gale tapped her paper cup against Aster's. "I suppose we do have other common interests we should discuss."

"Right." But neither spoke of enchantments or plans. Aster looked over the remaining food and decided she didn't have room for more. Still, she wasn't quite ready for real life to return. "You never told me your family name. Unless it's Alcorini?"

Gale wrinkled her nose. "It is not. I borrowed that from a famous witch who lived a hundred years ago. Seemed like the sort of thing a fake one would do." She pulled her knees up to her chest and wrapped her arms around them. "I don't really have one now. It's just Gale. Or Nightingale. I don't have a family anymore, and I don't like to pretend that I do."

Aster shifted closer, until she could have touched Gale's hand. "I'm sorry. Do you miss them?"

"Often." Gale smiled sadly. "I miss them, but not everything they still carry with them. The people of Bright Hollow don't much care for witches. I don't regret what I am, or using magic to save them. I hope I'll do more good in the world as a witch than I could have stuck in a tiny village for my entire life, but it's hard. Especially at this time of year."

"Do you hate them?" The question was out before Aster had considered that it might be too personal, but Gale didn't seem upset by it.

"No. A part of me wants to, but I can't. They made me who I am, and I still hope that someday they'll break free of their cage as I've tried to do." She brushed a tear from her cheek and turned to Aster. "You know, I was horrified when Jes told me you'd killed people who had hurt you. I wondered how someone could do something like that. But when I consider the curse and remember the people it killed—my dear friend Willow, children, people I knew all my life, who were like family to me—I think I understand. I want to find the person who cursed us." She shivered. "I swore before God that I'd never kill anyone, that I'd heal and not harm, but it's more complicated than I ever expected."

"It is. I'm sorry. I shouldn't have asked."

"No, it's good." Gale wiped her cheeks again and smiled, warm and genuine in spite of the shine in her eyes. "I don't talk about it with anyone, really. Jes and Cas know what happened, but not all of what it meant. And it's complicated for Madrigal. I don't like her to know I have mixed feelings about my freedom, so..." She shrugged. "Thank you."

"Of course." Aster surveyed the mess of half-eaten treats and discarded sandwich crusts, then got to work packing everything away, unsure of what else to say. Gale joined her, and soon the room was back to what it had been before.

"Where did the books go?"

"Oh." Gale returned from the kitchen, where she'd carried the plates. "I have plenty of storage space. Doesn't really do to leave evidence of my work lying around." She crossed to the bookshelf, and open the cupboard beneath to reveal the sweaters Aster had found there before. Then Gale closed the doors and whispered something under her breath, and when she opened the cupboard again the shelves were packed with books and papers. "I returned some to the library today when I was out, too."

Aster raised an eyebrow. "The library has books on magic?"

Gale glanced back at her, sly and secretive. "Not the library you've been to."

Aster decided not to ask, curious as she was. She wanted to know everything about how Gale had gone from her old life to becoming a witch, how she'd fallen in with someone like Jes, how she and Madrigal had met. But that was the past. It only mattered if there was a future, and Aster couldn't be sure she had one of those, with Gale or without her. The present was what she had, and it would have to be enough.

They took turns visiting the outdoor toilets in the yard behind the building, which served the businesses and flats surrounding it, then cleaning their teeth at the kitchen sink with water they'd hauled up from the well. Nothing here was as convenient as it was at home with its indoor plumbing and spacious rooms, but it felt comfortable, like they'd been following this routine for years.

Only when Gale's hand brushed against hers as they passed in the kitchen did the newness of it all strike Aster with a lightning bolt of excitement and that nervousness she was so unaccustomed to. And when Gale went behind the screens that divided the room and returned dressed for bed, her body free beneath the white cotton and her dark hair flowing over her shoulders, the world seemed to shift in a pleasant but terrifying way.

When Gale offered to let her borrow a nightgown, Aster

declined. Her clothes felt like armour, and she was accustomed to sleeping in them.

Once everything was attended to and Gale had commanded the fire to burn low, they stood side by side, looking at the narrow bed in the corner.

"Well," Gale said.

"Well."

Aster allowed herself to imagine sharing the space. They'd both fit if they positioned themselves properly. Back to front, arm around, the scent of Gale's hair on the pillow. Or maybe one girl on her back and the other on her side, and then—

Don't. A pang of pain unrelated to her scars squeezed at Aster's chest.

There was a good chance she'd be dead in a week unless Gale managed to pull off a miracle. Spending time with her was making Aster regret not experiencing some aspects of life more fully. Not only physical pleasure, which she'd had fleeting experience with when she was away from the prying eyes and gossiping tongues of the city, but falling into something deep and unexpected with another person, knowing them in ways most others never would, fighting and forgiving and growing together.

Her life had been about seeking justice and preparing for the life that would follow when the wolves were dead, and there had been no time for intimate friendships or romance.

Now that it seemed there might not be a life to follow, it was tempting to think of grabbing on to what she could of those things with a girl who might have been everything to her under other circumstances, to take what time she had left and make the most of it, to burn bright before her fire went out.

But it wouldn't be fair to Gale, who had already lost so much. She deserved better than to be consumed in Aster's dying flames.

"This'll be fine." Aster took one of the folded blankets from the end of the bed and set it on the floor as a pillow. "It won't even be the least comfortable place I've slept in the past month."

Gale's brow furrowed. "But you're my guest."

Aster bit back a laugh. "You're doing all the work to save my life right now. Rest while you can."

"Very kind of you." Gale offered a thin smile. "I thought rich folks would demand the best spot as their right. I much prefer a person with real manners. Shall I put out the fire?"

Aster watched the low flames burning in the fireplace, holding back the darkness. "You could leave it. I don't mind."

"All right." Gale got into bed and lay on her back, looking up at the ceiling, and pulled a blanket up to her shoulders. "Goodnight, Aster."

"Goodnight, Gale." Aster lay down on the floor rolled onto her side, facing the kitchen doorway. The floor beneath her created pressure points on her hip and arm. She tried to relax into it as she had so often before, but no matter how long she lay still, sleep wouldn't come. When she reasoned Gale might be asleep and wouldn't feel badly about her discomfort, she rolled over, slow and quiet, and tried to find a better position.

She told herself to mind her own business and leave Gale with her privacy as she slept. But she let her eye open a crack, and found Gale still lying on her back, her eyes closed. Tears had wet the skin at her temples, and her lips moved in silent whispers.

Aster sat up, but didn't go to her. If she was talking to Madrigal—but no, she always spoke aloud to the ghost.

Gale rolled onto her side and wiped her eyes. "Am I keeping you awake?"

"No, the floor's doing that." Aster crawled closer. "Are you all right?"

Gale tucked one hand under her head. The firelight flickered in her eyes, and her nose and cheeks had reddened as though she'd been out in the cold. "I was praying. Do you think that's silly?"

Aster smiled and sat beside the bed, legs crossed. "You've

convinced me you speak to a ghost. Who am I to say your God isn't also listening?"

"I wonder sometimes." Gale sighed, long and heavy. "I was raised to seek God's will in all things, and I believed I was doing that when I chose to pursue magic, even though it went against everything we believed at home. I still believe this is the right path for me, but the world is so much more muddled than it seemed when I was growing up. So many things seem right and wrong at the same time, and I don't know which way to turn."

"Saving me, you mean?"

"That's one thing," Gale said. "Maybe it's selfish for me to want to save you. Maybe someone bringing you back was wrong in the first place. But you dying again is wrong, too. You've lost so much, and the thought of everything being taken from you again angers me. You were taught to believe things someone thought best for you, but you deserve a chance to find your own way, to have freedom you never knew you were missing. I think God would want that for anyone."

"I hope so." Aster began to scoot back toward her makeshift bed, but Gale reached out and touched her shoulder.

"There's room up here," she said, and rolled over to face the wall, leaving space on the mattress behind her. "If you want."

Aster wanted to resist, but strength of will only went so far. She climbed into bed and pulled the blanket over her, shaping her body to Gale's. Her clothes and Gale's nightgown separated them by several layers of fabric, but when Aster rested her arm over Gale's waist, Gale's hand found hers, skin on skin.

There was no more to it. No movement, no more quiet words.

But as she lay with her head on the pillow next to Gale's, the scent of pine and lavender surrounding and soothing her, Aster decided that if tonight was to be one of her last nights alive, this was a fine way to spend it.

CHAPTER TWENTY-FOUR
GALE

Madrigal appeared as Gale made her way up a wide, tree-lined avenue the next morning. True to her word, the ghost hadn't returned the night before, or even during the brief time Gale and Aster had spent breakfasting on leftover pastries and carefully not discussing or speculating about anything of actual importance.

"Don't fiddle with your sleeves," Madrigal said, not unkindly. "You're showing your nerves and it will make you stand out." She turned to take in the houses, family homes of brick and timber that were a little closer to the factories than wealthier folks might have preferred, but nicer than those in Gale's neighbourhood. "Is this where the inventor lives?"

"Next street over, I think." Gale kept up her pace and forced her hands to rest at her sides, though for some reason they felt awkward no matter what she did with them.

Jes had reluctantly agreed to let her speak to her friend Henry, but only if Cas agreed and accompanied her. Gale hadn't told her she'd be too frightened to speak to a brilliant stranger alone anyway and had accepted Cas's presence as though it were a concession on her part and not an absolute necessity.

She'd declined his offer to pick her up in a cab, preferring to let the long walk soothe her nerves.

Bare-limbed oaks reached out over the street, casting thin shadows across the road and sidewalks that had been cleared of snow. There were few people out. Most were probably busy preparing for the celebration of whatever Eve it was in their household, cooking or shopping or wrapping gifts if that were part of their tradition. Still, Gale kept her voice quiet and tried not to look like she was talking to herself.

Madrigal had no need to lower her voice. "Did you have a good evening with your guest?"

"It was quite pleasant." Gale turned to Madrigal, just for a second. "You really weren't listening in?"

"Not this time. I wondered whether things might get unprofessional and decided I'd trust you to tell me anything relevant."

Gale smiled. "Nothing too unprofessional. We had a lovely supper, talked for a while. There wasn't much I could tell her until after this meeting, so we just got to know each other."

She thought of waking well past sunrise and finding that she'd rolled over in the night, that Aster now lay on her back and Gale was the one with her arm around her guest, and decided not to tell Madrigal about that part.

Or about Aster almost poisoning both of them because she'd found an old jar labelled *TEA* that Gale was using to hold dried burnberry leaves, which were beneficial in the tiny doses she added to her pain potion but would have had them both choking on blood if they'd consumed the tea Aster had so thoughtfully made.

Madrigal had lectured her enough on properly labelling everything and not leaving it to memory. There was no need to let her say "I told you so" now.

"You really like her," Madrigal said.

"I do. When Jes told me about the murders I thought my positive first impression of her had been wrong, but it wasn't. She's interesting. Lost for the moment, but she'll find her way through." Gale paused. "I'm not getting attached. I know how long the odds are of us saving her."

"Good. I'd hate to have to remind you." Madrigal walked backward in front of her, hands clasped behind her back. "They're not just long odds. They're—"

"I know. But I can't give up when there are possibilities left to explore."

They turned the corner onto a dead-end street. Gale stopped. "That's it." She nodded to the house at the end of the road, which would either contain the answer to her prayers or the greatest disappointment she could currently imagine. She stared it down until she heard footsteps on the sidewalk behind her.

"Cas."

"Gale. Madrigal." He couldn't be certain the ghost was there, but he tended to assume. Madrigal returned the greeting, and Gale passed it along.

He'd dressed well this morning, as Gale had aspired to do. Her fitted coat covered most of her dress, and she wore several layers of petticoats beneath to give the skirt fashionable fullness. The skirt was long enough that her shabby boots were hardly noticeable.

Cas offered his arm, and she took it, holding tight as they started toward Henry's house.

"You're not scared, are you?" Cas asked.

"Could you blame me if I were? You and Jes have talked about the mysterious Henry enough that he's become a bit of a legend in my mind, and I'm well aware of his feelings toward magic."

"Don't worry about that too much," Cas said, but Gale wasn't reassured by the false confidence in his voice. "It's not like where you come from. He doesn't have religious objections, but practical ones. He likes things he can understand—physical forces, gravity, melting points, leverage and whatnot. Predictable and measurable things."

"Science," Gale offered.

"Exactly. Magic is more of a mystery and an art, proven to exist but not obeying the laws he's so fond of. He doesn't understand it, and therefore doesn't trust it and would prefer to ignore its existence entirely." He glanced down at Gale and patted the gloved hand that rested on his forearm. "You've overcome worse, even in your own heart. This should be no trouble at all."

"And what of ghosts?" Madrigal asked.

Gale's steps slowed, and Cas with her. "Madrigal wonders whether he'd be comfortable with her being there."

"I haven't told him anything about you, and I'm not sure he'd believe me if I did," he said, speaking directly to Madrigal, though he wasn't looking at her. "That said, Jes told me to ask that you wait outside, or wherever you're comfortable. I can't stop you if you want to come in, and neither he nor I will know the difference. But she thought it best that there be no apparent magic, no ghosts listening in. We try to keep things honest with Henry, at least when it can't get him in trouble."

Gale braced herself for an outburst, but Madrigal only sighed. "I have no wish to go where I'm not wanted. I'll listen as I can."

Before Gale could object, she vanished.

"She's gone." They resumed their walk toward the end of the street. "I feel terrible."

"I do, too. You'll thank her for me later?"

"Of course."

The street felt lonelier without Madrigal there, even with Cas on her arm. Gale tried to imagine what it was like to be a ghost, present but removed from the world, unable to touch it or influence it directly, either unwanted or completely invisible almost everywhere she went.

It's no wonder she's desperate to leave.

The two-storey brick house at the end of the street sat alone, a monarch on its throne while the houses that lined the sides of the street stood like courtiers seeking its favour. It wasn't a particularly grand home compared to some in the city, but its broad frame and fenced yard seemed quite a lot for one inventor to occupy all alone.

They passed through the gate and between rows of bushes so overgrown they had to walk single file up the path. Gale shoved her hands deep in her coat pockets to keep them from trembling.

"Worst he can do is say no," Cas reminded her.

"That's exactly what I'm afraid of."

Jes had made no promises except that she'd set up a meeting with the one person she knew to have done any work with artificial limbs and organs. Gale tried not to let her hope or her fear carry her away.

Cas knocked three times. It was several minutes before the door opened and a bare-faced young man not much taller than Gale herself peered out at them. His shirt was untucked, his trousers creased, and his hair mussed, but Gale knew enough from Jes and Cas's stories to feel herself lucky he'd dressed in proper clothing for their visit.

He squinted at her. "This the witch?" His voice was husky but not unpleasant.

"I am." Gale held her hand out. "Nightingale, but you can call me Gale."

Henry offered her hand a half-hearted shake and stepped aside to allow them to enter.

The house beyond the foyer was a mess, but not as bad as Gale had expected. Henry led them through a large wood-panelled entryway strewn with half-full—or perhaps half-emptied—boxes, past a wide staircase leading up into darkness, and into the parlour, where a pair of mannequins dressed in old armour stood at attention on either side of the cold, empty hearth. A huge mirror in an ornate gold frame hung slightly askew over the fireplace, a bright spot against blue papered walls.

Henry sank into a green armchair and gestured for his guests to take the sofa, putting their backs to the big front window. "Jes said in her message you have an interest in mechanical organ replacement?"

To the point. Gale appreciated that given the current state of her nerves.

"Hearts specifically," she said. She sat and folded her hands in her lap, leaving her gloves on to hide her missing finger. Henry knew what she was, but he didn't need extra reminders of that reality.

Henry leaned forward. "Why?"

"I have a friend whose heart isn't working. I thought a replacement might be in order, and… well, other options are obviously limited. Cas had told me you were working on this sort of thing, so it seemed worth a shot."

"Indeed. I was working on it, but quite some time ago."

"Before the clockwork soldiers?" Cas asked.

"Hmm." Henry glanced at the mannequins as though he'd forgotten about them. "I do need to get back to those someday. Balance is such an issue. Before them, and before a certain jewellery-making project a friend came to me about a few years ago."

"And the hearts?" Gale asked, hoping to keep the conversation somewhat on track.

Henry folded his hands and leaned back in his chair. "The heart is essentially a mechanical pump, which interested me. Much simpler to understand and recreate than other organs. I made good progress, had some working prototypes I was pleased with."

The skin on the back of Gale's neck prickled. "But?"

"But," Henry said, sounding disgusted, "all it was good for was display, a fascinating curiosity I could sell to that school of medicine if I ever needed the money, and nothing more. There would be too many problems putting it in a living person, recovery and infection and such. Power is the biggest issue, though. The heart beats. It pumps when I can get it going. But even if one could keep the patient alive long enough to make the swap and manage everything that would come after, its owner would have to remain bedridden forever, connected to an engine to power it. I couldn't find anything else to..." His voice trailed off, and he looked from Gale to Cas and back again. "No. I see where this is going. Absolutely not."

"Henry, please," Cas said, his voice low and soft. "Just listen."

Gale pulled her shoulders back and sat up straighter. "I understand that you don't care for magic, Mister Ward, but—"

"Call me Henry, please. My father is Mister Ward, and I'd prefer you not invoke him here." The bitterness in his voice told Gale not to ask more.

"Henry, then." She offered her most engaging smile. "My friend's condition is such that I can't help her with magic alone. We need technology to save the day."

"How marvellous." Henry leaned forward again, hands dangling between his knees. "Tell me, if your friend is in such terrible shape, how is she alive to be waiting for this miracle you propose?"

"It's..." She looked to Cas.

"Better to get it all out," he said.

Gale swallowed hard. "Blood magic."

Henry's eyes widened.

"But we're trying to get rid of it!" Gale added. "Out of her, and then out of the world. That's the whole point. It's why we need you. We want to rid the world of that particular power, but we'd like to do it without costing an innocent life."

Henry arched his thick eyebrows. "How innocent?"

Gale hesitated. "She's the assassin who tried to kill Jes."

To her surprise, Henry laughed out loud. He turned to Cas. "She's joking, right?"

"Not at all."

Henry chuckled again. "Bet Jes deserved it, too. Fascinating woman." But he sobered as he looked back to Gale. "That doesn't sway my answer, of course. I understand what you're trying to do, but—"

"Please listen first," Gale said. "Think of it. Your brilliant invention, finally in use and saving a life. Not a dead end in your research and experimentation, but the beginning of something that will make history. Not a prototype gathering dust in your attic, but real progress."

Henry scowled at Cas. "Did you tell her to say that?"

Cas pressed a hand against the lapel of his jacket. "I promise I didn't. I do remember you working on the heart, though. Amazing stuff, and you were so excited in your letters when you wrote about it."

Henry leaned forward with his face in his hands, covering his eyes. "Curse you, Cas," he whispered. Then he looked up at Gale. "I'm working on something else now, and I don't want to take time away from it."

"But surely a life is more important—" Gale began, but Cas reached out to touch her arm. He shook his head.

This is the best we're going to get.

She fell silent, knowing she'd never be able to explain exactly how important this particular life had become to her, or how much it would mean to save Aster with her own magic.

Henry stood. "If you'd like to come upstairs, I'll show you what I was working on. And you can see whether you could..." He paled. "If you could enchant it into working."

"Really?"

"Really." But Henry didn't sound particularly excited. He led the way out of the room, and Gale hurried after him. Cas followed more slowly as they made their way up the stairs and into a room so large Gale suspected it had required the knocking down of a few walls to create it. Wooden crates lined two of the walls. Against the others stood an odd assortment of tables, all of them covered with miscellaneous bits of metal, odd rubber shapes, and a huge pile of dark-brown fabric.

A claw-footed bathtub sat in the corner, its insides stained a sickly green.

Cas stood with his hands behind his back and took it all in. "Good to see you're settling in and getting organized."

Henry shrugged. "Haven't been here long."

"Nearly a year and a half," Cas said, without a hint of derision or judgement.

"That's what I said." Henry dug into one of the boxes near the door, setting its contents on the floor as he went deeper—an astonishingly realistic wooden foot, a cuckoo clock with five hands, and what appeared to be a real mouse, dead and stuffed, holding a tiny violin in its front paws.

"It's not going to change the world, you know." Henry's voice was muffled, as his head was now deep in the crate. "What you're doing is illegal. Until that changes, or until the king decides to let his mages turn their attention to enchanting medical devices, we can't let on that this even happened. I'm not keen on the idea of wasting away in prison for aiding a witch, and I doubt you're willing to have your neck stretched just to prove this can be done."

"I'll settle for seeing my friend's life saved," Gale said.

Henry emerged and brushed a bit of dust from a white cotton bag that was small enough for him to hold in one hand. He tossed it to Gale, and she scrambled to catch it.

Her hands shook as she picked at the drawstring's complicated knot. "Is it not fragile?"

Henry frowned at her, bemused. "A heart is useless if it's going to break easily. Here, give it to me." He took the bag and untied the string, then pulled out a misshapen lump of greyish fabric with bright, silvery metal wires tracing over its surface in a tight, uneven grid pattern. He handed it back to Gale.

She examined the device carefully. It didn't look like a heart, though she supposed it would be the right size if it were filled with blood. It was impossible to see what lay beneath the fabric, but she felt lumps and a few harder bits inside.

"Attaches inside the body like the real thing," Henry explained, pointing to several round entry ports at the top made of the same metal that was woven through its surface. "You've seen the electric lights they're using in theatres?"

Gale nodded. She hadn't seen them, but she'd heard.

"This metal conducts the same power without overheating. Fantastic stuff. From a mine in Miklovia. Expensive, too."

Gale cradled the precious heart in both hands. "I'm sure Aster will find a way to repay you if this works."

Henry nodded, though he hardly seemed to have heard. "I've got the whole thing set up to beat quite efficiently on a mechanical level, coordinating the chambers and sending the blood where it needs to go." He frowned at the heart, looking like a disappointed schoolmaster. "But the rhythm depends on the power supply. I considered fiddling with that to make it beat faster or slower, but it seemed pointless given the existing obstacles."

Cas stepped closer. "An interesting problem if one had a different kind of power to work with."

Henry scowled at him. "I suppose. I don't like it. But if you want to try, go ahead. Take it. And let me know what comes of it, if anything."

Gale slipped the heart back into the bag, which she tucked into her pocket. "Is this the only one?"

"It is." Henry looked over the mess on the tables. "Miklovium is an incredibly versatile material, but rare. Even if this worked, even if it wasn't going to get you arrested, I doubt I could make another."

Gale swallowed hard. "Good to know."

One shot. One chance to enchant the heart and find a way to make it replace the dark magic that was keeping Aster alive.

It seemed impossible, especially for a witch with so little

experience, but it was one more chance than she'd had a few minutes earlier.

And though she knew of no other living witches in Queen's Run who would help her, there was at least hope that the wisdom of a hundred dead ones would shine a light on her path.

"I've been thinking about Eamon's vessel."

Gale turned to Aster, curious. "And?"

They crossed the street, passing a spiced tea vendor on the corner without stopping. The streets were busy, bustling with folks out enjoying the fine winter weather, all their cares apparently forgotten as the holiday season swept them up in a wave of good cheer, friendly greetings, and the little paper-wrapped gifts handed out to strangers by folks who celebrated Langnaak. Aster waited until they cut through a quieter side street before she spoke again.

"You said that a blood witch can't hold magic in himself, that it's all in his external vessel."

"Correct. Likely something he's had for a long time. They grow stronger with age."

Aster added that detail to her frustratingly limited knowledge of magic. "Does he need to touch it to use it?"

"Not necessarily," Gale said. "It's far more effective if he does, but he might draw some power as long as it's nearby. Not more than an arm's length from his reach."

"Then it would be something he always has on him even if he

didn't anticipate needing his magic. I can't imagine him leaving it at home in the basement, or letting me take it on hunts. Probably not his dagger."

Gale nodded thoughtfully. "That'd be my guess, too. The blade only channels magic to his vessel once you've brought it home to him. Have you figured it out?"

"No." Aster sighed and picked a crumb off her sleeve. She'd left her coat in the carriage the night before, but at least the dress was warm, and it looked presentable enough after she'd hung it to air out while Gale was at her meeting. "There are too many options. I know it's not his keyring, because he left it when he went to meet Roddy. He usually has his cane. And the ring his wife gave him. And a pocket-watch, though I can't remember whether he has more than one of those."

"Or it could be something he keeps better hidden," Gale said. "But those are good options to keep in mind."

Aster waited for her to say more, hoping she wouldn't have to, but Gale didn't speak again.

"If I broke it," Aster continued, "it would make it easier for the mages to take him. Without his vessel, even any enchantments he'd placed on the house would disappear. He'd be defenceless. The police could probably do it. No more hiding the evidence in that basement room, no protective spells."

Gale turned to her, frowning. "Does he use many of those?"

"Not that I remember."

"Right." Gale sighed. "Well, keep thinking about it. It would be wonderful if we could see him arrested for the murders without drawing the mages' attention to Queen's Run, but not until we've figured out how to keep you from dying along the way."

"And you think we'll find those answers?"

"We'll try."

They reached the end of the street, which opened onto the square at the heart of Queen's Run. The massive buildings that stood on its four sides—the central bank, the library, a row of offices, and the headquarters of the Queen's Herald newspaper— stood quiet and sleepy under a heavy blanket of high clouds darkening the city even earlier than expected on the eve of the longest night of the year.

The bank's outer doors were open, but the newspaper appeared to have shut down for the holidays, and though the library never closed out of respect for Kritsa, the Ignatite goddess of wisdom, there didn't appear to be anyone coming or going. Only the birds were active, with pigeons fluttering in a noisy flock at the base of the statue in the centre of the square and a murmuration of starlings swooping overhead in their perfectly choreographed dance.

The library had stood for over a century, its stone facade keeping guard at one end of the square. Towering columns flanked its recessed doors. Beneath them, a pair of massive stone dragons lay on their bellies, their tails curved around their bodies and their front claws gripping the edges of their stone plinths. One had its eyes open and teeth bared, ready to defend its literary hoard. The other took a more restful position with its eyes closed and a dreamy smile curving the worn-down scales around its mouth.

Aster had visited many times. The library held an extensive map collection as well as its shelves of publicly available books and the more restricted collection of older scrolls and documents kept locked away in a separate section in the back. Even if specific memories had faded, a sense of warm familiarity flowed through her as she stepped inside and breathed in the cool, dry air with its heady scents of leather, parchment, ink, and deeper hints of mossy forests and vanilla that hovered around the older books.

Rows of shelves extended away from the door, guarded by a thin old librarian who looked as dangerous as either of the dragons outside. He cast a sharp look at the two young women from behind his desk as they entered, but didn't speak.

Aster glanced around at the well-ordered shelves of books. It took a map—or a fearsome guide like the man at the desk—to navigate all the topics one could research here, but even then they wouldn't find what Gale needed outside of a locked room.

"Are there books on magic in the private collection?" she whispered.

"Hardly." Gale cast a glance over her shoulder. The library seemed empty aside from the librarian. "Stick close."

It felt strange to Aster to not be the one making plans and hunting down information. Staying behind at Gale's quiet flat for much of the day with nothing to do and no idea whether Madrigal was watching her had been a gentle form of torture. When Gale had returned with a heart in her pocket and a head full of ideas, Aster had her boots on before Gale had finished asking her whether she felt like a trip to the library.

They passed through the Private Biography section in the far right corner of the room. Aster had never visited this area, filled as it was with tales of dead folks whose descendants thought them grand enough to have the story of their exploits commissioned for the edification of the masses. Most of the collection looked untouched. Gale slipped into the space between the last two shelves and stood facing the blank, parchment-coloured wall, her back to Aster.

"Turn around," she said, speaking over her shoulder. "Keep watch."

Aster did, though there was nothing to see but books.

Gale murmured something behind her, speaking the language of magic, her voice somehow musical even at a whisper. "Let's go," she added in plain Andonian.

When Aster turned, an open door had appeared in the wall with a narrow stone staircase beyond it lit by candles in sconces on its wood-panel walls.

"What is this?"

Gale ushered her through, then followed. When Aster looked

back, the door had closed and presumably vanished on the other side.

"Secret library," Gale said, no longer keeping her voice quiet. "There were a few witches on the committee that planned and constructed this building way back when, and they built the enchantment into the structure as it went up. It's incredible, really. Like Madrigal's shelf but on a far grander and more complex scale. The normal library has an attic, and if anyone accessed it there would be nothing there but empty space, cobwebs, and the underside of the roof. But this way…"

It wasn't necessary to say more. They'd reached the top of the staircase.

Another version of the library's attic stood before them, just as the contents of Gale's bookshelf had changed when she'd spoken the right words. Walls closed off the lower reaches of the roof, leaving a room with a pleasant peak to its ceiling. The space was filled with the vague, ghostly shapes of furniture under dust covers made of thin fabric that revealed hints of what lay beneath. Tall bookshelves lined the walls, and in the centre, a pair of large tables plus several armchairs would have given the place a cozy, well-used feel if it hadn't been for the air of silent neglect that left it feeling like a relic of the past.

"I know, I know," Gale said. Aster turned and realized she wasn't talking to her but to one of the chairs—or someone invisible sitting on its dusty cover. "But she can't get back in here on her own, even if she heard the words, and no one downstairs can hear us. You said yourself this place practically doesn't exist without… Well, they're not going to tear the building down to find it, are they?"

Aster stepped closer. "May I speak?"

She addressed the empty chair, but waited for Gale to answer.

"She says you may," Gale said, speaking cautiously, like a person expecting a pair of territorial dogs to break into a fight.

"Hello, Madrigal," Aster said, hoping she was looking at the right spot to meet her eyes. It felt strange and awkward, but it was time to stop letting Gale do all the arguing on her behalf. "I apologize for the intrusion, and I promise I'll never speak of this place to anyone. I'm glad to be here, but I know it's not for me. I only want answers, as Gale does, and to be of some help if I can."

A long silence followed from Aster's perspective, but judging by the changing expressions on Gale's face, she assumed the young witch was getting an earful from her mentor. She didn't seem bothered, though, and finally she glared back at the empty space.

"Well, she's here now," Gale said, "and nothing has changed. She needs my help, and I need yours. You can go if you want to. Let me muddle through this myself and fail. Then she'll be dead and you can give her that piece of your mind directly. I'd really appreciate it, though, if you'd help me learn something useful." Another pause, and Gale's expression and voice both softened. "I haven't forgotten. But isn't this what you wanted? Me eager to spend every last scrap of time and energy on learning what you have to teach?"

Aster stepped back, again feeling like she was intruding on what was none of her business even when she herself was the topic of discussion.

"Thank you," Gale said at last, and pulled the cloth from over one of the bookshelves, then the next. Aster joined her, and soon they'd exposed more than a dozen shelves of books, scrolls, and papers, plus one of the big cherrywood tables in the middle of the room.

"What can I do to help?" Aster asked.

Gale looked around. "Can you read the old language?"

"No."

"Then there's nothing you can do until I find some spells to play with." She removed the cover from one of the chairs and pulled it closer to the table but didn't sit. "I might need you to answer questions about the enchantment and your injuries. In the meantime, please don't touch anything on the shelves. Madrigal is provisionally fine with you being here, but I'd rather not upset her more."

"Of course. Will you thank her for me?"

Gale smiled, though the tension didn't leave her eyes. "No need. She heard that."

Aster tried to stay out of the way as Gale crisscrossed the room, gathering materials from several shelves, lost in quiet conversation with her invisible companion. When it seemed Gale truly had no immediate need for her, Aster made her way around the room, taking in as much as she could.

The books on the shelves came in an astonishing array of bindings, sizes, thicknesses, and general conditions. A few volumes looked professionally printed, but most were clearly hand-bound in leather or thick paper, and many seemed to be stacks of loose notes tied together with twine rather than proper books at all. Aster made a loop around the room, looking them over, hands folded behind her back to keep herself from touching the books or the other items on shelves toward the rear of the room—black kettles and pots, a wide bowl made of silver polished to such a smooth shine that it looked to be made of liquid, and a selection of bottles containing leaves, stems, and roots that were labelled in unfamiliar script. A sign above them read REFERENCE ONLY, NOT FOR USE in clear, modern Andonian.

"Blood loss, yes," Gale said, and Aster turned to find her seated at the table, pointing to a page in a large book. "But if there were something to at least hold her together long enough for true healing…" She trailed off, listening, and Aster decided it might be best not to hear more.

Aster leaned in closer to look at the markings on the bottles, and a small collection in one corner caught her eye. There was nothing familiar about the handwriting on the glass jars, and she couldn't read the language, but they gave her a strange feeling nonetheless. Aster tuned out the sounds of Gale and Madrigal's seemingly one-sided conversation and examined it.

Warm. I'm warm and happy. Nothing matters except... except...

But there was nothing more. If there was a memory bringing those feelings, it was buried too deep for her to catch more than that hint of it.

She moved slowly past the shelves again, letting her eyes wander, searching for anything that would offer another scrap of that goodness and peace.

"But if I could get a better feel for the natural rhythms of her current heart," Gale said, louder than she'd been speaking so far, and Aster turned. The witch was looking over a massive tome set open on the table in front of her, but had turned it to her left so Madrigal could look at it. "At what it responds to, what signals it's getting? That could come later, adjusting it as needed once we've got it working, but it's something to consider before I set the whole thing up. A heart is no good to her if she ends up fainting every time she climbs a flight of stairs."

Aster's stomach fluttered. It truly was incredible—not only that someone so young could be so brilliant, but that she'd turn her keen interest and obvious talent toward the needs of a stranger and an enemy. Gale was clearly in her element here, working on what Madrigal seemed to think was an impossible problem, defying the odds, reason, and perhaps Death himself in her mad quest to make right what the wolves and Eamon had done to her all those years ago.

Death.

Aster's skin chilled as she wondered whether Madrigal had met him. She'd never had much use for any gods, but ghosts and magic fuelled by souls had suddenly brought such notions far closer to home.

She passed the table and uncovered one of the armchairs to sit in, reasoning that she'd only been explicitly told not to touch what was on the shelves. Gale didn't look up until Aster pulled the chair closer and sat across from her.

The mechanical heart sat at the centre of the table, fenced in by open books and the notes Gale had been writing. Aster itched to pick up one book in particular. Its cover extended well past its pages on the front, which would allow the soft leather to wrap back around and contain the paper. Probably a good thing, too. Even without flipping through the pages, it was obvious that while most of them were bound properly together, someone had turned it into a scrapbook of notes on different kinds of paper, parchment, and vellum that strained the bindings until the pages refused to lie flat. The ones Gale had opened it to were covered from top to bottom and edge to edge in black ink, the messy script practically screaming their author's enthusiasm for whatever they'd been writing.

Gale caught her looking. "This place holds the knowledge of generations of witches, hidden here when they thought their homes were unsafe or brought by their siblings in magic after their deaths so they could live on by teaching new generations. There aren't many of us around to use it these days, but I'm glad it's here." She nodded to the book. "That one belonged to Draxilla of Golemburg. She might be my favourite teacher here, aside from Madrigal. Some of the writings are so dry, but not hers. A little hard to decipher at times, but I wish I'd had a chance to meet her. She passed away not long before I met Madrigal."

Aster glanced at Gale's notes. "Will yours be part of the collection someday?"

"I hope so." She listened, then smiled. "Madrigal says I need to do something worth reading about first. And I won't be called Nightingale of anything until I've settled somewhere for longer than a few years."

"And how's that coming?" Aster perched on the edge of her chair and rested her elbows on the table. "The doing of significant things, I mean. Not the settling."

"Not bad for a start," Gale said with forced cheer that made Aster's hopes sink. "The enchantments to make the heart move are the easy part, relatively speaking. Thanks to Henry and some theoretical notes on human anatomy, I know how it's supposed to function. It's only a question of making it do what it was made for, which is much simpler than working from nothing." She gestured toward another book, this one larger and tidier. "In fact, I think we're ready to give it a try."

She stood, and Aster pushed her chair back to stand as well. Gale checked her notes, held her hands over the heart, and spoke.

"Glear'ech rolumn arpetch."

Her voice rang through the attic library, the words clearer than any spell Aster had heard from her, and that feeling came back, warmth and joy pushing back against the doubts and fears that crowded her mind as she waited to see whether she might have even the slightest chance of living out the week.

The spell went on, Gale's voice rising and falling, weaving magic that hung thick and dazzling in the air. Aster's gaze drifted from the mechanical heart to Gale's face, and the rhythm of the dark, magic-given heart inside her stumbled as she took in the fierce determination of her expression, the grace with which Gale held herself as she practiced an art Aster couldn't begin to understand. Gale seemed more than herself as she called on the magic she carried within her, commanding it by her will and her knowledge. It was a part of her even when she hid it from those who feared her for it, forever connecting her to the energies of the universe and the witches who had come before her.

Eamon had great power, but he'd given up so much to claim it. He stole what Gale accepted as a gift, killed for what she used to preserve life. For those sins magic would never again be truly his.

The heart on the table shuddered, then picked up an unsteady series of pulsing contractions as it struggled to push air through its chambers. Aster watched, holding her breath, as the rhythm steadied.

Gale lowered her hands and leaned on the table, head hung low.

Aster rounded the table and took her by the arm, guiding her into a chair. "Are you all right?"

"I only need a moment to recover. But look."

They watched Henry's mechanical heart pulsing on the table. It was strange but lovely—at least until Aster remembered it was intended to beat inside her for the rest of her unnatural life.

She sat on the arm of Gale's chair, her legs weak. "You did it."

"I did." Gale waved her hand, and the heart went still. Aster's blood froze, and she sucked in a hard breath.

Gale glanced up at her and rested a hand on her thigh. "Aster?"

Aster didn't answer. She was thinking of Eamon, of the regret in his eyes as he stole back his power, showing her why she needed him to keep her alive.

Gale took Aster's hand and squeezed. Its feverish warmth brought Aster back to herself.

"Sorry," Aster said. "I suppose I hadn't thought about you shutting it off once it was going. Best if I stay on your good side after you've fixed me, right?" She tried to keep her tone light, but failed miserably.

Gale didn't speak until Aster looked away from the unbeating heart and met her gaze. "I could do it that way," she said. "I could make it so you rely on me for every breath, so you have to keep me happy if you want to live. Protect me, protect Jes, do as I tell you." She stood, not letting go of Aster's hand, and turned to face her. "But I said you deserved freedom, and I meant it. I'll admit that I'd like to know you better and under kinder circumstances, but if you're going to stick around, I want it to be because you want to, not because I'm holding your leash. I think there's been enough of that, don't you?"

Aster squeezed her eyes closed and took a long breath. "Agreed."

"Good. The enchantments will make the materials strong and will keep the heart beating until they fall apart. Probably long after you've died of other causes."

Aster decided not to try to picture that. Instead, she looked up into Gale's eyes, drinking her in and trying to believe the impossible. "Thank you."

Gale looked away. "Don't thank me yet. Like I said, this is the easy part." She released Aster's hand and turned back to the books. "Healing is one of the most difficult challenges a witch can face. Magic is about power, intention, and knowledge to varying degrees. But beyond that, life resists being pushed in directions it isn't inclined to go. Pure magic influences, it doesn't force the way blood magic does."

"I see. So speeding up natural healing would be simpler than cursing someone to grow a second nose?"

"Precisely." Gale motioned for Aster to stand next to her. "It's why blood magic is used for those sorts of curses, why it's managed to hold you together for so long. That's not to say my sort of magic can't do great damage or accomplish the seemingly impossible, but blood witches have reasons for making the sacrifices they do." She flipped through another book, opening it to a detailed diagram of the insides of a human body with its heart and circulation laid out. "Still, we can try as long as I know exactly what needs to happen. My anatomy lessons seem so long ago, and I didn't get deep enough into my studies to have seen inside an animal's body. The next step is figuring out how the blood vessels and everything else connect to the heart. I can imagine it in theory, but I don't think it's enough."

"What does Madrigal think of all this?" Aster asked.

Gale's expression darkened. "I'd rather not say yet. Not while we're making progress. Not while there's hope."

Numbness threatened to steal over Aster's body and mind, but she fought it off.

Madrigal had experience and knowledge, but Gale had determination, and that had to be enough.

As long as we're fighting, we haven't lost.

"What do you need, exactly?"

Gale chewed her lower lip and flipped a few pages in the anatomy book. "A real human body to examine, I suppose. Dead, obviously." She paled slightly. "Fresh."

Aster checked her watch and considered the problem of bodies and the ways a person might dispose of them. The longest night of the year would begin soon, and then every business and school in the city would be closed for the holidays.

"The answers might not be here in your books," she said, "but I think I know where you can find them."

CHAPTER TWENTY-SIX
ASTER

The Von Maris Memorial School of Medicine didn't take security as seriously as Aster had feared.

After a quick return to the flat, she and the witches had made their way to the north end of the city, Gale following Aster through the shadows like she'd been born into them. With Aster in her dark cloak, Gale clothed in a deep blue dress and a black scarf covering her head, and Madrigal as invisible as she always was, they'd made their way across the gardens that surrounded the school without notice.

Now, thanks to a loose lock on a ground-floor window, Aster slipped into the dark and silent halls of the school, then reached out to help Gale climb in.

"Wait," Gale whispered, and crouched beneath the window. "Madrigal can't go far enough to look through the entire school, but she'll tell us if there's anyone nearby."

Aster paced the wide hallway, unable to keep still, willing to rely on her ears to tell her if anyone was coming. Soon enough, Gale pulled a candle from her bag and lit it with a touch of her fingers. "She says the basement is this way."

Aster followed, though she'd already had an idea of the layout of the school. Eamon had hosted several fundraisers here, convincing the wealthy that surgery was the way of the future and that improvements to the school would set Queen's Run above every city in Andonia as a shining beacon of wellness and knowledge.

He'd done it, too. The new wing had been built, the basement anatomy studio improved, new equipment purchased. The world was a better place for his presence, even if it was also a far worse one.

Gale's enchanted candle burned with a bright and steady flame that illuminated the olive tile of the floors, the spotless and undecorated white walls, and the windowed doors of the rooms they passed.

"I won't be able to completely cover this up when we're done," Gale whispered. Her wide eyes reflected the candle's flame as she glanced over her shoulder and into the dark corners of the ceiling as though something might be waiting there to attack. Her free hand gripped the strap of her satchel tight. "They're going to know someone was here."

They reached the end of the hallway, and Aster pushed the heavy door at its end open, then held it for Gale to pass through. "I really think that's the least of our problems at the moment. As long as they don't know it was us, we'll be fine."

The chill of the grave rose from the basement to greet them as they descended the wide wooden stairway, and the candle's flame trembled as Gale's hand shook. Aster didn't ask whether it was the cold or her nerves.

"I'd have thought someone who ran with wolves would be more comfortable with criminal activity," Aster said, trying to lighten the mood.

Gale shot her a dark look. "*Accustomed to* it isn't the same as *comfortable with*. And mutilating bodies isn't quite in the same league as anything I do for Jes."

Another set of double doors at the bottom of the stairs was

unlocked. Beyond them the candle's light picked out the shapes of a row of four waist-high metal tables in the centre of the room, three with long lumps shrouded in white sheets on top of them.

A haunting chill trailed up Aster's spine like ghostly fingers, and she stopped before she reached the first table. "Madrigal? We're alone here, right? Just the three of us?" Her voice echoed eerily through the dark room.

It still felt odd to speak directly to nothing, but asking Gale to relay the message when the ghost was perfectly capable of hearing her seemed needlessly rude.

"She says we are," Gale said a moment later. "Apparently these people all died elsewhere and were probably safely in Lord Death's lands before their bodies were buried." She turned sharply to Aster. "Buried?"

"Buried," she said softly. "Occasionally people will donate their bodies to the school after death, but it doesn't happen often enough to be a real benefit. No one talks openly about where the rest of the corpses come from, but there's good money in acquiring them." She looked back to Gale and found she'd closed her eyes.

She decided not to disturb her. She wanted—needed—Gale to go through with this, to examine what might lie beneath the scars on Aster's chest and figure out how to connect a heart to whatever remained once the enchantment was gone, but it had to be her decision.

Aster moved closer to the nearest table and touched the upper edge of the white sheet, then forced herself to pull it back. A middle-aged man lay on the table, his skin pale and bloodless, his eyes mercifully closed. The cool air kept the bodies fresher than they might have been otherwise, but the scents of lye soap and turning meat threatened to bring bile up in Aster's throat.

As did the gaping slit in his throat.

The resurrection man.

The wolf.

He didn't look familiar to her, but that didn't mean anything. She knew her own work—clean, like he'd been opened with a scalpel rather than the larger blade that would have done that kind of damage in a single stroke.

Aster held her breath as she looked down at him. She didn't feel sad, exactly. She'd meant for him to die, and he had. But this man was nothing now, his spirit burned up for the sake of her own healing.

Four in the basement. Madrigal had guessed dozens over the years.

For that, she did feel sorrow, and guilt that settled in her chest, threatening to claw its way out through her flesh and bone.

She covered him and moved on to the next body, a young woman, thin, her skin sallow and loose as though she'd lost weight in the weeks before her death.

The third body had no face. Some lecturer had already been at it, removing the skin to display the musculature beneath, slicing out half the lower jaw to leave the tongue hanging down the side of the throat, which had also been opened to expose its inner workings.

It didn't trouble Aster as much as she might have expected. But then, she had seen more than enough of the insides of her own body recently. At least this person had been dead before it happened.

But she pulled the sheet back up and decided not to offer it as an option even if the chest might be intact.

When she turned back, Gale was standing beside the second body. "We're going to need tools," she said, her voice hollow and dull. "Something to open the, um..." She swallowed hard and dropped her satchel to the floor. "The ribs. And finer tools to remove the heart. Whatever you can find."

Aster folded the sheet down to the body's waist, revealing a wheeled wooden tray of instruments beneath the table. "I could open the body for you," she offered. "I don't mind."

"All right." Gale held the candle steady, but looked away when Aster lifted a set of what looked like long garden shears and set them on the table.

"I know," Gale said, answering something Madrigal had said. "But when that time came I intended to put people back together, not chop them open. This isn't the same at all."

Aster took a sharp knife from the tray and sliced across the skin beneath the collarbones and well below the ribs, then connected the lines down the middle of the chest. Even after all the lives she'd taken, she supposed she'd never done so much visible damage to a human body. It was strange to work so slowly, and somehow more disturbing than the thought of killing.

Like butchering a deer, she told herself, though she'd never done that, either. Rabbits, but it wasn't the same.

She didn't look at the dead woman's face as she opened the chest, cutting away tissue that covered the bone and viscera, or when she used the shears to make cuts down either side of the breastbone and carefully separated the flat slab of bone from what lay beneath. When she lifted it away, the hole looked like a far tidier version of the damage she'd seen in herself when Eamon had withdrawn his magic—no broken bones, the blood already drained away, organs intact. Her stomach heaved, both from the memory and from the sight of the exposed heart encased in a thin, pale membrane.

Gale turned and leaned in close, though, obviously fascinated in spite of her misgivings. "That's it," she whispered. She laid a hand on the corpse's brow. "Bless you, stranger. I hope you're happy where you are now."

Aster slid the tray of tools closer, then took the candle and held it high enough to cast light over the body without being in Gale's way. Now that the decision was made and the deed irrevocably done, the witch seemed calmer and more confident. Her hands, which had to feel as ice-bitten as Aster's from the chilly basement air, didn't tremble at all as she examined the heart.

"We don't know what's left of Aster's," she said. "I'm thinking we should try to…" She paused to listen. "True. In that case I should convince the tissues to grow into the artificial heart rather than relying on clean cuts and sutures. That'll give me at least some leeway if parts are present but damaged." She listened again for a full minute, frowning with concentration, and nodded. "I've got my notes, but I can work through it without."

Aster found she needed to look away when Gale started cutting. It was one thing to open a cold, unfeeling body. It was quite another to imagine herself lying open like that, to see Gale's capable hands slicing the heart free, removing it and setting it on the table.

"Hopefully that's the least we'll have to work with," she said. "Aster, would you reach into my pocket and take the artificial heart out?"

She did, feeling detached from her own body, and set the heart on the table next to the one Gale had removed from the corpse. She wondered what hers looked like as it beat inside her. Had Eamon's magic formed new muscle? Or had it created an invisible barrier containing her blood and forcing it to move as it would if she'd been truly healed and whole?

The thought made her want to tear it from her chest, whether Gale was ready or not.

Gale glanced up at her and frowned.

"Something wrong? You look odd."

Aster tried to smile, but felt more like a cornered animal baring its teeth. "It's nothing." She watched as Gale measured the space between the ribs with her fingers, then the new heart, and a troubling new thought came to her. "Thinking about that mechanical heart being in her and then in me is a little off-putting. Silly, I know. I'd be lucky for that to be a concern."

"No worry at all," Gale said. "I can call the blood out of it and back into the body. Won't even be contaminated if I do it correctly, though I don't suppose a bit of dirt would matter to her."

She seemed to be leaving something unsaid, but Aster didn't push.

Gale set the fabric-and-metal heart gently into the corpse's chest and debated enchantments with Madrigal. Aster tried to focus on the cadence of magic's language instead of exactly what they were talking about and how it related to her. By the time Gale spoke the first spell, it had become something like a song. Magic hummed through the air, and Aster looked down to find the gory mess inside the body moving, its vessels stretching toward the tubes atop the heart and growing, vine-like, into them.

Dark circles formed under Gale's eyes, giving the appearance that she hadn't slept in a week, but she pressed on.

Then she spoke the spell she'd used in the library, and the heart began to beat.

Gale's hands dropped, and she disappeared over the edge of the table. Aster set the candle down and crouched in a single motion, barely catching Gale before she hit the floor. She held her gently and sat with her legs crossed, cradling Gale's head in her lap.

"Madrigal?" she asked, but there was no answer she could hear.

It was only a few seconds before Gale's eyes fluttered open. "It worked, didn't it?"

Aster didn't answer, assuming Gale was speaking to Madrigal. After a few moments Gale took a deep breath and pushed herself up onto her knees.

"Slowly." Aster offered herself as support when Gale continued her attempts to stand.

"I'm fine," Gale said, sounding confident even as she struggled. "That took a lot out of me, but there's plenty of magic left."

Gale leaned heavily against her, and Aster wrapped one arm around her waist as they looked down at the blood-streaked mechanical heart beating in the chest, under-filled and struggling. She poked at the heart and sighed. "They drained a good portion of the body's blood already, and what's there is in fairly nasty condition, so we're not getting the full effect."

"But you understand the mechanics of attaching the heart to a body now," Aster said. "That's good, right?"

Gale's chin trembled. "It's something. It's better. It's a thing I know that I didn't know before. It's..." She looked away from Aster into the darkness, listening. Then she sobbed. "I know, but we've come so far."

Aster didn't want to ask, but she had to know. "What did she say?"

"That I've done well." Gale's voice came out low, rough, and entirely defeated. "That I've made great progress along this path, but we've now come to the edge of a chasm I can't hope to leap across without magic like Eamon's. Doing this with dead tissue has helped me learn the technique, but commanding it to do the same while you're alive would require more power and skill than I have access to. And even if I did..." Her words trailed off.

Aster looked down at the body and the eerily lively false heart. She imagined herself lying there.

And remembered what had come before it—the cutting, the blood, the loss of the old heart.

"Even if you did, the procedure would kill me," she said, if only so Gale wouldn't have to. "You can give this body a beating heart, but you can't bring her spirit back. Even if you could properly heal my wounds before you did this, and even if you found a less invasive way to put the heart in, I'd die in the time between you removing Eamon's enchantments and getting this heart into place."

"Right." Gale pressed her lips together as tears streamed down her cheeks. "Madrigal thinks Eamon was able to bring you back because he had a fresh soul in his possession to trade to Lord Death in exchange for yours. Whether Death had a choice in the matter isn't clear, but—"

"But it doesn't matter when we can't make that kind of deal."

"Not without me stealing souls and ruining myself as a witch," Gale said.

Aster let the truth of it sink in. She'd known after Eamon's demonstration that she had no chance of living without his magic. Gale had given her a spark of hope, but that had vanished, leaving her exactly where she'd been before. It hurt more now, though, for reasons Aster couldn't quite place. Maybe it was because she was over the initial shock, or because hope had set her up for a harder fall.

Or maybe I feel like I have more to lose now.

She brushed Gale's tears away. "It's all right."

Gale sniffled and blinked hard. "We need more time. Better advice. There has to be a way to keep you alive through this. Henry couldn't do it, but he didn't have magic on his side."

"There isn't time," Aster said, and cleared the lump from her throat. "Eamon and Roddy will kill again, and soon. I can't let that happen."

"I know." Gale stepped away and turned back to the body. She murmured more words in the language of magic, and the mechanical heart went still. Another spell followed, and the blood that marred its surface drew back into the body. When Gale pulled the heart out, it was once again spotless. Blood that had dotted the table, too, drew back into the body. Gale placed the corpse's rightful heart back into place.

"Help me," Gale whispered. "Both of you. I can't cover our tracks, but I also can't leave her like this. There's no life here to fight me. I think I can manipulate her flesh."

She spoke another spell with a mournful rhythm to her

words, and the blood vessels inside the body slowly connected themselves to the heart.

Aster steeled herself and placed the breastbone back into place, then held it steady as Gale spoke another spell. Nothing happened. Then, as Gale repeated the spell with more force and obvious effort, the bone knit together. Thicker lines where the blades had broken through made it clear that damage had been done. Aster closed the skin, positioning it carefully to match up the edges. Gale's voice wavered as fresh scars formed along the lines where Aster had cut, painfully raw to look at. The process was slow, and Gale frequently paused to catch her breath and listen to whatever Madrigal was telling her.

Aster hoped Gale would find a way to do this for the living someday, even if it seemed clear that it wasn't going to work for Aster herself. She'd said living tissue was far more difficult to manipulate, but Aster had no doubt Gale would find a way if she wished to. Even the laws of magic and nature would have no choice but to bend in the face of her beautiful, stubborn will.

If only I could be around to see it.

"Told you they'd know we were here," Gale said, looking down at the raw, freshly mended wounds. She wavered on her feet, looking ready to collapse. Aster pulled the sheet back into place and hauled one of Gale's arms across her shoulders to support her weight.

"What do you need?"

Gale took a long, sighing breath. "Home. My vessel. I didn't think I'd have to drain myself quite this much, but it'll help. Rest. A cup of tea."

"Home, then." There was more Aster wanted and needed to say, but it would have to wait.

CHAPTER TWENTY-SEVEN
ASTER

By the time they got back to the flat, Aster was supporting most of Gale's weight. She took the keys from her and unlocked the door, then helped her into the cold, dark room. Moonlight from the window behind the dividing panels picked out the shapes of Gale's day-to-day business space and glinted off the glass sphere on the table, but it looked like the set for a play after the audience had gone home. Still, lifeless, waiting to be useful again.

Aster hoped it would be soon. She'd considered things on the long, silent walk back, and her path forward had become clear.

Eamon needed to be stopped before he could hurt anyone else, and Roderick Bates would have to go down with him. There was no more time, no matter how badly Gale wanted it. When Aster went to the police, they'd call on the king's mages for help if they believed even a fraction of her story. It wouldn't be easy, given Eamon's paranoia and intense preparation for just such an attack, but they would win in the end. They'd take both witches' heads for their crimes, and Aster would die with Eamon even if he didn't decide to revoke the enchantments before his death.

It would be better for Gale, who would return to her quiet life of fortune telling until she'd learned enough to do as she wished with her magic. Slow and steady and relatively safe, not this mad scramble to outpace a killer and learn to work miracles in the space of a week.

They passed into the living area of the long room, shedding cloak and coat as they went, and Gale caught a second wind as she went to the cupboard beneath the bookshelf and took a small, dark object on a gold chain from a box. She clasped it in both hands and curled up at the head of her bed, kicking off her boots before she pulled her stockinged feet up under her skirt.

Aster lit the fire with kindling and one of the matches that were probably only on the mantel for show most days. Gale needed to hold on to whatever magic she could.

"Are you sure?" Gale asked, clearly not speaking to Aster. "But you'll come back?"

Aster left them to their discussion.

The kitchen stove fire came next, and Aster busied herself making tea, careful to use the correct leaves out of the multitude on the shelf. When she returned to the other room with two cups, she found Gale sitting up straighter, still looking exhausted but far stronger and brighter than she'd been minutes before.

"Good stuff in there?" Aster nodded toward Gale's hands.

"The best." Gale opened her caged fingers. It took Aster a few seconds to understand what she was looking at—not a piece of jewellery, but what appeared to be a rat's skull carved from obsidian. Gale looked down at it with an affectionate smile. "Not conventional for a vessel, I'll admit, but it works." She slipped the chain around her neck and tucked the skull under the bodice of her dress, then accepted one of the cups from Aster.

Aster sat on the bed, her back to the wall, her knees touching Gale's crossed leg through layers of cotton and wool. She wanted to ask for the story of how such an odd item had come to be but decided to leave it for later.

Then remembered there wasn't going to be a later.

Still, she left it, and they sipped their tea in silence. Part of her wanted the story, wanted to learn everything about Gale that she could before she left to go to the police, to soak herself in knowing this strange and surprising person who had somehow convinced her that not everyone who ran with wolves was a monster. But a larger part was content to sit on a sagging mattress as the crackling fire warmed the room, sipping tea in the most comfortable silence she'd ever experienced.

"I'm not ready to give up," Gale said when the tea was gone and the cups set on the floor.

"Nor am I," Aster said. The evenness of her voice surprised her given how her heart lifted when Gale spoke, how her stomach pitched and rolled at the breaking of the quiet bubble that had shut out the problems at hand. "But it's time. I won't let another person die for the sake of Eamon's magic, and I won't risk letting him take control of me."

A tear rolled down Gale's cheek, and she wiped it away with a savage flick of her wrist. "It's not fair."

"No." Aster's heart seemed to be swelling, tearing, and crumbling all at once, and she marvelled at how a thing made of such dark magic could feel so real and true. She took Gale's hands in hers and traced her fingertips over the ghostly veins visible beneath the pale skin at her wrist. Her throat thickened, and her voice became heavy. "I can't thank you enough."

Gale looked up from their entwined hands, meeting her gaze. "Don't thank me. I failed you."

"But you tried to give me something Eamon never even attempted—freedom and a chance to choose my own path. You offered me the truth even when it stung me, even when it made me want to hurt you for revealing it, after I'd spent my life with someone so intent on burying my pain that he stole parts of me to do it."

Gale leaned her head on Aster's shoulder. "I'm glad you're not angry with me."

Aster smiled, though Gale couldn't see it. "I am, though. A little. A week ago I would have been angry about dying, but I had only a vague sense of the future I'd be losing." She swallowed back the tightness in her throat and willed herself not to cry over what had never been hers to begin with. "Now I can see what might have been. What I might have wanted when the hunt was over. That does make me angry, in a sad sort of way."

Gale drew in a long, slow breath. "What would you have wanted?"

"You. This." Aster's stomach tightened painfully. She had no memory of ever confessing such a thing to anyone.

"I hoped that's what you meant." Gale sniffled. "Madrigal would say it's for the best—not that she wants you to die."

"Doesn't she?"

"No. She's always been wary of anything or anyone she thinks might steal my time and attention away from magic, and I think she knew you were a threat before I did. She wanted me to turn you away, but she doesn't wish you ill. Not now, anyway."

"She has been helpful." Aster wondered whether Madrigal might have the good grace to meet her in the borderlands when the time came. It would be nice to meet her face to face, to thank her for trying.

We go on, she reminded herself. If she'd ever doubted it before, Madrigal was proof. No one knew what lay beyond the veil, but there was something. A pleasant thought, but it didn't make the idea of seeing those mysteries revealed before she was ready any more appealing.

Gale lifted her head and trailed her fingers down the scar on Aster's face, studying it as though she were memorizing the shape of the line. "She'd say this never would have worked anyway. You and me."

Aster took Gale's hand and pressed it harder against her cheek. "She's probably right. But I would have liked to find out."

Aster wasn't sure who started it, whether it was Gale leaning closer or herself shifting her weight to bring their faces together, or if both happened at the same time. All she knew was that her mouth was on Gale's, that the young witch tasted like warm tea, that her lips were soft but firm. She let go of thought, of hope, of regret, and once again let the moment become everything. Her fingers tangled in Gale's hair, desperate to hold her close.

But Gale pulled back, touching a finger to her lips.

"What's wrong?"

Gale smiled sadly. "Nothing," she whispered. "Absolutely nothing." She held Aster's face in both hands, gentle but surprisingly strong, and pulled Aster into another long, deep kiss.

Aster's body warmed as it awakened. She wanted to draw this out, to burn every movement and every touch into her memory, but there was no time. The top buttons on the bodice of Gale's dress opened easily, and she brushed her fingers over the exposed skin at Gale's collarbone.

Aster's dress was newer, the buttonholes tighter. Three of the buttons popped off and clicked to the floor as Gale tugged at the fabric, trailing kisses down Aster's throat to the upper reaches of the scars on her chest. Every movement was eager but unpracticed.

And to Aster's mind, unbearably perfect.

They rolled down onto the mattress, knocking the pillow to the floor. Gale pinned Aster beneath her, then pulled her own dress over her head, leaving her in a fitted chemise that left her arms and upper chest bare. Her skin glowed in the light of the fire, and the thin fabric clung to her breasts as she leaned in and pressed her parted lips to Aster's again. Aster grabbed on to her hips, then slid her hands upward, tracing each curve, attentive to every lovely shift in Gale's breath.

With a wave of her hand Gale made the fire burn lower, leaving the room bathed in a warm glow as she pulled back, leaving Aster room to sit up.

Aster cupped Gale's cheek in one hand and traced her lips

with her thumb, then let her fingers move down the smooth curve of Gale's throat, brushing the gold chain that disappeared beneath the fabric of her chemise. She wanted to tell Gale that she was beautiful, that she was frightening and fascinating and perfect, but the words wouldn't come. Instead she opened the remaining buttons of her dress and pulled her arms from sleeves, cursing the tight fit of the heavy fabric. She'd barely freed herself before Gale pushed the straps of the loose shift down over her shoulders and her arms, letting the fabric fall, exposing Aster to her waist.

Gale's gaze swept over her, leaving her feeling raw and undone in the most perfect way.

Gale pressed a hand to the scars that covered Aster's breastbone, and Aster's heart beat wildly beneath. Gale smiled and leaned in close enough for Aster to feel her breath against her lips. "Does it always race like that?"

Aster's voice came out a breathy whisper. "No." She pushed herself up to catch Gale's lips again with her own, fighting to keep her head above waves of desire that threatened to drown her.

They separated, but only for long enough to shed the remaining layers of cloth that separated them, to reveal every soft curve, every scar, every aching part that longed to experience everything that would soon be lost to them. Only Gale's vessel remained, dark and strange, and Aster's bracelet around her wrist.

Everything but Gale slipped from Aster's mind, and for once she was glad to forget.

CHAPTER TWENTY-EIGHT
GALE

Gale fought against the weight of her body and the warmth of the fire that threatened to lull her to sleep as she lay next to Aster, tangled in her arms, breathing her in. It felt right, like a beginning rather than the ending they both knew it to be. She knew the longer she lay still, comfortable, and happy, the harder it would be when it ended, but all she wanted was to freeze time.

"I have to go," Aster said, but she didn't seem to be attempting any such thing.

Gale held her tighter. "Just a little longer." She glanced at the clock on her nightstand. Midnight had passed hours before. In a few more the sun would rise, but for now the sky remained black outside the windows, and it seemed possible to pretend the longest night of the year would last forever.

Aster drew another breath and gently disentangled herself. "I might have waited too long already. Eamon and Roddy probably have their next victim chosen—several, maybe, if altering my enchantment would take a lot of power. I'll go to the police, and if I can get them to believe me about how dangerous he is, they'll call in the mages. And then..."

She left the thought hanging, unfinished.

It's not fair, Gale thought. She wondered whether Aster felt the weight of it pushing her back toward the bed as the blankets pooled around her waist, leaving the scars on her lean, muscled back exposed. Her hair was a mess of wild curls, and to Gale she looked like a warrior goddess. Flawed and imperfect like the gods in tales from Jatlind or Kardav, not like the polished and untouchable God she herself had grown up knowing.

She knew she couldn't possibly love Aster after knowing her for such a short time, but her heart seemed disinclined to listen to reason.

We should have more time. More of this. Even if it's not forever. At least long enough to find out what it could be.

Aster looked down at her hands, frowning, and touched each of the charms on her bracelet one by one.

"What are you thinking about?" Gale asked.

"Justice. Whether it's come to find me, after all the lives I've taken. I always thought I was doing the right thing. Jes's family killed my grandmother. Their fight with Eamon hurt me, made the enchantments necessary. The scars were their fault, and the missing memories. I made them monsters in my mind, and I felt no guilt about slaying them."

Gale propped herself up on one elbow and reached out to touch Aster's arm. "Eamon made sure you didn't know better. I don't doubt that at least some of them deserved it."

Aster winced and looked away, but Gale didn't amend the statement. She knew her boss well enough to know that Jes wouldn't have deserved a knife to the back, that no one was merely the sum of their past crimes. Gale herself didn't regret the deaths of that family any more than Jes seemed to, but it didn't make Aster the sword of justice.

Aster was human, confused, and hurting. She deserved to know and feel all of it, even the hard parts. Eamon had protected her from pain and guilt all her life, and what good had it done?

"And maybe some didn't," Aster said. "I can't know. I don't remember what happened that day. What if one of them tried to stop what happened?"

"Then you were wrong. There's nothing you can do about it now." Gale spoke the truth as gently as she could. She wanted to tell Aster she could make amends, but it would have been false consolation. The only action left was to see Eamon finished and his evil removed from the world.

"Thank you for not lying to me." Aster turned to her with a sad smile. "Eamon would have told me I was right all along, that it was the cops' fault for not catching the wolves first, that we had no choice but to do it ourselves. He'd try to ease my guilt until he could make me forget it."

"But?"

"But every hunt was mine. Every kill. He controlled me even without the perfected enchantment he has planned for me, but I also made choices." She turned her hands over, examining invisible bloodstains. "At least Jes will be safe. You'll thank her for me? Even if I never use that heart, I appreciate her help."

"I will."

"Good." Aster brushed Gale's hair back from her face, her fingers pulling at the tangled strands. "I hope he knows before the end that he failed. He wanted so badly for them all to die."

Gale tilted her head to one side. Her hair fell forward, tickling her bare skin. This idea that Eamon wanted Jes dead even after Aster was willing to let her go had seemed minor before, but now that it was all they had left, it shone a little brighter. "He does know how to hold a grudge, doesn't he?"

"He does." Aster flopped back on the bed, apparently having given up her attempt to escape its pull. "He always told me it was all my idea, that revenge burned in my heart, and he facilitated my education and travel. I never questioned where that came from, but I was a child with no memories. He could have said no. We could have moved on. They'd never have found us."

"A bit like poking a den of sleeping bears, wasn't it?" Gale stared up at the ceiling. "He put you in danger just to see them dead."

Aster rubbed at the scar encircling her forearm. "He was making me into the weapon he needs to keep feeding his power, and I wouldn't have agreed to kill anyone else. But once my training was done and I'd proven myself, he didn't stop."

Gale watched her without speaking, not wanting to derail Aster's thoughts. She'd done all she could. If there were more answers, they were locked away behind the enchantment that held Aster's memories captive.

"He still wants every one of them dead," Aster said. "I suppose he was willing to put me in danger because there's no one he could hire who'd do the job as well as I can."

Gale sat up straighter, feeling as though a bolt of lightning had shot through her. Her thoughts whirred like one of Henry's mechanical contraptions. "Wants, or needs?" She rolled out of bed, padded across the floor, and knelt beside her bag to dig through the books she'd taken from the library.

There had been something. Something she hadn't known was a piece of the puzzle, if only she could shake off her mind's sleepiness and remember what it was.

She abandoned the bag a moment later and went to the shelf, too preoccupied to worry about her nakedness.

"It's here somewhere," she muttered, pulling books free and placing them on the floor as she rejected them. "I've been so focused on breaking enchantments and giving you a heart that I abandoned everything else, but there was something in one of my other lessons..."

She stood in the centre of the room, the warmth of the fire kissing her bare skin, the book in one hand as she paged through it with the other. Aster sat up and watched her, looking wary and unwilling to hope.

"Here," she said, and brought the book to her bed. She sat and showed it to Aster, though she couldn't possibly read the old Andonian script written on the page. "I don't think it's about their lives or his power, it's about what they know. I didn't think of this before because this is a book on illusions, not memory enchantments. I probably wouldn't have found much on those anyway. Not many respectable witches want to involve themselves with—"

"What does it say?"

Gale tried to keep her voice from trembling. "It says the greatest danger to a lie is those who know the truth. An illusion works best on those who don't know what they're supposed to be seeing, who are willing to believe. A witch could enchant a hovel to look like a castle to those who had never seen what was there before, but if someone familiar with it came and revealed the truth to people who were willing to listen and believe, the illusion might shatter."

Aster traced a finger over the page. "So if a witch wanted that illusion to hold forever, they'd do well to get rid of anyone who might destroy it with the truth."

Gale closed the book. "It's not the same thing. What Eamon did to you isn't anything like an illusion, but the deeper principles could be the same."

"Jes and her mother could be the last keys to breaking down the walls around my memories," Aster whispered. "Good enough reason to want them dead. If that's the case, though, he was risking more than my life when he sent me after them. They could have told me everything."

"Would you have believed them?"

"No. He warned me never to speak to them, and said if I did they'd only spout lies to save their own necks."

"He set you up to guard your mind against the truth. But you'd listen now."

Aster leaned forward, fingers peaked against her lips as she stared into the fire. "It doesn't change anything. Eamon still needs to be stopped. I'm still going to die when he does, if not sooner."

"But speaking to Jes might unlock your memories." Gale set the book aside and took Aster's hands in her own. "If you find out what he's hidden from you and why, we might find something that could help—details about the enchantment, perhaps. Or if you have a memory that identifies his vessel with absolute certainty, we could find a way to steal it. Then his magic would still exist, but he wouldn't be able to use it to withdraw the enchantment, and we'd have a little more time." Gale didn't know whether such a thing was possible, but it felt good to hope. "We have to try."

Aster smiled, more sadly than Gale liked. "Or maybe I just find information that will help the mages bring him down, and I die knowing who I was and who I really am."

"I know who you are." Gale cupped Aster's chin in one hand and tilted her head until their foreheads rested together. "You are a warrior, and a person who has formed herself from the ashes of what she's lost over and over. A person worth saving, with or without her memories. I know this seems impossible, but it's all we've got."

Aster thought for a moment, then stood and reached for the clean black dress she'd laid out over the back of one of the chairs. "Do you know where Jes is?"

Gale grinned, then pulled Aster in for a quick kiss before she retrieved the clothes that had been scattered across the bed and the floor. Energy prickled at her skin—excitement, apprehension, and hope she knew would end again in disappointment but that she had no desire to chase away.

"She'd never trust me with that information when I was getting close to you," she said. "But I know someone who does."

CHAPTER TWENTY-NINE
ASTER

Aster waited on the dark street in front of Bellawick's Curiosity Shop, watching the light snowfall accumulate on her cloak. She had no doubt Gale was being as quick as she could while she tried to explain everything to Cas, but each second that passed on the face of the grandfather clock for sale beyond the window seemed to take its time in coming.

She tried to occupy her mind by thinking about what the next step would be if Cas refused to let her speak to Jes, but there was nothing.

It was Jes or straight to the police.

Jes or death without knowing the truth about what Eamon had stolen from her with his enchantments, without ever being truly free from the threat of his control. Pain, blood, and whatever came after.

All of it might still happen if she did speak to Jes, but at least there was a chance something would change.

After the longest quarter-hour of Aster's life, Gale returned to the shop door followed by a young man who struck Aster as strangely familiar, though not in the same way Gale had been on their second meeting. Gale had felt like a forgotten friend. This friend of Jes awakened her defenses as only an enemy should.

"You again," he said as he stepped out of the shop. He held the door for Gale, then closed it. "You'll forgive me for not offering to shake your hand. My manners come a little undone when people try to murder those I care about."

"Cas," Gale said, speaking under her breath. "Please. You promised."

His expression didn't soften. "Gale told me you need to speak to Jes, and why. She didn't convince me of why Jes should want to speak to you."

Aster looked to Gale, but the witch wouldn't make eye contact. A test, then. He had told her not to help.

"I'm not going to kill her, if that's what you think."

Cas smiled without any warmth. "Most people offer a bit more than that."

"I am going to finish off a man who wants her dead. The king's mages will see him removed as a threat, and his head will no doubt roll at their earliest convenience."

"Which is nothing more than you offered for the last favour she did for you." Cas leaned back against the window and braced one foot against the brick below it. "We know who you are, who he is, and where you live. We could report him ourselves."

Aster gritted her teeth and held tight to her temper. "Then what about information on her mother's whereabouts?"

Cas considered it, not looking impressed. "Is that something you have to offer?"

"Yes." She had only a vague idea, but Eamon had mentioned Embercliffe, and she felt she'd known more, once. Specific information might be among his papers, if she lived long enough to search for it.

"That information might be enough to get you an audience," Cas said, pushing off from the wall. "But anything else is probably going to cost you a lot more." He stalked away, and Aster fell in several paces behind him.

Gale caught up and walked beside her. "He's not usually this prickly."

Cas glared back at them. "Of course I am."

But Aster didn't feel any true anger from him toward Gale, and Gale showed no sign of being bothered by his performance. She hadn't asked Gale much about her relationship with Jes and whatever other wolves moved in her circles these days. There hadn't been time. She'd expected a strict hierarchy, her bosses keeping Gale under their thumbs and taking unreasonable percentages of her fortune telling fees, but this was something different.

More like siblings.

Aster had none of her own she could compare this to, but it seemed to fit. Gale had lost her family, but she wasn't alone. Jes and this Cas person weren't the sorts of people Aster would have expected someone as kind and gentle as Gale to adopt as a replacement, but maybe she'd underestimated the wolves.

A little, anyway. She wasn't going to give them too much credit just yet.

The Grand Dahlia Hotel stood in austere splendour at one corner of Midtown Meet, a dark edifice of stone distinguished from its neighbours by its height and the red-and-white striped awning that extended over the sidewalk, welcoming guests and offering brief shelter from the weather to those who scurried past every day, avoiding the critical gaze of the elderly but imposing doorman. Aster had never stayed in the hotel, having always slept at home when she was in town, but she'd visited the restaurant several times and enjoyed the wildly varying menu that shifted every time they hired a new chef with a different cultural and culinary background.

Fuzzy memories, faded as they all became with time, but good ones.

As they passed into the lobby with its curving double staircase leading up to the second floor, the scents rising from bouquets of exotic flowers near the desk masked any hint of what the cooks might be preparing for guests who were awake in the deep hours long before dawn.

Cas led Aster and Gale through without stopping at the desk, and the attendant, a generously formed young woman in a skirt and jacket that matched the awning outside, busied herself with paperwork as they passed.

Aster took another look at the hotel lobby, noting the freshly laid carpet in a design of clear Kardavi origin with its swirling patterns and deep hues, the polished brass accents on the railings and the desk, and the armchairs in proper little seating areas for those who didn't wish to invite guests up to their rooms. None of it showed signs of age or wear.

"Not a cheap place to stay," she noted when they'd climbed the stairs and passed by the restaurant, headed to the back staircase and the hotel's upper levels.

Cas glanced back at her. "For most people, sure."

Aster's teeth clenched involuntarily. "So she's got cops *and* hotel managers in her pocket?"

"You make it sound so crude," Cas said. His suit was a little rumpled, his face still lined with creases from his pillow, and he seemed to lack the energy to put much fight into his words now that he'd completed his share of the negotiations. "She has skills that benefit people, and in return they do things for her. As it happens, her work at the shop allowed her to connect the manager with items for a collection of a personal nature. Nothing criminal at all, just good business."

"Plus she's willing to stay on the fourth floor," Gale added.

Aster laughed. "The haunted one, right?" She paused. "Oh. I'd always thought that was a load of rubbish."

"Likewise," Cas said.

They climbed the back stairs, their steps echoing off the

polished wood steps that glowed under the light of gas lamps on the wall. "As it turns out," he said, "people having nightmares on this floor wasn't simply a result of them buying into existing stories—they were being visited by a true ghost, and not a happy one. But Madrigal was able to convince Miss Artendale to allow Jes's presence."

Aster shivered. "Does Jes have those dreams?"

Cas paused at the top of the stairs. "She does, but says she doesn't remember much about them. Typical for what ghosts inspire, apparently. Jes doesn't have nightmares, though. Seems to me her sleeping self is on quite good terms with the spirit, even if her waking self doesn't know much about it."

She'll probably use that connection to get good seating on the train to the afterlife, Aster thought, but kept it to herself.

They stopped outside room 408, the suite at the end of the hall.

"Weapons?" Cas asked.

"She doesn't have—" Gale began, but stopped and sighed when Aster pulled the dagger from her boot and the coil of wire from her pocket, then reached under her cloak and removed her belt and its knives from the waist of her black dress. Cas took them from her with an even glare.

Gale gaped at her, and Aster could only imagine what Madrigal might be saying.

"Wait here," Cas ordered, and unlocked the door to enter. The lock clicked behind him.

"Is Madrigal still with us?" Aster asked. Gale had said the ghost was with them before they reached the shop but hadn't mentioned her since.

Gale shook her head. "She's gone to speak to Christine— Miss Artendale. It's a lonely thing, being a ghost. Christine wasn't a witch and can't anchor herself to magic to visit other places in the living realm like Madrigal can. She's just here. Alone. Lost."

Aster wanted to ask more about the ghost, but the door to 408 opened. Cas stepped out into the hall.

"She'll speak to you," he told Aster. He kept his tone even, but obviously wasn't pleased. "Gale and I are to wait out here."

"It'll be fine," Gale told him. "Really."

Aster left them to their discussion and entered the suite. The rooms beyond were dimly lit by a few lamps, the curtains drawn tight against the night.

Jes stood with her back to the room, but glanced over her shoulder as the door closed, then turned. She wore a dressing gown of charcoal velvet, but stood with the posture of a queen dressed for court. Aster stepped closer, hands held out to her sides to show she'd come unarmed.

"Well," Jes said, and moved away from the window.

Aster took stock of her, feeling as though it were for the first time.

A few years older than Aster or Gale—younger than Aster had expected, just as Gale had said. Dark hair coiled into a loose bun at the back of her neck. No jewellery, simple silk slippers on her feet. Not fancy, but put-together. Respectable even at this hour. She'd obviously been awake before Cas entered, either because she hadn't gone to bed or had risen unaccountably early, and had recently ordered tea brought up. She poured two cups from a porcelain pot with pink roses on the side.

Refined. Unthreatening, but Aster prickled with wariness.

"I didn't think we'd meet again so soon," Jes said.

Aster struggled to remember anything from their first meeting in the park or the conversation Gale said they'd had in the jail. There was nothing.

"I didn't think you'd agree to see me."

"I almost didn't. Sugar?" Aster nodded, and Jes continued serving. "I asked Cas to wait outside, to come if he heard trouble. But if you wanted to hurt me, I'd be dead before he came in, wouldn't I?"

"Before you could scream." Aster accepted the delicate porcelain cup Jes offered and sipped, her best manners on display. Now that Jes was close enough that Aster could see her eyes, something moved in her memory, far too deep to be of any use. A hint of recognition, nothing more. "He took my weapons, but you'd be dead already if that was what I'd come for."

"Very good. I'd hoped we could get the threats and posturing out of the way quickly." Jes paced slowly across the plush floral carpet, saucer in one hand, cup in the other. "Cas told me what you want. I hate to disappoint you, but I don't know how much help I can be. As I said before, I was only a child that day. I did what I was told. And I remember very little." She smiled sadly. "I should remember more. My favourite uncle died that day. My mother—Mav—was sent away after it was all over, and it changed our lives forever. But I think I already told you that."

"You may have. I don't remember us speaking."

"No. And that's where I come in, isn't it? The last potential key to your memories. The only one you haven't murdered, save for my mother, who you'd planned to hunt in…"

Aster gritted her teeth. Valuable information was a high price to pay for a meeting that would only lead to further negotiations with a crook. "Embercliffe."

"Interesting." Jes frowned, though not at Aster. "Sit, please."

Aster perched on the edge of a chair and sipped her tea, feeling a bit like an attack dog that had been ordered to heel. "Gale hopes that speaking to you will jog something that opens the floodgates, so to speak. You don't have to know everything. Just something that will connect me with what's been hidden."

"Very well."

Aster set her cup and saucer down. "Just like that? Cas thought you might want payment of some sort."

Jes tilted her head to one side and narrowed her eyes, assessing Aster carefully. "Gale hasn't asked you for money, has she?"

"I've offered, but she hasn't taken much."

Jes touched her fingers to one of her temples, as though the thought gave her a headache. "Of course she hasn't. And you have no way of getting me any before we speak because your time's up."

Aster's fingers tightened around her teacup. "It is. Lives are at stake, and not only mine. This is a small thing for you to give me, isn't it? One conversation, a few memories?"

"Hmm. Valuable to you, though." Jes sat in the other chair and crossed her legs at the ankle, looking more at ease than Aster felt. "You must understand that I can't afford to do favours for every murderer who tries to stab me. Can't afford a lot of things. As it turns out, Mav wasn't wrong about it being less risky and more easily profitable to go after the poor and ignorant. I won't go back to that, but here we are."

Aster decided not to offer a comment on the value of more honest employment. Jes would only point out that her own work history involved a wealthy father and the aforementioned murder.

"If you survive this," Jes said, "I'll expect you'll find a way to repay me with a bit of your family fortune. Enough to fund my operations for… let's say a year."

Aster swallowed hard. "Fine." She decided that if she died in the next few days, disappointing Jes would at least be one great consolation.

"What we're doing tonight is honest business, Aster." Jes set her empty cup and saucer on a table beside her chair. "You came to me of your own free will. I'm not lying to you or making false promises, and I'm not the monster you still want me to be."

Aster forced herself to relax as she reached into the pocket of her dress and pulled out the money she'd taken from home. It wasn't enough to fund anything for long, but it was a show of the good faith she was faking more than feeling. "Tell me what you remember."

Jes leaned back in her chair, fingers interlaced over the front of her dressing gown, and looked toward the ceiling. "I was with my family. I would have been, what, eight years old? It was a time when the curses had been going on for long enough to hurt badly, but nowhere near the end. Things were as hard for my family as they were for anyone else. People were guarding their resources more carefully than ever. In some cities we faced sickness we had no hope of talking our way out of, in others there was no food to be bought even if we had coin to offer." She looked to Aster. "These aren't my memories, exactly, but what I remember Mav telling me. All I knew was that she and her brother and cousins were always angry and sniping at each other, disagreeing about what to do or where to go next."

"It's fine," Aster said, barely whispering so as not to break the spell of the story Jes was slowly weaving. Nothing was triggering her own memories yet, but she couldn't shake the sense that there was something there, that this had to be why Eamon forbade her to speak to the wolves or believe their lies. "Keep going, tell me anything."

"The family was contracted to find someone. All I knew at the time was that the journey to central Andonia was longer than I liked and almost duller than I could stand, but I didn't really mind because the grown-ups seemed happier than they'd been before. The crops and forests were dying, and the horses almost starved on the way. Finally, we passed a village and got free of the woods, then travelled along a road that looked like no one had used it in years." Jes frowned, then nodded to herself. "Yes, I remember sitting next to Pietr as he drove, and I made a game of spotting the tracks and pointing them out to him. We found a little farm at the end of the road, and things were growing. It was autumn, coming up on what would have been harvest time in better years, and there were apples, pumpkins, a little field of wheat, grass growing in a pasture with a few cows..."

Jes trailed off, her gaze becoming distant, her voice wistful.

"There was a barn and a house, both painted white. I was sent to play with the calf out in the field, a darling thing with big brown eyes. It was hours before they called me in. When they did, I met this lovely lady. She seemed ancient to me at the time, but I suppose she wasn't really. Glowing skin, warm like yours. Short hair streaked with silver. Kind eyes, but she seemed afraid. She wore a green dress and a purple apron, and her house smelled of the herbs that hung in bunches from the ceiling."

Something moved deep in Aster's memory. *Rosemary, crowthorn, chamomile, sage...* A gentle voice speaking, a scarred hand pointing to hanging bunches of plants that Aster would barely recognize if she saw them again. Laughing eyes, a dark, rich brown that was nearly black, with deep lines at the edges carved by laughter that Aster could almost hear.

Then it was gone.

"I'd say we were there about a week before the man came," Jes said, and the creases between her eyebrows deepened. "I was happier there than I was most times during my childhood, free to play in the barn and collect eggs while the grown-ups did whatever they were doing."

Aster's jaw tightened until bolts of pain shot into her temples. "Eamon told me that part. Wolves using my grandmother as their servant, taking her food, sheltering in her house."

Jes raised one eyebrow, but seemed unbothered. "Maybe. But as I told you once before, whatever he told you isn't the whole truth. We were there at someone else's behest—someone who had wanted Mav and the others to find this exact woman. I don't suppose they asked why he wanted her. Not if he was offering enough coin for it."

"He who?" Aster felt certain she didn't want the answer, that she already knew.

"A young man. Strong, healthy, with black hair and a thick beard. He carried a walking stick with a pretty ball in its head."

"Glass?"

Jes nodded. "Clear, sort of green-gold with air bubbles worked through. I suppose he looked pleasant enough, but I hated him on sight."

"Why?" Aster's mouth had gone dry as the image of a younger Eamon stepped into her mind—not as a memory, but something close to it.

"I don't know." Jes looked to her, head tilted slightly. "Mav had taught me from birth to trust my instincts, and they told me to stay away. I didn't need more than that."

Aster nodded, feeling a grudging sort of kinship over this. Jes relied on her gut to evade the law and danger, Aster to fill in blanks left by missing memories. But it was the same skill, the same sense.

And now they were both using it to do whatever they could to survive.

"Was he leaning on the cane?" Aster asked.

Jes frowned again. "No. It was more like an affectation, like the ridiculous sorts who carry riding crops around their country estates even if there are no horses nearby. A prop. There might have been a slight limp, but nothing that really stood out."

A vessel. Aster's heart skipped. An object he'd had even before he'd needed it and kept using even when a sturdier cane might have helped him more. It wasn't a memory, but it was worth paying for ten years of Jes's dirty business if it gave her the key to stopping Eamon.

"I said that week was the best part of my childhood," Jes said, slipping back into the story. "But when he came, I wanted to leave. And we did. The job was done, I suppose we got paid, and that was to be the end of it. But after we left, we met a girl coming toward us on the road, younger than me, too small to be out on her own. She wore a tattered cape with a hood—not dark like the one you're wearing, but bright red like a cardinal's feathers against the barren grasses. Mav asked her where she was going."

"My grandmother's house," Aster whispered, feeling she'd given the answer before. She searched for more. All that came to mind were feelings, physical and emotional, a swirl of cold and hunger and loss. But her lips kept forming words. "My mother and father are dead, and I'm to ask her to take me in."

There was no more.

Jes leaned in closer, watching with keen interest.

"I spoke to you. So did Mav. Then the grown-ups talked while you and I sat by the road and rested. And I—"

"You braided my hair." As Aster looked deeper into Jes's eyes, she remembered them in a younger face, a smiling girl. "You talked to your mother an told me you were going to escort me to my grandmother's house. That it wasn't safe for me to go alone."

Jes looked away. "That was all they told me. I found out many years later that they'd decided a young man who wanted your grandmother so badly might pay for you as well. I didn't know anything was wrong until we came to the house and I heard the noise inside."

Aster's breath hitched, though she didn't remember why. Then a piercing scream rang through her memory, sharp and pained and despairing.

"I haven't liked to think on any of this," Jes said, and cleared her throat. "And haven't had reason to. Mav wouldn't let me go inside. You ran through the doorway, though, quick as lightning, and Mav sent the others in after you."

Aster closed her eyes again and followed the scream, freeing her mind to make more connections, letting thoughts come as they wished.

The scream.

A white house.

The familiar scent of herbs, but something strange and sharp mixed with it.

Grasping hands, her feet aching as she ran to the house, her own cries ringing in her ears because that was Grandmother, and someone was—

The floodgates opened, and she remembered.

CHAPTER THIRTY
ASTER

The memories came in a flood of images, sounds, and sensations, none of them in order or connected to any other.

There were shouts. Screams. Panic. Her grandmother lying on the floor of a cottage that felt familiar in the memory, a single room with heavy beams beneath the roof and comfortable old furniture Aster barely saw. Her focus was on Grandmother on the floor, arms spread out at her sides, blood at her wrists and ankles where someone had—the memory blurred where Aster's young mind had refused to take something in.

Too many people in the house, anger. Pain, hiding, then the memory skipped back to running in through the door.

Aster tried to pull herself to the surface, back to the present and her body, but as she did, the memories began to fade. So instead she let herself sink deeper, though it felt like drowning.

It was all there, or at least as much as she'd understood at the time. Eamon had done a fine job of hiding it all away, but with Jes's memories to unlock the door, his dark enchantment proved to be brittle, easy to shatter if one knew its weak spots.

A stranger appeared in her mind, her dark eyes laughing, a

cheerful song on her lips on a day long before the one at grandmother's cottage. Aster's heart swelled with adoration and childlike love.

Mama.

Then the laughter and song were gone, replaced by those same eyes in dark, sunken spaces over hollowed-out cheeks. Mama, lying in bed, her breath coming in hard rasps. Father beside her, not moving at all.

People Aster hadn't remembered, hadn't thought of except to wonder who they might have been, in more than a decade. Now her heart felt as though it might shatter as her childish grief returned, amplified as it echoed through empty years of forgetting.

Another stranger came, though Aster tried to cling to the memories of her parents. A man sleeping in a dark room, trying to bargain, and then his throat slit clean. The same face on a table in a cold basement, waiting to be taken apart.

Other wolves.

Other children playing in a village she'd forgotten existed.

Jes, seen through the bars of a jail cell.

It all came at once, snatches of faces and sounds and smells, with no sense of time or logic.

Then the tidal wave settled, and the memories began to sort themselves into a rough order. Aster kept her eyes closed and ignored the tears on her cheeks and the heaving breaths in her chest, trying to focus on anything from the day she died.

Into the house. I usually ran in with flowers in my hand and Mama at my back after walking the long road to grandmother's house, but today I was alone until I met the nice people coming my way. Grandmother is screaming. There's a man, a stranger with a black beard. He has a knife. He's saying strange words, hurting her. They both see me. Grandmother shouts for me to go, but the men from the road are at my back, blocking the door. And I don't want to leave her. They're all shouting—the men and the stranger.

Aster struggled to remember their words, but it was like listening underwater, everything muffled and distorted.

She waited for the memories to settle more, and a few phrases surfaced before vanishing again into the confusion.

"Know what you both are... will pay good money if we turn you in, unless you want to..."

She focused on her body, on the hotel room she'd left behind, until she could speak. "Your family saw that Eamon was using magic. They were trying to blackmail him," she said, her eyes still closed against the full intrusion of the present world.

"Sounds right," Jes said. She sounded far away. "Never took any of them long to spot an angle they could use to squeeze a bit more coin out of a person."

Aster felt her way back to that day at her grandmother's house, ignoring tempting but irrelevant threads of memory that had been stolen over the years—the death of a wolf, a bruised heart after a girl in Embercliffe called her ugly, nights spent crying for a lost family she couldn't picture in her mind. There wasn't much more to recall about that day. To a child, it had all been confusion and terror. But there were knives flying through the air, and a pair of heavy axes. Aster running to her grandmother, trying to protect her, pain in her arms, her legs, her head as the blades and heavy objects struck, as someone hauled her off her grandmother and cut clean through her arm with an impossibly sharp blade before the memory vanished.

She couldn't see her injuries, and time had dulled the memory of the pain, but there it was.

Not the wolves. Not an accident, either.

Aster's entrance had interrupted what should have been a drawn-out sacrifice. Eamon had attacked her as he had the others. There had been blood everywhere, and more pain than her mind could process.

They didn't harm me. Eamon did. Only him.

None of them were blameless. If the big, bad wolves hadn't

hunted down her grandmother, Aster might have lived out the curse and the rest of her childhood under her care.

But Eamon had sent them. Eamon had staked her grand-mother to the floor and had barely begun torturing her when the wolves came back. And Eamon's magic, his knives, his power that brought down the house, had killed Aster. Every word he'd spoken to her about it since, every bedtime story about how he'd saved her from the wolves, every scrap of hatred he'd sown in her heart before he sent her to destroy the last keys to her damning memories, had been a lie.

She wanted to hate him for it, but felt nothing but emptiness.

She forced her eyes open and found Jes still sitting next to her but looking away, giving her a measure of privacy. She handed Aster a lace-trimmed handkerchief, and Aster wiped away the tears that wet her face, then blew her nose.

"You can keep that," Jes said, somewhat unnecessarily.

"He was killing her," Aster said. Her voice cracked. "He was torturing her, cultivating pain and fear before he took her soul. I suppose he got it."

Jes looked to her. Her eyes shone with tears, and for the first time Aster saw a human there and not the mask of a soulless criminal. "I am sorry. Truly. Mav was never clear on all the details. She fled with me when the fighting started. Said it was to keep me safe, but I suppose that's part of why the family wouldn't take us back after. But I played my small, ignorant part."

Aster took a deep, shuddering breath. The memories were still flitting through her mind like ghosts, impossible to ignore but no longer threatening to pull her under. New details came—Eamon's eyes, one of the wolves having bright red hair, Jes holding her hand as they walked and Aster feeling like the girl could be a big sister to her. Crashing noise, her breath stolen, the sky opening up where the house's rafters had been.

"I know you didn't—" Aster began, but her voice failed her.

Jes laid a hand on her forearm. "Not that time, no. But I was raised to keep doing these things, hurting people, stealing from easy targets who couldn't afford the loss. Just as you were raised, I suppose, to seek justice by killing those who were there that day." She leaned in closer. "I'm still doing as I was taught, but I've turned my skills to those more deserving of the treatment."

"And no one is more deserving of mine than Eamon." Aster stood, though her legs felt weak. "You and Gale should get out of town for a while in case things go badly. I'll go to the police, then get into the house, tell him you got away, and steal his vessel before he suspects anything. He won't be able to fight back or hide his secrets without magic."

"And then?"

"Then Gale tries to fix me before he's executed or the enchantment breaks down. If she can't, I suppose I get to enjoy the best sleep of my life." Aster choked back a laugh.

Don't fall apart, she ordered herself.

Not yet.

Her memories churned again, and the wolf's words echoed through her, over and over.

Know what you both are. Know what you both are.

"Eamon, the man with the black beard. He was alone when he arrived at my grandmother's?" she asked.

"He was. I can't imagine anyone wanting to spend time with him."

The hairs on the back of Aster's neck stood on end. "Why would one of your uncles have said, 'We know what you both are,' then?"

Jes frowned and stood, then stepped closer. "Your grandmother was a witch. I thought you knew." She looked to one side, trying to remember. "Somebody of… what was the town called? Golemburg?"

Aster opened her mouth to object, but couldn't.

Her little farm had been alive and well during the curse. The herbs, the familiarity of Gale's warm, bright power…

Gale.

Aster gasped as another more recent memory came, of Eamon explaining why witches could become such stubborn ghosts. *Magic makes for a powerful spirit, and sometimes a tenacious one.*

And wasn't a powerful spirit exactly what Eamon wanted to fuel his dark magic as he perfected his control of Aster's mind? She'd thought he'd kill more innocent people to do it, but that was wrong.

Not more victims. Just the right one.

She'd asked Eamon about witches after she met Gale, never naming her but connecting the question to a fortune teller. She wanted to linger on the wonderful ease with which the memory came to her, but there was no time.

Not when she'd left the business card in her desk, easy enough for Eamon to find if he became curious about why she hadn't returned yet.

She ran for the door. "Go, now. All of you, before Eamon knows anything is—"

But when she threw it open, only Cas was standing there.

"Finally," he said, checking his watch. "Did it work?"

"Where's Gale?"

"She said you two left in such a hurry that she forgot something important at her flat. Left about twenty minutes ago, said she'd be back. Why?"

Aster gritted her teeth. Memories were still coming, all of them interesting and none of them relevant, and focusing on the present took more effort than she liked. "She's in danger. Eamon wants Jes dead, and if he finds out Gale exists, he'll want her for far worse. Is there a meeting place she'd know to go to?"

Jes stepped into the hallway. "There is."

"Good. Give me my weapons, then go there. I'll find her and send her after you, and then you all need to leave town."

Cas handed her things over, and Aster slipped her dagger into her boot, the wire into her dress pocket, and the belt with the comforting weight of her knives around her waist. Without another word, she pulled her cloak tight around her shoulders and hurried to the stairs.

There was no sign of Gale in the stairwell, in the restaurant, or in the lobby. Aster dashed into the street, ignoring the irritated glare of the doorman, and looked both ways, but there was no familiar blue coat on the lamplit streets.

She turned toward Gale's home and ran.

CHAPTER THIRTY-ONE
GALE

The flat was dark and cold when Gale returned. She shivered, closed the door tight behind her, and made her way to her bookshelf.

"There you are!" Madrigal appeared beside her, looking peevish and surprisingly red in the face for someone who didn't require blood or a beating heart. "I convinced Christine to step into the borderlands with me, and when I tried to return you were gone."

Gale decided not to waste breath on an apology, but an explanation seemed in order. "I was so excited about Aster speaking to Jes that I forgot to prepare for what comes next. What if they uncover something that gives us the key to saving her as well as finishing Eamon? And me standing there without this."

She picked up the little cloth bag containing the mechanical heart, lifted her skirt, and stowed the heart in the secure pocket beneath it. Once that was safe, she dumped the books out of her satchel and packed the rest of what she might need—bandages, a potion to dull pain, needles and catgut thread that would support her magic by physical means if necessary.

320

She told herself, over and over, that none of it was likely to be necessary, to not get her hopes up, but she couldn't help it.

She hoped. At least for the moment.

Madrigal watched with her arms folded across her chest, her face now lined with weariness more than anger. "Gale."

"Madrigal." Gale stopped and faced the ghost. "I'm not ready to give up."

"I know. But—"

The door to the flat burst open and crashed into the wall. The sound of splintered wood hitting the floor came at the same time as heavy bootsteps, then the crash of the table hitting the ground. Gale gasped and spun on her heel, heart pounding.

The screens that had divided the room fell, and a large man stood in their place.

Bald and bare-faced. Burly. His black suit jacket straining at the shoulders and unbuttoned.

He grinned as he slipped two fingers into his waistcoat pocket to touch whatever hung at the end of a gold watchchain.

"Hello, miss. Would you be…" He pulled a crumpled business card from inside his jacket. "'Orianna Alcorini'?"

Gale glanced toward the bookcase. Her vessel was hidden behind its enchantment, safe as long as she didn't try to retrieve it. "I'm not open for business."

"Ah, well then." He stepped toward the fireplace and swept one arm across the mantel, sending candles and jars of herbs crashing to the floor. "Good thing I'm not here for business."

Gale edged toward the door until the stranger moved again, blocking her progress in two steps. Gale retreated toward Madrigal.

"I didn't feel him coming," Madrigal said. "He's hidden himself." Gale didn't answer. The less this fellow knew or suspected about her, the better.

"What do you want?" she asked.

He clucked his tongue. "Not much of a fortune teller, are

you?" His gaze fell to her hands, which rested at her sides, fingers splayed, ready to call on her magic to defend herself. He smiled. "A friend of mine has a daughter who's been acting strange lately. I've been trying to keep an eye on her, but she's given me the hardest time." He tossed a familiar business card onto the floor between them. "He was concerned enough last night that we went through his daughter's things and found this. We never imagined there was another witch in Queen's Run."

"You're mistaken." Gale's voice cracked.

"I don't think I am. You're very good at hiding yourself in plain sight, Miss Alcorini." He scooped up her satchel from the floor and pawed through its contents. "Potions, eh? What else have you been up to?"

When Gale didn't answer, he threw the bag into the corner of the room. Glass shattered, the sound muffled within.

"You'll come with me now, miss."

Gale let go of her habitual hold on her magic, opening its channels within her, letting it flow.

"Defence," Madrigal said, at the same moment as Gale shouted, "*Alehia aldomor ic'lieni dorsuma,*" and released a burst of magic that had taken down large and powerful men before this.

The stranger took a step back and winced but didn't fall.

"Adorable," he muttered. He reached into his waistcoat pocket again, and the room filled with a brewing storm of power. "Eamon will want you alive, but I suppose I could still give you a look at how real magic is done."

"Blood witch," Madrigal spat. "His vessel—"

"I know," Gale said, trying not to look at his watch.

She kept her voice to a whisper, focused her intentions on protection and deflecting harm from blood magic. She hadn't practiced defensive spells as faithfully as she'd promised Jes she would, but she understood the theory. Physical protection. Mental protection. Shield her own magic. She set her intentions on all of it as she pleaded with her power to set barriers, speaking its language without stopping to think or translate.

Her magic obeyed, but as the stranger's power moved through the room, knocking over chairs without physical contact, sending the blankets flying from her bed in a demonstration of what were surely the least of his abilities, it felt like building a fortress of straw in the face of a tornado.

She shouted *"Alehia aldomor ic'lieni dorsuma"* again, hoping only to distract him—if not from his own brewing spells, then from what she herself was doing to protect herself.

This time he only laughed.

His spell sounded nothing like the clear tones in which Gale spoke to magic. He used the same words, but heavy and mumbled and spat out like a curse.

God, let me live, Gale prayed. *And let me not live to regret it.*

The sound of clay pots breaking in the kitchen nearly vanished under the roar of a dark spell. The blood witch closed his eyes and raised his hands.

Gale focused on the first spell that came to mind—the illusion Madrigal had made her work on days before. It came easily after those hours of practice, and a dozen greyish-pink mice raced across the floor toward her enemy, then up his trouser legs.

There was nothing to them. No weight, no substance. But it took his focus from his spell for a second.

Gale darted past him and ran for the door, her spells still on her lips.

CHAPTER THIRTY-TWO
ASTER

Aster took the stairs up to Gale's flat two at a time, trying to ignore what she'd seen from the ground—the open door, the darkness beyond.

Cas and Jes thundered up after her, and Aster turned on them as she reached the top. "I told you to go," she snapped.

Cas stood two steps below her, glaring. "She's been ours longer than you've known she existed."

Aster spun on her heel and passed through the doorway. Arguing would feel good, but it would waste time she couldn't afford.

The door hung from its lower hinge, its upper panel cracked. The room beyond was a ruined mess. Gale's carefully laid-out work area and her living space lay open to each other, with the colourful scarves blown into the kitchen and the crystal ball cracked into pieces in front of the dark, cold fireplace. Pages torn from old books lay scattered across the floor.

Aster moved slowly through the flat and into the kitchen, ready for a fight, but there was no one there.

"By every god," Jes whispered.

Aster stepped back into the larger room to find Cas examining the fireplace and Jes standing in the middle of the mess. She'd pulled on a long coat over her dressing gown, but her neat hairstyle had come loose as she'd run after Aster and she looked far less composed than she had in her room at the hotel.

"You have to leave," Aster told them. "This is Eamon's doing. If he has Gale—"

"He does." Cas came closer, holding a scrap of paper covered in thick, scrawled script that he handed to Aster. "This was on the mantel."

Aster,
Your father is most concerned about you. Excellent work finding us a witch. I suppose you'd better come home if you'd like to see her again. Your father will, no doubt, insist on giving you one last chance to redeem yourself.
Or you can leave her to us.

Warmest regards,
Roderick

"I didn't find Gale for them," Aster said, not looking at either Jes or Cas. "I swear."

"We know." Cas took the note from her, scanned it again, and handed it to Jes. "But that doesn't change what's happened."

Jes crumpled the note and shoved it into her pocket. "What are we going to do about it?"

Aster looked around at the mess and tried not to imagine the fight that had caused it. There was no blood on the floor, but that seemed like a small mercy. She'd felt the effects of one of Roddy's lesser incapacitation spells and could imagine how much more he'd have thrown at a witch. She'd be unconscious, unable to move, unable to feel until they wanted her to.

"*We* aren't doing anything," she said. "You two are going to get out of town."

Jes lifted her chin. "Are we?"

"Please." Aster held her hands out, offering peace even as she refused to back down. "You've broken Eamon's hold on my memories, and I'm grateful. But 'one last chance' means he still wants to fix my enchantment, which means turning me into a monster willing to kill without remorse to bring him more power."

Cas stared evenly at her. "You've felt remorse?"

"I do now." Aster looked from him to Jes and back. "Don't go to the police yet. If Eamon has Gale, we can't get the mages involved. They might come in time to save her, but then they'd put her to death. I'll have to figure out how to finish Eamon off myself." The thought made her physically ill. This wasn't slipping a blade into a stranger, but the face-to-face betrayal of someone she'd once loved, who she thought still might love her in his vile, twisted way.

"And this 'warmest regards Roderick' fellow?" Jes asked.

"I'll have to deal with him, too."

Jes and Cas exchanged a long glance.

"There's nothing you can do for now," Aster added. "I intend for Gale to walk out of that house alive. She'll need you then."

"We're no good to her if you fail," Cas said. "Surely more bodies, or at least someone waiting outside if there's trouble would make it more likely that she survives."

Aster's temper flared, and she tamped it down as well as she could. Working alone had the advantage of not needing to deal with emotional or stubborn people, and she vastly preferred it. Still, they wanted the same thing she did. She moved closer to Jes.

"If I fail," she said, fighting to keep her voice even, "Eamon will kill Gale and finish his improvements to my enchantment. If he does, I won't be able to see you as an ally or someone I've done business with, and I won't have any qualms about killing you, or how I do it." She glanced at Cas. "Or how many others I have to kill to get to you."

Neither answered, and neither moved toward the door.

"Please," Aster said. "If the worst happens, I don't want your blood on my hands."

"We're not leaving the city," Cas said.

Jes nodded. "Not without Gale."

They think I'm going to succeed, Aster thought. She supposed their faith should be encouraging, but couldn't let herself dwell on anything besides her next steps.

"Fine." Aster took a long breath, steadying herself. "But stay away and be careful."

Cas laid a hand on her arm. "Good luck. I wish you well."

Aster forced a weak smile. "Just this once?"

"Sure."

A cold wind blew through the open doorway as Aster stepped out into the dark.

She supposed she'd be dead by sunrise. All she could let herself think about now was how she'd take Roderick and Eamon with her—and how she'd make sure Gale lived to see another day.

By the time Aster reached the old black house on Greybaud Avenue, nearly everyone in the city was either tucked safely in bed or enjoying the warmth and light of an all-night celebration as they awaited the coming dawn. The fresh dusting of snow had covered slushy streets with a layer of fresh white that sparkled in the lamplight, and the air was sharp with cold.

A single set of boot tracks stood out against the snow on the pathway leading to the front door. There was no sign of Roddy, but he hadn't been home for long.

Aster looked up at the house, searching for some sign of what she should expect. All she found were the empty, staring eyes of its windows, a hint of light around the edges of the parlour curtains at the cracked-open window, and the front door left slightly ajar.

She wished she'd brought more weapons along and wondered if she might sneak up to the attic before anyone realized she was there.

Roddy. Eamon. Destroy their vessels, steal their power. And if the enchantment doesn't vanish right away, kill them before they can start over.

Newly surfaced memories welled up as she looked at the house. The strongest were of returning from hunts, in pain and exhausted. She'd been thinking of the kill each time, and half a dozen recollections spooled out like thread, each shouting for her attention.

The accomplished swindler who took such pride in the fine horses he bought with his ill-gotten money. He'd offered no information, but had begged for his life.

The jewel thief who had so recently existed in Aster's mind only as the cut diamond-shaped charm on her wrist. She'd been Aster's first kill and hadn't felt her death creeping up on her as she slept. There was guilt buried in the memory, and the seed of Aster's desire to tell the rest of them why they were dying even when Eamon had ordered her not to.

The old couple who had left behind simple cons and thefts in favour of selling human flesh to slave ships bound for other lands. He'd offered to pay Aster off. His wife hadn't put up a fight at all.

Each one was a part of her history and herself that had been lost, that she desperately wanted to reclaim before she died even if they revealed her ugliest facets, but they meant nothing now. There was only time left for saving one life and ending two others.

Three. I'm ending three.

A familiar sense of calm settled over her as she faced her final hunt.

She hoped Gale's God was watching over her as she pushed the door open, cast one last look over her shoulder at the hard and beautiful world outside, and stepped into the house.

CHAPTER THIRTY-THREE
ASTER

"Close the door, dear."

Aster did, and followed Eamon's voice into the brightly lit parlour. She sank into calm focus, afraid of what might be lurking beneath its surface if she allowed herself to think of anything else.

Roddy stood in front of the white sofa near the window with Gale's still and silent body in his arms. Her head was tilted back, exposing the delicate skin of her throat, and freshly melted snow glittered in the cascade of dark hair that hung over Roddy's arm. He stared back at Aster, daring her to make a move.

Aster's focus cracked, but didn't shatter even as her chest tightened.

A porcelain cup clinked against a saucer, and Aster looked to Eamon. He sat in his chair next to the fire, tea in hand, his cane resting against the chair beside him. Aster didn't want him to see her paying special attention to it, but all it took was a glance and a simple recollection for her to confirm that the glass ball at the top was the same as the one she'd seen that day at her grandmother's house.

Ordinary. Necessary. Ever present, within reach if he needed to draw on the magic he couldn't hold within himself.

"I'm here," Aster said. "Let her go, and I'll hear whatever you have to say."

Eamon set his cup and saucer on the table beside him and pushed himself from the chair, leaning on his cane. "I doubt she'd be going anywhere in this state. Roderick was more liberal with his application of magical force than I'd have preferred."

"I'll wake her when I want to wake her." Roddy looked down at Gale with a strange mix of tenderness and hunger, and it took every ounce of Aster's willpower to not launch herself at him and tear his eyes from their sockets. He dropped her roughly on the sofa and turned his back to Aster, raised his left hand, and whispered a few strange words.

Gale didn't wake. Instead, the parlour window slammed shut and the heavy lock on the front door thudded home.

Aster's heart pounded.

Eamon looked toward the ceiling. "That's all of them?"

"Of course," Roddy said. "Every door, every window. No one will see or hear anything from the outside, no one comes or goes until I say so."

Or until you die, Aster thought, and the idea warmed her.

"Weapons?" Eamon asked. He spoke cordially, like he was offering to take her cloak.

Aster removed the throwing knives from her belt and set them on the table.

Roddy patted her down roughly. "That's all."

Aster didn't allow herself to think of anything, wary of giving her secrets away.

But Eamon frowned at her, disappointed. "The dagger in your boot, dear."

Aster crouched and pulled the dagger out. Eamon took it and studied the slender blade. "I had this made for you. Did you think I'd forget it?"

"I'd hoped."

He sighed and set it on the mantel. "We'll take the witch to the basement, Roderick."

Roddy picked Gale up again as though she weighed nothing. "Don't try anything," he said, speaking to Aster. "Long as you behave yourself, she lives. You harm me, I snap her neck and drain her for what her spirit's worth. Understood?"

Aster gritted her teeth and stepped aside. "Sure."

There was no point playing the part of the innocent daughter or the penitent sinner when they already knew so many of her secrets. But as long as Roddy had his hands on Gale, he held the power. The time for fighting would come.

Roddy's steps fell heavy on the wood floor as he followed Eamon toward the basement. Eamon unlocked the door, then stood aside to let him pass.

"After you," he said, and motioned for Aster to follow Roddy. Her feet seemed to be made of stone as she dragged them across the floor, and she wondered whether this was what criminals felt when they took the final walk to their executions—hopeless, empty, but not nearly numb enough to ease the terror.

The lamps were lit, blazing bright, casting faint shadows in the enclosed stairway as Roddy took the first step down. Aster ached to push him down the stairs. But he still had magic on his side, and Gale in his arms.

He was turned sideways to make his way through the narrow passage. Aster watched Gale's closed eyes and parted lips.

Then Gale opened her eyes and met Aster's gaze. She winked slowly, then closed them again before they reached the bottom.

Aster held back a gasp. Gale had protected herself. Not completely, but it was something.

A faint chill gripped Aster from head to toe, as though the warmth of the lamps had forgotten to reach a patch of air on the stairs. It vanished, leaving goosebumps covering Aster's arms.

Neither Roddy nor Eamon said anything about it, but it had been there.

Like a ghost.

Madrigal couldn't do anything practical to help, and unless Gale recovered quickly, she wouldn't be much help in a fight, either. But the idea that the ghost might be there eased Aster's nerves even as the thought of soon meeting her beyond death made her stomach twist into a tight knot.

The bottom of the stairs. The hallway. Aster's heart was thundering now, and she struggled to keep her breath even. Panic would be the end of everything, but she felt its frozen fingers tangling in her hair, tracing up her spine, gripping her heart.

The door to Eamon's chamber of horrors stood open, a gaping maw at the end of the corridor. The scent of dried roses and death wrapped itself around Aster and threatened to suffocate her as she followed Roddy into the dungeon. She didn't look up or acknowledge the bodies that still hung there but took in what might be more useful. During the time she'd been gone, Eamon had tidied up the mess from her last visit, and every knife and torture implement was locked away, the cupboard that had held them closed tight. His new blade lay on the workbench, gleaming in the warm lamplight, but it was no good to her.

The last thing she wanted was to deliver Roddy's soul to Eamon's vessel when he died.

Roddy dumped Gale on the table.

"Careful," Aster warned. Roddy sneered and slammed Gale's left arm against the rough wooden surface, then used both hands to slip the leather cuff around her wrist.

Gale sucked in a long breath, arching her back off the table. The fingers of her free hand scratched at its surface.

"Not yet," Roddy grumbled, and reached across. Gale pulled her arm away, then tried to snake it back under him.

Reaching for something.

Aster ran at him, throwing her weight against his unmovable

bulk, grabbing at his arm before he could stop Gale's movement. He snarled and turned, catching Aster across the chest with one arm and casting her across the room as though she weighed nothing. Aster hit the wall and tensed, ready to rush back at him.

Eamon stood in the doorway. Aster waited for the pain, the sensation of his enchantments draining from her, but nothing came.

Roddy glared at him. "Eamon, you'd best take care of your—"

His words became a guttural cry as Gale pulled a golden watch free from his waistcoat pocket.

His vessel.

He grabbed for the watch, but Gale swung it by its long chain over the far edge of the table.

Aster braced her boots against the stone floor and ran the few steps across the room. In the same motion she pulled the hidden loop of wire from her dress pocket and gripped the flat bits of wood at its ends in both hands, letting practice and instinct take over.

He was a different kind of wolf. Nothing she hadn't dealt with before.

The sound of the watch shattering as though the entire thing had been made of glass filled the room.

Powerful magic, Gale had said, but fragile.

Aster launched herself upward, bringing her arms down over Roddy's shoulders like a child jumping onto a trusted adult for a piggy-back ride. She pinned her knees to his waist, pressed the wire to his throat, and hauled backward.

Roddy clawed at the wire, but Aster braced herself and pulled harder, slicing through the thick gristle of his throat, releasing his blood in a thin stream. He reached for her, and she dodged, still holding tight until he crashed against the wall, pinning her, knocking her breath out before he stumbled forward.

She fell, dropping to the floor in a crouch, searching the room for a weapon. She'd need to finish the job before Eamon could stitch him back together with magic as he'd done for her.

Roddy staggered toward Eamon, bright blood pouring between his fingers as he tried, without magic, to stem the flow.

Eamon murmured something under his breath, and a cold gust of pure magic blew through the room. A fresh memory rose in Aster's mind, herself as a child feeling that chill for the first time and feeling as though her nightmares had stepped into the waking world.

The enchanted dagger rose and flew into Eamon's open hand, and with a well-aimed thrust, he drove it into Roddy's chest.

Aster tried to scream.

Roddy fell to his knees, gripping Eamon's forearm, then collapsed to the floor.

When Eamon pulled the blade free and turned to Aster, his eyes were bright and he stood straighter than he had before, the ball of his cane still gripped in one hand.

"Thank you, Aster," he said. "I was wondering how I'd tidy up that loose end. You really are extraordinarily gifted in these matters. It will serve you well in the future."

"There is no future," Aster said. "I remember everything you said to me the last time we visited this room. There will be no meddling with my enchantment. No more killing. No more power delivered to you."

Eamon paled. "You're wrong, my dear. Roderick figured out the solution, but I can work the magic alone. I'll just need to make you comfortable in one of these cells until you stop fighting me, and all will be well." He scowled as he turned to Gale. "You did something to protect her mind?"

Gale didn't answer, but she opened her eyes and glared at him. The effort of breaking Roddy's vessel seemed to have taken any energy she'd recovered since his attack, and his death hadn't fixed anything.

She said enchantments would disappear with a blood witch's death, but perhaps other spells were different.

"Interesting." Eamon frowned and touched her cheek. Gale's lips twitched, but she didn't pull away. "You defended yourself against blood magic, if imperfectly. That takes skill. It would be a shame to kill you." He drummed his fingers against the head of his cane. "I'll tell you what, Aster. I'm tired of fighting. If you'd be so kind as to step into one of those empty cells, I'll let your friend go as soon as the effects of Roderick's spell have worn off."

Aster laughed. It wasn't funny, exactly, but the idea that she'd once respected this snake tickled some deep, dark place in her mind. "Would you? How kind. I'd have expected you to make that promise, lock me up, then kill her anyway." The urge to laugh vanished. "Or would you find a way to work the new enchantment without her, then have me kill her for you once I lacked the desire to do anything but your will?"

Eamon stepped back from the table, and Aster circled away from him. "I've only wanted what's best for you since the day I saved you," he said. "I swear to you that once your enchantment is finished, you will be perfected. No scars of the past. No guilt. No pain. No fear."

"No choice. No humanity." Aster added, mimicking his tone. "I'd rather die than serve you." She stepped between Eamon and Gale. "How many witches have there been between my grandmother and this one?"

Eamon's head jerked back as though she'd slapped him.

More distraction. Put him off his guard.

Aster took a step closer to him—all she could take without moving into his dagger's reach. "I spoke to Jes. I remember everything. You paid the wolves to find my grandmother so you could feed off her pain and take her soul. *You* killed me." The words came out sharp as his dagger, dripping with poison. "You may have brought me back to life, but I only died because of your desperate, pathetic desire for power."

Eamon bared his teeth like a cornered dog. "The criminals and this witch have poisoned you against me." He murmured something under his breath, and Gale's back arched off the table as her face twisted in a spasm of pain.

"The poison is yours." Aster grasped at memories as they flew past—the deliberate attacks toward her and the wolves, the screams and shouts, a younger Eamon shouting his spells as she ran toward her grandmother and tried to shield her. "You couldn't possibly think you'd buried it forever, that I'd never remember what you did to me."

"I thought you were their brat!" Eamon's voice became a desperate cry, full of pain and regret. The hand holding the dagger trembled, and he turned away from Gale. "I meant to hurt them by hurting her, and only realized my mistake when I dug your body out of the rubble and looked into your eyes. So I brought you back. I'd lost so much and imagined a better future with you. You were to be my second chance. My new family."

There. His weakness. His pain.

Eamon had insisted that Aster be trained to kill without risking a fight, but her teachers had prepared her for the worst, and she remembered everything she'd learned from them about exploiting weakness in any form.

"What did happen to Winifred and Claudia?" she asked, letting a mocking tone come into her voice. "You said the curse took them. I believed you until I found out what kind of monster you really are. Did you sacrifice your daughter for magic? Did you—"

Eamon shouted a string of words in old Andonian, low and snarling, and a blast of stinging air like a desert sandstorm hit Aster full force, scraping her skin and stealing her breath. She stumbled back and crashed into the table, barely keeping herself from falling on top of Gale. Objects from the shelves flew through the air, and Aster leaned across the table, protecting Gale's head and torso with her body as she shielded herself as well as she could with her arms. Something hard hit the arm that protected the back of her head, and the sounds of shattering glass and ceramics rang in her ears.

Memories of the first time she'd met Eamon became clearer, and the fear and confusion she'd felt then threatened to overwhelm her.

Eamon standing in the middle of her grandmother's cabin, guarding the older woman's tortured body.

Knives from the kitchen flying, blades-first, toward the intruders.

Heavy books, iron pots, and papers flying about, injuring the enemy and obscuring Aster's view of anything more.

Pain as her thin clothing failed to protect her from the attacks, as Eamon efficiently dismembered a child to teach her supposed family a lesson.

Aster breathed in the scent of Gale's skin, focused on Gale's breath and her own, and willed herself to remain in the present.

Think.

Eamon had the knives, the needles, the other implements of torture available to him in the cupboard, but he hadn't called for them. This was a tantrum, not his final attack, and only a hint of what he could do.

He still wants me alive, even after all this.

She undid the leather cuff that bound Gale to the table. When Eamon's storm blew itself out, she stepped away, circling the outside of the room, forcing Eamon to face her as her boots crunched over the remains of the jars and crockery that had sat on the shelf. She stepped on something that squished beneath her foot, and she kicked it away. An eyeball rolled toward the wall and stopped, staring at her.

Gale still didn't move, save for her lips.

"I would never have harmed my sweet Claudia." Eamon spoke in a pained rasp, his breath heaving from the effort of his work. "I would have used my magic to reshape the world to her liking if my faithless wife hadn't stolen her away from me." Eamon pointed the dagger at Aster. "You sound like her. Winifred never understood my methods, my quest, my potential. It was too much, and she was too weak. She fled with my poor girl."

Aster's heart hammered, and she tried to catch her breath. "But you found them, didn't you?"

"I did. Too late to save Claudia from the plague that took her." His mask of rationality and civility cracked, and a mad grin split the blackness of his beard. "But Winifred learned to respect my work in the most personal way possible. I loved her. I did. And it made the sacrifice so powerful." He stepped closer, blade in hand. "The question is whether you become the next one, or whether we erase all of this and start over. No guilt, no regrets."

He looked to Gale, adjusting his grip on the knife.

Aster lunged and grabbed his cane by its shaft, wrenching it free from his grip. It came more easily than she'd expected, and she swung it with more force than she'd needed.

The glass ball smashed against the wall, sending glittering shards tinkling to the flagstone at Aster's feet. The wood cracked near the top, and she held tight to the jagged-tipped length of hardwood, ready to run Eamon through with it before his enchantments failed and she fell apart.

But his magic didn't disappear, and when she turned back to him, he was standing as straight and strong as before, glaring at her.

Eamon shrugged out of his jacket and laid it on the workbench, leaving him in a fine white shirt and perfectly pressed trousers. "You really need to pay better attention," he said, and raised his right hand.

His magic froze Aster's arm from fingers to shoulder, and the makeshift spear clattered to the ground.

Aster's scars burned like fire.

Aster fought to stand, then shed her cloak. The pain grew more intense as she moved, but she *could* move, and nothing else mattered.

But when she forced her body toward Eamon, he cursed and spat out a different spell.

"It's so hard, isn't it?" he asked, voice dripping with sympathy. "So tiring to keep fighting me. Think of how it will be when these broken parts of you are fixed."

A harsh reply formed behind Aster's lips, then died there as her thoughts sank into a warm pool of magic and dissolved until all she could cling to were the words Eamon offered her.

"Fixed," she repeated.

"Right." Eamon smiled. "Step behind that door over there, just for a few moments, and think of how happy you'll be. No scars, no fear, no needless worry about what you should or shouldn't do."

It did sound lovely, and Aster wondered why she was fighting at all.

"Aster."

Gale only managed a whisper, but it was enough. Aster looked to her and frowned, confused. A memory came to her—Gale in a jail cell, speaking between the bars, saying she looked nicer when her scars weren't covered. Touching her face by firelight, caressing every old injury like she was memorizing them.

The haze of Eamon's magic threatened to drown the memory, but Aster clung to it.

"You can't erase what you did to me," she whispered. "I know you're using magic against me. I won't believe a word you say." She paused, fighting for her next breath. "And I never will."

It was a lie. The temptation to sink back into his persuasion had become overwhelming. But it wasn't the truth. Though it felt like madness to keep fighting, she took another shuffling step toward him. Glass crunched under her boot.

"You're a liar, Eamon."

The liquid haze thinned like fog in sunlight.

"You've only ever cared what was best for you. Not for me. Not for anyone else."

Eamon lifted one hand toward her and his mouth twisted into an ugly grimace. The haze abated and the pain grew worse, digging deep into Aster's skin and muscle. She pushed back her sleeves. The scars had melted into ugly, freshly scabbed wounds but had not begun to bleed.

Sweat shone on his forehead as Eamon raised his other hand, twisting his fingers around his dagger's handle, slowly drawing his hands toward him before reaching again, like he was fighting to pull water toward himself.

He's drawing it back, but—

She glanced at Gale. Her eyes were squeezed tightly shut, and her lips were still moving.

Not praying, but speaking magic. Fighting at Aster's side though Roddy's spell had robbed her of the strength to stand. Holding the enchantment in place as Eamon tried to draw it from her.

Or part of it. The pain continued to grow until Aster's

stomach turned, and she retched hard enough that it bent her in half and sent fresh waves of pain through the scar on her head.

"I will never stop fighting you," she said, her voice stronger than before. "If you take my weapons, I'll tear your throat out with my bare hands." Her left leg weakened, and she fell to one knee as a flood of warm blood flowed toward her boot. "If you take my memory, some part of me will survive, as it has always survived. That part will fight to bring itself back until the day I die. Or the day you do."

Eamon darted forward and raised his knee, connecting with Aster's nose, bringing a blinding flash of sharper, fresher pain that erased her thoughts. Only instinct and memory made her roll as she fell, and when her mind cleared she was back on her feet.

Control it. Fight it.

The pain didn't lessen. She told herself it didn't matter and fought to focus on what did.

There was no way to win the fight as long as he had magic up his sleeve. He'd shared so little over the years, and he'd surprise her again soon enough.

She'd been wrong about his vessel. The cane might have been with him the day they met, but it had been as Jes had said—an accessory, an affectation, or something to lean on if his missing toe gave him trouble. He'd simply been too vain or too stubborn to trade it in when he needed something stronger.

Aster gulped a breath that felt like it cracked her ribs open and tried to remember more from the day she'd met him.

He'd worn a suit, of all things, to walk into the woods and murder a harmless witch. Cane. No rings. Nothing else she recognized as being with him since then.

Nothing she could see.

But then Eamon moved closer, and she looked away from the play of light on his dagger's blade to catch the duller gleam of the gold chain at his throat.

Winifred and Claudia. His loves, his loss, his disappointment, his sacrifice, always worn close to his heart.

Not out of love or for the sake of memory alone.

Aster reached for her cloak and flung it at Eamon, then ran toward the cupboard that held Eamon's weapons as a gust of magic sent it flying away. He spoke. She dodged, but the blunt force spell hit her arm, breaking her already uneven stride, sending her crashing into the wooden door. It opened, and weapons clattered to the floor.

Before her fingers could close around the handle of a butcher's knife, Eamon let out a spell that came as an enraged roar. His magic tore the knife from her, whipped it through the air, and plunged it into her right thigh as the other weapons scattered out of reach.

Move. More. Faster.

Aster fell to her knees, and the soft impact echoed through bones that should already have shattered. A long chunk of broken pottery sliced into her knee as she landed on its pointed end. A groan escaped her, though she hated to give Eamon the satisfaction.

"I didn't want this," Eamon said. He crouched in front of her and plunged his enchanted dagger into the muscle of her shoulder. Not to kill, but to draw from her pain. The fresh wound barely registered against the agony that already enveloped her from skull to toes. "I gave you so many chances. I loved you."

Aster ground her teeth together and forced herself to look into his eyes. "That wasn't love."

He twisted the blade, separating muscle from bone, spilling blood that soaked warm and heavy into Aster's dress. Tears filled his eyes, even as they lit up with the thrill of fresh power.

Let me be quick, Aster thought, praying to no one in particular and to anyone who would listen. If Lord Death was real, there had to be someone else out there who could help. *And let me be strong, just for a little longer.*

The pain didn't abate. But when she reached out her right hand as though to touch Eamon's cheek in supplication, she found she still had control of muscles that screamed for mercy as her movements pulled at her seams. They obeyed her, remembering the training Eamon had paid such good coin for. He pulled back, but too late. Aster's hand dropped, and the ends of her fingers tangled in the golden chain, gripped it tight, and pulled until it snapped.

At the same time, her left hand searched the ground for a weapon and found the thick, razor-edged piece of ceramic. Its edges bit into her flesh as she gripped it tight.

Gale's voice grew louder, speaking the musical cadence of her magic even as Eamon shouted more of his own twisted form of the same language.

The strength drained from the hand that held Eamon's locket. Slower, perhaps, than Eamon had wished, but as long as his vessel survived, his magic was stronger than Gale's, his experience in the craft more vast.

The locket fell to the floor and opened, leaving Winifred and Claudia's solemn portraits staring up at her as Aster's wounds opened at skin level. Within her, Eamon's dark enchantment rose up, becoming a palpable thing that fought to escape from her body. The pain became the roar of a crowd, and individual slices of agony became indistinguishable from each other, blending into a single senseless entity that threatened to drown out thought and will and consciousness.

Aster brought the blunt end of the ceramic shard down on the locket, striking Winifred's portrait. It wasn't a good hit, or a strong one, but the glass shattered, the hinge broke, and Eamon's incantations turned to a long howl of pain and loss as the tiny portraits caught fire and burned to nothing.

Almost done.

Aster couldn't feel her right hand anymore and didn't dare look to see whether it was still there. Gale was nearly shouting now, but Aster felt the enchantments unravelling, the dark magic receding as inexorably as the ocean's tide. Eamon wasn't pulling it now.

He didn't need to. Aster had finished the job for him.

Eamon turned to run from the room, and Aster released herself into her final hunt, embracing the pain as she launched upward and brought her makeshift weapon down again, driving the pointed end into his back, forcing it through cloth and flesh until the blade found its resting place between the ribs next to his spine.

Her fingers lost their grip, and she fell to the floor, gasping as her ribs cracked, her thigh bone shattered, and her heart ceased its frenzied hammering.

There was no fear this time, no regret over how she'd spent her last breaths.

Eamon fell to the floor and crawled toward the doorway, blood blooming against his white shirt as he reached and struggled to pull her weapon free. Gale still spoke, but the words grew muffled.

Aster listened until black fog filled the world around her, covering everything.

CHAPTER THIRTY-FIVE
ASTER

There was nothing.

And then there was a bit less of nothing. The thought made no sense, but the realization that she'd had a thought at all gave Aster something to anchor herself to.

I exist. I am... somewhere.

She took stock first of what there wasn't—pain, anger, fear. The dungeon had vanished, and what took a distinct lack of shape around her was grey, like the thickest mist imaginable. There was light, but no source of it. Ground to support her, but no horizon. The fact that she could see, though, and the fact that she could tell she wasn't floating implied a physical presence, and after what felt like quite a long time, she found control of her head and looked down.

She wore the dress she'd worn into the dungeon, but it was as clean as it had been when she'd put it on. And when she pushed back her sleeves, finding the fabric softer and more pliable than it had ever been before, her skin was whole and unmarked, as though it had never faced the trials of life. Not healing, but absence of injury. She marvelled at it in a way that felt somehow distant and passionless, turning her arm over, flexing her fingers, spinning in a slow dance and feeling not a single ache or twinge in her muscles.

It was good. There was no sense of victory or great meaning in this place, but this was better than the vaguely remembered shadows of what had come before.

As she completed her spin, another figure emerged from the fog. A stranger, lithe and lovely, her hair like a flow of dark honey and eyes that showed no shock at Aster's presence. If anything, this woman seemed to recognize her. She held her hands folded in front of the skirt of her green dress, and her feet were bare.

"Aster," she said, and gave her a sad smile. "We meet at last."

There was nothing familiar in the warm tones of her voice, but Aster knew her anyway. "Madrigal?" She'd thought there was no pain here, but her voice caught in her throat as the realization hit her more fully than her peaceful awakening had allowed thus far. "I'm really dead?"

Madrigal stepped closer, and Aster caught the shine of tears in her eyes. "Just moments ago. Gale asked me to come look for you."

Aster stepped past Madrigal and searched the fog. She thought she caught the sound of a distant voice calling her name, but it could have been her imagination.

"This is the borderlands," Madrigal said. "All who die pass through here. Lord Death will come soon to take you."

Aster took a long, calming breath, then realized she didn't need to. Her heart wasn't racing. Panic wasn't filling her, nor was the urge to fight the god when he arrived. There was sadness, a deep ache at the loss of what she'd never have when she left the world behind, but it was a peaceful sort of melancholy.

"Will Gale be all right?"

Madrigal arched an eyebrow. "Is that all you want to know before you go?"

"Yes." She listened again but heard nothing from the world she'd left behind. "If she's safe, I have no regrets. And no desire to stay here as you have. Even if she could see and hear me, I wouldn't do her any good."

It was an unfamiliar feeling to not want anything more, to not fight and cling and seek victory. Not bad, but strange.

Madrigal watched her closely, then nodded. "That's as it should be."

"You didn't answer my question."

"No." Madrigal flickered and vanished for a moment, then returned. "I don't think Gale is in physical danger. You did your job better than I'd hoped."

Aster turned again, slowly. "But Eamon's not here. He's still alive."

"Barely, but yes."

Aster opened her mouth to speak, but Madrigal held up a hand to silence her.

"My lord."

A chill ran through Aster as she turned and a tall figure in a floor-length robe the colour of the grave—not quite grey, not quite brown or black, but its own fathomless hue—stepped into view, his face shadowed by a deep hood, his hands hidden under long, loose sleeves.

"Madrigal," he said in a resonant, deep, and surprisingly pleasant voice.

The ghost's eyes widened. "Yes."

"It's time we spoke. But I believe there's other business to be tended to first."

Madrigal paled. "Of course, my lord."

Lord Death, who needed no formal introduction, turned to Aster. "Are you ready?"

"Almost." Aster made herself look deep into the shadows beneath his hood and caught the hint of a very human-looking jawline and a grim but well-formed mouth. "I'd like to go back and see Gale, the way Madrigal does. Just to say goodbye."

Lord Death tilted his head gently to one side, and Aster felt as though he understood her completely. "She won't be able to see or hear you," he said. "Nor will I allow Madrigal to speak to Nightingale until this is over. Do you understand?"

Hearing Gale's name on Death's lips sent a shiver through Aster. "I do."

"Very well."

Death's pale left hand emerged from his sleeve as he raised it into the air and waved away the fog, revealing the dungeon as Aster had left it. For a long moment all she could do was stare at her own body, which she barely recognized as the one she'd occupied for so long. It seemed like a strange thing now, lying there face-down on the floor, completely separate from her. Eamon, who lay motionless by the door, looked just as strange and distant, like a defeated enemy from a history book rather than her own life. She turned instead to Gale, who had climbed from the table and was crawling toward her body through the pools of blood and piles of debris. She seemed to be regaining her physical strength as the effects of her enemies' spells ebbed, but sobs wracked her body and tears streamed down her cheeks.

"Madrigal!" she called, her voice raw and cracked. She turned Aster's body over, revealing a dress soaked in blood and a face mutilated by injuries that had never been allowed to truly heal. Aster's eyes stared up at the bodies that hung above it as Gale reached into the pocket beneath her skirt and pulled out the artificial heart, and Aster understood why she'd gone back to her flat without protection.

She was only caught because she still hoped. No sense of guilt accompanied the thought, but it brought a hint of sorrow that vanished quickly. Eamon was defeated. Gale would live. All was well.

Aster placed her hands on Gale's shoulders. They passed through, and Gale didn't seem to notice at all. She was focused on reaching for one of the knives Eamon had scattered across the floor, on steadying her trembling hands to slice open the front of Aster's dress, on pushing aside scraps of bloody flesh and splintered bone to make space for the mechanical heart.

Then she reached out to close Aster's eyes. What had been a scar on her face was now an open gash, and the skull above was caved in on one side. Gale brushed aside a lock of gore-soaked hair that stuck to the corpse's cheek and rested her hand against the lifeless flesh with all the tenderness of someone admiring a sleeping lover.

Gale's lips parted, revealing gritted teeth. She squeezed her eyes closed and sobbed again, sharp and aching, and the sound vibrated through Aster's spirit. Then she visibly steeled herself, setting her jaw and straightening her shoulders, and looked down at the heart.

"Madrigal would call me a fool for this," she whispered to Aster's body. "But I promised you I'd do everything in my power."

Eamon groaned. Gale ignored him, raised her hands over the heart, and began her incantations. Her voice remained weak and shaky, but Aster felt the magic more strongly than she ever had when she was alive. It wasn't a faintly familiar thing now, but an essential force drawn from the core of the world, taking on Gale's distinct essence, directed by her intentions and guided by her knowledge.

And, Aster suspected, by her grief.

Madrigal knelt by Gale's side and laid her hands on her shoulders, and Gale leaned into her touch as though she knew, deep within, that her mentor was with her. Aster wished she could offer the same.

Lord Death stood over Eamon, watching the proceedings.

Gale worked with her eyes closed, and the body began to respond. Ruined flesh grew into the mechanical heart, forming connections. Clean, bright blood from the floor drew back onto the body, leaving its mark only in the shifted patterns of the dust and dirt it left behind. It was as it had been with the other body, but now the words came without hesitation and the tissues grew together more easily.

Aster looked to Madrigal, whose attention was firmly on her student. She smiled, proud and sad at the same time. "Not even looking," she whispered. "She's working by the feel of the magic, improvising her words, speaking to magic in its own language. Pure connection. Masterful." She looked to Aster, then down at the heart as it took on a full, rounded shape and began beating with a steady, mechanical rhythm. "I've never known her to have such passion for this work, even when she was saving her own life."

Gale paused, opened her eyes, and watched the heart. Aster watched it, too, and waited to feel some renewed connection to her body. There was nothing.

"But she can't save me," she whispered.

"No, and she knows it as well as you or I. It's the attempt that matters now. The care. The last gift she can offer you." Madrigal blinked, and a tear slipped from each eye. "I owe you an apology, Aster. I told Gale to stay away from you."

"You knew she was in danger," Aster said, and watched as the bones knit themselves back into ribs, though they were covered in webs of visible lines where the breaks healed. "You were right."

"It wasn't only that. I knew from the first moment you shared that you would be a problem for her. She's always craved connection. Wanted someone to share her life with, someone to support and challenge and love, who would do the same for her. I believed that would only distract her from her studies. I still believe that would have been the case, but..." Madrigal's voice trailed off, and she shook her head sadly. "Perhaps I underestimated the power of devotion as a motivation toward greatness.

She's a real witch, now. Everything I ever hoped my apprentice would be."

She glanced toward Lord Death, but he said nothing.

Neither Madrigal nor Aster spoke as Gale sliced away more of the dress and the layers beneath, then worked without guidance to bring the rest of the body back together. She moved slowly, adjusting broken bones with skilled hands, pulling ravaged muscle and skin into place as her voice carried the magic that closed old wounds and formed new scars. With Aster's life and spirit gone, the dead flesh complied as easily as an inanimate object might have, with the injuries still visible but everything appearing, as far as Aster could tell, whole and freshly healed. But the tissues remained dull even when the veins filled with blood, no different from the corpse she'd practiced on.

Gale's voice was fading, her hands trembling. Dark, hollow circles formed under her eyes, and her lips cracked as though she hadn't taken a drink in days. Her skin took on a yellowish hue, and bruises blossomed beneath her skin.

"Make her stop," Aster demanded, not sure whether she was speaking to Madrigal or the god lurking behind her.

"I can't," Madrigal said. "Don't worry, she'll faint before it kills her. But she's made for magic now. Witches rely on it like anyone else relies on breath or blood, and she's emptying herself for you."

"But it will come back?"

Madrigal reached out and laid her hand on Aster's. It felt warm. Alive. "In time, it will. Her grief won't help, but she's too strong for this to be the end."

The skin closed and the old scars re-formed, though they appeared raw and barely healed.

The room fell silent save for the ragged breath of the two living humans as Aster sat next to the cast-off shell of her living self and tried to decide how best to say goodbye. A deep ache spread through her chest—not grief for herself as she'd been, but for the life she might have lived.

Gale rocked unsteadily on her knees, then laid her head on Aster's chest and closed her eyes.

"Come back," she whispered. A tear dripped from the end of her nose onto the painfully fresh scars covering Aster's breast-bone. "Please."

CHAPTER THIRTY-SIX
GALE

Gale lay with her cheek against Aster's cool skin and sank into nothingness. If there was magic left in her, she couldn't find it. She felt ancient and dusty and had neither the energy nor the desire to make herself do anything but breathe.

I failed you.

The heart beat against her ear, regular and meaningless.

I'm sorry.

Eamon groaned, and she forced her eyes open. He struggled to lift his head.

"Help me, witch."

Gale decided she could spare the energy to sit up after all. "You," she whispered, and forced herself to her feet. She stumbled and grabbed the edge of the table, then used it to drag herself closer until she stood over him.

"Please," he said. "You can save my life. I'm no danger to you or anyone now."

Gale glanced back at Aster's body. "You've done plenty of damage, though."

Eamon drew in a slow breath. Gale hoped it hurt. The wide end of a massive shard of broken crockery still protruded from his back, perhaps the only thing keeping him from bleeding to death.

"Aster died more than a decade ago," he said. His voice came out thin and pained, but he didn't seem to have any intention of shutting up. "This isn't murder. It's undoing what I suppose you'd call my old sins. Let me start over. No more magic."

"Old sins." Gale's thoughts came to her slowly, as if the world outside the dungeon had ceased to exist and her mind needed to rebuild it before past hurts and future plans could be true concerns. "What other old sins scar your soul? A curse, maybe, on a town in the mountains last spring? I'll listen if you want to clear your conscience."

She looked down at him, then at the body of the one who had brought her to this wretched place. Blood witches. A rare thing.

But Eamon appeared genuinely confused. "Many sins, but not that."

Gale leaned harder on the table. Knowing he'd done it wouldn't have made her next decisions easier, but it would have been so good to lay that question to rest.

"In spite of what you believe," Eamon said, "I used my power to make the world better. I didn't do that sort of work."

Did that help you sleep at night? Gale wondered. *Knowing you manipulated and controlled her, but it was never technically a curse?*

But she didn't ask. He'd only defend himself, and his justifications would anger her when she needed a clear head.

Gale considered her options. Aster would have pulled the weapon free if she hadn't lost her grip, and the blood loss might have been the end of him. But she was dead, and now Eamon's life rested in Gale's hands.

She stared down at him. "I made a promise to God a long time ago, when I lived in that mountain town. Swore I'd heal all, that I'd leave judgement in God's hands because no human deserves that power. I meant that oath with every fibre of my being, and I swore it on my own soul. I suppose that would mean I have to help you."

"Oh, thank you," Eamon whispered. He reached for the hem of her skirt.

"Shut up," Gale snapped. Something sparked deep inside her, shining through the emptiness. It warmed her and strengthened her, but it wasn't magic. "I made that promise when I believed all the ill in the world came from people choosing their will over God's. I've learned a few things since then, though." She frowned. "A lot of things, actually. And I've learned them by making my own choices, still seeking God's will but walking that path without a map. Do you know how frightening that is? To be responsible? To not know?"

He didn't answer.

"But it's good, too. I've seen love in the darkest places and loyalty among people I once would have condemned, found power and joy where I was once forbidden to look. And I think…" She paused. "I think sometimes we do have to judge for ourselves. Aster might have been wrong in following your orders, but she was right about one thing. Justice doesn't always come to those who deserve it. Not in this world."

Eamon reached for her hand, and Gale pulled it away. "What good will it do you to let me die?" he asked. "You aren't a blood witch, and I don't believe you'd have the will to become one even if you had the knowledge." A fine sheen of sweat shone on his brow. "You can't claim my soul and trade it for hers as I did when Aster died the first time."

"Claim?" Gale clung to the edge of the table and crouched. Eamon flinched. "I wouldn't touch your soul for the sake of every good thing in the world. You belong to…"

The words trailed off, and Gale froze in place.

He's here. He has to be.

Lord Death would have come for Aster. But Gale imagined even a busy god might want to stick around to make sure a snake like Eamon wouldn't find a way to lose himself in the border-lands if he died.

Eamon had stolen so much from Lord Death. Dozens of spirits that should have moved beyond the veil had instead been consumed. It was quite a debt.

Everything she'd been taught, everything she'd promised to become, said this was wrong. She didn't care.

"I wouldn't touch it myself," she repeated, and stood. "But I might be willing to release it for the right price. Lord Death? Are you here? Will you speak to me?"

Silence followed. Gale waited, tense, unsure of whether to feel afraid or foolish.

"I am."

The voice came like a whisper she felt more than heard, and every hair on her body stood on end as fear won out. She'd spoken to a ghost before, but a god was another thing entirely. Her frail and temporary mortal body trembled.

Eamon's eyes widened, and Gale knew she hadn't imagined the voice.

"You know this man," she said. No physical form accompanied the voice, so she spoke to the room. "He's stolen from you many times. A friend once told me that those who do evil in this world run from you after their deaths."

"This is true." The voice was stronger now. Interested. It made Gale feel like screaming, laughing, and fleeing all at once, and her heart seemed to be trying desperately to hammer its way out of her chest.

"I could help him," she said. "I don't have much magic left in me, but I could probably keep him alive until he gets to a hospital. It's what I've sworn to do." Death didn't answer. Gale steeled herself. "Or I could leave and let you take him, depending on what it's worth to you."

"Don't!" Eamon cried. "Please. You don't know the—"

"I said shut up," Gale said, cold and calm.

"You would dare to bargain with Death?" The disembodied words came not as a challenge or a threat, but with genuine curiosity. Still, the very existence of the voice made Gale tremble.

She straightened her shoulders and told herself she wasn't afraid. "I don't wish to. But I suppose I have to try."

A long pause followed before Death spoke again. "If his life were yours to offer, I might be free to consider it. But I wonder whether you understand what you're asking of me."

The unearthly voice sank into Gale's body, chilling her bones. "Please tell me, then."

"Your lack of action does not make his soul yours to give. He must die by your hand if you wish to upset the balance in your favour." The voice was closer now, more specific, coming from just behind Gale's shoulder. She didn't dare turn. "You must sacrifice not only his life, but a part of yourself—your oath, your certainty, the bright shine of your soul. You, who has sworn to preserve life without judgement, must take it without hesitation for your own purposes."

Gale's breath caught in her throat.

"Release this man's soul to me now," Death said, his voice moving closer to Eamon, "and I will allow the balance to shift in your favour so that Aster may return to life." A dark swirl of fog appeared, then coalesced into the form of a human figure in a dark robe, his face completely lost in shadow.

Eamon sobbed.

"Will I be like him if I do this?" Gale asked, finding herself less afraid somehow now that Death had a body she could speak to. "Will I stop being a vessel?"

There were some risks she wouldn't take. She could too easily imagine what it would be like to lose her power, to crave it as she did now, and to find ways to justify killing to feel it flowing through her again.

"No. This transaction has nothing to do with your magic."

Only my soul, Gale thought. *Fantastic.*

"The cost will be to your integrity, and your faith in who you believe yourself to be. Small costs to some people, but not to you." He spoke gently, but the words weighed heavy. Gale had sinned before in the eyes of her people but had taken on *witch* as part of her identity when she realized her people were wrong to fear it, and it hadn't changed who she believed herself to be.

There would be no such comfort with the words *killer* or *oathbreaker*. She would commit the sin of considering herself like God, believing herself worthy to judge one life more valuable than another, and turning her back on God's will.

So be it.

Lord Death moved toward Aster's body, and Gale followed. "She'll return to weakness and pain," he said. "You have done much for her, but the damage remains. For most of her life she's lived with corrupted magic that held her together and numbed the pain. There will be no dark enchantment to hide the agony of true healing, and no assurance that she will ever be free from it. Is that what you want?"

"No." Gale closed her eyes to shut out Death's dark form and Aster's body at his feet. She imagined Aster returning to life, screaming, cursing Gale for not letting her remain at peace and begging her to send her back. But when she tried to imagine not giving Aster the chance to live, it was no better.

"Well?" Death asked. "You need to decide. A body without a spirit isn't good for long."

Gale looked down at Aster, then crouched beside her and traced her fingers over the fresh scar that ran down her face. "I don't want her life," she said. "I'll offer you Eamon's, but what I ask in return is that you let Aster choose." Tears burned at her eyes. "I'll understand if she wants to rest now that her work is done. But if she comes back, I'll do everything I can to help her once my magic returns."

"Done." The god's voice shook the room. When Gale looked up, he was gone.

Gale took a deep breath, picked up the razor-sharp knife she'd used to cut Aster's clothing away, and shut out the screaming voices of her parents, her community, and her own conscience as she walked toward Eamon.

"Don't." Eamon grabbed her skirt and looked up at her, begging. "Please. You say you lived in the cursed town—I didn't curse them, and I don't know who did, but I have connections. I can help you learn the truth and bring them to justice if that's what you want. I'll never harm another soul. I'll never use magic again."

Gale hesitated. It pained her to think he might be her last connection to answers. But knowledge and justice wouldn't bring back the dead of Bright Hollow any more than they'd brought back Aster's grandmother.

And she knew better than to trust him.

Numbness descended over Gale as she reached for the makeshift blade Aster had driven into him. Its edges bit into her skin, and she welcomed the pain.

She twisted it as she pulled the shard free, opening the wound wider.

Eamon cursed and kicked with his legs, still trying to escape, dragging himself desperately through the doorway. Blood flowed freely from the wound on his back, but it was still only the end of Aster's work. Not enough to upset the balance in her favour.

Gale dropped Aster's weapon and gripped the knife's handle tighter.

"God forgive me," she whispered, "though I know what I do."

She caught up with Eamon in two unsteady steps, grabbed the hair at the back of his head to lift his chin, and drew the blade across his throat.

CHAPTER THIRTY-SEVEN
ASTER

The room vanished again, and Aster stood in the fog of the borderlands with Madrigal and Lord Death. Peace returned, leaving Aster with curiosity but no real sense that what came next mattered.

That in itself troubled her.

I should be bothered, she thought, *about what happens to Eamon. To Gale. To me.*

"Concerns of the living," Lord Death said, as though he'd read her mind. "The dead know how little mortal matters mean in the grander scheme of things." He looked to Madrigal. "Some take longer to learn this truth and require time to let go."

The witch turned away.

A scream echoed through the borderlands, and though she couldn't see Lord Death's face, Aster felt him smiling.

Eamon, or something very much like him, shambled toward them. Like Aster, his death wounds had no effect on his spiritual form. But a dull shock rolled through Aster at his appearance nonetheless, and she stepped back from him.

Everything about him was wrong.

His eyes were black from lid to lid and corner to corner, and dull. Flat. Dark-green fluid dripped from them, and from his open, shrieking mouth. Weeping sores festered on every bit of exposed skin. His black beard, so fine and well cared-for in life, had faded to a strange, sickly blue in its spirit form and grew in mangy patches. His limp was gone, but he stumbled as though the muscles in his legs had wasted away.

His dark eyes could see, though, and his steps and his screaming both halted when he saw Lord Death.

"I won't go," he said. His voice came out thick and mucosal, the sound of a man slowly drowning from within.

Aster looked down at her hands, at the clear skin that had been bloodied so many times in life, and wondered how much worse Eamon's crimes were for his soul to have become this.

Eamon turned and stumbled away.

Lord Death sighed and reached out a hand. The distance was too great by any physical measure, but he caught the back of Eamon's shirt and hauled him closer. Death's hands were strong and surprisingly lively, and Aster caught the flash of a well-muscled forearm before his sleeve fell back into place to cover it.

She looked to Death's face again, searching the shadows, but saw no more than she had before. She suspected, though, that he might not be as fearsome as the living supposed, that once one stood properly before him and laid their eyes fully on him, Death might be quite lovely.

At least for most.

Eamon struggled as Lord Death pulled him closer.

"Aster, help me," he begged. "Lord Death, please, I didn't know. That is, I didn't fully understand—"

Lord Death waved his other hand and Eamon's mouth snapped shut, held tight by five stitches of thick, dark thread sewn through his upper and lower lips. Rough ropes appeared out of the fog and wound themselves around him, pinning his arms to his sides and binding his legs together, and Lord Death dropped him to the ground.

Aster didn't ask what would happen when Lord Death took him from the borderlands. She couldn't find it in herself to care.

The fog thinned, allowing Aster to see Gale. She'd dropped the knife and lay again with her head on Aster's chest, listening to the useless beating of the enchanted heart.

"He needs your decision, child," Madrigal said. She spoke to Aster but watched Gale with the shine of tears in her eyes.

Aster looked down at her body. Gale had done a remarkable job, giving back everything that had been lost, repairing what would have taken months or longer for a body to heal itself, if such a thing had even been possible. She'd poured herself out, given over her magic to give Aster a chance.

And yet.

She closed her eyes and marvelled at the strength of her spirit body, the complete absence of pain, how easy it would be to forget that suffering existed at all.

"How bad will it be if I live?" Aster asked.

Lord Death stepped closer. "I can't say for certain. I expect your body will continue its work of true healing, but with so many fresh wounds, with weakened flesh in a world where disease lurks around every corner... even with a witch by your side, you may experience the kind of suffering that leads many mortals to cry out to me for mercy." He stood beside her, hands folded in his sleeves, and watched as Gale took a trembling breath and closed her eyes. "But you have suffered before. You have died before and returned to fight similar battles. The only question is whether you want to do it again."

"We've met, then?"

"We have. But no mortal is permitted to remember me if they return from these lands."

"And did I choose to go back that time?"

"No," Lord Death said, his voice hard. "That time there was dark magic to compel you. Your grandmother's soul was released into my care, and you were stolen from me."

"She's…" Aster remembered her grandmother easily—tough and sharp-witted but unfailingly kind and generous, always ready with a tight hug and a delightful story when Aster came to visit. "She's all right?"

"Of course."

Her parents would be, too. If she went with Lord Death, Aster would see them again. She imagined feeling their arms around her, hearing her father's booming laugh that she'd forgotten for too long. Her heart ached for them.

Aster crouched and hovered her hand over Gale's tangled hair. It was the closest she could come to touching her.

"That was all she ever wanted for me," she said. "To give me the freedom to choose for myself."

"And now you must," Lord Death said.

Aster looked to Madrigal. The witch's skin appeared paler than it had before. "You'll guide her through this if I return? And help me?"

Madrigal's jaw tightened as she glanced at Lord Death. "I'm afraid I can't promise anything. You have to choose now, or the choice will be made for you."

Aster tried to remember life—not only the pain, the lies, the insults and injuries, but the other things. The way the days lengthened after the longest night, building toward the first breath of spring blowing through the city. Crocuses in the garden. Sparrows in the bushes outside the window.

Not everything in life was worth returning for. She'd happily leave small talk and gossip and fundraisers behind forever. But there was another kind of life waiting if she chose to return, far different from the one Eamon had wished for her. One full of good magic and laughter, freedom and friendship. Maybe even love.

To die would be to end my story without knowing how much better things might have been after the long, dark night.

She knelt beside her body.

"There is no life without pain," she whispered. "But I want it. I want the good that comes with it."

"Very well." Lord Death offered no hint of whether this pleased him.

The fog darkened, and the last thing Aster saw before it closed over her was Lord Death dragging Eamon's struggling form by the back of his jacket, paying no attention to him otherwise as he lowered his head to focus on what appeared to be an intense discussion with Madrigal.

CHAPTER THIRTY-EIGHT
ASTER

Aster's gasping, ragged breath burned into lungs that screamed for mercy. She forgot where and who she was as everything disappeared in the undertow of sensation—aches, stiffness, lines of searing pain that tangled together in a net that pinned her to the ground, a dull thud in her skull pounding out a steady and terrible rhythm. She gritted her teeth and released the breath in a long, low groan.

A weight lifted from her chest, leaving her exposed skin cold but easing the pressure.

"Aster?" Cool hands rested on her cheeks. Then again, more intensely, Gale's voice breaking with hope. "Aster?"

Aster forced her eyes open. Everything came to her blurred and whirling in a dizzying attack of light, colour, and form, but with another breath, Gale's face came into focus. Dark circles ringed her eyes, her rounded cheeks had lost their rosy glow, and her sallow skin was lined with dirt and tears. She wiped her nose on her sleeve, but it didn't quite do the job. There was no magic in her, no sparkling energy. The goddess was gone, leaving only the girl.

She was the most beautiful thing Aster had ever seen.

Aster tried to reach a hand up to touch her cheek, but her arm was too heavy.

"Gale," she whispered instead. "Are you all right?"

Gale laughed and wiped her eyes with the other sleeve. "I think I am, if you are."

"Your magic?"

"It will come back. My vessel is safe at home, and I've got ingredients for potions to replenish it and speed things along. I think the effects of that thug's spell have worn off." She frowned and touched Aster's cheek, fingers barely brushing her skin. "I'm more concerned about you."

Aster made herself smile, though it tugged painfully at the fresh scar on her face. "You're only saying that because I died."

Gale reached for Aster's cloak and covered her with it, then took her hand, slowly and gently. "Did you… what was it like?"

The answer was there. Aster opened her mouth to speak it, and suddenly it was gone.

"I don't know," she said. "I remember that things happened, but not what they were or what it was like. Eamon is gone. You saved me. Madrigal…" She lifted her head, though it made the ache worse, and looked around. "Is she here?"

Gale followed her gaze. "No. She disappeared after you died. I asked her to go find you. Not very nicely, I think. I hope she's not sulking."

"No." Aster laid her head back down on the hard stone. "I know she was there. She's good, isn't she?"

"One of the best." Gale drew her knees up to her chest, crossed her arms over them, and rested her chin on top, close without quite touching. She looked smaller than Aster remembered. Younger. "What did she say to you? Where is she?"

Aster struggled to remember, but there was nothing. Only a vague sense that someone else was there, that it had been terribly important.

"I don't know," she said. "I think... I think she said she was proud of you."

A frown crossed Gale's brow, then vanished as she looked toward the door and Eamon's body lying in it. "We should get out of here. Find someone who can take care of this mess. Get you to a bed so you can rest."

"Your bed," Aster said. "Your home, where you can fix yourself. Or anywhere but here."

"Agreed." But they didn't move. Aster supposed neither of them could yet. The thought of standing was as daunting as the idea of climbing a mountain.

Aster slowly stretched her left arm out across the floor. "Maybe in a few minutes?"

Gale gave her a weary smile and lay on her side. She rested her head on Aster's upper arm, one of the few places on her body where there were no scars. "Does that hurt?"

"No." It was a lie, but one that would keep Gale close. Every fibre of Aster's body hurt, but she had no regrets.

She closed her eyes and focused not on the pain, but on Gale's breath and the beating of her strange new heart.

We'll get up, she promised herself.

Soon.

She'd barely closed her eyes when the sound of soft footsteps reached her from the corridor. Gale picked up the knife she'd used to kill Eamon and climbed to her feet, and Aster forced herself to follow, holding the cloak up to cover herself as the scraps of her ruined clothes fell away. Her body didn't want to listen, and she only managed to stand by thinking through every motion and demanding that her limbs obey her in spite of the feeling that everything might fall apart again.

A wave of dizziness hit her as her heart beat steadily, offering her nothing extra to support the effort.

Gale stepped toward the door without magic or the foresight

usually offered by Madrigal's invisible presence, and swung the knife as someone stepped into the doorway.

Cas jumped back, easily avoiding her strike, then stood still, taking everything in. Aster could easily imagine his shock as he looked over the mutilated corpses hanging from the ceiling, the fresh pair on the floor, Gale looking frightened out of her mind, and Aster herself likely looking as horrid as she felt.

But only mild surprise showed on his face. Jes joined him a moment later and frowned as she looked over the mess.

"You told me you'd stay away," Aster said.

"And you believed us?" Jes clucked her tongue. "I thought you had more sense than that."

Aster sank back to the floor, legs crossed, leaning forward. All she wanted was to lie down again, but there was only so much weakness one could show in front of enemies.

Or whatever they were now.

"We did consider taking your advice," Cas said. "It didn't suit us." He offered Gale his arm, and she leaned heavily on him.

Jes paced the room, barely disturbing the debris that covered the floor, avoiding the pools of Eamon's and Roddy's blood. "We'll need to get rid of all these bodies. I know people who will help."

"For a fee?" Aster forced a dark smile. "Or did you help yourself to a few valuables on your way down?"

"Hardly." Jes crouched in front of Aster. "Nothing goes missing, nothing looks like a crime scene when the police come by about your father going missing. You'll come up with a story about him leaving town, perhaps with that fellow." She nodded at Roderick's body. "The other corpses vanish, too, and we'll seal off this room before the cops come. But yes, at your expense. We're not running a charity for wayward vigilantes."

"I'll cover it from my personal account." Aster looked up at Eamon's victims. "But those ones need proper burials. They deserve that much."

Cas nodded. "I'll get in touch with Halivund and Bunker. They'll help with that, and they'll know someone trustworthy to brick in the door."

The world swam around Aster as exhaustion and the haze of pain threatened to overtake her. She laid her head on her arms, letting the conversation go on around her without really following it. She only looked up when she felt a gentle touch on her shoulder.

"Come on," Gale said. "We're going to get out of here. I'm going to replenish my magic, you're going to get a massive dose of my pain potion, and you're going to trust my friends to take care of everything else."

Aster wanted to object but couldn't think of a good reason.

She let Cas help her to her feet and leaned on him as Gale led them to the door, pausing only long enough for Aster to take Eamon's keyring from his pocket and hand it to Jes.

The new key to the dungeon had disappeared with his other enchantments. Aster brushed its dust from her fingers and forced herself to walk away.

CHAPTER THIRTY-NINE
GALE

Madrigal's home in the forest was as Gale remembered it at its best—a fine little log cabin with symbols of protection painted on the doorposts, a lush and wild garden where herbs and vegetables grew ripe and healthy in every season, chickens clucking contentedly as they chased any pests that dared breach the property line. Dawn had arrived, sending yellow rays of light through the hazy mist that covered everything.

The only problem was that this version of the cabin didn't exist anymore, and Gale had no recollection of travelling here. A dream, then, but a pleasant and peaceful one.

She walked the stone paths between overgrown flower patches, letting the blossoms kiss the open palms of her hands, and found Madrigal sitting in the orchard beneath a tree that bore yellow apples, purple pears, and a single bough of bright cherries.

"This is different." Gale sat on the soft grass next to her mentor, her legs tucked beneath her skirt. She was dressed in flowing white fabric so light it barely whispered against her skin. It made her wish she could wrap her waking body in anything so lovely. "I haven't seen you in a dream since just after we met for the second time."

Madrigal smiled. "Dreams are important. I don't like to disturb yours, or your rest. But we need to speak."

The sky darkened as a heavy cloud passed before the sun. Gale's stomach clenched. "Is it about Aster?"

"No."

That only left one option. Gale swallowed back her apprehension. "You can't leave."

"It seems that's no longer true." Madrigal leaned back against the tree and traced her fingers over the abundant curve of a perfect apple. "After my death, I stayed in this world out of anger against you, and out of my own stubborn unwillingness to leave business unfinished. I couldn't bear the thought of not passing my knowledge on."

A chill wind blew through the orchard, sending a flurry of leaves blowing toward the gardens.

"You still have so much to teach me," Gale said. Her heart fluttered at the thought of going on without Madrigal at her side.

"I do. I suppose I could decide to be unsatisfied, to chain myself to you and this world again as I pursued some new purpose. But you're a true witch, now. You speak the language of magic not only with your lips, but with your mind and your heart." Madrigal took Gale's hands in hers, and for the first time since her death they felt warm and alive. "You did what I believed impossible. You understand what you want from this path you walk. You have much to learn, but that was true of me until the day I died, as it has been of every witch. We never stop seeking and learning, but you don't need me for that anymore."

Hot tears spilled down Gale's cheeks, but she held her voice steady. "I want you, though." She wiped her face on the back of her wrist, and the tears vanished.

Madrigal closed her eyes and smiled. "It's good to hear you say that. I know I've been hard on you, but I've come to think of you as more than my student. In a world where things were different, we might have grown old as sister-witches."

Invisible claws dug into Gale's heart, tearing it in half. "We should have been. If only I'd chosen better the first time we met—"

Madrigal laid a hand on hers. "*If only* is a dangerous place to live. There is only what is, and I forgave you for all of that long ago. There is nothing left for me here, Nightingale. If I were alive, I would be releasing you from your apprenticeship now. My work is done, and there's nothing to tie me to a world I can't enjoy as I did when I lived. I don't belong here, and haven't since I died. It has been a pleasure to teach you, to watch you grow. Even to fight with you."

Gale squeezed Madrigal's hands and imagined she'd never have to let go. "I know I've been a terrible apprentice. I wish I could go back and change things."

"I wouldn't want you to." Madrigal stood and stretched, and in the next moment the two were walking side by side through the woods on the gentle slope of the mountain. "You've been challenging, frustrating, and stubborn, but all the best witches are. Magic is intention and will as well as power, and you have all of them in abundance."

"I'm glad you haven't hated every moment."

Madrigal chuckled. "No. Only most of them." She bumped Gale's shoulder with her own. "My business is finished, and I thank you for that. You don't need a teacher hovering over your shoulder. And if I'm guessing correctly, your time and attention will now have demands unrelated to magic lessons and fortune telling."

Gale threaded one arm through Madrigal's and pulled her close, savouring her solidity and warmth. Their time alive together had been so short and so burdened with uncertainty that they'd never shared much friendly physical contact.

"I may not need a teacher," Gale said, speaking past the thickness in her throat and the ache that spread through her chest. "But I still need my dearest and most constant friend."

"I know." Madrigal drew in a trembling breath. "But you'll have me in my notes. You'll have the wisdom of the library to guide you, and you'll find other witches and other friends. You'll do great things, even without me."

They walked on, across the babbling creek. Its icy water wet Gale's feet, but they dried as soon as she stepped back onto the rocks on the far side. "Has he told you what waits beyond the veil?"

She remembered every detail of her meeting with Lord Death. His warnings haunted her, and she had no desire to meet him again any time soon, but she didn't fear him as she once might have.

"No. No one on this side is meant to understand that mystery." Madrigal didn't sound at all fearful. She turned her face toward the breeze that blew through the forest. "I won't abandon you. If you insist that I stay, I will."

Gale's stomach clenched as she caught the unspoken *if I must* at the end of the statement, and she drew in a long breath as she made her choice.

"You've given me so much," she said, willing herself not to cry. "It would be selfish of me to ask you to turn away from what you've wanted for so long. If you can love me enough to stay, I can love you enough to let you go." She turned, clasping Madrigal's hands in hers. "I will mourn you as I was never allowed to after you died. But I will survive. I will do my best to honour your teachings as I go on." Her breath hitched. "And I swear I will never forget you."

"Thank you." Madrigal dabbed at her eyes. "This is the right thing. I know it is. But damned if it doesn't hurt."

Gale laughed through her tears. "Not for long, I hope. Not for you, at least."

The canopy of leaves overhead shifted from summer green to

autumn gold. "I have no doubt that what lies beyond death's true door is beautiful," Madrigal said. "Peaceful. Restful. This world is a mess, and so are the people in it."

Gale saw no reason to argue.

"But it has its own beauty." Madrigal caught a yellow oak leaf as it drifted toward the ground. "I hope you'll enjoy it to its fullest, in ways I forgot to when I was alive. Your life is your own, my dear Nightingale. Promise me you won't waste it in mourning for too long."

The sky went dark, and the forest fell into shadow.

"I promise," Gale said, though the bottomless well of grief opening within her felt as though it might tear her soul in half.

Madrigal pulled her into a tight embrace, and Gale breathed in the earthy scent of herbs that had surrounded her mentor in life, trying to fix it forever in her memory.

CHAPTER FORTY
ASTER

ster rolled over in bed, squinting against the sunlight streaming in through Gale's window.

"Where's the clock?" she muttered.

Gale shifted beside her. There still wasn't much room in the bed, but thus far neither of them had found a reason to sleep anywhere else.

"I moved it," Gale answered, and yawned. "A person who's recovering from death shouldn't be worried about whether a few cogs and gears say it's time to be up and about."

Even without the clock, Aster had plenty of reason to get out of bed, most of it radiating from her bladder. She groaned under her breath and pushed herself up, moving slowly so as not to startle her injuries into making themselves known beyond the constant haze of relentless ache that had plagued her since her reawakening.

It had been a week. Getting to Gale's flat had been the first challenge and the greatest. With no potion to ease her pain and no magic that Gale could direct toward the cause, the carriage ride had been a gauntlet of bumpy roads that had jostled every freshly healed bone and newly mended muscle.

Aster had lost consciousness twice and had no regrets about the few moments of relief either of the incidents provided.

Since then, the stairs had been the bane of her existence—not only the climb to the front door, but the repeated journeys to the shared toilets in the yard out back and a single trip to the steamy halls of the public bath up the street the previous afternoon. She'd allowed Gale, who insisted she'd seen far worse in the clinic during her healer's training, to carry a chamberpot down for the first few days, and then her pride had overcome the pain and insisted she was better off forcing herself up and down to take care of things herself.

She looked back at the bed where Gale lay with her eyes half-closed. Though she kept herself busy, she slept more than seemed healthy. Her magic had returned and restored her physically, but Madrigal's departure had left a hole in her that Aster couldn't do anything to fix.

It might've had something to do with the choice she'd made to take Eamon's life, too, but after explaining the details to Aster, who remembered nothing of the time she'd spent dead, Gale had refused to speak about that at all.

But she let Aster hold her when the sadness overwhelmed her, and that was something. They'd both come out of the dungeon broken in their own ways, and Aster supposed it would be some time before they found out what normal was supposed to feel like.

Aster dressed, forcing her limbs to move faster than they wanted to, and tied a scarf around her neck before she stepped into the sharp, cold air.

No coat. She'd be sweating by the time she made it back up, anyway.

With every jarring step down, every damnably freezing moment in the little outhouse that emptied into the public sewer, and every ache in her arms as she pulled herself back up, a part of her longed for the indoor facilities she'd taken for granted back home.

But it would never be home again, and she'd never suggested to Gale that they might be more comfortable there no matter how true it might be.

By the time she returned to the third-floor flat, Gale was up and dressed and had hot water ready for tea.

"We did sleep the morning away again," she said. "It's becoming a habit. Not that I'm complaining, mind you."

"We need it." Aster moved closer and Gale turned to wrap her arms around her, gently enough to not hurt. Aster returned the embrace and placed a gentle kiss on Gale's shoulder. "How bad is yours today?"

Gale relaxed and leaned into her. "Better," she said. "Or maybe just the same. I'm glad for Madrigal's sake that she's gone, but I keep expecting to see her sitting by the fire, and I keep thinking I hear her voice. The empty places hurt, but knowing she's better off now makes it easier. How bad is yours?" She pulled back and looked into Aster's eyes. "Don't lie."

"The same. Stiff and sore, but I think I'm healing."

Gale frowned. "Did last night make it worse?"

Aster pulled her into a long kiss—a proper one, gentle but deep. "If it did, it was worth it. You almost made me forget to hurt for a while."

Gale smiled. It was good to see. "Then we'll need to try that again. But first, I want to see about a note I found in one of your grandmother's books. I'm going out later to speak to a contact about a new ingredient to try for the analgesic potion. Highly illegal, of course."

Aster sank into the single chair beside the kitchen table. "Is it safe for you to meet with someone like that?"

"I'll be careful."

Not what I asked, Aster thought, but decided not to argue. She had no right to tell Gale what to do. She only wished she was strong enough to go along to watch her back.

I will be, she promised herself. *Soon.* Between her grandmother's books from the library and Gale's magic, she was in good hands.

A knock sounded at the door as Gale handed Aster her tea, and Gale went to answer it. Aster held her breath and swallowed the bitter concoction. Finding a balance of ingredients that brought calm and eased pain without knocking her out or bringing hallucinations had been a difficult process and promised to continue to be so for some time. Gale seemed to enjoy the challenge, though.

Voices entered, accompanied by stomping boots. Jes, Cas, and an unfamiliar young man greeted Gale as Aster walked slowly out of the kitchen, dragging the chair with her.

She needed a cane, but the connection to Eamon was still too strong and fresh in her mind.

Cas took the kitchen chair, leaving the armchairs for Aster and their friend as Gale and Jes sat on the unmade bed.

"Aster, this is Henry. He wanted to meet you."

"Oh." Aster held out her right hand, and Henry shook it. "I owe you my thanks. And my life."

"Ah. Well. Very good." Henry pulled his hand back and didn't seem to know what to do with it. He settled for resting it on his leg and tapping out a quiet rhythm on the floor with his heel.

"How are my favourite reckless fools today?" Jes asked, without any hint of either irritation or affection. Melting snowflakes sparkled in her dark hair and over the shoulders of the black coat she wore buttoned to her throat.

Aster let Gale answer. She was grateful to this trio for everything they'd done but still felt like an outsider among them.

"Better," Gale said. "I'll be back to work soon enough, I imagine."

"If Aster repays me as she promised, I might consider allowing you a little more time to rest. So you're at your best when you return, of course." This time the corners of Jes's eyes gave away the hint of a hidden smile.

Aster wouldn't dare accuse Jes openly of affection toward her employee, but even among wolves, things were not what she'd always imagined. Jes and Cas had been frequent visitors over the past week, bringing food and the newspaper, and Aster had been surprised after a few days to realize she looked forward to seeing them.

"Of course," Gale said. "Any word on other things?"

Jes looked to Cas. "We heard from Tom about the investigation."

Aster leaned forward in her chair, ignoring the shifting landscape of pain within her. "And?"

"They're not closing it," Cas said, "but they're also not looking at you with any kind of suspicion."

Aster nodded. "Not yet, anyway."

Cas laid a hand on her forearm. Aster barely felt the light touch, but appreciated it nonetheless. "We took care of it. You don't need to worry."

"Thank you."

"What of the bodies?" Gale asked.

"Returned to their families now," Jes said. "There's to be a memorial service in the square tomorrow for them and all those who were never recovered."

A weight lifted from Aster's chest. Cas had arranged to have the bodies wrapped in clean sheets and placed outside of town, and the hunt was now on for a savage killer who seemed oddly respectful of his recent victims once his dark deeds were done. Roddy had been placed among them and would likely be buried in an unmarked grave when no one stepped forward to claim him.

As for Eamon, Aster didn't know what had become of his body. She'd imagined him being fed to hogs, or buried deep in the woods, or tossed into the sea. In the end, she'd decided it didn't matter as long as the truth of his crimes never came back to haunt her. His disappearance had caused quite a stir in his social circles, but Aster supposed that would die down soon enough.

It would be as great a scandal when the house went up for sale and Aster eventually vanished from society as well, but she didn't particularly care about that, either.

That part of her life was over, and she felt no urge to grieve for it.

Henry was watching her with great interest. She pulled back the sleeve of her blouse and held her arm out toward him. "Go ahead."

Henry pushed his hair back from his face and gingerly pressed the tips of two fingers to her wrist. "Remarkable," he whispered, and looked to Gale. "It's as you expected?"

"We're still working out the finer details of the enchantment," Gale said, her eyes lighting up as she spoke of her magic. "The challenge is getting it to respond to her needs so she doesn't faint on the way up the stairs, but we're almost there."

Or in other circumstances. Aster allowed herself a second to think again of the previous night. The enchanted heart picked up its rhythm as the rest of Aster's body remembered.

Henry beamed. "Remarkable. Simply remarkable."

He didn't ask Aster how she was feeling. She hadn't expected him to, and she didn't mind.

"You didn't tell me the cost for taking care of all of the bodies," she said, speaking to Jes. "I don't imagine it will be easy for me to free up any of Eamon's money for a few years. Not until he's declared deceased instead of missing."

"Don't suppose it would help if Eamon proved himself dead a

bit sooner than anticipated?" Cas asked, examining his nails as he spoke.

"If he what?" Aster asked.

Cas shrugged, and Henry looked at him with such open shock that the effort of not laughing at him washed away some of Aster's anxiety over the question.

It'll be fine, she reminded herself, and realized with some surprise that she trusted these people. They knew the worst of her and hadn't batted an eye at the murder bits save for where it threatened them personally. They could have demanded every coin she had to her name and the signing over of Eamon's estate in exchange for not turning her in, but they hadn't. Cas, and even Jes, both of whom had once seen her as an enemy, now sat in this cozy little room asking after her welfare and protecting her interests as though it were the most natural thing in the world, trusting her in turn to take care of the financials as that was all she brought to the table... at least for now.

This was the closest Aster had ever had to a big, post-holiday family get-together. A month ago, she would have considered stabbing anyone who dared suggest she'd experience such a thing with a loosely formed pack of wolves.

Now she found herself hoping next year would bring the same, if with less blood-soaked excitement in the lead-up and significantly less pain in the aftermath.

She was lost in her thoughts when Henry said something and the others laughed. The downstairs neighbour thumped on the ceiling at the noise, and Jes stomped back, which for some reason made Gale laugh even harder, loud and genuine in a way that would have been impossible even a few days before.

She was healing. They both were.

Aster leaned back in her chair and took it all in—the joy, the warmth, the pleasant stirring in her enchanted heart as she watched Gale wipe away tears and turn to her, a warm smile on her lips.

Her return to this world had brought pain that would surely last for some time. New hurts would come. There would be challenges and surprises, but for once she relished the idea of not knowing what might come next.

It was life. True life now, and hers to do with as she wished.

THE END

AUTHOR'S NOTE

Here we are again, safely at the end of another story, and I can't thank you enough for coming along on this journey. If you enjoyed *Scars and Seams* and would like to help other readers discover this series, please consider leaving a review on your retailer or review website of choice. Your recommendations really help!

There's more coming, and you'll be seeing these characters again. But next time (fate, the universe, and editor permitting) we're going to visit a different part of Andonia to meet a young woman with a questionable destiny. For updates, visit my website and sign up for my newsletter!

Until then, take care, and mind you don't step in any blood puddles on your way out.

-Kate

ABOUT THE AUTHOR

Kate Sparkes is the author of the Bound Trilogy and the All the Queen's Knaves series (as well as some steamy urban fantasy set in Newfoundland under the name Tanith Frost). She spends her days wondering what she actually did with all that time when she was supposed to be writing, then scrambling to catch up.

It's not a great system, but it's what she's got.

ACKNOWLEDGMENTS

This book was, to say the least, a challenge, arriving in my brain filled with massive possibilities, alternate storylines, and tempting variations on the rhythm of the series. I couldn't have made it the best possible version of itself without the help of the following wonderful folks:

The amazing author Krista Walsh, who reads my drafts and dries my tears, then cleans up my mistakes once the dust has settled.

Laura Fischer, Mike Lowden, Trisha Poole, Margie Scheiner, and Kathy Dunlavey, who read various versions of the story and told me where I'd gone wrong. Your interest and enthusiasm keep me going.

Joshua Essoe, for edits and infuriatingly tempting "but what if" moments.

The incomparable Stefanie Saw, for the gorgeous cover art that says so much about all of these stories.

My family, for giving me time and space to get my ideas onto the page.

And a special thanks to Minnie, who will not read this

because she is a cat, for keeping me company in my office every day and reminding me to take breaks when her fluffy belly needs some scritchin'.